Nadine Gonza* ██████████ ████ author. A lawyer by profession, she lives in Miami, Florida, and shares her home with her Cuban American husband and their son. Nadine writes joyous contemporary romance featuring a diverse cast of characters, American, Caribbean and Latinx. She networks on Twitter, but lives on Instagram! Check out @_nadinegonzalez. For more information visit her website: nadine-gonzalez.com

Joss Wood loves books, coffee and travelling—especially to the wild places of southern Africa and, well, anywhere. She's a wife and a mum to two young adults. She's also a slave to two cats and a dog the size of a small cow. After a career in local economic development and business, Joss writes full-time from her home in KwaZulu-Natal, South Africa.

Bromley Libraries

30128 80481 984 8

Also by **Nadine Gonzalez**

Miami Famous
Scandal in the VIP Suite
What Happens in Miami...

Miami Dreams
Exclusively Yours
Unconditionally Mine

Also by **Joss Wood**

Murphy International
One Little Indiscretion
Temptation at His Door
Back in His Ex's Bed

South Africa's Scandalous Billionaires
How to Undo the Proud Billionaire
How to Win the Wild Billionaire
How to Tempt the Off-Limits Billionaire

Discover more at millsandboon.co.uk

THE REBEL'S RETURN

NADINE GONZALEZ

SECRETS OF A BAD REPUTATION

JOSS WOOD

MILLS & BOON

All rights reserved including the right of reproduction in whole or in part in any form. This edition is published by arrangement with Harlequin Books S.A.

This is a work of fiction. Names, characters, places, locations and incidents are purely fictional and bear no relationship to any real life individuals, living or dead, or to any actual places, business establishments, locations, events or incidents. Any resemblance is entirely coincidental.

This book is sold subject to the condition that it shall not, by way of trade or otherwise, be lent, resold, hired out or otherwise circulated without the prior consent of the publisher in any form of binding or cover other than that in which it is published and without a similar condition including this condition being imposed on the subsequent purchaser.

® and ™ are trademarks owned and used by the trademark owner and/or its licensee. Trademarks marked with ® are registered with the United Kingdom Patent Office and/or the Office for Harmonisation in the Internal Market and in other countries.

First Published in Great Britain 2022
by Mills & Boon, an imprint of HarperCollins*Publishers* Ltd
1 London Bridge Street, London, SE1 9GF

www.harpercollins.co.uk

HarperCollins*Publishers*
1st Floor, Watermarque Building,
Ringsend Road, Dublin 4, Ireland

The Rebel's Return © 2022 Harlequin Books SA
Secrets of a Bad Reputation © 2022 Joss Wood

Special thanks and acknowledgement are given to Nadine Gonzalez for her contribution to the *Texas Cattleman's Club: Fathers and Sons* series.

ISBN: 978-0-263-30373-5

0222

MIX
Paper from
responsible sources
FSC™ C007454

This book is produced from independently certified FSC™ paper to ensure responsible forest management.

For more information visit: www.harpercollins.co.uk/green

Printed and Bound in Spain using 100% Renewable electricity at CPI Black Print, Barcelona

THE REBEL'S RETURN

NADINE GONZALEZ

For Ariel and Nathaniel. You colour my world.
I love you both.

A special dedication to my sister Martine: thanks for
holding my hand through this crazy journey.

Prologue

"It doesn't grant wishes, you know."

That pearl of wisdom was rolled out in a smooth male voice with a touch of twang. Eve Martin steeled herself against its charm. Leave it to a man to point out the blatant obvious. Yes, she was staring, mesmerized, at a multitiered champagne tower, but with good reason. Eve had started her evening staring at tap water filling a chipped porcelain mug. She'd been prepping for her nightly pity tea party when bleak hopelessness gripped her. For longer than she cared to admit, she'd watched water splash over the rim of her mug and swirl noisily down the drain, like her hopes, dreams, ambitions and every well-laid plan she'd hatched since age twelve. Once she'd been on the rise, labeled an up-and-comer in her field, 30 Under 30, and all the rest. Now she was on a Slip 'N Slide into oblivion. Well, she refused, flat out refused, to go out like that.

Stubbornness beat hopelessness any night of the week. On this Thursday night, it got her out of her pajamas and out the door and into a cab on her way to town. She'd asked the driver to take her to the only address she knew, the Texas Cattleman's Club. It wasn't until they'd pulled up to the lively venue that she understood her mistake. All she'd wanted was to enjoy a glass of wine at the bar, a simple pleasure she'd missed all those weeks in the hospital. But from the look of things, a very fancy party was underway. Eve fidgeted in the back seat, unsure of what to do next. Her driver was no help. In his late twenties, roughly her age, he wore a baseball cap and a smirk. Arms folded, he waited for her to get out of his cab. If she asked him to take her home, she would have had paid sixty dollars cash for a round trip to nowhere. God only knew she didn't have money to waste.

Ultimately, a third party settled the matter. A valet attendant stepped forward and opened the passenger door. Likely mistaking her for an invited party guest and eager to keep traffic flowing, he extended a hand. "Good evening, ma'am. Welcome to the Cattleman's Club."

With those words, she was granted access into the gilded sanctuary of Royal elite. Eve shuffled along with the others through the grand lobby to the grand ballroom. She felt lost among the chatty guests and wandered around aimlessly until she spotted the colossal champagne tower at the center of the room. She drifted toward it and watched, mesmerized, as an attendant atop a ladder poured bottle after bottle over a pyramid of long-stemmed glasses. From tap water to sparkling champagne, her night was looking up. Who knew? She might even have some fun tonight.

"It doesn't grant wishes, you know."

One glance at the wise guy was all it took to disprove that statement. Standing beside her in a well-cut navy suit, hands in pockets, head tilted to better catch her eye, was a tall man with dark hair, buttery brown skin, and brown eyes that outsparkled the best sparkling wines. For someone, somewhere, he was most definitely a wish come true.

From atop the ladder, the attendant raised the last bottle of champagne with a flourish. "Cheers, everyone!"

Eve did not need any more prompting than that. Suddenly very thirsty, she reached for a glass. To her horror, the entire champagne edifice came crashing down. Shattered glass turned the air around her into a glistening prism. Champagne splashed onto her cherry-red dress. Champagne dowsed her shoes, swirled around her ankles and flowed between her legs. Shocked, her own glass slipped from her hand and shattered at her feet.

While everyone around her scattered, she stood rooted in place. When would she learn? Stubbornness trumped hopelessness, but nothing was stronger than fate. Eve should have known better than to leave the safety of her bunker and tempt fate tonight. Her only wish now was to disappear.

One

Love at first sight was for suckers, right? In any event, that was the hill that Rafael Arias Wentworth was prepared to die on until he'd laid eyes on her. She stood motionless, staring at a champagne tower at the center of the grand ballroom. She was striking in a candy-red dress and hair gathered low in a cinnamon bun, yet all he saw was smooth, rich caramel skin. Who among this who's who of Royal was she?

Rafael reasoned away the feelings she inspired. He was still flying high from another experience. Earlier this evening, he had driven to the outskirts of town to visit a car dealer. Not the type who sold family-friendly sedans in an air-conditioned showroom. This one invited private customers into a nondescript building surrounded by a chainlink fence and guarded by massive dogs that turned out to be sweethearts. The owner was a young guy named Manny Suarez, a high-end car restorer. Rafael had reached out to him from Miami weeks before he'd decided to come back to town. Now it seemed they'd found the perfect car. After patiently answering about fifty questions, Manny told Rafael to put up or shut up. Rafael did not hesitate. He dropped a quarter of a million dollars on a 1969 Camaro convertible. He would have kicked the tires, but there were none. The rusted tin can rested on cinder blocks. It looked as if it had been drawn out of a lake. Its beauty, however, was untarnished.

He'd left the dealer's garage feeling energized. Running late for the cocktail party at the TCC, he gunned through the streets of Royal. He drove an expertly restored 1972 Jaguar XK-E. Classic convertibles were his weakness. Apparently, so were women in red.

Tonight's party was a business obligation. Rafael could not skip it, but he had no intention of staying late. He had a plan for these sorts of events: grab a drink, make the rounds and then slip out, hopefully unnoticed. But then he saw her and…*bam!*

Love or not, he was going to pass. There was only so much room in a man's heart, and tonight he'd fallen for the classic lines of a vintage Chevrolet. He dropped his glass of tequila and lime on the tray of a passing attendant. He was leaving before he did anything stupid, but not before getting the name of his sweet, caramel candy apple. That would be useful information in case he were up for falling in love some other night.

He approached her, ready to say hello. She didn't notice. She stood staring at the champagne pouring down the pyramid. He said the first thing that came to mind. "It doesn't grant wishes, you know." All he'd wanted was to coax a smile out of her. Instead, she'd glared at him. Then two things happened in quick succession, like thunder following lightning. A ladder crashed into the tower. The tower collapsed. The crash. The crunch of glass. The splash of champagne. Rafael was oblivious to it all. He recognized this woman. She was without a doubt the infamous Evelyn

Martin. A part of him must have known. The feeling she'd stirred in him wasn't love, but something just as violent.

There was no time to dwell on any of it. All hell broke loose in the ballroom. Beside him, a man dabbed frantically at his suit with a cocktail napkin. A woman bemoaned the state of her designer shoes. But Eve Martin stood unflinching in the face of catastrophe, and Rafael had to admit there was something badass about that. Even so, she couldn't stay here.

"Come with me." He draped an arm around her rigid shoulders and dragged her along. He marched her out of the ballroom, her eyes downcast, her jaw and neck tight with tension. In the lobby, he asked if she was okay. No answer. Was she in shock?

"Talk to me," he said. "Say something so I know you're alright."

She took a deep breath, as if bracing to face a firing squad. "I'm going to die of embarrassment."

"Is that all?" he said. "I'll call off the paramedics then."

She dabbed her wet forehead with her fingers. "I'm a wreck."

He had a feeling this statement had more to do with her state of mind than her appearance. "Would you like to go to the ladies' room to clean up?"

She shook her head. "No."

Staff members had cordoned off the grand hall. Others were handing out towels to the soaked guests. He grabbed two and handed her one.

"It was an accident," she said, her voice catching.

He wiped his hands dry. "A freak accident."

She bunched the towel to her chest. "I didn't mean to…"

Rafael narrowed his eyes. "Didn't mean to…what?" He laughed. "You think you're to blame?"

"I grabbed a glass!"

"That's how it works," he said. "They pour the wine, you grab a glass."

"I might've grabbed it the wrong way."

She had either a martyr complex or just a warped sense of reality. "Sorry to break it to you, Calamity Jane. You're not that powerful."

"What happened then?"

"The ladder toppled over."

"Oh…"

"Oh, yeah," he said. "It was dramatic as hell. Sorry you missed it."

"That's okay," she said with a sigh of relief. "I've had enough drama. Thanks."

"I think we're done here." Rafael slipped his phone out of his pocket, ready to text his code to the valet. "What's your valet code? I'll have them bring your car around."

"Never mind. I'll grab a cab."

He pocketed his phone. "Do you need a ride? I'll take you home."

"No," she said firmly. "I'm fine. Thanks."

"You're not fine," he said. "You're soaking wet."

"My feet are wet. I think I'll survive."

"Don't be so sure," Rafael said. "If my darling grandmother is right, you'll catch pneumonia and die in twenty-four hours."

"Your darling grandmother is wrong. And you've done enough tonight. Thanks."

"Before you go handing me a medal, Evelyn, you should know that I'm using you as a shield."

The sparkle in her eyes fizzled out. "You know who I am?"

Rafael didn't answer. She really shouldn't be surprised. Everyone in town had read up on her. They knew exactly who she was and were likely keeping tabs on her, down to her address and Social Security number. Having people know you, or think they did, by reputation or otherwise, was not a good feeling. He knew it well.

"And who are you?" she asked.

There was no time to answer. Paul and Jennifer Carlton, of Carlton Realty Group, P&J for short, were fast approaching. "I'm going to whisper something in your ear. Do you mind?"

She opened wide eyes. "I'm confused. Why, exactly?"

"I need your help." He lowered his head and whispered in such a way that an onlooker might suppose they were engaged in a private conversation and back off. "Pretend we're deep in conversation. Act like you're into it."

"I'll do my best," she said.

His plan failed. The elegant couple that he was trying to avoid accosted him with air kisses, shoulder clasps and prying questions. "Rafael!" they cried in unison.

Evelyn swiveled around. "Rafael..." Recognition dawned.

"Is it true you're sniffing at the Richardson property?" Paul asked.

Rafael skirted the question. "Paul, Jennifer, have you met Evelyn Martin?"

A cursory acknowledgment before resuming their interrogation.

"Many of our clients are interested in that property," Jennifer said. "If the motel goes on the market, get ready for a bidding war."

Paul had a suggestion. "How about we grab a drink and discuss this inside."

Evelyn spoke up in a clear voice. "Sorry, we're leaving. There's been a freak accident."

The *"we"* undid him.

"Oh?" Jennifer eyed Evelyn as if she'd just teleported in and hadn't been standing there the whole time. "What happened? And why is your dress all wet?"

"A champagne tower collapsed," Eve replied.

"Goodness!" Jennifer exclaimed.

Rafael spotted the tiny beads of liquid that added shimmer to Evelyn's otherwise unadorned sheath. "We need to get you out of that dress."

She shot him a look. Okay, he conceded. This time the "we" was overkill.

"Just take me home, please," she said to him. "I can manage the rest on my own."

Paul's and Jennifer's heads turned with each response that he and Evelyn volleyed at each other. Rafael had to get rid of them. That pair traded in gossip. Pretty soon all of Royal would be making up stories. He'd been down that road before.

"I should take Evelyn home before she catches pneumonia," he said. "Nice seeing you two."

"Good night," they said.

Rafael watched them go. "Ready?"

Evelyn looked as if she were still weighing her options. He caught the exact moment she gave in. "Sure," she said. "Tonight is a bust. Lead the way."

Her words were soaked in disappointment. Rafael felt for her. She hadn't gone through the trouble of coming out just for her night to end like this. That wasn't right. He looked around and spotted a server wandering about with a tray of champagne glasses. He waved him over, grabbed a flute and offered it to her. "You deserve it."

She hesitated before taking the glass. "I thought we were leaving."

"In a moment," he said. "The valet will send word when my car is ready. In the meantime, I know just the spot where we can wait. Follow me."

Two

Rafael Wentworth was crisp like money. Was it any wonder? He belonged to one of the oldest families in Royal, going back generations. Eve wasn't an expert in all things Royal—that was her sister Arielle's wheelhouse—but that much she knew. Cammie Wentworth had very generously taken in Eve's nephew while she was indisposed. Rafael's name had clout, and he knew it. He hadn't bothered to introduce himself because he'd assumed she knew who he was.

Rafael had asked her to follow him and she had, no questions asked. He led her out a side door and down a trail to a far-off bench under a magnolia tree. Moments later, Eve found herself sipping champagne under the wide Texas sky in the company of an heir to a great fortune. It was the last day of a very long, very taxing January. The night was balmy. He slipped off his jacket and draped it over her shoulders. "I like how you handled P&J."

"You mean that couple? Is that what you call them?"

"It's what everybody calls them."

She frowned. "Somehow, I doubt it. They seemed harmless enough."

"You naive little thing."

"I'm anything but that."

"Okay, then," he said. "Can't deny we make a good team. Maybe it's our South Florida connection."

"Do we have a South Florida connection?"

"So everyone keeps telling me."

Admittedly, she knew very little about the man except that for a while he was a person of interest in the delicate matter that had brought her to Texas in the first place. He had quickly cleared his name, but Eve should have known that wouldn't be the last she'd hear of him. After all, he was Cammie Wentworth's brother. Cammie was one of the first people Eve had met in town, and their lives remained entangled to this day.

"Don't read too much into it," Eve said, trying not to read too much into it herself. "Miami has a way of making bedfellows out of total strangers."

He cracked a smile. "I couldn't have said it better myself."

Eve pulled her phone from her purse, tapped on the navigation app and handed it to him. "Take me to this address and we'll call it even."

He only glanced at the screen. "I just left that area."

What was a Wentworth doing way out in her neck of the woods? "Really? What were you up to?"

His smile grew sly. "One day, if you're good, I'll tell you."

Eve smiled, too, for the first time in…what? Six months? It made her cheeks ache. "May I ask you something?"

"Shoot."

"Why did you come out tonight? You obviously don't want to be here."

He let out a heavy sigh. "It's the cost of doing business in this town."

Eve raised her champagne glass. Moonlight danced in the bubbles. "Is it really such a burden?"

"I think so," he replied. "At the end of a long day, the last thing I want is to stand around making small talk."

He sat with his elbows on his knees and his hands folded under his chin. She couldn't help but think of those Renaissance statues, perfectly symmetrical, exquisitely chiseled. "So, what *do* you want?"

"A steak, a bottle of red, a cigar…my bed."

It all sounded so good. What she would give for all those things, minus the cigar.

"I'm curious," he said. "What did *you* come out for?"

"I wanted to have fun."

What else could she say? After months in a hospital, she had wanted to wear her old clothes and feel like her old vibrant self. That would be giving too much away. Most people didn't need a profound reason to head out for a drink on a beautiful night.

"Fun?" he said, leaning into the word as if he had difficulty catching its meaning.

She spelled it out for him. *"F-U-N."*

"I'll let you in on this secret." His voice dipped to a smoky whisper. "No one has ever had fun at a country club. It's not allowed."

"That's not true! It's beautiful here."

Music and chatter wafted their way. The party had resumed. No one would allow a puddle of champagne to wash out the night.

Rafael got up and pulled on the knot of his tie. "That's how they get you. But don't be fooled. This club is for small talk and social climbing. That's all."

"You're crazy."

"Darling, it's Texas law," he said with a tip of an imaginary Stetson hat.

Eve let out a thin peal of laughter, and that in and of itself was a minor miracle. This morning she had cried in her coffee. These last few months had been so trying. She'd lost her sense of humor, her ability to laugh at herself and others.

"Think I'm kidding? Check the TCC bylaws," he said. "It specifically states no member shall have any fun of any kind. They'll escort you out if you do."

"I'm not a member, so I'm in the clear."

"You're not?" he said, rolling up his sleeves. With the moonlight streaming on him, adding a streak of silver to his ink-black hair, he was, possibly, the most beautiful man that she had ever set eyes on. "How did you get in?"

She'd just…walked in. It didn't occur to her that the club wasn't open to the general public. Eve took her glass to her lips and tried to hide her panic. Would they escort her off the premises now?

At first, Rafael didn't seem particularly invested in her answer. When her silence dragged on, though, his interest grew. "Evelyn," he said, "is there something you're not telling me?"

"I go by Eve, not Evelyn."

Eve was suddenly very hot. It didn't help that her damp dress clung to her body like plastic wrap.

"Eve," he said. "What are you not telling me?"

"I didn't know the rules," she said in her defense. "The only club I belong to is a gym."

"So…what did you do to get in?"

"I didn't do anything!" she said heatedly. "My cab pulled up around front. It was holding up traffic and the doorman whisked me in."

"He *whisked* you." He laughed, the smooth, rich laughter that was stored in oak barrels for decades, only to be shared with the best of friends. It left Eve feeling a little drunk. "This is so good I need popcorn."

"Oh, stop!" Eve punctuated her cry with a stomp of the foot. The soggy sole of her stilettos made an unpleasant swish sound. She slipped them off and wiggled her toes in the grass. Might as well get comfortable, too.

"Eve Martin, you are a wild woman."

She wasn't. That was the thing. She was the definition of boring and stable and predictable. Her little sister, Arielle, was the fun and spontaneous one. At the thought of Arielle, a ball of pain hardened in Eve's chest. She took a long sip of champagne to ease it down.

"Actually," he said, "I kind of like you."

Well, that was kind of nice. "I like you, too."

"You know what?" he said. "I wonder if we could marry our two visions for tonight."

True to her nature, Eve stomped a spark of interest just as quickly as it flared. "We can't marry anything."

"That's a shame," he said. "I just had a great idea."

So many warning bells were chiming, she could hardly hear her own thoughts. "What is it?"

He looked into the distance and pointed west. "I'd like to take you there."

She strained her neck and spotted a grand house on a hill. Light poured out from every window. It looked inviting enough, the sort of place that might serve a hearty farm-to-table dinner. Was that the plan? A late meal?

"I'm not going anywhere with you," Eve said. "I'm a mess."

She yearned for her bed. Which bed, though? Not the lumpy one at the Airbnb or the hard one she'd left behind in Miami. Certainly not the hospital bed she'd been confined to for weeks upon arriving in Royal. There it was. She was bone tired and didn't have a comfortable place to rest. That was the root of her problem.

"You're not a mess, and even if you were it wouldn't be a problem," he said. "It's an inn."

Eve fell straight through the trapdoor of her imagination. What was he thinking? "If you think this night ends with us in a hotel room, you're out of your mind."

"It's not a hotel," he said. "It's an inn. Trust me, I know the difference."

It was a room with a bed. "Are you trying to say people don't have sex in *inns*?"

"They do," he said, unfazed. "But only in the dark and in the missionary position."

"What?" A dam cracked, and laughter cascaded freely from her. It felt so good to laugh again, almost like flying. "What rule book are you reading from?"

He joined her on the bench. "Do you trust me, Eve?"

"No," she said. "I don't."

Eve didn't trust him, but she wanted to trace the line of his jaw with her fingertips. One thing had nothing to do with the other.

"Could you try? For one night."

"No." Her mother, and her grandmother, for that matter, didn't raise a fool.

"That's fair," he said. "But do you know what's waiting for us over at the Belleview Inn?" he said. "A steam shower, room service, laundry service, TV, Wi-Fi and a balcony with a view of a rose garden. We can have dinner and engage in adult conversation. Does any of that appeal to you?"

All of it appealed to her. Following her hospital stay, Eve was referred to rehabilitative therapy. She was only three weeks into an arduous course of physical therapy and had pushed her body beyond its limits tonight. She felt drained, exhausted. And she was wet and hungry. She needed a shower. Room service, even at a modest inn, sounded decadent. Although she knew better than to say yes when a charming man invited her up to a hotel, motel, or a Holiday Inn, that was exactly what she intended to do. She blamed the champagne, the preferred elixir of the god of bad choices.

Rafael checked his phone. "My car is ready. What do you say?"

"I say let's go."

"Fearless," he said, almost to himself. "I like it."

They walked to the valet station where the car was waiting. Rafael Wentworth drove a classic sports car, the type only seen in films set in Italy. It suited him perfectly. He held open the door for her, then got behind the wheel. "You've had enough excitement," he said, revving up the engine. "Let's get you out of here."

They drove off into the night, leaving the Texas Cattleman's Club behind.

Three

After arriving at the inn, Eve fidgeted in the passenger seat. Rafael wondered if she were having second thoughts. He was a hotelier by profession and could not drive by a property without checking it out. They needed a shower and a good meal. A room at the nearby inn was a practical solution. If she didn't feel comfortable, he was prepared to drive her home.

"Hey," he said. "We can leave."

She froze, her hand on the door handle. "But...we just got here."

"You look uncomfortable."

"I need to get out of this dress, that's all."

"And a little nervous, too."

She waved away his concerns. "It's just how I look."

That wasn't true. He'd seen her scared, shocked and amused. Never, in the arguably short time he'd known her, had he seen her look this antsy, and he didn't like it. "You really can trust me, Eve," he said. "I've been accused of getting one Martin sister pregnant. I'm not trying to push my luck."

Her hand fell away from the door handle and she looked all at once scared, shocked and not in the least amused.

Rafael rushed to apologize, only managing to spit out a limp string of words. "Oh, shit, sorry. I didn't mean that."

But as his wise maternal grandmother would have said, *Lo que sale de la boca, del corazón sale.* Things that come out of the mouth come from the heart. He'd thought he was over the whole Royal mystery baby mess. Apparently, he was still pissed and resentful as hell. His resentment extended to the whole blessed town.

Rafael hadn't been back in Royal since leaving for Florida in a huff at age seventeen. He'd returned at the request of his family. His father, Tobias Wentworth, who was the reason he'd left home in the first place, was turning a leaf and wanted to reconcile. Although he wanted nothing more than to leave the past behind him, he'd finally relented. Naturally, Royal welcomed him with a scandal.

Not long ago, his half sister, Cammie, and her fiancé, Drake, had taken custody of an abandoned baby. All that was well and good and had nothing to do with him. While Drake and Cammie fostered the child, authorities worked to track down the baby's parents. Normally, he would have applauded the effort except, for some reason, his name topped their list.

The child was the son of Arielle Martin, a budding freelance photojournalist from South Florida who had reached out to him a few times seeking a comment on a story. As small-town logic would have it, that connection was enough to make him the father of her infant son. Rafael hadn't wasted any time and cleared his name with a paternity test. It was water under the bridge now—except he was about to book a room with Arielle's sister, the very woman who had brought the baby to Royal in search of his father.

This could very well be a bad idea.

Eve released her seat belt with a snap. "We're going inside. I want the night you promised. Do you understand?"

It was an order. Normally, Rafael did not respond well to orders. This time, he did not hesitate. "Yes, ma'am."

At the front desk, the night manager recognized Rafael and made a fuss, offering a free upgrade to a suite.

"A two-bedroom suite," Eve insisted.

The manager reassured her. "Two very separate rooms, ma'am. Please wait here a moment. I'll be right back."

He went off to program their key cards. Eve eyed Rafael with suspicion. "Why was he fawning over you? Are you a frequent flyer or something?"

"A professional courtesy," Rafael replied. "I'm in the hospitality business."

"Interesting," she said. "I didn't know."

"I'm opening a luxury guest ranch in town with accommodations similar to this, but better."

"You're here to check out the competition, aren't you?"

He raised a finger to his lips. "Shh."

She smiled. "Sneaky... I knew you had a motive for coming here."

He winked. "Just not the motive you thought."

She rolled her eyes. Her long lashes fanned the high slopes of her cheeks. In the intimate light of the inn's lobby, her caramel-colored skin was smoother than Rafael could have ever imagined. She was of average height, reaching his chin and no higher, and she was thin to the point of frail. A good gust of wind could knock her over. Then he recalled that she was in the hospital those weeks that he was being ruled out as her nephew's father. She must have had a rough time.

Rafael was glad the tension that had built up in the car was subsiding. He wanted to make her laugh again, the way she'd laughed when they were alone in the garden. Her laughter had leaped out as if springing from a sealed cave. He'd wanted to take her in his arms and hold her close until she settled down.

"Incoming!"

Lost in the fantasy of holding her, he didn't quite understand what she was saying. "What's that?"

"Just…shut up."

She stepped up to him and brushed her lips to his in a whisper of a kiss. Rafael tensed, the muscles of his abdomen tightening. "Act like you're into it," she murmured through clenched teeth. With every nerve ending in his body setting off sparks, he didn't have to rely on dormant acting skills. He pulled her close and kissed her hard, deep, and slow. She gripped the lapel of his suit jacket and opened to his kiss. He heard her groan just before she tore herself away.

"I think we're good," she said, her voice shaky.

He was shaken, too. "How the hell do you figure?"

"I kissed you to create a distraction," she said. "P&J just walked in."

Paul and Jennifer Carlton were the most annoying couple in Texas, but at this moment he was making plans to send them a fruit basket and a bottle of wine.

"Here I thought you wanted to test that sex-in-an-inn theory."

"Stop thinking that," she scolded. "They're right over there. Don't look now, though."

He wouldn't dream of it. Her swollen lips had his undivided attention.

"Okay… They've entered the dining hall. You can look now."

"Nah. I'll take your word for it."

The manager returned. He was a little red in the face from what he'd undoubtedly witnessed.

Rafael plucked the key cards from his hand. "I'll take those. Thanks."

"Anything else, sir?"

"Send up laundry services, will you?" Rafael said. "And your best bottle of tequila."

The manager cleared his throat. "Certainly, sir. Enjoy your evening."

Four

In the elevator, Eve kept her eyes pinned to the tip of her pointed-toe stilettos. She could lie to him, not herself. The truth thrashed around in her chest. She had wanted to kiss him. All night, she had wanted to kiss that smart mouth, mess his hair and breathe in the scent of his skin. She'd seized on the flimsiest excuse to do it. It was as simple as that.

Now she stood as far away from him as physically possible. They rode to the top floor in unyielding silence. Just as the doors were about to split open, Rafael slammed on a button and the doors jammed in place. She startled and looked up at him.

"Listen, I…" His voice trailed off. She darted a glance his way. He looked as uncomfortable as she felt. "That was a really shitty thing for me to say about your sister, and I'm sorry."

"Alright."

Eve hoped he wasn't waiting for a more nuanced response. His quip about Arielle had stung. For a moment she'd panicked, not knowing what to do or say. Apart from the police and journalists still on the case, no one openly discussed Arielle. She was the stranger, the outsider, who had blown into town to dig up old secrets and stir up past resentments before mysteriously taking off.

"I never met your sister," he said. "She'd reached out to me, twice, requesting an interview. Each time I turned her down. She wanted to dig into my past, my ties to Royal and the Wentworth family. I don't want to think about my past, let alone meet with a stranger and discuss it over coffee."

Her sister was a photojournalist with dreams of someday having features in *Vogue* and *Time*. She had come to Royal to investigate a 110-year-old story with ties to the country club that was the beating heart of the town. To support herself while in Royal, her sister had taken a job at an assisted living facility. According to her diary, she became interested in one of the residents with a storied past. "I think she was more interested in Harmon Wentworth than you... Is he your great-uncle?"

"We're related, but we're not close."

"She was all about small-town America. I guess she was trying to find out what made Royal so special—and probably dig up any secrets or scandals along the way."

Rafael's lips curled with a sardonic smile. "There are enough family rifts in Royal to fill an encyclopedia."

"So I gather."

"Anyway, I am sorry." He lifted his thumb off the button. Eve rushed to press it, freezing the elevator in place. He searched her face. "What's going on?"

"I just want to say, it's alright. Apology accepted." Eve felt sorry for everyone who had been dragged into her sister's drama. Somehow, Arielle's personal choices had become everyone's problem to solve, including Eve. It was maddening and frustrating and yet, as one of her sister's two surviving relatives, Eve had no choice in the matter. There was no way out for her; she was duty bound to see this through to the end.

"But are *we* alright?" he asked.

"We're fine." She released the button. "Now let's get off this elevator."

She followed him down a quiet hall to their suite. He unlocked the door, switched on the lights and dropped the key card on the console table in the foyer. She rushed in ahead of him. "I love it."

"It's not bad," he said.

The layout was simple. The two bedrooms opened to a common sitting area. The decor was traditional and tasteful. Bay windows offered views of a sprawling garden.

"We should take notes." Eve went to the writing desk and picked up a pad and pen. "First impression—views are to die for," she murmured as she wrote.

"You're being generous."

She capped the pen. "You're being a hard-ass."

"It's just rolling grass." Rafael flung open the door of the hall closet, found a terry-cloth robe and handed it to her. It was soft. She couldn't wait to slip it on. "Need help with that dress?"

"Actually, yes." She turned on her heel and gave him her back. "Help me with the zipper."

She could use an extra set of hands. It had been such a pain to pull up.

When he gripped the tab, her breath caught. He took his damn sweet time inching the zipper down and sending a thrill up her spine. Not trusting her voice, Eve thanked him with a curt nod. Then, clutching the robe to her chest, she scurried off and locked herself in one of the bedrooms.

In the en suite bathroom, Eve gingerly stepped out of the stiff red dress and let it collapse onto the marble tile floor. She let down her hair, also stiff with styling products. She was working on releasing her bra when she heard the knock on the bedroom door.

"Yes?" She peered at Rafael through a narrow crack of

the door. She had grabbed a towel and wrapped it around her torso, but with the memory of their kiss still expanding in her mind, she might as well be naked.

Rafael's gaze swept down her throat and across her bare shoulders. "Hand over the dress. Laundry service is here."

Eve slammed the door in his face. She rushed to the bathroom, picked the dress off the floor and carefully rolled it into a ball. At this point, it was a biohazard and ought to be bagged and labeled as such. Rafael was leaning casually against the doorframe when she returned. She handed him the dress through the crack. "Here you go."

"Thank you, miss," he said. "I'm ordering dinner. How do you take your steak?"

Oh, God… Just the thought of a good steak made her mouth water. "Actually… I'll have a grilled salmon and asparagus."

"Really?"

"Yup."

"Is that what you want?"

"No. It's what I should have."

"Any reason?"

"Just…trying to clean up my diet."

There was no way to bring up her new heart-healthy diet without dampening the mood.

"You're disciplined," he said. "There are plenty things I'd like to try, but I'm not starting tonight."

Maybe a little too disciplined, she thought with a frown.

"Are you sure?" he said. "It's okay to change your mind."

"Fine! I want the steak," she blurted. "Medium well."

"Medium rare," he said with a grin. "You can trust me on this. I know beef."

Trust was the theme of the night, she thought, as she slammed the door in his face for the second time.

Five

The shower was strong. Hot water needled Eve's shoulders and back, but did nothing to ease the tension in her muscles. She tried wiping the slate clean of all thoughts of Rafael: his face, his inky-black hair, warm almond skin, his fingers around her wrist, or working the zipper down her spine. And then there was that kiss. Eve pressed her forehead to the glass shower door and relived the moment the fake kiss had turned real.

She was in a hotel, no, an inn, with a gorgeous man who touched her, who kissed her, in such a way it made her melt. What was she doing hiding behind locked doors? Eve stepped out of the shower and toweled off. If she could change her mind about the steak, couldn't she change her mind about other things?

Rafael wasn't in the sitting room when she stepped out in her robe. Eve heard the shower running in the adjoining bedroom. She picked up the pad off the coffee table, curled up on the couch and added to her list.

Robe: super soft.
Complimentary toiletries: top notch!

A moment later, the door to his bedroom swung open and Rafael came out, barefoot and wearing a robe that was larger than hers. Stripped down like this, he looked more relaxed than he had all night. More touchable, too.

"You look cozy," he said.

Eve tucked her feet beneath her. "People may not come here for wild sex, but the robes make up for it."

"Ha!" he said. "You should add that to your list."

She held up the pad. "It's all here."

"May I see?" She handed it to him and he silently reviewed the growing list. "You have an interesting rating scale."

"I'm not in the hospitality industry," Eve said. "My first impression is that of the average guest."

"Very useful."

"What properties do you own?"

He dropped the pad on the coffee table. "Miami Sky and Sky Blu in Fort Lauderdale."

"Are you kidding?" Those were two trendy and frankly sexy South Florida landmarks. Miami Sky was the preferred spot for after work drinks with colleagues. Not that she'd be hanging out with colleagues anytime soon. "Why haven't I ever heard of you before coming to Royal?"

"I'm not the attraction."

She wasn't sure about that. Looking up at him now, all she saw was damp, smooth, golden skin. He was hard to miss. Although he claimed to have never met Arielle, Eve wondered if her sister had ever crossed paths with him. She must have attended those famous Sky Blu pool parties.

There was a knock and a voice announced room service. Rafael raised his eyebrows, his excitement palpable. "Are you ready to eat?"

She was more than ready. "Can't wait."

The food at the Belleview Inn was phenomenal. Either the chef was a genius or Eve hadn't had a decent meal in far too long. After dinner, she updated her list. *Food: fabulous!*

Rafael shook his head. "You're too easily impressed."

"Says the man who wolfed down his steak!"

They migrated to the couch to savor slices of tres leches cake. Rafael had insisted on dessert. Later, he asked, "Have I done right by you?"

She dragged a finger through the icing and took it to her lips. "I think so."

He set down his plate and stretched out, all long limbs and languid gestures. "Now it's time for some adult conversation."

Eve fidgeted with the knot of her robe. "I think I'll pass on that."

"Sorry. That's not an option," he said. "Review the minutes. It's on tonight's agenda."

That agenda was trash. "I've got an idea. How about we write a new one?"

"No chance," he said. "I have questions that I want answered."

"Was that your plan all along? Feed me and get me to talk?"

"It's a good plan. Works every time."

And it looked like it was going to work now. "What do you want to know?"

"Who are you, Eve Martin? Aside from the mystery woman who showed up in Royal with the mystery baby?"

According to her medical chart, she was a Black, unmarried, college-educated female, age 28, with a family history of coronary artery disease and a recently diagnosed heart defect that had landed her in a coma. None of that was sexy, thrilling, or exciting—all things she wanted to be tonight.

"Go on," he said.

She bought herself some time. "You first."

"Me? Depends on who you ask."

"I'm asking you," she said. "Maybe I was too quick to size you up. Seems to me you're a good guy."

Rafael used a cloth napkin to dab at cake crumbs on her

chin. It reminded Eve of the way he'd tended to her in the club lobby, so unexpectedly tender. "I'm not all that good," he said softly.

"You've been good to me."

All her adult life, Eve had avoided men like Rafael. She'd played it smart and chosen her dates from a pool of "nice guys." What she'd gotten was a string of dull dates and luke-warm sex—no crazy night escapades or kisses that made her head spin.

He got up from the couch and returned with the bottle of tequila and the bowl of lime wedges that room service had delivered earlier. He filled two tumbler glasses with ice and set up a bar on the coffee table. "I brought you here, kept you up past your bedtime, made you eat steak, drink—" he poured her a glass "—and drink some more."

She took the glass from him, their fingers brushing. The ice and the tequila sparkled in the overhead light. "You forget I made some decisions along the way."

"I'm just saying." He sank down to the carpeted floor and reclined against an armchair. "Maybe don't let your guard down around me."

Eve slid off the couch and joined him on the floor. "I'll make my own mistakes, thank you very much."

He raised his glass. *"Salud!"*

"Cheers." She took a sip of tequila. The chilled spirit warmed her heart.

"Were you and your sister close?" Rafael asked.

"We were sisters," she said with a sigh. "Nothing could change that, obviously. But we weren't exactly close."

"It's the same with my half sister," he said. "But we're trying."

Eve joined her hands on her lap. Since he'd brought up Cammie, perhaps it was time for this conversation. Rafael's sister was her baby nephew's temporary legal guardian. After Arielle had died, Eve came to Royal to reunite Micah with his father. Only, she fell sick and was hospitalized within hours of her arrival, leaving her baby nephew in need of care. Cammie Wentworth, by virtue of being in the right place at the right time, had offered to foster him.

"It's sort of awkward meeting you like this," Eve said. "Your sister is my nephew's guardian."

"Ah!" he said. "I was wondering who that little kid was."

Eve saw right through him. No amount of humor would make this less awkward. "Your sister is a very good person. She's been a lifesaver."

He looked at her steadily. "She's the best. I'm the problem child."

"I can see that."

"Cammie and I didn't grow up together," he explained. "What came between you and your sister?"

"There was the age difference between us. It wasn't that great, but add to that a stark difference in personality. We were always competing with each other."

"For guys?"

"Ugh!" Eve groaned. "Only a guy would think that."

Rafael bowed slightly. "I apologize for dumb guys everywhere."

"We competed for everything except guys," Eve said. "Arielle was a butterfly, drifting from adventure to adventure. She thought I was a bore. You can say we led competing lifestyles."

"You…a bore? Where did she get that?"

"She wrote it in her diary."

"She wrote 'Eve is a bore' in her diary?"

"Not those exact words," Eve said.

Arielle was a crafty writer. Her exact words: *If only Eve could get out of her own way, get some new friends, get away for a weekend, get laid, get a job she actually likes. Sheesh!*

"I think you're plenty fun."

"Just wait until I bore you to tears with my lists and spreadsheets."

"You're organized," he said. "I can appreciate that."

"Well, my sister couldn't. It drove her crazy."

"Sounds like classic sibling rivalry," he said. "Family isn't always the best judge of things, Eve. I can tell you that."

"More than petty rivalry," Eve said. "We were hell-bent on proving the other wrong. I wanted her to see that my orderly way of life was the best, the most secure. And it kills me because, in the end, when she returned home from Texas, pregnant, scared and ashamed, the way she looked at me…" Eve's throat tightened. "I could tell she thought I'd won." Eve's voice cracked. She paused to take a breath. "I didn't win, you know? I didn't win a damn thing."

"No one wins this stupid game," Rafael said quietly. "No one."

"Well, I lost big time," Eve said. "After giving birth, my sister had some…heart problems. Meanwhile, I had my own problems. Things were a mess at work and soon after she died, I lost my job under a hailstorm of false accusations of fraud. My face was on the local news and my accounts were frozen. It was hell. The lawyers doubted the court would let me keep Micah. So I hopped on the first bus to Texas, collapsed, ended up in the hospital bed and lost Micah, anyway."

"And that's when Cammie stepped in?" he asked.

Eve looked down at her hands.

Rafael let out a low whistle. "That's a lot."

Eve agreed. It was a whole helluva lot. She hadn't even shared the most harrowing details. After meeting with the lawyer and faced with the prospect of losing custody of Micah, Eve had sat sobbing in her car for an hour before hatching the plan to flee west. It was imperative she reunite Micah with his father. What choice did she have? She was facing possible criminal indictment. If it turned out that she wasn't free to raise him, she had to make sure he was left in good hands. Unfortunately, she couldn't just call the man. Arielle had never shared his identity, and Eve had not wanted to pry. Then her sister had died suddenly and it was too late.

That afternoon, she drove home and, heart pounding,

started to pack. She tossed her clothes and important papers into a suitcase and grabbed the tin with the ten grand in cash that she'd inherited from her grandmother. She stuffed Micah's diaper bag with packets of formula, diapers and a dozen onesies. As she'd packed the bag, she found the most important thing hidden in a side pocket: a diary that Arielle had left behind. It detailed her time in Royal. It likely held the only clues Eve would ever have to discover the identity of Micah's father. When she was about ready to leave, she sat with the baby to collect herself and cried some more. It had been the worst night of her life.

"So, you see," she said. "I don't blame you for being upset where my sister is concerned. I know how it feels to be falsely accused of something. It's terrible, and no one should have to go through that."

He studied her awhile. "A simple paternity test cleared my name. It wasn't quite so easy for you. What happened there?"

"Don't you know?" How she'd lost her dream job under criminal allegations was a part of her past that she'd rather not think about, let alone discuss with a stranger over tequila.

"I might have heard a few rumors."

"Allegedly, I embezzled hundreds of thousands of dollars from the financial firm that gave me my start."

Rafael refilled his glass. "Stealing from a greedy investment banker isn't really stealing, is it?"

"Stealing is stealing."

"Alright," he said dismissively. "But you didn't steal anything."

Eve raised her chin, defiant. "How do you know?"

"You're not that clever."

Ouch! That stung. Eve couldn't even hide it. "I was pretty good at my job."

"Am I wrong?" he asked.

"Dead wrong," she fired back. "It wasn't a complicated scheme! I could've come up with it."

"Maybe," he said coolly. "But you couldn't have executed it."

"I can do whatever I put my mind to."

In the back of her mind, Eve knew her outrage was misplaced. He was, in a strange way, taking her off the hook. Why was she so desperate to hang on?

"Sorry to take a swipe at your criminal credentials," he said. "But you nearly passed out at the thought of tipping over a champagne tower at a country club. You really want me to believe you embezzled money from one of Miami's most powerful financiers?"

Well…he had her there. "In any case, they caught the person who tried to frame me. I'm in the clear."

"All's well that ends well," he said with a crooked smile.

He picked a wedge of lime from the bowl and brought it to his lips. Eve watched, transfixed, and once again fell straight through the trapdoor of her imagination. She was in the lobby again, kissing him. For all his talk about his grandmother, Rafael was not the type of guy you brought home to meet your own grandma. He was good for making a woman *feel* good. And there he sat at arm's reach, unguarded and practically undressed. Eve could *never* embezzle hundreds of thousands of dollars, not from a greedy financier or anyone. But maybe, just maybe, she could pull this off.

Eve rose to her knees and loosened the knot of her robe.

Rafael set down his glass on the coffee table with a definitive tap. "What are you doing?"

"I'm letting my guard down."

The sides of the robe fell open. His heated gaze raked her body. "Eve…" he said. "What did I say about that?"

She was far from caring. "I want the night you promised."

He leaned his head back against the seat of the chair, watching her through narrowed eyes. "Pretty sure I didn't promise this."

Eve drew her robe shut. "My mistake then."

Before she could tie the belt, he caught it and tugged her

to him. She fell forward into his arms. The kiss in the lobby had been the slow, getting-to-know-you sort. By now, though, they knew each other just fine, and this kiss was rough and demanding. His hands roamed her body. Eve tried to straddle him, but he eased her away. "Eve, we have a dilemma."

"What's that?"

"Either we call our man downstairs and ask him to send up a box of condoms or—"

She silenced him, first with a finger to his lips then with her mouth pressed to his. "Just kiss me."

With adept hands, he pushed the heavy robe off her shoulders. Then he eased her away again and took in her naked body. "Where?"

"Wherever you like."

He lowered her onto the floor and pressed a kiss in the dip at the base of her neck. "Where else? Show me."

Eve pointed to her navel and he followed her fingertips with his lips. Next, she guided him to her hip. Slowly, methodically, he pressed hot kisses all over her aching body. His tenderness and care soothed her aching heart. Eve twisted and arched her back, doing whatever necessary to meet his mouth wherever it wandered.

Kissing on the lush carpet: exquisite.

Six

Eve curled up in bed. She dreamed of Rafael's fingers grazing her skin, soft laughter in the dark and kisses pressed into her eager body. She dreamed of coming so close to pleasure only to be denied, again and again, until the denial was its own pleasure. Then she woke up shivering and alone—not just in bed, but the hotel suite. She called out to Rafael, and the only response was silence. There was a note on the bedside table. She read it twice, still a little hungover from all that tequila.

Eve, sweet, something's come up. I have to go, but I don't have the heart to wake you. A few things:

> *Your dress is in the hall closet.*

> *Call room service and breakfast will be delivered.*

> *When you're ready to go, contact the concierge.*

A car is waiting to take you home or anywhere you need to go.

> *Everything is taken care of.*

Here's my cell number. 954-333-1100
Call me.
—R.

So…he'd bolted. Maybe he wasn't such a good guy, after all. Was it any surprise, really? This must be his MO, abandoning women in hotel rooms, sneaking out while they slept. She wouldn't have pegged him for that sort of guy. For whatever reason, the idea didn't take root. She wanted to give him the benefit of the doubt.

Eve climbed out of bed. On the bright side, she did have an entire suite to herself. Last week, she'd moved out of her Airbnb host's guest bedroom into their renovated detached garage. She had more privacy, but not much more space. Here, she had so much space she could do cartwheels—although her physical therapist would not approve.

Eve called for room service. The order had already been placed, and within fifteen minutes the food was delivered. Say what you like about the Belleview Inn, the service was prompt. There was a bit of everything, mostly healthy options like oatmeal, yogurt and fruit, but also bacon—crispy, crunchy, salty, tasty bacon. She reached for a strip then dropped it. Her life was oatmeal. No bacon, no more steak or liquor, and no escapades with sexy strangers allowed. She poured herself a glass of orange juice and wandered the connected rooms. Everything looked different in the morning light. Eve took in the pale yellow wallpaper, thick maroon drapes, heavy wood furniture and framed paintings of horses. *Decor: traditional to a fault.*

The bed in the second bedroom was pristine. Rafael had slept with her last night, and the bed they'd shared was a crime scene. He'd kissed her everywhere then scooped her into his arms and carried her to bed. They fell asleep, limbs intertwined, skin-to-skin. It took all Eve's willpower to keep from climbing back into that bed and under the sheets just to feel him again. But she couldn't indulge in this fantasy. She'd had her fun; it was time to get back to reality.

After breakfast, Eve poured herself a bath and tossed a floral-scented bath bomb into the warm water. She had to wash Rafael Wentworth's scent off her body. Where best to do it than in a claw-foot tub?

When Eve finally made it home, she pulled on a pair of pink leggings and a matching top, holdovers from her hot yoga days. She had a physical therapy session later that afternoon, and for once she was looking forward to it. It seemed she couldn't sit still one minute without feeling Rafael's lips tracing circles on her breasts. If she shut her eyes, even briefly, his phone number blinked in the back of her mind like a neon sign.

She had to forget the happy-go-lucky Rafael Wentworth. They were too different. Tonight, while he'd likely meet with friends for dinner, she'd eat ramen in bed while applying for random jobs online. She was fine with it. Eve was no longer interested in comparing her life to anyone else's. This was what she had to do to stay afloat. Her focus was on building a secure future for herself and her little nephew.

She sent a text message to Cammie, her nephew's benefactor, for lack of a better word. She wanted to visit before therapy. Holding the baby would help her reconnect with her priorities.

Eve's love for Micah was tethered with guilt. There was nothing she could do to sever the two emotions. It had been that way ever since the nurse had placed her newborn nephew in her arms. Arielle was not well, and the infant needed skin-to-skin contact. The joy of new life coupled with anxiety over her sister's declining health had overwhelmed Eve. She held Micah close and sang to him, just like her grandmother had sung to her. Skin-to-skin contact: the fabric of family.

Arielle wasn't well, but no one had expected her to die. The heart attack that took her life three weeks after Micah's birth had even shocked her doctors. Yet unexpected death and soul-wrenching heartache was the one thing life had prepared Eve for. She'd lost her parents in a fatal accident not too long ago. All that being said, she would not lose Micah. She refused.

Micah was her heart. She would move heaven and earth to ensure he had the future that he deserved. She hadn't come to Royal to have fun or flirt with gorgeous men. She had one specific task: track down Micah's father. According to Arielle's diary, he was a TCC member. A DNA test had ruled out Rafael, but that left a sizable portion of Royal's wealthy male population. Unfortunately, that was the only clue she had.

Eve touched the hollow of her neck, the very spot where Rafael had planted a kiss. She'd keep the memory alive, but resolved to shelf the man away for good. She could handle only one life-shattering event at a time. Given the opportunity, Rafael Wentworth would shatter her heart. She knew his type. His rushing off this morning had made it all the more clear. He was not one to get attached. When he was ready to move on, he'd leave a big, gaping wound in her life for her to stitch up on her own. Eve had nursed enough wounds, both physically and emotionally, and would not survive another.

Her mind made up, she grabbed her keys and her bus pass and set out for the day.

Seven

It had killed Rafael to leave that note for Eve, but his options were limited. A 4:00 a.m. phone call got him out of bed. The news hadn't been good. Scaffolding at the construction site of his newly acquired property had collapsed. The luxe guest ranch was still under construction and not yet open to clients. The main house with reception, offices and a few permanent suites was complete. The restaurant was half-finished, and his Michelin-starred chef was busy creating new recipes and testing them on the staff. Rafael hoped to have everything up and running in six months. It would be tight, but doable. But that meant overseeing everything himself.

Eve was in deep sleep, her face soft. He didn't have it in him to wake her.

Like a thief, he'd crept out of the suite, stopping at the front desk to make the necessary arrangements. On the drive to the site, he worried as much about the accident as he did about her waking up alone and confused at the

Belleview Inn. Eve and her air of mystery. Eve and her scandalous past. Eve and her uncertain future. Eve with skin like caramel.

Weeks ago, Cammie had wanted to introduce him to her protégé of sorts, thinking that two outsiders from Florida might hit it off. His sister wasn't wrong, but he and Eve had more than Miami in common. They were outsiders in every sense of the word. Rafael even understood her reasons for dressing up and heading out last night. It was his preferred way of coping with life's ups and downs, a method he'd perfected over the years. He knew how isolating it could feel to be the odd one out in this tightly knit community, and he wasn't going to let her twist all alone in the wind.

He intended to call her as soon as he got a chance. With all the chaos on the construction site, the opportunity didn't present itself until midmorning. It was too late. The Belleview Inn front desk clerk informed him that his guest had checked out an hour ago.

He took a break around noon and drove out to the car shop to finalize the purchase of the Camaro. The location was just as odd looking in the daylight as it had been the night before. A gravel path led to the concrete block of a building. The blinking neon OPEN sign over the metal door was the only indicator that it was a place of business, and not home base for a garage band. Manny clasped him on the shoulder. "Good thing you left your top hat and tails at home this time. You can join us for lunch."

With the accident at the construction site, Rafael hadn't bothered to dress for work. He'd stopped by the residence, slipped on a black T-shirt, jeans and a pair of boots. Manny wore a denim button-down shirt and cargo pants. They were roughly the same age and both successful in their own right. Manny had worked in one of the most prestigious shops in Dallas before relocating to his hometown of Royal.

Inside the "showroom," several cars were lined up. The Camaro was draped with a canvas cloth.

"I'm excited for you, man," Manny said. "Want another look?"

"What do you think?"

With a yank, Manny revealed what looked like a carcass of a car dragged up from a swamp. Rafael winced, hit with buyer's remorse. The harsh light of day revealed cracks and dents he might have overlooked the night before. What on the mother-loving earth had he agreed to purchase?

"Hey! Show some respect," Manny said. "This is a 1969 Camaro—"

"No, it's not," Rafael interrupted. "That's what it used to be."

"Once upon a time this beast tore up the asphalt."

"No doubt. But *today* it's a rotting tin can."

"Having second thoughts? It happens. You gotta have faith, bro," Manny said. "If you can't see the beauty in this, I can't help you."

Rafael considered the curved contours of the car's rusted body. He saw the beauty. He wasn't willing to admit it, though.

"When I'm done with this tin can, it'll fetch north of five hundred grand at auction. So you can get in on it now for the low, low price that we agreed on last night or you can drive off in your pretty car and have a nice life."

"What's your plan for the engine?" Rafael asked. No amount of trash talk was going to throw him off.

After a lengthy discussion, Rafael tossed the pen he'd used to sign the papers at Manny, aiming for his head. The next thing Rafael knew, they were seated at a round table in the back of the garage, eating barbecue with a pair of mechanics and talking about cars. It was a welcome distraction. He worried about Eve, wondered if she'd gotten home alright. And why hadn't she called him? He didn't have her number, and with no way to reach her, he was at a loss.

After lunch, Rafael drove slowly along the busy streets. She lived in this part of town, didn't she? Too bad he hadn't memorized her address. He considered asking around. She was such a polarizing figure in Royal that he could likely get her address from anyone on the street. Or…he could ask his peach of a sister. The idea struck him between the eyes. Eve's nephew was in Cammie's care, his darling sister's care. Damn it! He should have thought of it hours ago.

Rafael pressed hard on the gas. Twenty minutes later, he pulled up to Drake and Cammie's ranch. Drake was Micah's official foster parent and Cammie was the primary caregiver. Or did he have that wrong? It hadn't occurred to him to ask before. It was a temporary arrangement, and complicated, too. His sister wanted children; she'd always been clear about that. Drake, though, had preferred his freedom. Honestly, Rafael couldn't blame him. However, by taking in Micah and helping Cammie through this time, Drake seemed to be coming around.

Rafael was mulling this over when Drake approached and tapped on his windshield, peering at him with his ice-blue eyes. Rafael climbed out of the car.

"Rafe! You're early, man," Drake said good-humoredly.

Rafael had started visiting Cammie on Friday afternoons. It was his attempt to meet his sister halfway. They were starting over. Cammie was just a kid back when he'd moved in with his father and teenage Rafe wanted nothing to do with her. The children of dysfunction, they had no prior relationship to fall back on, no well of childhood memories to draw from in bad times. Rafael had left his father's house at seventeen when it was clear he had no place in the Wentworth clan. His very existence was a black mark to the Wentworth name. When he left for Florida, he vowed never to return.

Cammie had reached out to him constantly over the years, then she started writing letters advocating on their father's behalf. Losing his third wife, the love of his life, had wrecked him. Apparently, he'd changed. The old man then reached out, pleading for another chance. It was time to stop ignoring them. And here Rafael was, back in Texas, far from the life he had built for himself and second-guessing his decision every day. However, he was committed to repairing his relationship with his father and would remain in Royal for as long as it took. He'd taken on projects to justify staying in town, even just to himself. The guest ranch and the Camaro were necessary tools. The projects kept him moving at a fast pace while he took on the slow work of getting to know his estranged father and becoming the brother Cammie deserved. He felt certain that this was something that he had to work through. His anger toward his family had served as armor. As a teen, he'd needed that extra protection. But as an adult, it only weighed him down.

Rafael had taken some measures, baby steps, really, to reconnect with his family. On Saturdays, he met his father for lunch, usually at the TCC's Colt Room. On Fridays, he visited with Cammie. They'd sit outside with coffee and talk. It had been awkward at first. He was the reason her family had blown up. Her mother left their father after he finally came around to acknowledging Rafael as his son. And yet, Cammie didn't resent him. He doubted he'd be so generous if it were the other way around.

He and Drake headed toward the house.

"Cammie is inside with Eve and the baby," Drake said. "Want to grab a beer?"

Rafael slowed to a stop. "What did you say?"

"Beer. Want to grab one?"

That wasn't the answer Rafael was looking for. He said yes to the beer and, heart pounding, dashed ahead of Drake up the front steps. He'd cleared the door when he realized that Drake had meant for them to grab a beer while Cammie visited with Eve. Well, too bad and too late for that. He followed the sound of voices into the kitchen. There she was at the kitchen table in pink leggings, hair in a floppy ponytail, golden brown skin flushed, no makeup and no lipstick to wipe away with a kiss. His heart fell into a ditch. *There you are, sugar plum.*

Cammie was at the stove stirring a pot. "Hey, you! I wasn't expecting you this early."

"I was in the neighborhood and thought I'd stop by and say hi." He sought Eve's eyes. "Hello, Eve."

"You just happened to be in this neighborhood?" Drake said.

"And how do you two know each other?" Cammie said.

Eve looked a little panicked. She cradled Micah in her arms.

"Everyone knows everyone in this two-horse town," Rafael said, teasing his sister and throwing her off their scent.

"Whatever!" Cammie fired back. "I'm glad you two have met. You've got a lot in common."

"So you keep saying."

Drake slapped him on the shoulder and handed him the beer that he'd forgotten about. "Don't stare," he whispered. "You'll scare her."

He couldn't help but stare. The woman before him now, soft, tender, unhurried, cradling a baby in her arms, was the same person he'd met last night, sharp, direct, bemoaning her former "30 Under 30" status. He had to wrap his head around that.

Eve's phone buzzed and she slipped it out of an invisible pocket of her body-hugging leggings. One glance at the screen and she let out a groan.

"What is it?" Cammie said.

"My therapist has to reschedule."

"You're in therapy?" Rafael said.

"Physical therapy," she replied without looking at him. "I'm still wobbly on my feet."

Last night he'd assumed that her heels were the problem. He knew about her long hospital stay. Even so, he hadn't suspected a physical impairment. Guilt wormed through him. He'd kept her up and fed her steak and dowsed her with tequila and made her body twist to his will. Just how oblivious was he?

"Are you okay?" he asked.

"I'm fine!" She followed that declaration with a look that said: *You know I'm fine!*

Rafael shook his head. He knew no such thing.

Her phone buzzed again. She looked at her nephew and made a decision. "Take him, please," she told Rafael. "I have to answer this. They need me to reschedule."

He went over to where she sat and lifted the baby from her lap. While she typed on her phone, he took in Micah with new eyes. He had a head of black curls and was as plump and golden brown as a loaf of bread. Micah stared at him with skepticism. He had Eve's eyes. Rafael tickled his chin to find out if he had Eve's smile, as well. Micah did not smile. Solid little kid.

"Look how good you are with him!" Cammie exclaimed. "Remember that first time? You wouldn't even touch him."

"I remember." Babies were cute and all, just not for him.

"You'll make a great dad someday."

Rafael raised an eyebrow. "Have you seen the cars I drive? There's no room for baby seats."

"You'll upgrade to a family sedan." It was as if she'd had his whole future mapped out.

Drake leaned against the counter. "Or get a truck like the rest of us."

Rafael was going to hurl up his beer. Now was probably not the time to bring up his expensive new purchase.

Eve returned. "I'll take him now." She waited as Rafael placed Micah back on her lap.

Drake spoke up. "Heard there was an accident on your property."

Rafael had forgotten how quickly word traveled in Royal. "Scaffolding collapsed on the site."

Cammie had abandoned the pot and worked a knife through a stash of herbs. "Was anyone hurt?"

He locked eyes with Eve. "No, but it dragged me out of bed at four in the morning."

"You couldn't have been happy about that," Drake said.

"God, I hated it," Rafael said. "You have no idea what it cost me."

Eve turned away, her cheeks the color of wine.

"You can't be everywhere at once," Cammie said. "You need help."

"I'm looking to hire an assistant."

"Don't you already have one?" Cammie asked.

His sister had visited the property and met his staff. "You mean Dan? He's overseeing HR and general management stuff. I need someone more detail-oriented for daily operations."

"We've used a local recruitment firm," Cammie said. "Remind me to get you the number."

"Sure," he said, already forgetting all about it. Eve was giving him a hard look, even as she bounced Micah lightly on her lap to the baby's delight. What was she trying to tell him? Her phone buzzed again and stole her focus. He nearly groaned in frustration. When had he become so needy? He needed to know what she'd wanted to say. On top of that, he needed to know why she hadn't called. And it didn't stop there. He needed to know more about her physical therapy and the nature of her injuries, if any. He needed to know if she had dinner plans. If she didn't, would she agree to grab a bite with him?

"Oh, no!" Eve cried. "They want me to come in *now*."

"What's wrong with now?" Cammie asked. She sprinkled the chopped herbs into whatever it was she was cooking. And whatever it was, it smelled really good. "Take my car. I'm not going anywhere."

Rafael had assumed that Eve had chosen not to drive last night, but that didn't seem to be the case. She didn't have a car, here, in Royal, Texas, where public transpor-

tation was a sort of practical joke the local government
played on its people.

"I can take you," he said.

Out of the corner of his eye, Rafael caught Drake laughing into his beer bottle.

"Big bro to the rescue!" Cammie cried. "It's settled. Rafe
will take you."

God, he loved his sister.

"No, thanks," Eve said, hugging Micah to her chest. The
little boy reached up and dug his chubby fingers into her
cheek. "I don't want to impose."

"It's no trouble," Rafael said.

Nothing she could ask of him would be too much. He
would drive across this state and back if she needed him to.
He wasn't sure his hard stare could convey all of that, but
he put in the effort.

Eve hesitated a moment. "Okay."

"It's settled," Cammie said. "Now go on, you two."

Eve held up Micah and spoke to him. "Auntie Evie has to
go to therapy now. Remember I told you about therapy? I'd
love to stay and give you a bath and read you a story. Next
time. Okay?"

Rafael watched as she planted a kiss on Micah's forehead and whispered a secret in his ear. A wave of tenderness crashed into him.

Cammie took Micah from her. "Don't worry about it.
We've got bath time covered."

His little sister was the most generous, bighearted person Rafael knew. She loved children. It made sense that Eve
would entrust Micah to her.

Drake ushered them out the door. "Go on. Don't get into
trouble."

Rafael and Eve walked to the car in silence, each aware
they were being watched.

"Thanks for the ride," she said.

"Were you ever going to call?" he asked.

"No."

"Why?"

"Not important."

Like hell it wasn't. "You thought I skipped out on you?"

"Yes and no."

He held open the car door for her. "You're not making sense."

"Don't worry, I'm over it." She climbed in. "There's something else I want to talk to you about."

Really? He could think of literally nothing else he wanted to talk about. The minute he joined her in the car, she grabbed his arm, digging her nails in his biceps. He welcomed the contact, but questioned her motives. "What's up?"

"Hire me!"

"What?"

"You need an assistant and I need a job. Hire me!"

So, that's what it was all about, Rafael thought, driving off Drake's property. She wanted the executive assistant job.

"You'll never find anyone more detail-oriented than me," she said. "I'll learn the business. I'll do whatever it takes."

Rafael stopped at a light. "You got the job."

She released his arm. "Well…don't do me any favors. You should go through your regular process."

"You're of two minds on everything, Eve. Anyone ever tell you that?"

"I'm a Gemini," she said. "I'm not asking for a handout. All I ask is that you consider my application."

"How about an interview?" he suggested. "Would that make you feel better?"

"Yes, it would," she said. "Then you can judge for yourself whether or not I meet your needs."

Rafael suppressed a laugh. She met his needs, and she damn well knew it.

"Where are we headed?" he asked.

"Wait a minute."

She pulled out her phone and tapped an app for directions.

She was the most app-dependent person he knew. "You really don't know your way around, do you?"

She clutched the phone. "It won't impact my job performance. I rely on GPS, sure, but I always find my way around."

"Settle down, Eve," he said. "The interview isn't until later."

If anything, she was overqualified with her extensive experience in finance. And last night had taught him one thing: they made a great team.

"Later when?" she asked.

"How about tonight?" he proposed.

"Is that when you usually interview candidates? At night?"

Her clipped tone cut him. He resented the implication. "It is, actually," he said. "I take the top two candidates out for dinner. I only hire people I'm comfortable with. My business is my life."

Her expression fell. "Oh."

Rafael's hands tightened on the wheel. He understood all that he was giving up to offer her this job. As his employee, she would be off-limits. He'd have to forget everything that had happened the night before and wasn't sure he could. Was it too late to take back the offer and help her find some other job? Maybe at his father's nonprofit?

They arrived at the therapy clinic. Rafael found a parking spot in a shady area of the lot, but Eve had only minutes to spare before her appointment.

"Today we're doing lower body strength training," she said. "Woo-hoo!"

He released his seat belt and faced her. "Why do you need therapy?"

"I was in the hospital awhile and it's like they say—use it or lose it."

"Why were you in the hospital?"

"Haven't you heard?"

No use pretending he hadn't heard the gossip. "They say you collapsed and fell unconscious. No one ever says why."

"It's too much to get into right now," she said. "And I promise I'm getting better. It won't affect my job performance."

"Oh, God, Eve… Enough with that."

She averted her eyes, looking out the car window at the bland outpatient clinic. "Sorry. I'm just anxious."

He reached for her hand, but thought better of it. "I understand."

"I have to go," she said. "They'll cancel my appointment if I'm late."

"How are you getting home?" he asked.

"Don't worry. I can manage."

"Manage how?"

"There's a shuttle bus for patients."

"It takes you to your door?"

"It takes me close enough and the walk is good exercise."

"I can wait here until you're done."

"Don't even think about it." She opened the car door. Before stepping out, she leaned in as if to kiss him and then stopped short. Had it finally clicked? He was no longer her potential lover. He was her future boss. Regret pooled in her brown eyes. She blinked and pulled away from him. "So, about that interview. Time? Place?"

"Tomorrow morning at nine. Does that work?"

"It works."

"Text me and I'll send you the address," he said. "You still have my number, right?"

That simple question brought back the note and the events of the night before that she refused to acknowledge. "Yeah. I have your number," she said, and slipped out of his reach.

Eight

Eve had her mind on her money. If she had to choose between good sex and a good job, she was going for the job. No doubt about it. Too bad the same man had the power to offer both. No, that wasn't quite true. He was offering one or the other, and she had made her choice. She'd seen the disappointment in his eyes. It mirrored her own. No one would ever hold her like he had, press kisses into her skin, whisper her name, tease her, tug her hair…

Eve's fingers trembled when she texted him a short, brief message later that night. This is Eve.

I'm sorry. Who?

She sent him an eye roll emoji. He sent her a photo of him biting into a monster burger. The message read: This is dinner.

She snapped a photo of her cup of low-sodium noodles and sent it along.

His response came quickly. Toss that out and come join me. I'll treat you to Royal's best veggie burger.

She took her phone and cup of noodles to bed. Nope! Sorry. I have a big interview in the morning with a certain Mr. Wentworth.

You have an interview with a certain Mr. Arias. And brace yourself, I hear he's a jerk.

Arias? Really?

If local gossip held a kernel of truth, his mother, Rosa Arias, was a local girl of Mexican descent. Tobias Wentworth got his mistress pregnant but had no intention of ever marrying her.

Arias. Really. Haven't you heard? I'm the big, bad, black sheep.

A wicked smile tugged at her lips. A wolf in black sheep's clothing is what you are.

He responded with a wolf emoji. Be careful. Don't get lost in the woods.

She tapped her thumb against the screen wondering what to reply next. Thankfully, he sent her the address and wished her good-night. Eve fell breathless onto her pillow. She should crave safety, but she didn't.

Earlier today, when Rafael had stormed into Cammie's kitchen as if it were the beaches of Normandy, her heart had tanked. She visited often and had never run into him in the past. Besides, he'd said they weren't close. In Drake and Cammie's kitchen, drinking beer straight from the bottle, he was not the perfectly put together man she'd met the night before. The country club member. An heir to the Wentworth fortune. Scruffy, unshaven, tousled hair, wrinkled T-shirt, plain jeans, and even a little grease under his fingernails. She could barely look at him for wanting him so much.

That night Eve went to bed early, but she did not sleep a wink.

Her alarm rang at six thirty on the dot. It took her a while to find an interview-appropriate outfit. Normally, this wouldn't be a problem. She had been dressing for the job she wanted instead of the sucky job she had ever since she was old enough to vote. Too bad she had left her collection of pantsuits back in Miami. For her interview with "Mr. Arias," she settled on a blue silk blouse, a navy pencil skirt and a pair of pumps.

Eve left her place with plenty of time to arrive at the guest ranch and freshen up in the restroom before the 9:00 a.m. interview. Unfortunately, she hadn't planned for the delays. The bus arrived twenty minutes late and broke down a few blocks from the appointed address. Rather than sit and wait for a new one to arrive, Eve hopped out and walked the rest of the way.

The Arias property sat on an impressive spread of land. From the guard gate, a long driveway to the main house extended under a canopy of leafy trees. It was 9:05. She was officially late.

This was not the first impression Eve had wanted to make. Her goal was to force him to see her as more than a charity case. Showing up sweaty and exhausted at a morning interview wasn't the way to go about it.

She ambled along the cobblestone walkway in her sensible heels. Her feet hurt. When she thought of the way she used to strut in stilettos along the crowded sidewalks of Miami's financial district with a cup of Starbucks in one hand and her phone pressed to her ear, it made her want to cry. As it was, she couldn't even safely carry her nephew until she built up adequate upper body strength. The rehab doctors had prohibited it.

Eve arrived at the main house and limped into the reception area. She breathed in the chilled air and soaked in her surroundings. The decor was minimal and modern, all tall windows, cream upholstery and cognac leather.

First impression: wow!

A receptionist looked up from a computer monitor. "Are you Eve Martin?"

"Yes." Eve stepped forward. "I know I'm late."

"Just by a few minutes." The young blonde woman rose from behind a smooth, curved marble desk. "What happened to you? Did you cross a desert to get here?"

Eve could die of embarrassment. "The bus broke down."

"Yikes!" The receptionist offered her a bottle of water. "Let's get you fixed up."

"But I'm late," Eve stammered.

"Exactly. What's five more minutes?" Her message was clear: better to show up fashionably late, than sweaty and on time. "I'm Audrey, by the way."

"Nice to meet you, Audrey."

From behind the desk she produced a pack of tissues, face mist and a compact mirror. "Here you go."

Audrey was young, barely twenty, and had all the can-do spirit that came with that age. "Don't mention it. I was super nervous when I interviewed with the great Rafael Arias Wentworth. Seriously, though, he is amazing and this is the best place I've ever worked. Seeing what you went through to get here, you must really want this job."

From the mountaintop of legal and medical bills where she was perched, Eve saw things differently. She desperately needed this job. She was living off meager savings and the modest inheritance from her grandmother.

Eve checked her reflection in the mirror and smoothed back her hair. She wore it in her signature bun at the nape of her neck. She blotted her face and reapplied lipstick. One spray of mint-scented mist and she was ready.

"Much better," Audrey said. "I'll let Mr. Arias Wentworth know you're here."

Mr. Arias Wentworth. That was a mouthful. Would she have to call him that? Would he call her Ms. Martin? How awkward would that be? She'd spooned with this man.

"Take the stairs or the elevator to the second floor," Audrey said, giving her one last push. "Good luck!"

Eve took the elevator, which turned out to be a mistake. It took her right back to the elevator at the Belleview Inn and that first real, heartfelt conversation they'd had. That took her back to the first kiss they'd shared in the inn's lobby. And that looped her back to the time he'd pushed off her robe and lowered her onto the carpeted floor. Her cheeks were burning when the elevator doors slid open. There stood Rafael Arias Wentworth, laid-back yet professional in a tailored blue blazer paired with a sky blue button-down shirt. His dark hair was slightly wet and brushed neatly. This was corporate casual Rafael, and she wanted to yank him into the elevator and leave lipstick stains on his crisp collar. Their eyes met, and she had no doubt he knew exactly what she was thinking.

This was getting off to a great start.

Nine

Rafael greeted her when she stepped out of the elevator. "Good morning," he said. "I was about to give up on you."

Eve didn't believe him. He would never give up on her. That type of certainty was odd this early in any relationship. "Sorry I'm late. It won't happen again."

"No worries," he said. "Come with me."

He led her past the deserted reception area to his office suite tucked behind a pair of frosted glass doors. His name was etched on the glass in straightforward print: Rafael Arias Wentworth.

"Take what you need and drop that heavy purse here," he said, pointing to a smooth suede couch.

"We're not doing it here?" she asked, rummaging through her purse for the mini tablet with her résumé. She didn't have a hard copy. The print shop was closed by the time she'd made it out of physical therapy.

"No, we're not," he said. "Let's go. Breakfast is waiting."

Breakfast! Her mood took off on a hot-air balloon. She'd munched on a cereal bar on the bus and now she was starving.

Rafael led her out of the office suite and took the stairs to the lobby. Eve had no choice but to follow. The stairs were steep, and the glossy marble tile looked slippery. She clung to the rail like a toddler. Her therapy diagnoses were disturbing: *abnormality of gait, general muscle weakness, and lack of coordination.* The goal was to regain her "prior level of function." Because she had yet to do so, the social worker on the case had marked her as unfit to care for an infant or child full time. With each session, Eve was getting stronger. Her endurance and balance had greatly improved. Still, uneven surfaces remained a challenge. She was working with her therapist on that, too.

Audrey smiled up at them from the reception desk. When Rafael wasn't looking, she gave Eve the good old thumbs-up. Eve cringed. She had no idea how much of her self-confidence was tied with her physical well-being. She'd always been athletic and capable, playing sports through high school and, in recent years, keeping up her fitness with rigorous gym classes. And here she was, clinging to a handrail, taking careful steps, while Rafael took confident long strides. When he reached the landing, she'd only made it halfway down. He swiveled around and raced back up, taking the stairs by twos.

"I'm sorry," he said when he reached her. "I should be more careful with you."

"No, you shouldn't," she said through clenched teeth.

"Yes, I should," Rafael insisted. "What's wrong with that?"

Nothing. Absolutely nothing was wrong with it, except that it made her feel weak and pathetic. This last year had revealed her greatest flaw: an inability to accept help of any kind with any sort of grace.

Rafael would not budge. He offered his arm and waited for her to take it. Reluctantly, she looped a hand around his elbow. To touch him again, even like this, made her flinch.

Together, they made it down the stairs. He led her out of the building through a wide door made of reclaimed wood. The vast property sloped west, and he pointed out the limits beyond a tuft of pine trees. A gazebo was set up with a round dining table. Rafael held out her chair and told her the chef was working out the kinks in the new kitchen. To keep things simple, he'd requested one dish: a Spanish omelet. "No sausage. No bacon."

"Thanks for that."

Rafael plucked a croissant from a basket at the center of the table. "You wouldn't meet with me for dinner, so I got creative."

Eve handed him the iPad opened to her résumé. He took it from her and set it aside. "There'll be time enough for that," he said. "How was your night?"

"Mr. Arias Wentworth," Eve said, "I can't tell you how to do your job, but you should start with the standard interview questions. Like… What are your strengths? Or… Where do you see yourself in five years?"

"What *are* your strengths?" he asked.

"Um…" She was distracted by the way he toyed with a butter knife. She imagined reaching across the table and mingling her trembling fingers with his strong ones.

"And tell me your weaknesses, while you're at it."

"I'm practical," she replied. "I have no trouble setting aside fantasy to focus on reality."

Rafael flashed a half smile. "That's not the standard answer."

"Alright." She tried again. "I'm stubborn. I won't give up on a problem until it's solved."

"That's more like it," he said, and slid the iPad across the table. "Why not just tell me what's here?"

"Sure," Eve said, suddenly nervous. She might have to peek at her own résumé to get the facts straight. "I attended FIU, both for undergrad and business school. Then I accepted an internship with the firm and gradually worked my way up."

He nodded his approval. "Very good."

"You know how the story ends, so it wasn't all that good."

Rafael tilted his head, studying her. Eve knew what he was thinking. She was the one to continually bring up the scandal—not him, not anyone, just her. Even when offered a fresh start, all she could do was dig up the relics of the past.

Rafael picked up the pot of coffee from the center of the table and poured her a cup. "Sugar?"

"Please."

He added two cubes to her cup and presented it to her like a gift. Her hand trembled as she took it from his hand to her lips.

"You may be overqualified for the job that I originally had in mind."

Eve shrugged. "It's this or bus tables, so…"

"Not true," he said. "You have options. Between Cammie, Drake and I, we can find you a job."

"No." Eve set down her coffee cup. She didn't want to work anywhere else.

"Audrey says this is a great place to work and you're a dream boss."

"Gotta love Audrey!" Rafael said with a low laugh. "Though I wish that were the case, it's not. I'm not a dream anything. I can be difficult, Eve."

"How so?" she asked, wondering who was sitting across the table from her this morning. Was it the black sheep or the gray wolf?

"I'm going through some things," he said. "Coming back to Royal, dealing with Tobias, getting to know Cammie… It's been hard."

She could only imagine. Rafael had inherited a mix bag of snacks: money, scandal, shame, loss and a name that worked like a diplomat's passport, providing access and immunity. She could not relate. The Martin name would not open any doors. Her father had emigrated from the Bahamas. Her mother was from Georgia. They were entry-level middle class at best. The family home was their one asset. When they died unexpectedly, she and Arielle had sold it to cover the cost of the funeral and other expenses and split the rest. Eve had inherited from her grandmother, as well. Grandma Martin had left her and Arielle exactly ten grand each. The old school Caribbean woman never trusted banks and squirreled away her savings in tin boxes. For sentimental reasons, Eve had kept her inheritance in the same blue Danish butter cookie box that she had received it. The cash had come in handy when her accounts were frozen. It was as if her wise grandmother had known that a woman always needed liquid assets. All in all, her family had left Eve and Arielle in good shape. The rest of it, though, the scandal and shame, they had brought on themselves.

"You and Cammie seem to get along," she said.

Rafael raked his fingers along his jawline. "It's work, though. I'm not a family guy, Eve. I've never had a traditional family, and I don't know how the gears work."

None of that changed the fact that he could be a dream boss. Would he be moody or temperamental at work because of his family drama? If that were the case, she wouldn't wilt. Eve had worked with some major jerks in the past. "If you have a bad day at work, don't worry about me. I can take it."

"I wouldn't take my crap out on you," he said. "That's not what this is about."

"What then?"

He leaned back, hesitated. The breeze tousled his hair and she was suddenly jealous of the breeze. "Opening a luxury guest ranch this close to the TCC makes good business sense," he said. "When this property came up for sale, I grabbed it. But Royal is Tobias's territory. Something about this doesn't sit right."

"Just to be clear—Tobias is your dad. Correct?"

"Don't call him that."

Oops! Eve reached for her coffee cup. "Noted."

"Sorry," he said, sheepish. "That came out harsh."

"Look," she said. "It's not my business, but the way I see it Royal is Arias territory, too."

A current of understanding passed between them. Eve got it now. This new endeavor was a monument to his mother disguised as a guest ranch for the discerning traveler. Rafael was putting down a marker. His goal was to raise the Arias name, flip Tobias the bird and remind all of Royal the son of scandal was back.

"I've been tossing money around like confetti on this project and…some other things. I need to be reined in. That's where your job would come in."

God bless the person who had to rein in Rafael Arias Wentworth. She bet wild horses were more readily tamed.

"Do I even have a job?" she asked testily. This interview had gone off the rails. There was no point beating around the bush anymore.

"The job is yours, Eve," he said. "Just take it already. Or are you going to demand a fitness test?"

The job is yours. Eve let out a long breath. She had a job. Praise God! Now it was time to get serious. She dropped her elbows on the table and interlaced her fingers. "In that case, let's talk money."

Rafael's eyes flashed. You'd have thought she'd asked him to talk dirty to her. Was money his love language? What a coincidence! It was hers, too.

"Alright," he said. "Let's talk. Give me your number."

"I'm not cheap."

"Shock me."

"Forty thousand."

"Come on, Eve. Is that a joke?"

"I've done the research," she said, offended. "Thirty-five thousand is the average salary of an executive assistant in Royal."

"You'll have more than administrative duties. I want you in charge of the budget."

Her heart fluttered. Was that what he meant by reining him in? Getting a hold on the budget? He was likely going overboard with the renovation. He could build this place into the Taj Majal and it wouldn't change anything. Her advice was to leave "family vendetta" off the budget.

"Is that something you'd be interested in?" he asked.

"Very much."

Spreadsheets, budgets and reports were her thing. She enjoyed making sense of numbers. It was assuredly the most boring skill set known to man, but Eve didn't care.

"Did I mention this job includes some travel? Are you comfortable with that?"

"I am, to some extent. I wouldn't want to be away from Micah for too long."

"I understand," he said. "An overnight trip now and then to visit a distributor or location site. Nothing more involved than that."

No adjoining suites. No dinners in bathrobes. No kissing on the floor. No falling asleep in his arms. "No problem."

"Knowing all of that, what's your number?"

"Forty-five thousand?"

"Oh, Eve." He balled up his cloth napkin and tossed it onto the table. "You can't tiptoe into negotiations."

The chef arrived with their omelets. Eve thanked him. It looked and smelled delicious. Too bad her stomach was in knots.

"Rafael," she said a moment later. "I don't have the winning hand here."

"Yes, you do," he said. "All signs point to you as the ideal candidate. I need someone competent who is willing to start right away. You're in a position to do that. More importantly, I need someone I can trust. So, from where I sit, your hand looks pretty good. Play it."

"I want sixty-five thousand to handle the administrative work, plus the budget and expense reports."

"Done."

Eve brightened. "Really?"

"The standard answer is, 'I can live with that.'"

She really could. This meant a decent life for her and Micah, whether they found his wayward father or not. In a gesture that was definitely not interview appropriate, she reached over and covered his hand with hers. "Thanks. You won't be sorry."

His expression clouded and something inside Eve collapsed. The elephant in the room, or gazebo in this case, had to be addressed. "Rafael," she said, her heart aching, "I want you, but I *need* this job."

His gaze did not flicker, even as the light in his eyes dimmed. "Am I the fantasy that you're setting aside to focus on reality?"

Eve did not reply. The answer was obvious.

Rafael withdrew his hand from beneath hers. "*Bienvenida al rancho*, Ms. Martin," he said. "Can you start on Monday?"

Eve didn't reply to that, either. The answer was obvious, too.

Ten

I want you, but I need this job.

Sitting across a table from Tobias Wentworth, Rafael stewed. Eve had said those words so matter-of-factly, almost without feeling. Well, he wanted her, too, but couldn't turn it off and on like she could. The slow fire they'd lit in the garden at the TCC had quickly grown wild and out of control. He thought about her every waking hour. He wanted to finish what they'd started at the Belleview. It wasn't the same for her; she could take it or leave it.

"Are those fries any good?" Tobias asked.

"Pretty good."

They were at their usual table at their usual meeting spot, the Colt Room at the Cattleman's Club. They'd met for dinner instead of lunch. Rafael had rescheduled on account of his late breakfast with Eve. Still, he ordered his usual burger and munched on the seasoned fries without tasting them.

"You're stabbing the damn things with your fork like you have something against them," Tobias said. "Looks personal."

Rafael stared at his silver-haired, blue-eyed "dad" who could always read his moods. Some things never changed.

Rafael had returned to Royal on the promise that Tobias was a changed man. He'd given up his money-hungry ways and started a charitable foundation to prove it. It had only taken the death of the woman he loved to bring that drastic change about. Much like it had taken the death of his mistress, Rafael's mother, for Tobias to acknowledge Rafael and bless him with the Wentworth name. Why did a good woman have to die just to nudge this man down the right path was the question Rafael wanted answered.

"It's been a tricky week," he mumbled.

Tobias cut into his steak. "I heard about the construction accident."

"Yeah, that was something," Rafael said. "But did you hear about the champagne tower that collapsed in the ballroom? That was a catastrophe."

"Oh, yeah," Tobias said with a chuckle. "I would have liked to see it."

For a cranky old man, Tobias could be good company.

"I heard from Cammie that you've taken on a mentee and doing a good job with it."

Tobias's nonprofit venture provided assistance and support to the children of first responders. Cammie had joined as the organization's director and was steering it well. Rafael's receptionist, Audrey, had received a scholarship and was putting it to good use. She worked mornings and attended evening classes at the local college. When Cammie brought up Lucas, a clever kid who was at risk of dropping out of high school, Rafael had offered to meet with him. Now he couldn't shake the kid off—not that he wanted to.

"You know how it is," Rafael said, brushing off the praise. "Give a kid some attention, and they end up clinging to you for life."

"No," Tobias said. "I don't know how it is."

Rafael felt a pang of something. It couldn't be guilt. Tobias's relationships with his kids were tenuous at best. At some point, there hadn't been any relationship to speak of, so really, this was progress. The man should be counting his blessings.

"Stick with me," Rafael said. "I'll teach you a few tricks."

As much as he loved his work, Rafael had never wished away a weekend. Yet he'd spent his Sunday just waiting for Monday to come around. He couldn't wait to see Eve. He knew that he had to stay away from her, treat her like any other employee, but he wasn't sure how he'd go about it. In the recesses of his imagination, he replayed the images of their night together. He was stuck on the moment when she had offered him her naked body. Eve didn't play at seduction. As with everything else, she'd been direct and matter-of-fact, and it was sexy as hell. With so much unfinished business between them, how could he pretend it wasn't killing him? How could he hide it?

Finally, it was Monday. Rafael left it to Dan to greet Eve and show her the ropes as he pretended to go about business as usual. Eve was in good, capable hands. Dan was his second-in-command. Originally from Houston, he had jumped at the opportunity to relocate from Fort Lauderdale to Royal to help set up the guest ranch. Rafael had intended to stay out of the way for now and maybe stop by her office to welcome her later in the day. Yet Dan called almost straightaway to conference him into their meeting. "Our new hire has some… concerns on what she calls the Cadillac of benefit packages."

Dan was a Black, gay, army veteran who, as he put it, did not tolerate foolishness.

"Is that right?" Rafael said.

"Yes, sir. It is."

Her voice came through the speakerphone loud and clear, combative as ever. Rafael nearly burst with happiness. He reclined in his desk chair and joined his hands behind his head. "Alright. Let's hear it."

"We'll begin with the actual Cadillac," Dan said.

Rafael had picked out the vehicle himself. "Eve, you object to a company car?"

"Did my predecessor have a company car?" she asked.

Rafael tossed the question to Dan, her predecessor. "Did you, Dan?"

"I had a company truck," Dan replied flatly. "That's more my speed. Would you prefer a truck?"

"No, I wouldn't," Eve said. "But a Cadillac..."

"It's not an Escalade or anything," Dan said. "It's a compact SUV, solid, reliable and very stylish."

"Fine!" she said.

Rafael had to mute the phone to laugh. Meanwhile, Dan moved on to the next topic. "We covered health insurance. No objections there."

"None," Eve said. "And thank you."

"Now to accommodations," Dan said. "Here are the keys to the residence. Suite 3A is on the top floor. The views are partially obscured, but I think you'll like it."

"A suite? Really?"

"We don't have anything smaller, Eve," Rafael said. "And the view is fine."

"Did my predecessor have a suite in the residence?"

"Didn't need one," Dan said. "My fiancé and I are renting a bungalow in town."

"I don't need one, either," Eve protested. "I live in town, too."

"You sure about that?" Dan quipped.

"Mr. Arias, I would like to speak to you in person."

Rafael could think of nothing he'd like more. "I have an open door policy, Ms. Martin. Come on by."

She stormed into his office moments later, looking pretty and fresh in a lemon drop yellow dress. Her expression was tart.

"It's too much!" she exclaimed.

"Good morning, Eve. Have a seat."

She ignored him. "Seriously, what are you doing? A car? A suite?"

"The package is tailored to your needs. In your case, you need a car and a shorter commute."

"A company car is a Nissan or Toyota, not a Cadillac."

"I like to buy American."

"You drive a Jaguar!"

"You know too much about me," he said with a laugh. She gave him a sharp look, cutting off his laughter at the source. "Why not let me help you?" he asked. "It makes no difference to me. At this point, it's all Monopoly money exchanging hands."

In his heyday, Tobias Wentworth had a reputation of being a hard-ass boss and a miserly one at that. Rafael was determined to run his businesses differently. That meant meeting his staff's needs and treating them like people from the start, not as a means of damage control when things went awry.

Eve came closer, her hands little tight fists at her sides. In a thin voice, she said, "I don't want to owe you anything."

"The suite is available. If you don't move in, it'll just sit there empty."

The intercom buzzed, and Audrey's voice crackled through the speaker. "Mary Richardson is on line 1."

Mary Richardson, along with her husband, Keith, owned the neighboring South Point Motel. Rafael had been waiting for this call. He asked Eve to give him a minute. She went over to the couch, but the call was over by the time she got settled. He'd been summoned by his neighbor.

"Don't get comfortable," he said. "We've got work to do."

Eleven

The South Point Motel had seen better days. Or was it that Eve was enchanted with the splendor of Casa Arias, just next door. Mary and Keith Richardson were plainspoken individuals. They were not at all enchanted with their new neighbor or his plans for their property. But, as Mary Richardson said, they were at the end of the road. It was time for them to retire. Their adult children were not interested in managing a run-down motel. After a family meeting, they'd agreed to sell. "How to go about it is the question," Mary said.

"How do you want to go about it?" Rafael asked.

"We could put it on the market and see what bites, but why play that game?"

"There's no reason we can't come to an agreement."

Eve didn't need a briefing to understand the appeal of the Richardsons' property. The motel stood at the corner of a busy intersection. On the drive over, Rafael shared his plan to convert the building into a day spa, the type of business that would attract clients. But his real interest in the motel was its access to the main roads. As it was, Casa Arias was accessible only by a narrow side street. It wasn't ideal. Joining the two properties would greatly increase accessibility.

"Hold on." Keith spoke up for the first time. "The way I see it, you need us more than the other way around."

Rafael slid a glance Keith's way. "Funny. That's not how I see it at all."

Eve could not turn away from Rafael. She saw something in those dark eyes, gleaming like a razor's edge. It sent a shiver down her spine. Try as Rafael might to distance and distinguish himself from his family name, he was his father's son.

The meeting was inconclusive. Rafael was uncharacteristically silent on the drive back to his property. Eve would pay for his thoughts. He'd been wrong earlier. She did not know enough about him, and she was endlessly curious.

He pulled into his reserved spot. She reached for the door handle and he reached for her, curling a hand around her wrist. His touch was light, but the ribbon of heat coiled up her arm and held tight. He hadn't touched her since, well, that night when he'd touched her all over. God help her; the memory of that night still held her captive.

"Sorry I pressured you about moving in," he said. "Just wanted to help. Didn't mean to make you uncomfortable."

He released her and stepped out of the car. She followed him into the main house and up to the second floor. He directed her to her office then walked away, leaving her feeling lost, disoriented and confused.

Eve was ready to leave for the day when Dan chased her down the hall. "Ms. Martin! Hold on! I have your keys. The car is serviced and ready."

He dropped the key fob in her hand. She stared at it, wondering whether her Airbnb host offered overnight parking.

"I'll show you to it," Dan said.

He took her to the employee lot. A sleek, red SUV caught

her eye. She loved it. Later, she'd sit Rafael down for a talk on what counted as reasonable business acquisitions and expenditures. For now, though, she couldn't wait to climb behind the wheel. "It's a beauty."

"What did I tell you?" Dan boasted.

"Tell me the truth," Eve said. "He buys these cars just for the chance to drive them."

"It's a lease, but yeah."

"Help me set up the Bluetooth?"

"No problem."

Dan did more than set up the Bluetooth. He adjusted the seat to her height, added the local public radio station to her list of favorites and entered her home address into the navigation system. She thanked him and wished him good-night. Once settled behind the wheel, she punched in Cammie and Drake's address and drove straight over. It had been a long day. She needed to hold her nephew.

Two weeks into the job and Eve was feeling settled, and that was unsettling in and of itself. She learned the ropes. She knew her way to the restroom, breakroom and gym. She'd joined the morning coffee circle led by Audrey. Her days were shaped into a routine. She worked until five and, if she did not have a therapy appointment, she took off to spend time with Micah. For the most part, Rafael's affairs were in order and it was a while until she encountered her first red flag. Eve was no expert, but a proposal from a local design firm seemed to run a bit high. She used that excuse to schedule an emergency meeting with her boss.

Rafael had been avoiding her or, as he put it, "giving her space." He assured her that he was only a phone call away. She could read him pretty well. These new roles they'd assigned to themselves were constricting. By taking this job, she'd hijacked the ship and changed the course of their relationship. They'd been on their way to becoming something other than employer and employee. When she heard his voice down the hall, regret tied a rope around her heart. When she ate lunch alone at her desk, she wished they could, if only for a moment, sit, talk and laugh like that first night. Honestly, she would be willing to dock one week's pay for it. Finally, she had a legitimate excuse to seek him out. When she called, he reminded her of his open door policy and told her to swing by whenever.

In her old workplace, where ninja warrior skills were required to leap from one rung of a ladder to the next, there was no swinging by anywhere to speak with the top brass. She swung by and found that he was not alone. A teenage boy in a pressed button-down shirt sat in one of the two leather swivel guest chairs. Rafael was seated next to him, his feet propped up on his desk. They were sipping milkshakes and watching a Michael Jordan documentary on the wall-mounted TV.

"What's going on here?" Eve demanded, true to her schoolmarm self.

Rafael swiveled lazily in her direction. Eve wanted to swivel in the opposite direction and run down the hall. The urge to go to him, kiss him, ball up on his lap and set her head on his chest had come on suddenly and in the most violent way. When Eve had asked for this job, it was with the understanding that she would pack away all the feelings he stirred up in her. She'd struck that deal with herself and had entered into it discreetly, advisedly and soberly. Nothing had changed. She couldn't afford to mess this up. Very soon, she'd finish PT, get her doctor to sign off to regain custody of Micah and would have to provide for him. She still very much needed this job.

"Ms. Martin," he said. "Come in. Meet Lucas, my…" To Lucas, he said, "What are you again?"

"You're my mentor," Lucas said. "I think the word you're looking for is *mentee*."

"I think the word I'm looking for is wise ass."

"That's two words." Lucas turned to Eve for confirmation. "Am I right?"

"Leave her out of this," Rafael scolded.

"He's new to this," Lucas said. "It's only been six weeks or so of mentoring. He's doing okay, but we'll see how it goes."

"This is Evelyn Martin, my new executive assistant."

Eve stepped forward. "Nice meeting you, Lucas."

The boy grinned and gave her a double thumbs-up with greasy thumbs, a crumpled hamburger wrapper clutched in one hand. Lucas would grow up to be a handsome man someday. For now, though, he was all curly dark hair, mischievous grins, brown sunbaked skin and long, wiry limbs.

Rafael's eyes were on her, as gentle as his tone. "What do you have for me?"

Eve blinked, her brain blank. "I...uh...flagged something on the design firm's proposal."

"Tell me," he said.

"They've proposed marble for the spa."

"Is that bad?" he asked.

Lucas slurped his milkshake. "Gotta have that marble bling!"

"Marble is expensive," Eve explained. "Plus, it's impractical. It's great for some areas but not the best choice for the spa treatment rooms."

"What do you suggest?" Rafael asked.

"Quartz. Far more resistant, equally beautiful."

He seemed doubtful. "Is it, though?"

"I thought you might have doubts so I went out and got samples." During her lunch break, she'd gone to the nearest big box home improvement store. Eve opened the small cardboard box she'd brought with her and produced marble and quartz square tiles. Holding them up like a TV infomercial host, she said, "See for yourself."

Rafael and Lucas roared. For a split second she thought her masterful presentation had earned her a standing ovation, but nothing could be further than the truth. Rafael and Lucas were focused on the television screen, where Michael Jordan had leaped across the court and dunked a ball into the basket.

Lucas punched the air. "The man can fly!"

Rafael fell back in his seat, undone. "It gets me every time. Every damn time."

The two switched to Spanish, praising the prowess of the legendary basketball star. Eve, incensed, held up the samples. "Excuse me!"

Rafael snapped to attention, contrite. "I'm sorry, Ms. Martin. You were saying."

The formal "Ms. Martin" grated on her nerves. "You're his mentor. Shouldn't you be teaching him something?"

Rafael snapped the remote control off his desk and hit pause. Lucas groaned in protest, but Rafael silenced him. "She's right," he said. "The first thing I'm going to teach you is to respect your employees' time. Go on, Ms. Martin."

Eve felt foolish. After all, she'd barged in and dampened their fun. "You could save up to fifty dollars a square foot. Not to mention the expense of upkeep."

Rafael patted his pockets and found his phone. He dialed a number. "Yeah, Jason, I'd like a revised budget proposal to swap out marble for quartz in the spa treatment rooms. Comb through for any other cost saving options, and we'll see you Wednesday... Sounds good." He ended the call. "Damn! I feel productive."

Lucas rested a hand on his shoulder. "Good job, *jefe*."

Eve folded her arms across her chest. These two were clowns! She couldn't help but think back at her own high school internships, mainly how dull they'd been. She was assigned thankless tasks, making copies and fetching coffee, for the privilege of adding a company's name to her résumé. She hadn't learned a damn thing except how to make herself small and stay out of the way. She did not know anything about Lucas, but she would bet his parents were not TCC members. Rafael was teaching him a lesson: you could be successful and accessible. There was no need for a gilded cage. Eve was learning something, too. It was okay to have a little fun at work.

She reached for the remote and pressed play. "It's the goofy Mr. Clean earring that bugs me."

Lucas came back to life. "It's the source of his power!"

Rafael stood, took the samples from her clutched hands and eased her into the seat he'd just vacated. "Chocolate or vanilla?"

He was offering her a milkshake. "Strawberry?"

The corner of his mouth curved into a teasing smile. "You got it."

That evening, Eve went to spend time with Micah. After a solid half hour of tummy time, she sat on the floor, scooped her nephew up and settled him on her lap. She rocked and hummed a sad little lullaby her Bahamian grandmother used to sing to her and Arielle. *Hush little baby...my trials soon be over...* She could not sing that song without thinking of the fate of her sister, whom she prayed was at peace. But Eve's trials were over, too.

She'd been through the worst of it and, finally, things were looking up. For the longest time, Eve had adopted a defensive posture, just trying to protect herself and Micah. Now was the time to go on the offense, gain ground and make up for all she'd lost. She claimed to want a better future, for her nephew and herself. It had been her singular focus all those weeks spent in the hospital, alone, depressed and scared. But she could see now that her priorities were as scattered as the colorful blocks flung about the nursery.

Eve made some decisions. She'd move into the suite at the residence. Dan had given her a tour just to further entice her. It was the exact layout of her tiny efficiency except triple the size, airy and bright. It had gleaming wood floors, a modern kitchen, and, naturally, polished marble surfaces. A large bay window faced west. As far as she could tell, the only obstruction was the fine tops of pine trees. Eve was sure the sunsets would be miraculous.

By moving into the residence, she would eliminate the taxing commute. The money saved on rent would go to paying off her debts. Win-win-win.

Eve had been wrong about Rafael. Men like him were good for more than one thing. He was a businessman, cunning when it suited him. Good at seizing opportunities. Good at making money. Those were the skills that she had to develop. Since he was so intent on helping her, maybe he could help her draft a business plan of her own.

Micah fell asleep in her arms. As his breathing steadied, Eve slipped out her phone and dialed Rafael's number for the first time. He answered straightaway, his voice betraying his disbelief. "Eve? Is everything okay?"

"I'm moving into the residence."

"You are?"

"Yes," she said. "How soon can I move in?"

"Now… I'll help you pack."

"No," she said. "I can manage."

She'd turned him down mostly out of habit, but she really didn't have very much to pack.

"You're sure you don't need help to pack the car? Then haul it all up to the third floor of the residence?"

He had a point. With her heart condition, she shouldn't be lifting anything heavy. Her doctor would not approve. "Okay! Fine! Come by tonight."

"Send me your address."

Twelve

Rafael ducked out of a dinner party hosted by a state representative to drive across town and help Eve pack. He couldn't wait to see her again. By his own clever calculation, he'd ensured that he would see her every day from this day on. His generous offer had a selfish motive, designed to keep her close. It wasn't the thing a good and charitable person would do, which made him want to call her and say "See? You were wrong about me. I'm not the Good Samaritan of your dreams." But that would freak her out and rightly so.

He pulled up to her address. Eve lived in a converted-garage-turned-Airbnb. It was as dreary as he'd imagined. Selfish motives or no, he could not allow her to stay here.

She opened the door, wearing heather-gray leggings and a small, tight, yellow T-shirt with a smiley face stretched across her breasts. The bright color played up her brown skin nicely. She took a step back. "Had I known this was a fancy packing event, I would have thrown on my one cocktail dress."

"The red one?" he asked, suddenly excited.

"No," she said. "The other one."

"That makes two."

"Who's counting?"

"I am," he said. "Just for accuracy. May I come in?"

She looked at him appraisingly. "I don't think so."

"I had a thing," he said, explaining away his dark suit. "I'll lose the jacket and roll up my sleeves."

"Please! I love when you do that."

Rafael played back the reel of every single one of their encounters until he found it: that night in the garden. She sat on the stone bench, moonlight adding sparkle to her soulful eyes. He'd draped his jacket over her shoulders, loosened his tie and rolled up his sleeves. He knew they were on the verge of something that night, some grand adventure, and had refused to let the night end.

"Come in," she said.

He stepped inside and shut the door behind him.

The kitchen, the bedroom, the tiny seating area were all crammed in one space. Rafael wasn't a snob. He'd lived in smaller places when he left home at seventeen. But at seventeen, he didn't care where he lived.

She pointed to the wine and water glasses lined up on the kitchen countertop. "If you could wrap those in newspaper, that would be great."

Eve folded laundry at the foot of her bed. He got to work, but she made a point not to look at him when he slipped off the jacket.

"Would you like something to drink?" she asked.

"Sure. Thanks."

She left the basket of laundry and went to the refrigerator, pulled out a bottle of fruit-flavored sparkling water and filled two glasses that he had not yet wrapped. "The first thing I did when I moved in was to buy stemware at the big box store to enjoy a cool beverage like a lady."

"I approve," he said. "Sounds like you've got your priorities in order."

"Speaking of priorities, I've been thinking," she said. "How did you get into the hospitality industry?"

"My friends used to call my crappy little apartment in Miami Beach a hostel," he said. "It was the one place they could crash, take a nap or a shower. The refrigerator was always stocked. After college, I applied for a job at a hotel and was hired on the spot. The owner was…kind. He took the time to show me the business. When he got sick and was ready to sell, he arranged for me to get a loan." Rafael took a sip of sparkling water and grimaced. "He became a father figure to me, you know? What he did allowed me to come back to Royal a success. Before you ask, the answer is no. I didn't take a dime of my father's money."

Rafael's hands were trembling. He pressed them onto the butcher-block countertop to steady them. Funny how her simple question had drawn so much out of him.

"How are things with your father now?" she asked.

He grabbed a delicate wineglass and wrapped it in the Sunday sports page. "We meet for lunch once a week or so. That's the long and short of it. We're never going to be the perfect father and son. We're not playing catch in his mansion's backyard."

"No one plays catch with their kids," she said with a little laugh. "That's what Little League is for."

"Are you close with your parents?" he asked.

"While they were alive. Sure."

God! What this woman had been through… "Sorry, Eve."

She brushed the condolence away. "My mother and I never did the typical mother-daughter things. She didn't teach me how to sew or wear makeup. She didn't even teach me much about bras. I had to sort all that out myself. But she loved me unconditionally. See my point?"

"Your mother was a lovely person. My father is Tobias."

"Well, that's true."

Her expression went soft. He turned away, taking a sip with a painful expression. She wasn't the only one who couldn't stomach pity. When their eyes met again, she was still studying him.

"You hate it, don't you?" she said.

"This sparkling stuff?" He set down the glass. "So much. Do you have anything else? Beer?"

"Sorry, I don't," she said. "They sell beer at the corner store."

He grabbed his car keys off the counter. "Great. Let's go!"

"Put away your keys. It's a short walk and parking is a hassle." She emptied their glasses into the sink. "Let's order pizza, too. Up for it?"

He was up for anything, apart from discussing the past. It was done, and there was nothing to be gained by digging up those old bones.

After calling the pizzeria, she and Rafael took off into the night. They argued about toppings on their way to the store and crusts on their way back. She paused to tie her laces just as Rafael brought up *tlayuda*, a Mexican tortilla. Having never tried it, Eve had no opinion on the dish. That didn't stop Rafael from launching into an impassioned defense of the street food favorite. Right then, a sprinkler embedded in the hedge that lined the sidewalk burst into action. A hard stream of cold water slapped her in the face. Eve cried out with outrage. The jet reversed course and struck her in the back of the head. She heard Rafael swear through the ringing in her ears. She was vaguely aware that he dropped the convenience store bag of snacks and grabbed her, pulling her out of the jet's path.

"Why am I always wet when I'm around you?" She caught the double entendre and tried, very clumsily, to walk the comment back. "God! I didn't mean for it to sound like that."

"Sound like what?" Rafael said distractedly. For some reason, he was undressing right on the sidewalk.

"What are you doing?"

He was very obviously unbuttoning his shirt. The slow

reveal of his smooth and sculpted chest had made up for the indignity of getting sprayed in the face.

"Covering you up. You're going to freeze."

He draped his dress shirt over her shoulders. His voice warmed her more than the thin extra layer, yet she reveled in it. Rafael raised her chin with the tip of his finger and inspected her face. With the back of his hand, he blotted her cheeks dry. The gesture was unexpectedly tender. The way he looked after her, those sudden displays of tenderness, got to her. Or maybe it was his bare, sculpted chest and the way his golden brown skin shimmered in the lamplight. Either way, he got to her—there was no denying it.

"Is this about your grandmother again?" she asked for the sake of making chitchat. "Because she's wrong. I won't catch pneumonia. I'll be fine."

"Take that back," he said. "Abuela Carla was never wrong."

She caught his use of the past tense. "I had an opinionated grandmother, too, you know," she said. "She would have fixed me a cup of ginger tea and told me to go to bed."

"Sounds like our grandmothers would have gotten along." He rubbed her arms, still trying to generate heat. It was wholly unnecessary. His shirt had wrapped her in his scent, and it warmed her to the core.

"If our grandmothers are looking down at us right now, they're probably wondering what we're squabbling about."

"Doubt it," he said, and scooped up the bag that he'd dropped to come to her aid. The muscles of his back rippled as he moved. "They're probably wondering why we aren't getting busy making babies."

"For the last time!" Eve cried, feeling defensive. "No one is trying to have your baby! Get that out of your head."

"Good! I don't even want kids."

The finality of his tone struck her. "Why not?"

"Not wired for it. That's all."

Eve vaguely remembered him saying as much during the

unorthodox job interview. She hadn't realized he'd made it a lifestyle. That said, she wasn't about to lecture him about the joys of procreation. She wasn't sure she wanted kids herself. That choice, however, was no longer hers to make now that Micah had been left in her care.

"My family can't seem to get it right," Rafael said. "Let the generational curse die with me."

"If you're cursed," Eve said, "I don't want to be blessed."

"Ha!" He gestured for them to keep moving. They were only steps away from her door. She trotted after him. Although she hated to admit it, the night air had a bite to it and Eve was starting to feel chilly. At her door, he took her key from her. "I got it."

Once inside, she stepped out of her sneakers and arranged them neatly by the door. She was only buying time to gather herself. Maybe it was the sight of this half-dressed man entering her place, taking their purchases into the tiny kitchen, looking around for her when she failed to follow him any farther than the foyer, but she was coming undone. All her reasons for holding back, good reasons, solid reasons, sound reasons, crumbled.

"I'll get you a towel. Where do you keep them?"

Never mind a towel. Never mind his shirt, for that matter. She stripped it off and draped it on the back of one of her two dining chairs. Then she stripped off her T-shirt, which was properly drenched and could very well give her pneumonia. It slipped from her hands and fell to her feet. Rafael went still. She had seen that look in his eyes the night she kissed him in the lobby of the Belleview Inn.

"Do you think?" She took a step toward him at the cost of losing her nerve. Her voice came out strained. "Could we… just one time…maybe?"

Silence swirled around them. Rafael studied her, unhurried. Her hopes shattered with each passing second. She was about to tell him to forget it when he answered, his voice hoarse. "We can definitely just one time…maybe."

Eve rushed to him, wrapped her arms around his neck

and pressed her sopping wet body to his. She must have knocked him off balance because they stumbled over together, landing on the carpeted floor. He brushed back her hair, took her face in his hands and held it as if she were a thing of rare beauty. A stone dislodged in her chest and the truth spilled out. "These last weeks have been terrible."

"Thank God!" He repeated the words under his breath in Spanish. *"Gracias a Dios!"*

"Rafael!" she scolded him.

His hands freely roamed her body. "I'm in hell, and I don't care who knows it."

She traced a finger down the length of his nose. "I'm in heaven now."

Rafael pinned her hands over her head and kissed her softly. Just as she eased into it, he withdrew and kissed her hard. Eve kissed back, hungrily, drunkenly, forgetting the complicated world just outside the door. In here, he was all hers. But then, as luck would have it, a brisk knock on her door brought everything to a screeching halt. A young voice cried, "Pizza!"

Eve groaned and Rafael buried his face in the curve of her neck. "Damn it!" he lamented.

No matter how they felt about it, the pizza delivery guy had done his job, and he wasn't going to leave until he got paid.

"Maybe he has condoms," she joked.

Rafael made a face. "*I* have condoms."

"Hey," Eve said. "You stocked up."

"After last time, I'm not taking chances."

Another knock on the door.

He pushed away, rising into a push-up. She missed the weight and heat of this body. "I'll take care of it."

She smashed his face between her hands. "You've got five minutes. Got that? And don't forget to tip."

He hopped to his feet. "Yes, ma'am!"

In the bathroom, Eve peeled off her soaking wet sports bra and dropped it into the sink. She caught her reflection in the mirror. Naked from the waist up, she looked wild. Eyes bright, lips swollen, cheeks taking on a raspberry flush. Most shocking was her hair. It had come loose from her ponytail. Eve's mother might not have taught her much about makeup, but she had obsessed over Eve's and Arielle's hair, always insisting they keep it neat and straight, never wild, never kinky, never a strand out of place.

She reached for a brush. For some reason, it was heavy as stone. She couldn't do it. She couldn't smooth out the lines and tuck the loose ends in place. What had she gained from following every damn rule in the book? Eve heard the front door slam shut. She put away the brush just as Rafael crowded the bathroom doorway. Their eyes met in the mirror.

"Knock, knock," he said.

She swiveled around to face him. "Just so we're clear. We're about to make a big mistake, aren't we?"

Rafael did not hesitate. "Oh, yeah. We're clear on that."

Eve loved the way he flew straight into the fire. "How about we make a deal?"

"Another deal?" he said. "Should I get my lawyer on the phone?"

Eve fell back against the vanity and gripped the edge of the countertop. "It's simple, really. You make me laugh and I'll make you—"

"Make me what?" he asked.

The answer she gave wasn't what she had cued up. "I'll make you feel a little less lonely in this town."

Rafael didn't say anything, but Eve knew she was right. Rafael Arias Wentworth was a charming, handsome, sexy, lonely man. He covered it with layers of charisma, but she saw through it. Like recognized like.

"Did you think this through?" he asked. "Sounds like a lopsided deal. I stand to receive far more than I'm asked to give."

"That's because you don't know the good it does me to laugh."

He rested his head on the doorframe and looked at her awhile. "Lucky for you, I love your laugh."

For all the heated glances they'd exchanged, it seemed to Eve they were seeing each other, bare and unvarnished, for the first time. He reached for the switch and killed the harsh overhead light and stood motionless in the soft light pouring in from the main room. Rafael in moonlight, in streetlight, in the pale light of a table lamp... He was unfailingly beautiful. Eve reached out to him. "Come here."

He kicked the door shut, came to her and hoisted her onto the vanity countertop. She worked on the buttons of the shirt he'd thrown on for the benefit of the pizza guy. Eve wanted to see him, touch him, explore his body. "You had your way last time," she said. "It's my turn."

"Well, now," he said in the dark. "Lucky me…"

Eve could swim in the currents of his voice. She swept her lips down the ridges of his throat. Her fingers found the hard knot of a nipple. She dipped her head and grazed it with her teeth. It was all it took to snap the thread that bound his self-control. Rafael cupped her breasts and returned the favor, his tongue circling her tender nipples before tugging them taut with his teeth. Eve arched forward, surrendering again. He slid his hands beneath the waist of her leggings and tugged them down her hips and, stepping back, down her legs. "So, you're always wet around me? I didn't know."

Eve burned with embarrassment. "Didn't think you caught that."

"Are you kidding?" With her leggings balled up on the tile floor, Rafael worked her underwear down her thighs.

"It was a joke."

"A joke?" He parted her knees and made room for himself. Her breath hitched as he dragged the back of a hand from a knee up. "I don't believe it."

With the pad of his thumb he proved her to be a liar. Eve leaned forward to kiss his parted lips then tilted backward until her hot skin met the cool mirror. Rafael buried his head between her thighs. She shivered at the feel of his tongue. He spread her wider, explored her deeper. Eve bit her lip and gripped his hair, but there was nothing she could do to slow the rush of pleasure that came embarrassingly fast. Rafael pushed away and gathered her in his arms, holding her, stroking her until she calmed down.

She whimpered and clung to him. "It's been a while."

"*That* I believe."

"Shut up!" Eve fumbled with the buckle of his belt, eager and impatient for more.

"Settle down, sweet," he teased.

He finished undressing, found the condom in his wallet and, with adept fingers, put it on. Eve was unsettled by the sight of him and undone when he took her hand and curled her fingers around him. "Put me inside you."

"Oh, my God…"

He kissed her forehead to reassure her, but made his demand clear. "Work with me."

Eve snapped out of her inertia and guided him inside her. Rafael braced himself with a hand on the mirror behind her and eased into her, slow and controlled. "Do you know what I think?" he asked.

She shook her head, her hair wild around her face. She didn't know anything except how good he felt inside her. "I think you need more than a good laugh."

Heaven help her. That was the truth.

Thirteen

The coast was clear. Audrey was not at her desk. Eve waited a moment then dashed, as fast as she could, across the reception hall. She'd almost made it to the elevators when she heard the young woman call out her name. "Eve! Come back here!"

Every morning, she and Audrey started their day with coffee and a little harmless workplace gossip. Audrey had a specific set of skills. She'd predicted Dan would be promoted weeks before it was announced. When Rafael expressed interest in the Richardsons' property, she was not in the least bit surprised. Generally, Eve enjoyed their chats. This morning, though, she worried Audrey would use those skills to see right into her guilt-ridden heart. There was no office gossip so juicy than the new executive assistant sleeping with the boss.

She and Rafael had agreed to one time, but the likelihood of them sticking to that agreement was slim. Eve had only left him a short while ago. They'd finished packing her things and drove to the residence in the small hours of the morning. After piling the few boxes and bags in her living room, he invited her to tour his suite, conveniently located down the hall. And then they tumbled into bed. Eve was certain that anyone with a little sense would pick up on it, let alone someone as perceptive as Audrey. It turned out to be a needless worry. Audrey was preoccupied with other things.

"You're coming tonight, right?"

"Where to?"

"The Cattleman's Club."

"Nope!" Eve's attitude toward the country club was simple: been there, done that. She had no desire to return and had the perfect excuse. "I'm not a member."

"You think I am?" Audrey said. "Tonight is the Valentine's Day fundraiser."

"Is today Valentine's Day?" Eve asked, alarmed. Had she really committed the cardinal sin of sleeping with someone new just before February 14? She would have to let Rafael know that he was under no obligation to buy her flowers.

"No, that's tomorrow. Tonight's the fundraiser. Everybody is going."

Eve walked backward toward the elevators. "Not me!"

"Come on, Eve! You have to go!"

"Not invited! This is the first I'm hearing of this."

"Everyone is invited," Audrey insisted. "We have a table for ten and ours is going to be the most fun." Before Eve could stop her, Audrey had Rafael on speakerphone. "Good morning, Mr. Arias Wentworth."

"Morning, Audrey."

Rafael's voice cracked through the speaker. As distant as it was, it brought him back to her. She could feel his hard body and smell his hair.

"Just wanted to clear something up with you. Eve, here, seems to think she's not invited to tonight's fundraiser."

After a moment's hesitation, Rafael said, "Is that tonight?"

Audrey looked as if she might faint. "You didn't forget, did you?"

"Oh, no! God no!" Rafael replied hastily. "Could you please ask Eve to come see me?"

"Absolutely!" Audrey ended the call with a triumphant look on her pretty face. "The boss wants to see you."

The door to Rafael's office was wide open. Eve knocked anyway. He looked up and tossed a file aside. "Ms. Martin."

"Mr. Arias Wentworth, Audrey said you wanted to see me?"

His mouth twitched with a smile. "Very much. Come in."

She took a seat at one of the chairs facing his desk. Sometime last night, she'd stood naked in this man's kitchen eating ice cream from the carton. He'd licked chocolate syrup off her fingertips and called her his "Candy Apple Eve." She'd laughed and planted a sticky chocolate kiss into the palm of his hand. The memory flickered before her eyes. Hard as she tried, she could not blink it away.

"I'll be honest," he said. "I forgot all about this damn fundraiser."

She would be honest, too. "Good. I have zero interest."

Rafael rose from behind his desk in one smooth movement and came to stand before her. He was never more handsome than when freshly shaved, hair damp, and wearing a crisp shirt. Even so, she preferred him as she'd left him an hour earlier: hair disheveled, cheeks rough with stubble, waving goodbye to her from bed as she tiptoed out the door.

"Here's the thing," he said. "We're duty bound to attend."

"I think you're wrong."

"Cammie will be expecting us."

He said *we* and *us* so liberally. It flooded her heart with irrational joy. Still, she held firm. "Surely Cammie isn't expecting *me*."

"I reserved a table a while ago and you're on my staff," he said. "She'll wonder why I excluded you. Think of the optics."

"I'd rather not."

"If you won't do it for Cammie, and the good children she's raising money for, do it for me. Just think of how lonely I'm going to feel at that country club surrounded by all those people. You did promise to help me feel less lonely, or don't you remember?"

"I remember." She glared at him. "You're never going to let me live that down, are you?"

"Never."

"I'm just done with that place," Eve said. "Don't you remember what happened the last time I was there?"

"You met me."

Eve let out a dramatic sigh. There was no way she was ever going to let him down. "I guess it's back to the country club."

"Welcome to Royal," he said. "All roads lead to the TCC."

He pulled his phone from the pocket of his charcoal-gray trousers. "You're going to need a dress."

"Can't I wear whatever?"

"No, you can't."

"Is this a fundraiser or the Met Gala?"

"Eve, sweet, I don't make the rules," he said as he absently scrolled his phone.

Next thing he had her speak with a personal shopper. Eve gave the professional her size and style preferences and was assured a few options would be delivered to her door by 5:00 p.m. Then she handed him the phone. "Thanks, but let this be the last time. Okay? This can't be a thing."

"What do you mean?"

"You taking charge, taking care of things."

"You mean taking care of *you*, don't you?"

"Yep." That was exactly what she meant.

"This doesn't count," he said. "The fundraiser is for a worthy cause. I'm doing this for the kids."

"Give me a break! You'd forgotten all about the kids."

"I forgot about the fancy dinner, not the kids. Never the kids."

"Good to know your heart is in the right place."

"Always," he said. "Now there's one more thing. As impatient as I am to stuff my face with shrimp cocktail tonight—"

"Don't be mean," she scolded him. "I'm sure they'll come up with something more imaginative than shrimp cocktail."

"You give them too much credit," he said. "But here's the thing. I need to make a quick detour before we head out to the club tonight."

Again with the *we*... "Are *we* going together?"

"That's a given," he said. "I'd be lonely without you."

Eve shot to her feet. "You're on a roll this morning!"

"That's because I had a great night!"

He was adorable. Eve felt the pull, tugging her toward him. This was dangerous territory. "About that," she said. "Tonight's event has a Valentine's Day theme."

He sat on the corner of his desk. "I'm aware."

"You're under no obligation to, you know, go all out and treat me like..." She grappled for the right word and drew a blank.

"My valentine?" he suggested.

"Yes."

"My candy apple?"

Eve's face caught fire. "Stop that."

"My caramel candy sweet?"

She had to get out of there. "I've got work to do."

He grinned at her. "Don't let me keep you."

The trouble was, she thought, on her way to her office, she so very much wanted him to keep her...and never let her go.

Fourteen

That evening, Rafael pulled up to Manny Suarez's auto shop. Eve looked out the passenger seat window, taking in the nondescript facade. "So, is this where you were the night we met?"

The night we met… He liked how that sounded. "You guessed it."

"And what is this place?"

"You'll see."

He got out of the car and came around to assist her. It was more than the gentlemanly thing to do. The seats of the sports car were low. Eve claimed to be progressing with physical therapy, yet she might still need assistance.

"Is this your pre-TCC ritual then? A drive to the wild side?"

He escorted her to the shop's door. "No, it just worked out like that."

He was here to finalize his selection of leather for the Camaro's seats. Manny flung the door open. "Bro! You brought a lady friend."

Rafael ignored the quip and introduced Eve to Manny.

"Good to meet you," Manny said. "Are you two heading off to the fancy Valentine's dance?"

"As a matter of fact we are," Rafael said.

"This is not a date," Eve said. "We're not dating."

Manny clapped. "Shot down!"

When Rafael swiveled to confront her, he lost his breath. Against the drab concrete gray walls of the shop, she was vibrant in a slinky red dress. This morning she'd told his personal shopper that she preferred color to black, and red was her favorite color of all. He'd made a mental note and filed it under miscellaneous things he knew about Eve. Tomorrow he'd order red roses.

She caught his eyes and spoke deliberately slow to ensure he caught her meaning. "We're attending the fundraiser in our professional capacity."

"Right," he said.

Manny tore open a bag of tortilla chips. "My wife made fresh guac. Want some?"

"Absolutely."

Manny entertained Eve with stories about his pet dogs. Something swelled inside Rafael. Her laughter was his, hard-won and prized. He wished he could hold her hand or touch her or display any form of affection without his gesture being met with a hard stare.

Back in the showroom, Manny tossed him a booklet. "Here are the swatches I wanted you to see. I have to put in the order by tomorrow so the suppliers in Italy can get it to me on time."

Rafael flipped through the booklet of leather swatches, ranging in color from cognac to deep bark brown. Eve approached and rested a hand on his wrist. "Those are gorgeous."

"Think so?" he said. "Pick one."

She tapped on a square of caramel-hued leather. His sweet, caramel candy apple Eve… "Good choice." He showed the swatch to Manny. "We'll go with this."

"What's it for?" she asked.

"You don't know?" Manny wiped his hands on a paper napkin. "You're in for a treat."

Eve looked to him for confirmation. "Really?"

Rafael was suddenly nervous. What would she think? He was burning steep stacks of cash on this project. That money could have easily changed her life or done a lot of good for someone. "We don't have time," Rafael said.

"But we drove all this way!"

"You got fresh guac out of it."

"That was good guac," she conceded. Nonetheless, she followed Manny to the back of the shop. He unveiled Rafael's car with his usual flourish. Rafael hadn't seen it in a few days. The strong, muscular build of the vehicle was all the more evident now that the old paint had been scraped off.

"You're…repairing an old car?"

"Restoring." Manny corrected her, defending his trade. "We're restoring a vintage '69 Camaro." He pulled up a photo on his phone and showed it to Eve. "This is what it'll look like when I'm done."

Eve studied the photo. "Hold up! You're going to make *this* look like *that*."

"That's what I do," Manny said.

"Like how? By magic?"

"No magic! Skill!"

She sought out Rafael. He braced himself for the blow of her disapproval. Instead, she looked amused. "There's no reining you in, is there?"

He grinned, relieved. "Afraid not!"

"I'm afraid to ask how much this will cost," Eve said.

"Don't be scared," Manny said. "I'll tell you. Homeboy is about to drop—"

"Look at the time! Eve, let's get going." She shot him a

look and he shrugged. "TCC rule number 110: Don't be late for dinner."

"I'm pretty sure that's rule number one."

"No," he said. "That would be pay your dues."

"Naturally."

Manny escorted them to the door. "Bye, kids! Have fun at the dance! Make good choices!"

They arrived late anyway. The cocktail hour was over, and the guests were seated for dinner. Tables were set up in the grand ballroom. Every table had a blooming red centerpiece in keeping with the night's theme, but wisely, no one had erected a champagne tower. Rafael paused at the entrance to tug at the cuffs of his shirt and adjust the links, readying himself for battle. In the past, his instinct and concern had always been to protect himself. Tonight, he had the added responsibility of protecting Eve. He'd led her to the lion's den. He would not allow anyone to tear her apart.

"Ready?" he asked.

She nodded. "Uh-huh."

He saw the fear in her eyes. "Just remember the golden rule—small talk only. Keep the chitchat brief and brisk."

"Got it."

"You look sweet enough to suck on in that dress."

She startled, eyes dancing. "Way to keep it brief and brisk, Mr. Arias Wentworth."

"I want you to know that's all I'll be thinking about all night. Got that?"

"Got it."

"Don't worry about them." He nodded toward the packed dining room. "Worry about me."

She very discreetly stroked his arm. "I'm a multitasker. I can do both."

Rafael pushed out a laugh. As it turned out, he could multitask, too. He checked out the dining room and clocked Tobias at the head table along with Cammie and Drake. In his classic black tuxedo, Tobias looked good but he was not the formidable man who had terrorized his youth. And yet Rafael felt pressure build inside him. It never failed. One look from his father could undo all his plans, leave him doubting his worth. Each time they met, Rafael had to mentally reset the clock. He was not a lost teenager. He was independent, successful, no longer cowering under his father's shadow or struggling to get out from under his thumb.

Eve stepped closer to him and placed a hand on his shoulder. "Are you ready?" she asked.

He glanced at her and fell headfirst into the depths of her brown eyes. A ribbon of heat wrapped around his heart. *I'll make you feel a little less lonely in this town.* He had not taken that promise seriously. After all, how could she? Feeling alone, apart, unwelcomed was part and parcel of his identity. He would not relinquish it. It had made him the man he was today. But Eve's hand on his shoulder made him want to reconsider.

"You two make an *adorable* couple!" a woman exclaimed. Before Rafael could do anything about it, P&J had accosted them.

"Is this date night?" Jennifer Carlton asked.

"No," Rafael said flatly. "This is a work event."

Jennifer winked. "I gotcha."

Paul Carlton voiced other concerns. "Have you heard from the Richardsons? My sources say they're ready to make a move. Now if you need a broker, I'm standing at the ready."

"I appreciate it," Rafael said.

"We're late as usual," Jennifer said. "Enjoy your night, you two!"

Rafael waved them off, but Eve stood petrified. He reached for her hand. "What's the matter?"

"They think we're a couple," she said. "And it's my fault. If I hadn't kissed you at the Belleview Inn—"

"I wouldn't trade that kiss for anything in the world."

"Yeah, but now you're linked to another Martin sister."

He really didn't like where she was headed with this. "I never met your sister," he said. "You, however, could put up a chain-link fence around me and I wouldn't mind."

They'd loaded so much baggage onto their leaky boat, they were sure to go under. Not tonight, though. He was going to paddle like hell to get them to shore.

Eve's eyes went misty, betraying her emotion, but her lips twisted in a smile when she said, "The poet laureate of Royal, Texas, has nothing on you."

"I've got skills," he said. "If you're ready, we should first pay our respects to King Tobias."

She nodded. "Let's do this."

Tobias rose to greet them. He clasped Rafael's hand in his and said, a little too loudly, "Good to see you, son."

"Tobias," Rafael replied, and pivoted. "Have you met Eve Martin?"

Tobias's cool blue gaze raked over Eve's face. "I've... heard of her."

Rafael felt Eve stiffen beside him. He wanted to tell his father to forget what he'd heard. "Eve is my new executive assistant. I'm lucky to have her."

"It's a pleasure to meet you, Eve."

"The pleasure is mine, Mr. Wentworth."

"Call me Tobias," he said eagerly.

His father's eagerness was, in a way, kind of endearing.

Eve went on to speak with Cammie. Heads close, they were swapping stories about Micah, their "Can you believe what he did today" stories. That, too, was endearing. Rafael would need a strong drink to flush all those warm feelings away.

He looked around for his table. It was clear across the dining room—thank goodness. Audrey caught his eye and waved him over. Rafael turned to Eve. "I think they're feeling neglected at our table."

"Let's head over," she said. "Bye, Cammie!"

Cammie stared at him, a quizzical look in her eyes. "Catch you later, Rafe."

"Sure thing," he said.

Eve waved to Audrey and, possibly without thinking, caught him by the arm and led him to their table. Rafael was conscious of the gazes that followed them and the rise of whispers. Not that he minded. They could say whatever they wanted about him. But if Eve didn't like it, he didn't like it.

Audrey, Dan and his fiancé, Robert, his foreman Bill and his wife, Sandy, and Lucas were seated at the table. None of them were TCC members. Each had expressed excitement beyond comprehension when he'd extended the invitation. Lucas looked sharp in an eggplant-colored suit that Rafael's personal shopper had picked out for him. The little snot was chatting up Audrey. "You know," he said, "I graduate high school in sixteen months."

Audrey rolled her eyes. "Eat your shrimp!"

Which brought them to the shrimp arranged in delicate crystal bowls, one at each place setting. "What did I tell you?" he said to Eve as they got settled.

"Who cares?" she said. "It looks delicious."

Rafael watched, mesmerized, as she brought a plump, pink prawn to her mouth and took a lustful bite. Last night, in the shower, those lips had tightened around him and he'd had to bite into his own flesh to keep from howling.

"By the way," Eve said, "I don't hate your new car. It'll look cool when it's done."

Rafael perked up. "You can say you love it."

"Love?" She rolled her eyes. "We're nowhere near love. Let's just see how it goes."

In sudden need of a distraction, he reached for his phone and checked the alerts before silencing it for the night. Thank God, too. Among the many messages was an email from Mary Richardson that read like a hostage note.

From: mrichardson@southpointmotel.com
To: raw@ariashospitalitygroup.com
Subject: Deal
We are ready to sell. We want this to be painless and quick.
No bidding wars. No middlemen. We want and expect no
less than 1.5 million in cash. If you are serious, let us know
by tomorrow.

Rafael let out a low whistle. It occurred to him that the
thrill was in the buying, restoring and renovating. Making
something old, new. Hotels, cars, it didn't matter. It was the
process that mattered, and that process began with the ne-
gotiation leading to a deal.

The waiter came around for their beverage orders. Lucas
was denied a beer. Eve ordered a glass of sparkling water.
Rafael asked for a whiskey then returned his attention to his
phone. He murmured, "Okay, baby."

Eve leaned close and whispered, "Yes?"

"Not you, sweet," he said with a low laugh. "But look
at this."

He angled the screen of his phone so that she could
read Mary Richardson's email. Her lashes veiled her eyes
as she read.

"Wow!" She smiled up at him. "P&J were right. What
are you going to do?"

"I'm going to show them just how serious I am."

He hit reply. Eve rested her hand on his; the brief contact lit him up.

"Wait," she said. "I'm sure Mary Richardson sent this
same email to at least five other prospective buyers. She's
tossing out bait. She's fishing."

"Here I thought you bought into her act."

"Mary is a shrewd businesswoman. No way she's letting
go of her life's work for one million five."

"She's no shrewder than you."

"Well, think about it. Why would she single you out?"

"You don't think I won her over with my charm?"

"No, dear." Eve patted his hand. "I really don't."

"Let's not leave her hanging then." Rafael typed up his response, offering twenty-five grand over asking price, but only if they were willing to lock this down.

"Look good?" he asked Eve.

"Yup."

"Hit Send."

She tapped on the button then grinned at him. He melted inside. He wanted to nuzzle her neck and breathe in her light, floral perfume. He wanted to love her. Those words stunned him. He wanted to *love* her. His sweet, caramel candy apple Eve... All he wanted was to wrap her in his arms and love her.

The waiter returned with their drinks just in time. He gave his glass a swirl and took a big gulp. Eve and Audrey were laughing at something Lucas had said. Rafael set the phone face up on the table to monitor his email as the night went on, but that wasn't necessary. It chimed right away with a response.

You've got a deal.

He nudged Eve. "We got it."

Eve clapped. "Congratulations!"

From across the table, Audrey waved her cloth napkin like a flag. "What's going on? What did I miss?"

"We're the proud owners of South Point Motel," Rafael announced.

"Well done!" Audrey cried.

"Good job!" Dan said.

"Watch out, Royal!" Lucas exclaimed. "We're taking over!"

"What do you plan to do with it?" Audrey asked.

"A spa," Rafael said. "And I'm putting you in charge."

Audrey's mouth dropped. "Wait. I'm getting a promotion?"

"Get ready," Rafael said. Audrey would earn a business degree in May. She was dedicated, loyal and smart. She would make an excellent project manager.

"Oh, I'm ready! Believe it."

"Well, shoot!" Lucas said. "Can I get her job?"

"In sixteen months," Rafael said.

Lucas was skeptical. "Is that a promise? Can I get that in writing?"

"Put a high school diploma on my desk and you've got a job. It's a promise."

Lucas snapped his fingers. "Best party ever!"

"Well now!" Dan said. "While we're at it, can I get a raise?"

Everyone laughed. The Arias table, a table of misfits and outcasts, erupted in chatter. Rafael didn't hear any of it. The same few words crowded his mind: he wanted to love her.

Fifteen

Maybe it was the rush of sealing the Richardson deal or the dreamy candlelight or the intoxicating scent of flowers or the string quartet playing classical renditions of country songs during dinner, or maybe it was Rafael's hand on her knee tracing lazy circles with his thumb. Either way, Eve was feeling fine.

Not long ago, she'd had to sneak into a party at the TCC. Tonight, she was a guest of Rafael Arias Wentworth and having the time of her life. How had all of this come about? She had taken a leap of faith or two. Eve thought of Arielle. Her life had ended prematurely, but she had squeezed a lot of living into it. It might not be the worst thing to follow her little sister's example.

After dinner, Eve excused herself from the table and went to freshen up in the restroom. She swept on lip gloss and fluffed her hair. As much fun as she was having, she couldn't wait to be alone with Rafael. Although they hadn't come to any agreement, it was clear they would spend the night together. She had not yet settled into her suite, had no idea whether the bed's mattress was soft or firm, and was in no hurry to find out.

On her way back to the table, Eve bumped into reporter Sierra Morgan.

"Eve!" she gasped. "Is that you?"

"It's me!" Considering that most encounters with the investigative journalist had taken place in Eve's hospital room, her reaction was understandable.

"I almost didn't recognize you!" Sierra exclaimed.

Eve laughed, self-conscious. "Is that good or bad?"

"It's excellent! You look healthy and amazing."

Sierra looked healthy and amazing, too. The petite blonde wore a classic little black dress with no Valentine's Day frills.

"Listen," she said. "I've been meaning to reach out to you."

"Oh? What about?" Eve asked, even though she knew full well. It could only be about one thing. Sierra was dedicated to crack the mystery of the identity of Micah's father. She'd stayed on the story well after the press had lost interest and moved on to other scandals.

Sierra drew Eve to a quiet corner. "I'm sorry to say I haven't made much progress finding Micah's dad. It's not for lack of trying. I've combed through Arielle's diary and followed up on every lead."

Ah! The diary… Truthfully, it was so much more than a diary. Arielle had also jotted some notes on the big story she was working on. It involved a feud between the Langley and the Wentworth families that was as old as the TCC itself. Though everyone thought it fascinating, Eve did not. In her opinion, it fell squarely in the category of other people's business. Grandma Martin would have cautioned her to keep her nose out of it.

"I appreciate that," Eve said. What else could she say?

"I know I'm overlooking something. Just can't put my finger on it," Sierra said. "Would you be open to meeting with me sometime soon? I need a fresh pair of eyes."

"Anytime," Eve said. "Not sure how much help I'll be. I've been through that journal hundreds of times. I found some clues that led me to believe Micah's father might be here in Royal, but not much else."

In a few cryptic passages, Arielle had written of a great love and necessary heartbreak. But then, her sister had a flair for embellishment. As per numerous accounts, no one in town recalled seeing her with a man.

"Two heads are better than one," Sierra said.

"So they say."

Eve was eager to wrap things up. With all of Royal's elite within earshot, this fundraiser was not the time or place for this conversation.

"I'll be in touch," Sierra said. "Enjoy your night."

"You, too."

Sierra returned to her table. Eve, though, had an urgent need for fresh air. She exited the dining room through the beveled glass doors. Out on the terrace, a few huddled men were smoking cigars. For all she knew, Micah's dad could be any one of them. After all, the diary had made clear that he was a member of the TCC.

She headed in the opposite direction, taking the stairs slowly down to the garden. Damn, stairs were still her weakness. All those hours of PT, when would her body be back to full strength? Getting healthy, getting strong, that was her priority.

Unlike Sierra, Eve was no longer consumed with finding this most elusive of men. If he did not want to be found, maybe he was not worth finding. However, her nephew would not be a baby forever. Someday soon, he would ask about his parents, wonder about his dad. Eve wanted to look him in the eye and tell him they'd exhausted every avenue. So, she would meet with Sierra and help in any way she could, but her conscience was clear. An investigative reporter and law enforcement professionals were on the job. The man didn't want to be found. What other explanation was there?

Eve walked along the garden path and came across the bench under the magnolia tree where she and Rafael had talked that first night. She lowered herself onto it and took her head into her hands, feeling like a fool. Like that first night, the music and chatter of the party reached her. She had nothing in common with those people. Sierra had delivered a timely reminder that her problems could not be shrugged off or ignored.

Eve took her fingers to her temples and drew slow circles to ease the tension building there. She needed a clear head to think. A bullet list was forming in her mind.

- Save money.
- Rent an apartment suitable for a baby.
- Look into day care options.
- Get the okay from her doctor to regain custody of Micah.

Eve had come to Royal desperate and determined to re-unite Micah with his father. At the time, she feared criminal prosecution and could see no other way forward. However, her circumstances had changed. She had landed on her feet and could handle things from here on out. If Micah's father ever showed up, great! Eve hoped the courts would see things her way and mandate supervised visits. She was not eager to en-trust her one and only nephew's care to the stranger who had abandoned his mother. In the fairy-tale retelling of Arielle's life, Eve would not allow that last detail to go overlooked. Her sister's great love had abandoned her. End of story.

Rafael joined Cammie at her table and dropped into the empty seat beside her. *"Hermanita, que bella estas."*

"Hey there, Rafe," she responded, mimicking his tone. "You're looking sharp tonight."

Rafael hiked the hem of his tailored pants to show her his black leather boots. "Do you approve?"

"It's like I always say," she said. "You can take the man out of ranch country but you can't take the ranch out of the man."

"Apparently so," Rafael said. "Where is Drake? What have you done with him?"

"Sent him to the bar to get me a fresh drink."

"Text him," Rafael said. "Tell him to bring me a whiskey."

She punched him in the arm. "I will not!"

Rafael rubbed his arm in mock distress. "Ouch!"

"You missed our coffee date this week," Cammie said reproachfully.

"Quit throwing shindigs like this and we can keep to our regular schedules."

From the corner of his eye, Rafael spotted J, of P&J, zig-zagging across the room toward him. *Oh, crap.*

"Finally! I got you alone!" she exclaimed. It was a funny remark coming from a woman who was forever stitched to her husband's side. "I can never get a word in without that woman running interference."

"That woman has my best interest at heart. I can't say the same of you."

Cammie tugged at his sleeve. "Who is she talking about? Not Eve, I hope."

Jennifer's face drained of color. "I mean nothing by it. It's just that we've been trying to speak with you—"

"All you ever had to do was call or stop by the guest ranch offices. Instead, you railroad me every chance you get, even when I'm trying to catch up with my sister."

Cammie wasn't done. "Eve Martin is a friend of the Wentworth family. As you ought to know, we are loyal to our friends."

"I didn't come here to cause trouble," Jennifer said. "I heard the Richardson property was suddenly off the market and wondered if you knew anything about it. That's all."

Rafael shrugged. "I guess you're just going to have to read about it in the *Royal Gazette* like everybody else."

"Alright then," Jennifer said. "You two look like you've got lots to catch up on, years of stuff, actually. I'll leave you to it."

Jennifer stormed off. Rafael grinned at Cammie and ruffled her red hair. "Damn, you're feisty."

She slapped his hand away. "You're not off the hook! Just how much time have you been spending with Eve?"

"You know I hired her."

"I know you moved her into the residence."

"You know she needed a place to stay."

"I know you're sleeping with her. That's what I know."

Rafael felt his jaw tighten. The way Cammie put it, you'd think he was doing something wrong, taking advantage of her. And yet he wasn't. For once in his life, he had someone else's interest at heart.

"Eve has been through a lot," Cammie said. "I mean *a lot*, and she's not at full strength yet. So I'm just going to make this as clear as day. If you hurt her, I'm going to hurt you."

"You already are." She had his hand in a death grip, her fingernails digging into his palm.

"There are so many beautiful women in Royal," Cammie said. "Any number of them would be glad to have you. I should know. They're blowing up my phone! Some are here tonight."

"Eve and I are friends," Rafael said. That was a thin slice of the truth. She may be the only real friend he had in Royal, but she was also the woman he was going home with tonight. "I would never intentionally hurt her."

"Your intentions mean nothing," Cammie said. "She's fragile, and you can unintentionally cause her harm."

"Eve is stronger than you think."

"Rafe," Cammie said, her tone softening, "Eve lost her sister, got accused of embezzlement, then landed in a hospital hundreds of miles away from home."

"Tell me about that," Rafael said. "What was she in the hospital for?"

Cammie frowned. "Not my place."

Rafael looked away, annoyed with himself that he had not gotten Eve to answer his earlier questions. He was still in the dark about so much.

"It's obvious, isn't it?" Cammie said. "She has a heart condition, much like her sister, who—in case you've forgotten—*died*."

Drake returned with Cammie's drink. Rafael lingered awhile longer, making small talk. But he just wanted to speak with Eve and finally get the details of her health issues, legal troubles and financial burdens. It was time for that difficult conversation. Cammie was right. Eve had serious problems. He'd been content to distract her, and that just wasn't good enough. He could do more.

Eve wasn't at the table when he got back. He spotted her across the room, apparently having a difficult conversation of another kind with Sierra, the investigative journalist from *America* magazine. Sierra reached out and squeezed her arm as if to reassure her that the sky wasn't falling. He watched, increasingly worried, as her expression darkened.

Eve and Sierra parted ways. Sierra returned to the party, and Eve darted out into the night. Rafael got up and chased after her. The ballroom opened to a terrace, which was empty except for a few guys huddled in a corner discussing fantasy football stats. He asked whether they'd seen a woman in red. One of them pointed the lit tip of his cigar toward the stairs. He charged down the stone steps and followed the garden path. He found her seated at the bench under the magnolia tree, head in her hands. He felt frustrated that with a few words the journalist had undid all the good he had done.

"Hey!" he called out. "What are you doing out here all alone?"

She startled. "Just needed some fresh air."

"Is everything alright?" He sat next to her.

She shook her head. "I feel like I'm playing the role of the girl who is back on track. Then I get a reality check and that whole facade comes crashing down."

"You *are* on track."

"Everything is up in the air," she said. "Micah still doesn't have a father or a permanent home. And here I am in this dress, at a party. I mean…what am I doing?"

"You're doing your best," he said. "They're not any closer to finding Micah's dad?"

"No," Eve said. "And it really isn't their responsibility to find him. It's mine."

"You can't do everything, Eve."

"I doubt he wants to be found. What's stopping him from reaching out?"

"He might not know."

"But when he heard about Arielle's death, he could've at least sent flowers."

"He might not have heard," Rafael said. "Eve, you can't make assumptions like that. Wait until you have all the facts."

"I've been waiting a long time."

"I know it's not easy, darling," Rafael said. "But nothing stays buried for long, at least not in this town. They'll find him and I'll help you through it."

"That's not how it should be," Eve protested. "You hired me to do a job. You didn't sign on to be my caretaker."

"I care," Rafael said. "I'm not going to pretend that I don't. Let me help."

If he told her the truth, how desperately he wanted to protect her and make the world new for her, it would scare her to death. She'd run.

She reached for his hand and squeezed it. "Thanks, but there's nothing you can do."

He came close to laughing in her face. Save for identifying Micah's father in a police lineup, there was plenty he could do. He had the money, the contacts and the influence to get shit done. And he had the know-how to do it right.

"Do you want to leave?" he asked. "If tonight's been too much of a strain, we can go, get you to bed early."

She pulled away from him. "Don't do that."

"Do what?"

"Coddle me."

"Lady, I'm trying to take care of you."

"By taking me home and putting me to bed with a cup of tea?" She stood and faced him. Fear and frustration had left her eyes. There was fire there. "You're my lover. Can't you think of anything better?"

Every muscle in Rafael's body tensed, forcing him to move deliberately and slowly. He got up from the bench and stood facing her a moment, then with a hand to her waist walked her backward toward the magnolia tree.

"What are you doing?" she asked, slightly panicked.

Rafael didn't answer until he had her pinned just where he wanted her. "I'm going to take you against this tree."

Her eyes widened with surprise and then delight. There she was, his fearless Eve.

"Okay," she said. "Just remember I don't belong to this club. If we're caught, they'll hand you a cigar and a beer, but they'll toss me out and ban me for life."

He cupped her face and dragged his thumbs across her high cheekbones. "I would burn this club down before I let anyone mistreat you."

Eve slid her arms around his neck and kissed him hard. The heady scent of magnolia mixed with the delicate floral scent of her skin enveloped him. *He only wanted to love her.* He broke the kiss, emotion rushing to his head. He was falling, falling, falling.

Eve ran her fingers through his hair and spoke to him in a soothing voice. "Arson, huh?" she said. "Who would've thought?"

Rafael let out a ragged laugh. Eve's laugh was forced; he

knew the difference. Rafael pressed his forehead to hers and she quieted down. A shudder ran through them, uniting them, and he knew this moment was more important than either of them would let on. She kissed him again, tenderly. He hoisted her up, hiked her skirt up and did what he said he would do.

Sixteen

Eve drew the pile of bills from the top desk drawer and reached for an envelope cutter. It was payday Friday, and she was grateful to have earned enough to finally start paying down her debts. She had no student loans and had always paid her credit card balance in full. However, she owed her lawyer in Miami and the medical center in Royal. Eve would likely be in the red the rest of her life, but she could get the creditors off her back. That was a step in the right direction.

Audrey poked her head through a crack in her office door. She had a date with a guy she'd met at the Valentine's Day dinner the week before, a medical student named Jamie, whom she firmly believed to be the "one."

"I'm out," Audrey said. "Any plans for tonight?"

"Physical therapy. We're going to focus on range of motion."

"Sounds hard-core," Audrey teased. "Don't overexert yourself."

"I won't. Bye!"

Audrey shut the door on her way out. Eve tore open the stiff gray envelope in which her pricey criminal defense lawyer sent all his correspondence, including invoices. She owed the firm five grand, but according to the balance sheet, she owed them exactly nothing. Zero dollars and zero cents. Eve reached for her phone and called the billing agency's toll-free number. This was the sort of mistake that would end up costing her more in the end; she just knew it. A clerk delivered the news in a flat voice. "There's no mistake. Your outstanding balance was forgiven five days ago."

"Why?"

"Our database doesn't have that information."

Eve lowered the phone. She could just call her attorney and ask. Would he bill her for that? Absently, she reached for one of her many medical bills. Her new health insurance plan had kicked in and would cover therapy and treatment going forward, but not the services she'd received prior to enrollment. She owed the local public hospital system tens of thousands of dollars. And yet…according to the notice, she owed exactly nothing. Her balance had been wiped out.

Trembling, Eve rose from her desk. There was no use calling another collection agency. She wanted answers and knew where to get them.

She crossed the hall to Dan's office. He was packing up for the day. Dan was not a chatty man by nature, and no amount of pressure would get him to spill beans of any kind. A Black man in his early forties, he wore his hair in the same buzz cut he sported during his army years. The framed photographs behind his desk proved it. Eve understood that for all her bravado, he was not the person she had to confront.

"Hey there, Eve!" Dan powered down his computer. "What's up?"

"I wondered if you could tell me what's going on with my medical bill." Although they'd run a background check on her, she didn't dare bring up her legal bills.

"Not really," he said. "Why do you ask?"

He seemed genuinely disinterested.

"My debt is wiped clean."

He patted the surface of his desk, searching for something under the blanket of scattered papers. "Lucky you."

"Here's the thing. Insurance doesn't cover services retroactively."

"Have you seen my keys?"

"No."

Her clipped tone made him look up. "Why are you mad?"

"I'm not," she said. "But I need to know if Rafael had anything to do with this."

"Why not ask me yourself?"

Rafael's voice rose from behind her. Eve shut her eyes and when she opened them, Dan looked away. In trying to avoid confronting Rafael, she had just provoked a whopper of a confrontation. There was a lesson in there somewhere.

Rafael stood out in the hall, his tie loose. He looked just as eager as Dan to end the day. Later tonight, after he met with Cammie for coffee and she wrapped up therapy, he was taking her out for tacos. A part of her did not want anything to interfere with those plans. Wasn't that the reason she'd sought Dan for answers, to leave him out of it?

"My keys were in my damn pocket all along!" Dan exclaimed. He grabbed his backpack and gingerly exited his office as if the floor were riddled with land mines. "Gotta run before traffic builds up. You know how it is."

Rafael wished him a good weekend and moved out of his way.

Eve didn't move from her post at his door. She studied Rafael's face. His expression was walled off, but he couldn't hide the truth. He knew what this was all about. Her fist tightened on the crumpled hospital bill in her hand.

"Want to talk in my office?" he proposed.

"Yes."

As soon as they were behind closed doors, she pounced. "I know what you did."

Naturally, he made a joke. "Isn't that the title of a horror movie?"

"I'm going to pay you back," Eve continued. "First thing Monday, I'll arrange for the money to be taken out of my salary in installments. We'll call it a consolidated loan."

He sat at his usual spot, the corner of his desk. "Call it what you like. You'd be paying me back for nothing."

"You paid off my bills!" Angry, she slapped the crumpled piece of paper on the desk next to him. He didn't glance at it.

"I had them forgiven. There's a difference."

"Forgiven...how?"

"My lawyers in Miami petitioned yours and convinced him to write off your case as pro bono work, considering the charges were dropped and you'd been unfairly accused. It was the only ethical thing to do."

Okay, fine! That was actually pretty decent. "What about the hospital bill?"

"Royal has a trust that covers the medical expenses of a few deserving patients each year. The board met this week, and my lawyers submitted your name for consideration."

"Then I'll pay you back your legal fees. None of your lawyers were working for free."

"They didn't work all that hard, either," he said. "It was a matter of making a few phone calls."

Eve dropped into a chair. "Is that how the rich get richer? By not paying for anything?"

Rafael raked the side of his face with his knuckles. His five-o'clock shadow was already filling in and it was only four. "We call it tapping into our resources."

She should feel grateful; instead she felt humiliated. There were only so many times you could say thank you to the same person before resentment kicked in. That was human nature.

"Would you rather I have it all reversed?"

"I'd rather we talk first!" Was it too much to ask he discuss his plans with her before putting on his white hat and charging off?

"I was going to tell you this weekend," he said, quietly. "It was meant to be a surprise."

"Rafael, you went behind my back because you knew I'd say no."

"This wasn't charity," he said. "You're not *indebted* to me or anyone. These resources exist. The average person doesn't know how to go about it and that's unfair, but it's smart to take advantage."

Oh, now she was average.

"On a side note," Rafael continued, "I could have very easily paid it all off. I've blown a quarter of a million dollars to restore a car. Money is not a problem."

"So you keep telling me," Eve said. She got it. He was filthy rich. Enough already! "How many times do I need to tell you that's not the point?"

He went around the desk and pulled a file from the bottom drawer. "This is not how I wanted to do this, but I might as well go all in."

Eve cringed. What was he getting at now?

He handed her the file. She flipped it open. Among other things it contained a science journal write-up of one Elizabeth Baer, MD, board-certified in cardiology. Eve's heart took off with a start. "What's this?"

"I've had someone look into it. Dr. Baer is the leading cardiologist with a specialty in hereditary conditions, which is what you have."

"I know what I have!" she snapped.

He toyed with a pen, waiting for her to say more. Eve dropped the file onto the crumpled bill. She wanted to scream and storm out. Instead, she held his gaze and said nothing. In her mind, she played a slideshow of all the good times they'd shared and the good things he'd done for her to remind herself that he was fundamentally a good person.

"Are you going to pass up an opportunity to better understand the disease that affects you and, possibly, your nephew?"

"Now you're being manipulative."

Rafael's demeanor changed. Those sparkling eyes went flat and that mouth, always quick to smile, was drawn in a grim line.

The hum of sadness filled her chest. "Rafael, you can't save me. You'll go broke trying."

Her life was a money pit. As soon as she cleaned up one mess or settled one tragedy there came another and another. What was he going to do? Spend all his leisure time calling lawyers and researching obscure medical conditions?

"I doubt it," he said. "Anyway, this isn't about me. Dr. Baer is one of the premier cardiologists in the world. She has an office in West Palm Beach. Currently, she's not taking new patients, but she'll make an exception. All I ask is that you think about it."

Eve's skin prickled. "It isn't fair for you to spring this on me."

"Sweet, I'm on your side."

Then why did it feel so uncomfortable?

"Think about it," he said. "I'll fly us out to West Palm Beach. Just say when."

"Rafael," Eve warned, "if you book a flight or pay for one more thing, I'm going to take you apart with my hands."

"Get into fighting shape," he said. "I'm not letting up."

Well, Eve was fed up. She stood and marched toward the door. He stopped her with one word. "Sorry."

She paused and turned to face him. He looked sorry, just not sorry enough. "Do you even know what you're sorry about?"

"For being the last card-carrying member of the patriarchy?"

Yeah. That summed it up. "I know I'm not easy," she said. "I would have put up a fight. That's no reason to go behind my back and pretend it's a surprise."

He nodded, looking properly contrite. Eve exhaled, feeling better that she'd finally gotten her point across. Now she needed a drink of water to calm down.

She moved toward the door. Rafael called after her. "Are we still on for dinner?"

"Obviously!" She tossed the reply without breaking her stride.

He'd promised her authentic tacos. If he thought he could piss her off and deprive her of tacos all in one day, he could think again.

Seventeen

Cammie poured him a cup of coffee, and they went out onto the back porch. Micah was napping, and the house was quiet when Rafael had arrived. His sister looked relaxed, barefoot and wearing jeans. He lit the cigar Drake had offered him and sat on the steps. The setting sun traced a fine red line over the horizon. Rafael wouldn't share this with anyone, but a part of him was rooted here in Royal. When he wasn't fending off rumors, railing against the TCC, or clashing with Tobias, he felt settled and calm in a way he never did anywhere else.

Cammie got him up to speed on the latest happenings in town, particularly the conversion of the Carrington ranch into a student training facility. Gabe Carrington had been his closest friend in high school. It was too bad that he'd relocated to New York City with his wife, Rosalind, shortly after Rafael had returned. Cammie talked and he smoked and nodded. From time to time he said, "Right." After his argument with Eve, he couldn't focus on anything. He just wanted to sit here, smoke his cigar and not give a damn about the world at large.

"Isn't that great?" Cammie asked.

To which he replied, "Sure, I'll contribute."

"Are you even listening?" she asked.

"Sorry. I might have spaced out."

She slipped off the porch rail and came to sit beside him on the steps. "What's the matter? Is it Tobias?"

Rafael shrugged and let out a long stream of smoke. "It's Eve. She's mad at me."

"But you two looked so happy the other night!"

"Well, she's not happy now."

"What did you do?"

"I had her debt wiped out, both legal and medical."

Cammie took another sip of coffee, mulled over his words. "That's actually pretty nice."

"I thought so."

Cammie blew a strand of red hair away from her face. She had freckles across the bridge of her nose. "What's the problem?"

Rafael stared into the distance. "I didn't tell her what I was up to. I just handled it."

"That's a very Tobias move."

"It was meant to be a surprise."

"A bouquet of flowers is a surprise," Cammie said. "A weekend getaway is a surprise. Paying off debts is a what-the-hell type moment."

"In a way, this is your fault."

"In what way?" Cammie said. "I asked you to be careful with her, not take over her life. You see the difference, right?"

"If I'd asked for her permission, she would've said no."

"You may look like your mom, but there's a lot of Tobias in you."

"Don't say that."

"Too late!"

She went back to sipping her coffee. Rafael drew from his cigar. "Fuck… That was a Tobias move."

"Thank you!" Cammie cried, nearly spilling her coffee down her T-shirt. "So, how did it go down? Did you two fight?"

"We exchanged words."

"Did she end things?"

"No!" Rafael snapped. He couldn't even stomach the idea. "We're getting tacos later."

"Tacos? Sounds like you're cool."

"We're not. You didn't see the look she gave me."

And Cammie hadn't heard the tone of Eve's voice, filled with outrage and pain. He knew he'd gone too far.

"Do you mean all of this is because of a look she gave you?"

"All of what?"

She drew a circle around his face with the tip of a finger. "The forlorn look, the sorry little frown, the woe-is-me attitude."

"Stop!"

"*You* stop!"

They were different people when they were alone together, behaving mostly like annoying teenagers. Even Drake had remarked upon it. The best part was that they were okay with it. Rafael understood they were actively making up for lost time, and it was nice. Jennifer Carlton was right about them. They had a decade's worth of stuff and more to catch up on.

"She called me manipulative," Rafael confessed.

"Damn!" Cammie exclaimed. "Eve packs a punch. Who knew?"

Rafael dropped his cigar in the ashtray and leaned his head on his sister's shoulder. "I fucked up."

Cammie pat his cheek. "Yeah, you did."

"What should I do?"

"Okay. What I'm going to say is going to blow your mind. Ready?"

"Go on."

"You apologize."

He pushed away from her. "I already apologized!"

"Alright, then. Now you wait."

"Wait for what?"

"For her to come around."

"Is that all? I need an action plan."

"Your action plan got you into this mess."

"Your job is to knock sense into me and tell me what to do."

"And your job?" she asked.

"Punch the boys who make you cry."

She laughed. "I'll go with that."

"I've got your back, baby cheeks."

"Quit calling me 'baby cheeks'!"

Cammie didn't have baby cheeks anymore, but she did once and that was all that mattered. The nickname was hers for life.

"You want advice?" she said. "Don't follow the Tobias playbook. Ask yourself, 'What would Tobias do?' Then do the opposite."

"Good advice," he said. In the back of his mind, he couldn't help but think they were being hard on their dear old dad. Tobias's marriage to his late third wife had been, by all accounts, a loving one—as hard as it was to believe.

"Speaking of Tobias, how are your lunches going?"

"They're going," Rafael said. "The trick is to avoid the hot topics. Once I get there it's all sports all the time."

Cammie pat his back this time. "He *is* trying, you know."

"I know," Rafael said quietly. "I'm trying, too. At the same time, I want to tell him to fuck off and go to hell. It's weird. You know?"

"Oh, I know. Trust me."

They fell silent. Rafael looked to the sky. He had so much shit to figure out. Right then, a scratchy sound came through the portable intercom Cammie carried around with her.

Micah was stirring. Drake's low voice followed. He made a soft cooing sound. Cammie cut the volume and put the monitor aside.

Rafael glanced her way and caught her silly little grin. "What's that?" he asked. "The state-of-the-art baby walkie-talkie?"

Cammie shrugged. "You'd be surprised to learn how much equipment a baby needs just to stay alive."

"They need love, too, I'm guessing."

She brightened. "Love, too. Yes."

"Hermanita—" he reached out and squeezed her hand *"—no quiero verte lastimada."*

Her smile went crooked. "I don't know what that means."

"It means—"

"No," she said, shaking her head. "I don't want to know, either."

Rafael let out a sigh and resumed staring out into the distance. "We're screwed up, aren't we?"

Cammie dropped her head on his shoulder. "Royally screwed."

First thing Monday morning, Rafael had a conference call with a team of engineers. The guest ranch was going solar. It wasn't as easy as it sounded. There were permits to secure and the matter of retrofitting new panels on old construction. Still, he would not be deterred. It was good for the environment, good for the bottom line and good press. There would always be a media outlet eager to publish a story on the hospitality industry's efforts to cut its dependence on fossil fuels. He wanted his company to be part of that story.

"This is my top priority," Rafael declared.

Right then his cell phone buzzed in his breast pocket. It was a call from Eve, which was odd. Normally, when they were in the office, she'd swing by or buzz the intercom. Since their fight last Friday, nothing was normal between them. They'd gone out to dinner and spent most of the weekend together, but each night she'd returned to her suite. Cammie had advised him to wait for her to come around. What if she never did?

Rafael hit mute on the conference call and answered his cell phone.

"Are you busy?" she asked.

"Not too busy for you."

"Good. I need help testing a theory."

"Where are you?"

"The Belleview Inn."

He liked where this was going. "To be clear, you're referring to the internationally known Sex in an Inn Theory?"

"That's the one," she said. "I bet if we tried really hard we could disprove it. What do you say?"

"I say give me ten minutes."

Rafael was giddy when he wrapped up the call with the engineers. Top priority or no, something even more pressing had come up.

Eve had booked a deluxe room and the Do Not Disturb sign hanging from the doorknob boded well for him. He knocked. She came to the door in lingerie, a delicate, pink matching set. Cotton-candy pink, bubblegum pink, stretched over lush caramel breasts. Her hair was wavy and loose past her shoulders. She looked him over. "You're overdressed for this experiment."

He returned the favor. "Give me a second. I'm having a moment."

She smiled. "Hate to rush you, but there's a draft and I'm freezing."

The tension that had been building in him all weekend broke. It was relief, more than anything else, that made him reach for her. The door slammed shut behind him. He buried his face in her neck and pinned her to him, hoping to hide the fact that his whole body was trembling. Their standoff had lasted three nights, three nights of waiting and, honestly, going a little crazy.

She was laughing. "I knew that would do it. You're obsessed with keeping me warm."

He kissed her at the spot that always made her shiver. "Now I'm obsessed with making you hot."

Kissing her hungrily, he blindly guided her from the foyer to the bedroom. They tipped onto the bed together. He ached to suck on her chocolate nipples through the veil of pink lace. But Eve slipped her fingers in his hair, like she loved to do, and brought his mouth to hers.

"Hey," she said sweetly.

He crushed her full lips with his kiss until he tasted sugar—and then a knock on the door. Rafael pulled away with a groan. This was fucking déjà vu.

"I ordered chocolate covered strawberries," Eve explained. "Sorry, I passed on the champagne."

Her wide brown eyes were filled with such eagerness it broke his heart. "That works for me."

He rolled out of bed, grabbed the goods, settled the tab and sent room service away. He found a condom in his wallet. Eve was sitting up when he returned. Her hands were linked behind her head.

"Don't get too comfortable," he said.

"Alright." She crawled the length of the bed and kneeled at the edge.

He tore off his clothes. She reached for him, asking for another kiss. He kissed her mouth then dipped his head, dragging his lips along the scalloped edge of her bra. "This stays on." He slipped a hand in the waist of the lace underwear. "This comes off."

"You're a demanding man, Rafael Arias."

But am I the man you love?

The words took up so much space in his mind that he came close to saying them out loud. To silence his mind, he covered her body with his and kissed her like the first night. His mouth trailed down her body, tracing a line straight down the middle until he met with liquid heat. Eve's fingers curled and tightened in his hair. Her back arched with each stroke of his tongue, but no sounds escaped her. That didn't sit well with Rafael. He licked and sucked and scraped her swollen bud with his teeth until she gasped and cursed his name. Only then did he pull away and crawl up the length of her body, triumphant. Her lips were parted, inviting, but he dipped his head and whispered in her ear. "That's not very nice what you just called me. I've been very good to you."

She pressed a kiss to the corner of his mouth. "And very bad."

Laughter rumbled through him. "Take the bitter and the sweet."

"Yes, please."

Rafael hooked an arm under her knee, eager to be inside her. She planted the palms of her hands to his chest. Though panting, she managed to deadpan. "Missionary? Really?"

Rafael laughed outright. "Darling, I don't make the rules."

He slipped on the condom. She snaked her arms around his neck. "So you keep saying."

His laughter rolled to a stop. The anticipation of pleasure tugged at every muscle of his body. "I need you. Hold me close."

Eve wrapped her legs around his thighs, taking him deep inside her. Rafael closed his eyes. He could not describe this feeling, scorching hot yet achingly sweet. That was Eve, thrilling him with every touch, every uttered word, every glance, every kiss. They rocked in smooth motion until crashing in pleasure. For a long while, they lay breathless and spent in each other's arms. Eve buried her face in his chest. Rafael stroked her back and whispered into her hair. "Sweet love, thanks for coming back to me."

Now that he had such wonderful memories at the Belleview, Rafael wondered, shouldn't he buy it? He asked Eve whether it was a good idea. She bit into a strawberry and shook her head. "This isn't Monopoly. You don't have to buy up every square you land on."

"It just feels so good being here with you." He wasn't serious about buying the place. After all, he'd checked and the inn with all the local charm belonged to a multinational conglomerate. But he wasn't kidding about how it felt to be here with her, like coming home.

"It always feels good," she said. "No matter where we are."

"That's true."

He drew her into his arms and held her close while they watched the midday news. Outside the temperature had dropped, and the weather reports predicted a dusting of snow. The program ended with a story of Gabe's ranch, now a training facility. Rafael told Eve about Gabe, his high school years and early childhood. He told her about his mother who died and the bullish way Tobias had reentered his life. "He took me in and gave me his name. It was the right thing to do, but I'd just lost my mother and didn't want to lose the name that linked me to her. Tobias didn't ask me or anyone else how we felt about it. He just did it. Cammie's mother took off, pissed. It was a shit show."

At some point, Eve had reached for the remote control and silenced the television. She rested her head on his chest and just listened. He was really killing the mood that she'd worked hard to create. Rafael was sorry about that and everything else.

"It's classic Tobias to take action for the greater good without taking into account anyone's feelings on the matter. I'm sorry I did that to you."

"You're not off the hook," she said. "I'm still angry for the way you went about it. You can't just push me aside and take action on matters that concern me. I won't stand for it."

"I'm on notice," he said. Rafael hadn't tolerated Tobias's BS. He expected no less from her.

"Good," she said. "I *am* grateful, though." She circled her arms around his waist and pressed her body closer to his. "I asked you here to tell you that."

"You could've just sent flowers."

"You know what? It was a toss-up between pink peonies and pink panties."

"You made the right choice."

"And you've lifted a great burden off my shoulders. I don't know how I could ever—"

Rafael brought a finger to her lips. He did not want her to carry on about finding ways to repay his kindness. "Please don't finish that sentence."

"I need you to understand," she said. "I depend on the kindness of strangers for just about everything. It makes me feel small. I wish you had met me before."

"When you ran with the 30 Under 30 crowd?"

"Yeah," she said with a laugh.

Eve reached for her phone on the nightstand. She tapped on the browser and pulled up an article by a Miami business magazine. She was recognized for setting up a database for a South Florida nonprofit organization. In the accompanying photo, her hair was pulled back in that tight bun she used to wear and her expression was fixed. Rafael kissed her forehead. "I think I like you better now."

Eve pinched the photo to expand it and studied it awhile. "I think I do, too."

"Have you given any thought about the doctor?"

He hated himself for bringing it up, but it was too important. Her health was on the line.

"Yes, I have," she said. "I decided it wouldn't be smart to turn down the opportunity out of spite. Although I'm tired of doctors and hospitals, I have to stay healthy for Micah."

Rafael held his breath. Eve was vacillating, and if he said the wrong thing, he could tilt this the wrong way.

"So, we can go whenever you're free."

"Seriously?"

She shrugged. "What harm can it do? If the office is in Palm Beach, it'll probably be like visiting a day spa."

Rafael doubted that. Not one to procrastinate, he grabbed his phone off the nightstand and dialed Dr. Baer's office. They scheduled a 10:00 a.m. appointment for Friday. "We'll fly straight to West Palm. When you're done, we'll head down to Fort Lauderdale. I'd love it if we could spend the weekend at my hotel."

She plucked a strawberry from the crystal bowl on the tray beside her, swiped it in the chocolate dip and brought it to his lips. "I'd love it, too."

Eighteen

Eve should have been elated to board a private jet to Florida. But the bliss of returning home was clouded by the true purpose of their visit. They were not headed to a resort hotel where she'd slip on a bikini and lounge by the pool. That would come later. Their first stop was a doctor's office where she'd slip on a backless gown and stretch out on the examination table only to be told she had six months to live. That's how it was going to go down; Eve was sure of it. Doctor visits didn't end with positive, uplifting news—not in her experience, anyway.

"What's going on in your mind?" Rafael said. "I'd pay to know."

Eve let out a sigh. "Just a little nervous."

Seated across from her, Rafael tapped the tip of his boot to the pointy toe of her shoe. "Where's my fearless Eve?"

Fearless Eve? She did not know who that was. Fear had her in a cage, mental and physical. Early on, her physical therapist had said her recovery could go faster if she would only push herself. "You're afraid," he'd said. "You can do more." At the time, she was afraid she might lose her footing and fall on her face, pass out and land in the hospital, or lose her life like Arielle. The same wheels were turning now. She was afraid to hope only to stumble into bitter, bottomless disappointment once again.

Rafael was watching her intently. Eve shifted in her seat, feeling uneasy. He patted his thigh and mouthed, *Come here.*

She shook her head. "Can't unfasten my seat belt. We haven't reached cruising altitude yet. Captain's orders."

"Don't worry. I'll keep you safe."

She sprang from her seat, abandoning the cold leather for the warmth of his lap. He kissed just below her ear. "What's wrong?"

Everything was wrong. Their first weekend getaway was for medical reasons. There was nothing sexy about it, but this was her life. Eve took a trembling hand to her throat. She pushed down a sob. Rafael cradled her in his arms. He let her cry without interruption. He did not try to console her. He simply let her get the toxins out. Eve surrendered to the torrent of tears, too strong to manage or control. It felt so good to be supported. All through her ordeal she had received help and assistance from government and nonprofit organizations, from the medical staff at Royal Hospital, even from strangers like Cammie and Sierra. What she had not had was a shoulder to cry on. She'd held Micah, but no one had ever held her.

Rafael stroked her hair. "I'll be brave for you," he whispered. "You can rely on me for this."

She pressed a palm to his chest. "I am grateful."

"I don't want you to be grateful," he said. "I want you to get well for selfish reasons."

She caught a flash of worry in his eyes. This relationship was meant to be light and fun. His role was to bring light to her life. She was not meant to darken his. Those were the

terms of their agreement. Now she worried something else
was at play, and she had to address it head-on.

She freed herself from his tight embrace and sat upright.
"Rafael, may I ask you a direct question?"

He leaned his head on the headrest. "Go for it."

"What's happening with us? Are we catching feelings?"

He peered at her with one eye shut. "What? Catching...
fireflies?"

She may be a straight shooter, but Rafael was a master
of deflection. *"Feelings,"* she repeated. For good measure,
she spelled out the word.

"I know what feelings are, Eve." He slipped a hand under
her loose cotton blouse and rolled his knuckles along the
grooves of her lower spine. "Do you feel that?"

"I'm serious!" she cried, although the back rub felt really good.

"You're too serious."

A moment later, when the flight attendant offered her a
cashmere blanket and poured them both French roast coffee, that all felt good, too.

"I need you to focus on *feeling* better," he said a while
later. "That's all that matters right now."

Eve agreed wholeheartedly, so why did her heart tank?
She dipped a biscotti into her coffee and pulled up her mental to-do list, the one she'd drafted the night of the fundraiser
then promptly abandoned the moment Rafael had pinned her
to the magnolia tree. She revisited it point by point, adding
one more:

• *Don't catch feelings for this man.*

Dr. Baer was a reserved woman, somber and soft-spoken,
with steel-gray hair and keen gray eyes. Eve spent three hours
in her office undergoing a battery of tests. Dr. Baer reviewed
the results and delivered somewhat hopeful news. "This is
not a severe case. There is no reason you can't manage your

symptoms now that you are aware of your condition. I am prescribing medication. I recommend moderate exercise and a plant-based diet. We'll follow up in six months at which time we can discuss other treatment options."

Eve was reluctant to accept the news on face value. "My sister died of this. Giving birth was too much for her heart and she couldn't recover."

She saw Arielle in her hospital bed, her life seeping from her body. She knew hours before her sister passed that she had lost her.

"You are not your sister," Dr. Baer said. "Remember that."

Rafael was in the waiting room when Eve stepped out. He said that he had gone out to handle some things while she was busy, but she suspected that he hadn't gone far. He looked a little bent out of shape. She rushed into his arms. On the ride to Fort Lauderdale, she repeated the doctor's words.

"Sounds like we got good news," he said. "Now we can relax and celebrate."

Eve could only think of sleep. It had been a grueling day.

When they arrived at the hotel, Rafael was greeted like an emperor. His staff seemed genuinely thrilled to have their boss back, and that was a rare and beautiful thing. Everyone, from the valet attendant to the general manager, wanted his ear. It took a while to make it through the lobby. She thought they were in the clear when they got on the elevator. Eve wrapped her arms around his waist and leaned on him. A woman raced across the lobby, heels clicking on the terrazzo floor. "Hey, stranger!" she called out. "Hold the elevator!"

The woman crashed into him, and judging by Rafael's reaction, he did not need a shield this time.

"Claudia!" He pulled the brunette into a hug. "It's been a long time."

"It's been ages! I'm happy to see you, but I'm so mad at you. Where have you been?"

"Good old Texas," he said, reviving his twang.

NADINE GONZALEZ

139

Claudia laughed and tossed back a lock of hair. "You're a Texas boy at heart."

"You may be right about that," Rafael said. "What are you up to?"

"It's Tatiana's birthday," she replied. "We're all meeting at the bar for drinks. Join us! It'll be like old times."

Rafael declined the offer. "Eve and I have plans."

Claudia opened wide eyes and took in Eve as if just now realizing that she and Rafael were not alone in the elevator. "Ah! Is this Eve?"

Rafael nodded. "Eve, this is Claudia, an old friend."

Claudia took a step back, disappointment tugging at the corners of her mouth. Even so, she managed to sound cheery. "Hey! Nice meeting you."

"Likewise."

Claudia got off on the twentieth floor, leaving behind the scent of her perfume. She and Rafael rode up to the penthouse floor, which was reserved for private residences. Rafael kept an apartment in Fort Lauderdale. Although he loved the Miami property, he said it could get rowdy. Fort Lauderdale was chill enough to feel like home. A home with room service, turndown service, laundry service and any other service you could think of including an in-room massage.

Eve couldn't put Claudia out of her mind. With the dimple in her chin and twinkle in her eyes, the glossy brunette looked vivacious and fun. If he'd gone off with her, he would've had a better time. Now that she'd seen him in his element, she understood there was little chance of him catching feelings for her. He would sooner catch a cold. With her sad stories, health issues and teary fits on private planes, she was nothing like Claudia. Rafael could cross out every item on her laundry list of problems, and she still wouldn't be like Claudia. The thought made her sad and tired.

Rafael gave her a tour of the penthouse. It was white, stylish and a little sterile. None of that mattered when you factored in the sweeping ocean views from every room. The bedroom was serene with a large bed dressed in white and few other furnishings. Rafael suggested she lie down awhile. Eve crawled onto the bed and sunk her head into a stack of pillows. All her negative thoughts dissolved into darkness.

She woke up hours later in a darkened room. Disoriented, she shuffled out of bed and stumbled down the dimly lit hall to the living room. She was bothered by the reigning silence. Had Rafael abandoned her yet again? No...no... He wouldn't. And yet her heart didn't settle until she saw the ruby-red tip of his cigar. He was out on the terrace that wrapped around the penthouse. Actually, he was in the sunken Jacuzzi out on the terrace, head back, blowing smoke into the night.

Eve squeezed her eyes shut and took a breath. Why had she freaked out, thinking he'd flown her all this way just to abandon her? Come to think of it, she'd been one erratic hot mess this entire trip. They were far from Royal, far from the responsibilities that she'd left there. She could maybe leave those cares behind for a day or two.

Eve headed back to the bedroom. She rummaged through her luggage until she found the bikini that she had ordered online and paid extra for overnight delivery in the hopes this weekend would have more to offer than a series of doctor visits. When she joined Rafael out on the terrace, he grinned up at her. The cigar in one hand, a tumbler with amber liquor and ice in the other, dark hair slicked back, he looked relaxed.

"Look at you," she said.

"Look at *you*," he tossed back. "How are you feeling?"

"Rested." She walked over to the edge of the hot tub and dipped a foot, the gurgling bubbles tickling the tip of her toes. "Listen. I need a favor."

"Anything."

"Whatever you do, don't let me think too much. Not tonight. Or this weekend. I need to get out of my head."

"Alright, darling," he said. "Whatever you need."

Eve exhaled, releasing the pressures of the day. "What are you drinking?"

"Whiskey." He raised the glass. "Want it? Come and get it."

"No, thanks," she said. "I'll have an iced tea."

"We make excellent mocktails here," he said. "How does a *nojito* sound?"

"Sounds delicious."

"I'll order," he said. "You'll have to get the door. My state of mind is very obvious right now."

"I'll get the door," Eve said. "I don't have those problems."

He took a drag from the cigar and looked at her through a screen of fragrant blue smoke. "But you cause them."

Eve bit back a laugh, loving the way his gaze skimmed her body.

"Is that new?" he asked, gesturing to her bathing suit.

She raised her hands to her hips. "You like?"

"Very much," he said. "You left the tag on."

"Oh!" She looked down and wondered how she'd missed the tag dangling between her breasts. Rather than pull it off, she reached behind her back, unfastened the bra top and let it fall to the side.

Rafael nodded appreciatively. "I was going to rip off the tag, but your solution works, too."

Eve didn't stop there. She looped her thumbs around the waistband of the bikini bottom and, with a little shimmy, lowered it to her ankles and kicked it aside.

"My God," Rafael groaned. "Eve, do you want to stop my heart?"

Eve eased into the water. "I need you alive for what I have in mind."

He dropped the cigar into an ashtray and reached for her. The strength of the whirlpool made his task easy. Eve drifted to him and soon she was in his arms, wet skin to wet skin, mouths thirsty only for each other. His hands were everywhere. "Don't think of anything except how this feels."

It felt amazing, absolutely amazing. She wrapped her legs around his hips, clinging to his body and his words.

"Don't think of anything except how much I want you," he said. "Promise?"

"Promise."

It was a promise she broke almost instantly, as she took in the twinkling city lights in the distance, the swirl of warm water all around them and the night that pulsed just for them. Could she be dreaming?

Rafael was too perceptive to let her thoughts wander. "Where have you gone?"

She pressed her forehead to his. "I'm here with you."

"Good." He kissed her again. "I can't think of anything but you."

Eve could feel his heart pounding in his chest. A current of fear moved through her just as strong as the water churning around them. She could not fall in love with this man, and yet she was dancing dangerously close to the edge. To break the mood, she splashed him with water. His grip tightened around her waist and he pulled her under.

The "nojito" came later. Then dinner. Then lying in bed, talking about nothing in particular while Rafael played with her hair. The next morning, Eve slept in while he met with his staff. In the evening, they took a boat and navigated the Intracoastal Waterway to one of Rafael's favorite seafood restaurants. At a rickety wood table, he pounded stone crab legs with a mallet and explained how their pail of "peel and eat shrimp" was better than standard-issue country club shrimp cocktail.

"If you've peeled it, you've earned it," he explained with a straight face. "It's that simple."

"Is that right?"

Rafael leaned back and joined his hands behind his head. "I'm telling you. It's all about the good old elbow grease."

He wore a plain white T-shirt and a pair of soft slouchy

jeans. He looked so good, the crisp white cotton contrasting with his golden brown skin. This quick trip had revived him, too, apparently. She commented on it, and he offered her a sad smile. "I'm torn between two cities. Royal is who I am. My roots are there. For better or worse, my family is there, too. Fort Lauderdale built me, made me the man I am today. Most people think I started out in Miami, but that's not true. It was here. Now I'm not sure where I belong. I've got a lot to figure out."

Eve understood. She was in the same boat, so to speak. Facts and figures had forever been her passion, but working alongside Rafael had given her a different perspective. She liked the hands-on nature of his work and enjoyed watching an idea unfold from conception to realization.

She unpeeled a rosy Gulf Coast shrimp. "I'm not sure what my next step will be."

A wrinkle creased the space between his brows. "You have a home at Arias Hospitality Group—always."

That was very reassuring, but staying on as his assistant was not her endgame. It was too soon to seek a promotion. Gradually, she could take on extra projects.

"Was your dream to work in finance?" he asked.

"No," she said. "I went to business school to start a business of my own."

"You wanted to be an entrepreneur."

"Not really," she admitted. Her dream was far less romantic. "I wanted to make my first million before turning thirty. Starting a business is the fastest way to do that."

Rafael took a swig from a chilled bottle of beer. "Do you know what happens when you turn thirty?"

She flashed a smile. "I haven't reached that milestone."

"I'll tell you," he said. "You stop caring about bullshit milestones."

Eve stopped caring about a lot of things. The rest of the weekend flowed by without a worry or a cloud in the pale blue Florida sky.

Nineteen

They arrived in Royal fairly early on Sunday afternoon, only four o'clock local time. Rafael knew Eve was anxious to see Micah and proposed they swing by Drake's ranch on their way home from the airport for a quick visit.

Drake greeted them with a grin at the door. "A little weekend getaway to Miami, huh?"

"It wasn't like that," Rafael said. "We had something to take care of."

"We never made it to Miami," Eve said, as if it made a world of difference. "We mostly stayed in Fort Lauderdale. Rafael worked the whole time."

"The whole time?" Drake looked him over. "Is that how you got your tan?"

"What can I say? I'm a whistle-while-you-work type of guy."

"I bet."

Cammie came down the stairs with Micah. "Hey, you two! What a surprise. I wasn't expecting to see you this weekend."

"I couldn't wait to see Micah," Eve said.

"Here he is," Cammie said. "He just woke up from a nap."

Eve went over to the sofa and, once settled, Cammie placed Micah in her arms. She cradled him close to her heart. He squealed with delight and burst into tears.

"He's fussy," Cammie said. "It's time for his bottle."

Drake had another idea. "I know what he needs."

Cammie and Drake parted in different directions. Cammie returned with a bottle of warm milk. Eve took it from her and slipped the nipple into Micah's pink little mouth and rocked him as he started to suck vigorously.

Drake returned with a small yellow teddy bear and handed it to Rafael. "Here you go, Rafe, my man."

"What's this?" Rafael asked.

"Yellow Bear."

The toy was the size of his hand. "Does it have a name?"

"That's his name—Yellow Bear."

"Original," he murmured.

"When it comes to kids, simplicity is key," Drake explained.

"And you're an expert now?" Rafael said, incredulous.

Cammie intervened. "Rafe, quit arguing and dangle Yellow Bear above Micah. He likes to grab at it while he's feeding."

Rafael sat next to Eve on the couch and did as instructed. He dangled the bear before Micah's eyes. The baby reached up to grab it.

Cammie slipped out her phone. "I'm taking a picture. You three look like a family!"

Eve shook her head. "No, we don't."

"Kinda do," Drake said, settling comfortably in an armchair.

Cammie snapped her fingers, demanding their attention. "Eyes on me. Smiles. Good. Got it!"

Eve had smiled for the photo, but quickly lowered her head. Rafael wondered what he was missing.

Cammie studied the photo she'd just taken and nodded appreciatively. "A damn good-looking family, too!"

Rafael felt his jaw tighten. Was Cammie projecting her hopes on them? Her dream had always been to have children, preferably with Drake. The tragedy was his bighearted sister had not found a willing partner in the man that she loved. But from what he'd gathered from their recent talks, Drake had done a full 180. It was all thanks to Micah. But the little one wasn't a miracle worker. Unlike Drake, Rafael wasn't going to suddenly change his outlook just because a cute baby had dropped into their lives.

He brought it up on the drive home. "Eve," he said, his eyes on the road. "May I ask you a direct question?"

"Go for it." She was less jittery now. Time with Micah always calmed her down.

"What are your long-term plans for Micah?"

"Oh." He felt her staring at him, but he could not meet her eyes. "You're asking because Cammie put you on the spot back there. Sorry about that."

"I'm asking because I want to know."

Eve had come to Royal in search of Micah's father. They'd yet to find him, but he was sure they would. When that day came, what sort of arrangement would they come to? She was very attached to her nephew. He couldn't imagine her just turning him over.

They stopped at a light, and he reached for her hand. "Sweet love, talk to me."

She very slowly withdrew her hand from his. He knew then that he had missed something back at Drake and Cammie's place. Somehow, he'd upset her. For the life of him, he couldn't think what that could be.

They drove the rest of the way in silence. He removed their luggage from the trunk of the car and loaded the elevator. They rode up to their floor. When they passed her door, she slowed to a stop and called out to him. "Rafael, wait."

There was an edge to her voice and he knew, whatever the argument, he'd lost.

"I'm going to regain custody of Micah," she said. "Just as soon as I reach my therapy goals and the doctor signs off on the paperwork."

Rafael cleared his throat. "Have you considered waiting until you find his father? There's no rush, really."

"I'm not waiting. He could go screw himself for all I care."

That edge in her voice was anger mixed with resentment.

"Are you worried about Cammie and Drake?" he asked. "Because they'll keep him for as long as you need. I think Micah's done them a world of good."

"It's dragged on long enough," she said. "They'd only signed on to foster for a short time. I expected to be done with PT by now, but the doctor overseeing my therapy is strict and won't sign off until I hit every single goal."

"Cammie doesn't mind. Far from it."

"I can't outsource my nephew," Eve said. "He's my responsibility."

"So what is your plan?" Rafael asked. "How soon is soon?" Even to his ears, his questions sounded curt.

"As soon as possible."

Eve surprised him with an elaborate plan that involved her moving out, getting her own place, securing day care and, because it was worth repeating, moving out.

"Eve, I thought you were happy here with me."

"I am." She went to him and slung her arms around his neck the way she liked to do when they went for long walks on the grounds and no one was around. "But I have responsibilities I can't shrug off. Please understand."

"You don't have to move out to do that."

She laughed off his comment. "Rafael, there's no room in your life for a child! You know that."

He had one more direct question for her. "Are you ending things with me?"

She shook her head. "Not really."

"It's yes or no, Eve."

"We can always see each other," she said. "It probably won't be the same."

He didn't want things to change between them. He liked it as it was. Something sharp was clawing at him inside. "You never shared any of this with me. When were you planning on telling me you wanted to move out?"

"I don't have any definite plans as of yet. My physical therapist thinks if I do well within a few more sessions, he'll talk to the doctors. And maybe I will ask Cammie to keep Micah a week or two longer, until it's all settled."

"A week or two?"

"Rafael, I can't let your sister raise my nephew so you and I can live free."

"No one is saying that—"

She stepped away from him and started pacing around furiously. "The only reason I let it go on so long is because I was afraid. I worried that I'd black out at a parking lot, leave him on the hood of another stranger's car and start the whole vicious cycle over again."

"I understand all of that, Eve," he said. "I knew this day was coming, but we could have talked about it."

This was rich coming from him, considering his past behavior. But Rafael felt something slipping from his fingers. It made him desperate.

"Rafael, this isn't about you," she said with exasperation. "This is about Micah. You don't understand what it's like to have children or care for children. It's like you said—you're not wired that way."

"And I've told you why."

"Or maybe it's just a choice you've made," she said.

"It is my choice," he said unapologetically. It was a choice that he had a right to make. If Cammie was right and he was more like Tobias than he'd wanted to think, it was probably for the best.

"Exactly," Eve said. "You're the lone wolf or the black

sheep or whatever else you call it, and it suits you. But I don't have a choice. My sister died and left me her son. I have no other family, and I have to do right by him. There are no other options for me. I'm not like Claudia."

"Claudia?" Rafael was genuinely confused. "What does she have to do with this?"

"You belong with someone like that," Eve said. "When I saw you with her, it all made sense."

At the moment, Eve was talking nonsense. "You saw her for all of five minutes."

"You know what I mean."

"I don't. If it's that clear-cut and we're so compatible, why aren't we together? She's single and so am I. Why aren't we riding off into the sunset together?"

"I don't know," she shot back. "Maybe you ought to consider that instead of spending all your time, money and resources trying to fix me."

Rafael drew a breath. "Look, we're exhausted," he said, as diplomatically as possible. "Let's head inside, shower and grab something to eat. We'll talk about this with cooler heads."

"No," she said. "I need some quiet time. I think I'll stay here tonight."

"Are you sure?"

"Uh-huh." She searched her purse for the keys that he'd never seen her use. He followed her into her suite and left her suitcase inside the door.

"May I come by and check on you later?"

"I'll be asleep."

Rafael didn't know how he managed to keep on standing when really he was in free fall. This was how it was going to end; he was sure of it. She would close the door on him, and there would be no way back.

Twenty

Hovered over her bathroom sink, her breath shallow, Eve was in the throes of an anxiety attack. It was over between her and Rafael. She'd understood it the moment they returned to Royal. Their joyride had come to an end.

She had Rafael to thank for her hard-won independence. He'd given her the job and even arranged for her to see the doctor. So now she no longer had any excuses. Each time she visited with Micah she felt guilty for not being more present or somehow doing more. Drake's comments about the Miami getaway had stung. He was only kidding and she knew it, but it didn't feel right to leave her nephew with Cammie while she and Rafael took off for weekend escapes.

In general, Eve wasn't fascinated with Royal's storied past, its feuds and drama handed down from generation to generation. However, it was well-known that Tobias Wentworth, Rafael and Cammie's father, had a solid reputation of being a ruthless, stingy, hard-ass businessman. In contrast, his kids were generous to a fault, giving without ever asking for anything in return. Eve loved them both, fiercely, but she could not rely on them forever.

She and Rafael were locked in the roles of generous bene-factor and damsel in distress. They couldn't carry on like this. At some point, he'd resent her or she'd resent him. He would certainly want someone on his level, and that wasn't her. The imbalance of power and privilege was just too great. Maybe it wasn't Claudia, either. It was his choice to make. There was no doubt in her mind that the generous thing to do was to cut him loose.

So now what? How do you break up with your boss? Was there any guidance on that? Office affairs were the worst. They seldom worked out. When things fell apart, you were stuck with your ex as a colleague or boss. Rafael was a good, decent man. He wasn't going to make things difficult. In the end of the day, he'd stuff down all his feelings and put on a friendly, impersonal mask. He'd call her Ms. Martin, and not in a sexy way. He'd duck out early on Fridays so there wouldn't be any awkward run-ins at the elevators. He'd be a perfect gentleman. He just wouldn't be her lover.

It began as early as the next day. The office suites were unnaturally quiet. Eve assumed Rafael had stayed away on purpose. Even though it hurt her, she was thankful. They needed a reprieve. Later, they could pick up again and carry on as before. For the moment, they needed space.

At lunchtime, Eve picked up a salad and ate at her desk. She didn't have an appetite and ended up pushing her plate aside and dropping her head on a stack of files. There was a hole in her heart that nothing could fill. She might have stayed like that, despondent and desperate, right up until quitting time if Sierra Morgan hadn't called. She wanted to meet for drinks. "We could talk and go over Arielle's diary, like we discussed."

"Yes. Absolutely."

"How about we meet at the Colt Room at five?"

The Colt Room was a wine bar at the TCC. Eve was beginning to think that all roads in Royal really did lead to the
country club. "Meet you there."

At four thirty on the dot, Eve grabbed her keys and headed
out. There was still no sign of Rafael. She did not hear his
voice down the hall or his rambunctious laughter. Not a peep.
Nothing. It gutted her. Was this her future? Rolling around
like an empty shell, going through the motions of daily life,
all the while knowing that there was someone out there who
could make her days bright? If only her hands were free to
grab the one he extended.

Rafael spent the morning at the Richardson property.
Mary Richardson very graciously showed him around and
led him through a point-by-point inspection. She showed
him the tiles that were missing from the roof, demonstrated
plumbing issues and pointed out the squeaky floorboards.
Rafael followed along with a heavy heart. He would've liked
to do all of this with Eve. It wasn't part of her job description to follow him around, but he had grown accustomed to
having her at his side. He couldn't stop thinking of the ob-
servations she would have made or the private jokes they
would have shared when Mary Richardson wasn't looking.
She would have no doubt drafted a quirky list.

He knew it was over between them and did not understand
why. They were good together. She thought he belonged with
someone like Claudia. Meanwhile, he couldn't picture her
with anyone else. Who could love or care for her better? Just
the thought of it pissed him off.

But what about Micah?

It had been so easy to overlook this point because Micah
had been safe and sound with Cammie. Realistically, that
couldn't go on forever. Eve said she couldn't outsource her
nephew, and he realized that was exactly what he had hoped
she would do.

"Are you alright?" Mary Richardson asked.

"Oh sure!" He accepted a glass of sweet tea when they reached the end of the tour.

"You're not having second thoughts, are you?"

"Hell no!" He checked himself. "Sorry, ma'am."

"That's fine," she assured him. "I curse up a storm, too. It's just that we're counting on the money."

"I promise you I'm not withdrawing my offer. We are going through with this."

"Good to hear."

"What are your plans for the future?" Rafael asked.

She reclined in a rattan chair on the porch. The motel was as much her home as her business. It was her whole life. "We have our eyes on a lake house."

"Sounds nice."

"It's time for us to walk away," she said. "We put so much work into this place and expected our kids to take over. Turns out: they have dreams of their own. We held on as long as we could, waiting for one of them to change their minds. Too long, really. We just couldn't walk away. At some point you have to ask yourself—do you own a business or does the business own you?"

"That's pretty deep for a Monday morning," Rafael mused. "Maybe too deep for me."

"Nah," Mary said. "You're a smart guy. Just think about it. You wouldn't pour all your money into one project. Well, that's what we did. We put all our energy into this motel and seldom took a day off. The goal was to secure the future. Meanwhile, the future is passing us by. Understand?"

"I think I do."

"What are your plans for this place?" Mary asked. "Are you going to tear it down?"

That wasn't his nature. For someone who swore up and down that he didn't believe in looking back, he liked to preserve the past. The motel was built at the turn of the last century. The architectural details made its charm. He would restore it and bring it back to its old glory. He made that promise to Mary, adding that he would invite them back for a visit when it reopened as a spa.

Mary nodded. Wisps of gray hair escaped her loose braid and glistened in the sun. "Looks like we picked the right man."

He'd stayed for lunch, and it was two in the afternoon when he took leave of the Richardsons. Rafael still wasn't ready to return to the office. He was not ready to see Eve again, to see the truth in her eyes. Eve was determined, a trait he normally liked. Except now she was determined to destroy the world they'd built together, and there was nothing he could do about it. Thankfully, another option came up.

Manny called and held up his phone to a car engine to let him hear it purr. "You'll want to hear this in person," he said.

"I'm on my way."

He tore through the streets, taking back roads to avoid traffic. He arrived twenty minutes later and Manny went through the production of unveiling the car. The old clunker was now a *Camaro*, with a new engine and its original electric-blue paint. He swept a hand along the grain of the leather seats, realizing with sadness that every time he admired the buttery caramel color, he would think of Eve.

Manny must have misread the crumpled look on his face. "Bro, don't get emotional!"

Rafael waved him off. "It's nothing."

"Where's prom date?" he asked.

"She's at work."

"That's too bad," Manny said. "She would've gotten a kick out of this."

"I think so, too."

"Bring her next time. She was good people."

"We'll see." Rafael looked around for a distraction. He tested the horn.

Manny came over and leaned against the car, hands in his pockets. "What happened? Are you two going through it?"

Rafael glanced at him and caught his knowing look. "Is it that obvious?"

"You look like someone stole your lunch money, your puppy and your brand-new bike."

"That bad?"

"Oh, yeah!"

"There's nothing I can say. I'm not really sure what happened."

One minute they were happy, the next she was making plans to move out. Frankly, he felt blindsided.

"That sounds about right." Manny went over to the mini fridge, pulled out two bottles of beer, cracked them open and handed him one. "Come on. Let's go sit outside and not talk about it."

Rafael pushed out a dry laugh. "Yeah. I'd like that."

Twenty-One

Eve sank into a leather banquette, across from Sierra. They had opted to take their drinks to a table for optimal privacy. Sierra looked smart as usual, her tousled blond hair framing her face, her eyes shining with intelligence and curiosity. But dread rose up steadily in Eve's gut like bile.

"There's a reason why I asked to meet with you at this bar," Sierra said.

"Really?" Eve said. "I just thought everyone liked to hang out at the TCC."

"True," Sierra said with a knowing smile. "There are other spots in town I like to go to when I'm not working. But this bar in particular, the Colt Room, does it have any significance for you?"

"None," Eve said, confused. "Why would it?"

Sierra produced Arielle's diary, face open. Eve took in the scrappy handwriting penmanship that she had made fun of back when she and her sister were in school. Her heart seized; she had to look away. Combing through the diary, discussing her sister, all of it was painful. It was necessary if they would have any hope of finding Micah's father, but it wasn't fun. This wasn't an exciting mystery she was aching to solve; it was a tragedy that pained her to relive. Honestly, her motivation was gone. Finding Micah's father was no longer her focus. The more time passed, the less it mattered. Her name had been cleared, and no judge would separate a child from his one surviving relative. She would have liked to tell Sierra to let it go. Eve was convinced the man didn't want to be found and with that arose a conviction deep within her that her family was complete and perfect without him.

Sierra tapped on a note in the margin of a page: one word, *COLT*, with little hearts drawn around it. She flipped the page. "Here it is again, underlined."

"I must have missed that," Eve said. In her feverish search for clues in her sister's diary, it shocked her that there were dots she had failed to connect.

"We can take it literally," Sierra said. "Maybe she took up riding. Was she a horse person?"

"Not that I know of," Eve said. "But when in Texas, right?"

Sierra laughed at the joke, but it came across as a professional courtesy more than anything else. "I thought it might have something to do with this bar."

Eve nodded agreeably. "Okay."

"There's happy hour on weekends. Maybe she came here once, had a good time and wanted to come back."

"That's possible, I guess."

She took in the brassy opulence of the Colt Room. It did not look like the type of place her easygoing sister would frequent, but then again, what did she know? It was obvious she did not know her sister as well as she thought.

"Are you alright?" Sierra asked, closing the diary.

"Oh, sure," Eve said. "This is difficult, but I'm okay."

"Is that all?" Sierra was ever the inquisitive reporter. "It's just the other night, at the fundraiser, you looked so happy."

"It was a fun night." Eve took a sip of lime soda to better evade Sierra's eyes.

"Sounds like both Martin sisters found love in Royal," Sierra said. "You and Rafael Wentworth make a cute couple."

Eve nearly choked. "How do you know? Did he say something to you?"

Sierra went red in the face. "It was in the *Gazette*."

Eve was glad they weren't seated at a bar height table; she would have fallen off her stool. "In the *newspaper*?"

Sierra pulled out her phone, tapped the screen a few times and pulled up a local newspaper's gossip column. Beneath the headline ROYAL'S NEW POWER COUPLE?, a photo of her and Rafael at their table at the Valentine's Day fundraiser, heads close, reading from the same phone. The camera caught them smiling conspiratorially. Other than that, there was nothing salacious about the photo—thank goodness. What if the photographer had caught them under the magnolia tree? That would have been a whole other story. Eve scanned the column. There was a quote from Jennifer Carlton. "Those two are inseparable! For sure they are a couple."

Heart sinking, Eve returned Sierra's phone. The image, though, was imprinted in her mind. She and Rafael looked so damn happy. What a cruel prank! It was as if the universe were taunting her with the image of the life she would never have. She drummed the tabletop with her fingers. "Great," she murmured. "Just great."

"It's a...great photo," Sierra offered.

"I know what it looks like—"

Sierra raised her hands. "No need to explain. I'm sorry I brought it up."

She looked so uncomfortable, Eve felt obliged to diffuse the tension. "What were you saying about the Colt Room? Maybe there is something to it."

"I thought so," Sierra said. "Except before you arrived, I showed Arielle's photo around. None of the bartenders or waiters remember seeing her."

"I'm not surprised," Eve said. "She would have preferred grabbing a beer at a college bar than sipping Chardonnay at the Cattleman's Club."

She was about to add that she and her sister were not the country club type, but the words never cleared her throat. She'd met Rafael here. Today she felt at ease, meeting with an acquaintance at the club for a drink. As much as anyone could feel at ease when their heart was splitting in two, obviously.

"I've been over it and over it," Sierra said. "It's a minor detail, but if feels big. You know?"

"May I ask you a question?" Eve said.

"Certainly."

"Why are you so…dedicated to this?"

Sierra took a moment before offering a carefully crafted answer. "I came to Royal to write about this club, its secrets and old ghosts. It's great and all, but your little nephew grabbed my heart. I was there from the beginning, you know. I was one of the first people on the scene when Cammie Wentworth found the little guy on her car."

Eve sat upright, but her inner walls were crumbling. Her imagination pieced together the scene when Cammie and Sierra discovered Micah abandoned on the trunk of the Mercedes. She was close to tears again, but this time she steeled herself. The time for crying had passed. If Sierra wanted to dig further, she would help her.

Eve racked her brain. "There's something else…"

Sierra leaned forward, eager. "Go on."

"Micah's middle initial is C," Eve said. "No middle name. Just an initial. We're a small family and no one's name starts with C." She had asked Arielle about it, but her sister had brushed her off. "I can't imagine it stands for Colt. That would be…ridiculous."

"Would it, though?" Once again, Sierra pulled out her phone. It seemed to have all the answers. Her prior research on the country club had not focused on the swanky bar. As to be expected, everything about the TCC, even a wine bar, had a story. "There's this blog I followed back when I was researching the club. It's chock-full of tidbits… Okay! It says here that members of the TCC would gather in the Colt Room for drinks after voting."

Eve imagined the members gathering to vote on a "no fun allowed" clause. She reached for a cocktail napkin to hide her smile. Rafael's words would forever make her laugh. That was something she would take with her.

"Well, now!"

Sierra's exclamation pulled Eve out of her Rafael-induced haze. "What is it?"

"Listen to this—one of the founding members is named Colter Black."

"That's an unusual name."

"There's more." Sierra perked up. "Colter Black donated the funds to build and stock the bar."

Colter… Eve turned the name over in her mind. Micah Colter Martin.

Sierra was positively giddy. "So much for my horse theory."

"Unless Colter Black has a great-grandson by the same name who crossed paths with Arielle while she was in town, I don't know what to make of it."

"You leave that to me," Sierra said confidently. "This is what I do. If there's a young Colter Black out there, I will track him down and swipe him for a DNA sample myself."

"It may come to that," Eve said dryly. "It still irks me that he hasn't made any effort to reach out."

"There's a chance he doesn't know."

"Now you sound like Rafael."

"Well then." Sierra set down her phone and picked up her wineglass. "He sounds like a pretty smart guy."

As luck would have it, Eve pulled into the residence parking lot only moments after Rafael had slipped into his reserved spot. He cut the engine and sprang out of the low sports car. She stayed put, her hands gripping the steering wheel. He looked disheveled. When he got closer, she saw that his eyes were bloodshot. This was her handiwork. She had managed to turn a joyous, outgoing man into this— whatever this was.

He held the car door open for her and helped her out. They stood facing each other for a while. She resisted the urge to reach up and smooth his hair.

"We made the papers," she said. "They published a picture of us at the fundraiser. They asked if we are 'Royal's New Power Couple.'"

He shrugged. "I wouldn't mind it if it were true, but we're not a couple anymore, are we?"

Eve didn't care so much about the headline. She couldn't get the photo out of her head. The photographer had captured an intimate moment. Her expression was one of a woman pampered beyond belief, content, not wanting for anything, happy at last. It had frightened her to see it, and it made arguing that they had never been a couple that much harder.

"Sweet love, come here," he said quietly.

It was a plea and she could not resist. Eve drifted to him. Even now, she could not keep her hands off him. She reached up and smoothed his hair. Slipping her hand down to his neck, she massaged the tension there.

His hand fell to her waist and he drew her even closer. "Couldn't we...just once maybe?"

A smile broke from the inside out. "Yes. Maybe just once."

His kiss was tender. When he pulled her into his suite a while later, and they frantically tore at each other's clothes, his kiss was still tender. She stepped out of her dress. He sunk to his knees, pressed his face to her flank, murmuring, "Eve, sweet Eve." He kissed her from freckle to freckle, connecting the dots. She bent forward to meet his mouth. Then all tenderness subsided, giving way to relentless desire. The world quieted around them and no sounds existed beyond their sharp breaths, the moans that escaped their lips and later the cries that spiraled out of her. As the sparks of their desire died down, Eve curled up to him in bed and listened to his heartbeat. That silk thread of tenderness returned, wrapping itself around them, tying them together.

Later, Eve slipped out of bed and quietly got dressed.

"Don't go," Rafael said.

"If I stay, I'll never want to leave."

"Stay," he said. "Move Micah in if you like. There's plenty of room in here."

She looked around for her shoes. "Yes, but there's no room for a child in your life. A baby is not a part-time gig or a sidehustle. You have to be all in. Does any of that sound appealing to you?"

Rafael propped himself up on an elbow. "I don't have to become Micah's dad to be in your life."

"Do you want to be anyone's dad, though?" she asked. Since they were on the topic, she might as well go there.

He raised his chin. Even in the half-light, she could see defiance stirring in his eyes. "Is that a deal-breaker?"

"It is," she said. This ordeal had made it crystal clear. Having lost her family, she wanted a second chance. Her life was wrapped around Micah, and there was room in her heart for more. "I know with most couples this conversation doesn't happen until months into the relationship. And I know it's not fair to dump all this on you like this. But it's worth asking if we even want the same things. If not, maybe it's best we end it now before anyone gets hurt."

"I want you," he said, without even a trace of doubt.

"I want you, too," she said. "Rafael, I'm so glad I met you. You've changed my life. I'm sorry I wasn't up front about my plans, but this was never meant to get so out of hand. From the day we met I thought you understood. The only reason I'm in town is because of Micah. If his father doesn't show up, I'll probably move back to Florida."

Despite the encouraging leads that Sierra was pursuing, Eve was committed to follow her own plans all the way through.

Rafael fell back onto the pillows and ran a palm over his face. "Now you want to move out of state," he said, speaking into the dark.

"Florida is home. There is nothing for me here."

"Nothing?"

She caught the mix of hurt and betrayal in his voice. She rushed to apologize and botched that, too. "Look, in a few weeks, you'll be over it. It'll be in the past."

"You think a few weeks will change how I feel?"

He couldn't conceive of it now, but she was right about this. He would likely move on to another project, something else neglected and timeworn to restore and make new again. He would forget her eventually—maybe not in a few weeks, but in time.

Rafael tossed back the sheets and got out of bed. Pulling her close, he stroked her cheek. "Sweet love… Nothing that you're telling me is real. Right now, it's just you and me—and we're happy. Why are you looking for the quickest way out?"

"Try to understand," she pleaded. "That's not what I'm doing."

Eve was reeling. How could he possibly think that?

"Yes, it is," he said. "Trust me. I'm an escape artist. I've done it more times than I can count."

Eve felt some shame when she walked out on him moments later, almost proving that he was right. Back at her suite, she poured herself a glass of water and went to sit at the bay window. Time passed and gradually, night slipped into day. In the distance, light scattered from behind the pine trees. This was the first sunrise she had witnessed in Royal, and it brought new clarity. She could not stay here much longer. She and Rafael would never resolve their differences. They could not go on like this, falling into bed only to fight afterward. Now that she was debt-free and had a little money saved up, there was no use putting off the move. In the morning, she would get in touch with a real estate agent who specialized in short-term rentals. It was time to get her plan in motion.

Twenty-Two

On Saturday, Rafael met his father for lunch. Tobias was seated at their regular table, a chilled glass of beer before him. The old man looked good, solid and healthy. His trim beard had a silver sheen. He was perusing the menu, although Rafael was sure he would order the rib eye with a side of baby vegetables to balance things out, a lazy attempt at lowering his cholesterol. Rafael just couldn't do it. He couldn't join him, order the burger and fries and start talking about the big game, whichever game that was. He couldn't pretend that everything was fine when it wasn't.

Rafael strode over to the table. "Let's go."

Tobias looked up from the menu. His blue eyes, piercing at times, were hazy with confusion. "Where are we going?"

"Never mind. Just come with me."

The waiter arrived looking just as confused as Tobias. "Anything I can help you with?"

"We're not staying." Rafael pulled out his wallet and

left a twenty to cover the beer. "We'll be back same time next week."

Tobias followed him outside and said, "What's gotten into you?"

"We're going to get some real food."

"There *is* real food here," Tobias objected hotly. "The best steak in Royal, if you ask me."

"Well, I'm not asking you." His car was where he'd left it. The valet had not yet taken it to the remote site. He retrieved his key. "Come on. We'll take my car."

A moment later, Tobias slid into the passenger seat. "Mind telling me where we're headed?"

"Nope."

Rafael drove in silence to a part of town he was sure Tobias hadn't visited in a while, not since he was courting his mother, anyway. The cobblestone streets were narrow. Most of the signs were in Spanish. The homes were modest, and the businesses could only be described as mom-and-pop shops. He pulled up to an eatery. Tobias dutifully followed him inside. Rafael ordered the special: *Lonche de carnitas*. The beer was served in plastic cups. They took their food to a table in the courtyard, hidden among terra-cotta pots spilling with ferns. Much to his surprise, Tobias dug in with delight, red-faced with joy.

"It's good, right?" Rafael asked.

Tobias grunted his approval. "Damn good."

"Maybe every once in a while we could come out here for lunch instead."

"I'd like that," Tobias said, looking very much like a man who just found a winning lottery ticket stuck to the sole of his boot.

"Good." Rafael took a bite of his sandwich and savored the fresh baked bread, grilled beef and onions. He washed it down with a swig of cold beer. It was a cool day, but Rafael felt as if his head was on fire.

They finished lunch in blissful silence. Tobias wiped his

mouth and said, "You want to talk about whatever it is that's making you this crazy?"

"No," he replied, avoiding Tobias's keen gaze. All trace of confusion was gone.

"Are you sure?" Tobias asked.

Rafael slumped back into his seat. He had to get it out or it would eat him inside. No amount of comfort food was going to do the job. "Eve doesn't want to be with me. She thinks I have a problem with her nephew."

"*Do* you have a problem with her nephew?"

"Not at all," Rafael said. "He's a fine little kid. I love the little guy."

"So?"

"She figures she'll be raising him someday. Someday soon."

"Ah!" Tobias said. "Cammie will miss the little guy. She's grown to care about him a great deal."

Rafael nodded. "I know."

"I guess it can't be helped," Tobias said.

"I'm afraid not," Rafael said. "Eve is making plans that don't include me. She doesn't think I'm up for it."

Tobias took a sip of beer. "Are you up for it?"

"Are you just going to repeat the last thing I say?"

"That's my strategy," Tobias said evenly.

"It's a good one," Rafael admitted. "What kills me is that she's right. I don't think I'm up for it."

"Do you love her?"

Something ripped inside Rafael, the veil that had been keeping his emotions separated, everything nice and tidy. "Yeah, I love her. All I want to do is love her. But do I see myself buying a house on a hill and settling down like Cammie and Drake? No, I don't. Hell, I don't even know what city I want to live in. I'm not that guy. I told her this on day one. I'm not wired for it. No offense, Dad." The word *Dad* had dropped from his lips like a stone, but it was rolling around out there and he couldn't take it back. "No offense," he continued, his tone softer, "but you and Mom did a number on me."

"Let's be honest here," Tobias said. "It was mostly me."

"Yeah." Rafael laughed. "I don't know why I looped Mom into this. She's a saint."

Tobias nodded gravely. "No argument here. I was a fool to have messed that up."

"You were young," Rafael said, surprising himself. His saint of a mother had often used this argument in the hopes of easing Rafael's resentment. It had never worked before.

"My mistake," Tobias said cautiously, "was not getting it right the first time. I've lived a long time, and now I know how important that is. There is no going back. The most you can do is make amends. But there is no repairing the damage done. I know. I've been trying."

Rafael looked up at the sky. There was just one lone cloud drifting by. "I know you've been trying, and I appreciate it. I do. I know I don't show it, but why else am I here in Royal? I have roots here, and I can't just walk away."

Tobias gripped his napkin. He held Rafael's gaze, even though tears turned those blue eyes to clear puddles. Rafael felt uneasy. Pain and resentment momentarily loosened its grip on his heart, allowing him to breathe freely for the first time in his life. He could very well pass out from the influx of oxygen.

"Do you want my two cents?" Tobias asked.

Rafael shrugged. "I'm not talking to hear myself talk."

"If you love her, then you have to support her. This must be difficult for her. The baby is not her child. She didn't ask for this responsibility, but she's showing up for it. That's a beautiful thing. The fact that she doesn't want to burden you is also selfless. The question is, what are you going to do?"

"Have you been meditating or something?" Rafael asked good-naturedly. "Suddenly you are so profound."

"Ah…" Tobias sighed. "I'm alone a lot. I've got lots of time to think."

Just then Rafael received a text message from Manny that instantly cheered him up. He glanced at Tobias. "Want to go for a joyride?"

"Son," Tobias scolded, "what did you go and do now?"

"You'll find out soon enough." Rafael rose from the table. "Are you coming?"

"Hell, yeah!"

"Alright, old man. Let's go."

"Watch yourself, young man," Tobias said, as he followed Rafael out of the restaurant. "Who you calling old?"

Over a lonely lunch at her kitchen counter, Eve learned that Royal's rental market was booming. The real estate agent had laughed at her laundry list of demands. Eve wasn't trying to be picky. It made no sense to move Micah from a palace to a shoebox. There was no matching Drake's ranch in comfort and style, but a bright space in a safe neighborhood wasn't too much to hope for, right? Wrong. Apparently, the chances of her finding a decent apartment at a decent rate were slim.

When she got off the call with the agent, she noticed an unread text from Cammie inviting her out for a stroll in the park with Micah. Eve rushed to accept. It was a fresh Saturday afternoon, and she needed an excuse to get out. She had nowhere to go. Although Cammie and Drake had always welcomed her with open arms, she didn't feel comfortable showing up at their home at all hours of the day.

Cammie was waiting for her by the fountain when Eve arrived at the park. Eve plunged her hands into the stroller and pressed her cheek to Micah's warm chubby face. He cooed in response. The rush of love was so overwhelming and comforting that she couldn't imagine giving it up for anyone or anything. The feeling confirmed that she was on the right path and doing all the right things, for her and her nephew's sake.

Eve, Cammie and Micah proceeded unhurriedly along the trail that circled the park. Cammie shared stories of Micah's attempts at eating green foods, mostly pureed organic peas that she brought fresh from the farmer's market. She showed Eve a short video of Micah shoving his hands into a bowl of green paste. Ordinarily, Eve adored these stories complete with the multimedia images. Sometimes, Cammie would send her a short video first thing in the morning and that alone would brighten her day. Today, however, she could only listen in silence, feeling increasingly uncomfortable.

Cammie was devoted to Micah 110 percent. Eve hadn't given this full consideration. She believed her ties to her nephew were the strongest because, after all, they were blood relatives. However, she could no longer write off Cammie's contributions as mere charity. Her attachment to the little boy was real. Not only real, it was deep. It was pure. It was love. For someone who had arrived in town knowing no one, Cammie had been God sent.

Eve stopped midstride. It took Cammie a few more steps before she realized that she was walking alone and talking to herself. She turned around and said, "Are you okay?"

Eve nodded, but she suddenly didn't feel so good.

"Oh, God! You're not well!" Cammie sprang into action. She steered the baby carriage with one hand and reached out for Eve with the other. She guided them both to the nearest park bench and tapped her back as if she were a baby about to spit up her peas.

"I'm okay," Eve said. "Really. It's just... I have something to tell you and it's not easy."

Cammie's expression fell. It wasn't long, though, before Eve caught the glint of steely Wentworth determination in her eyes. "Don't worry," she said. "Whatever you have to say, I can take it."

Such a strong family! Cammie's reaction was so similar to Rafael's. Eve could hug her.

"I just wanted to say thank you."

"Is that it?"

"For now." Their eyes met, and a current of understanding passed between them. "From the bottom of my heart, I really want to thank you. I owe you and your brother a debt of gratitude that I simply cannot repay."

"Oh, Eve, I don't know about that. You crash-landed into our lives and made everything better. Maybe I should be thanking you for the privilege of caring for Micah. Do you know how long I wanted a child in my life? This was a blessing for me. It made me think. It made me realign my priorities. It made me grow. Every day I wake up grateful for this opportunity. Plus it opened Drake's heart. We're now planning on starting a family of our own. We couldn't be happier. I know it won't last. I know..." Her smile was uneven, betraying what it cost her to make that statement. "Could we not talk about it just now? It's such a nice day."

"How about some ice cream?" Eve proposed, trying to recapture the levity they'd lost. "There's a truck over there."

She pointed at the string of food trucks only steps from where they were sitting. Cammie was game. "Sure. Let's do it."

They walked to the trucks and back. Micah started to fuss, and Eve didn't hesitate. She scooped him out of the stroller and bounced him on her lap.

Cammie cheered. "There you go! I knew you could do it."

"I guess therapy helped."

"It also helps to trust the process. You're going to be fine."

Cammie received a text message. She tapped on the screen and her jaw dropped.

"What is it?" Eve asked.

"I can't believe my eyes!" Cammie exclaimed. "Look at this!"

Between Micah and the melting ice cream cone, Eve had her hands full. Cammie angled the phone so she could see the photo on the screen. Rafael and Tobias in the restored Camaro, top down, wind in their hair, both men looking tan and flashing matching smiles. Cammie started to type an answer then stopped. "We can do better." She tapped on the camera app and switched to selfie mode. "Let's send a photo back."

"Let's not."

Eve shifted out of the shot. Cammie caught her with her free hand as she'd done moments earlier. "Don't run! You're part of the family."

That sounded lovely, but she doubted it very much. Rafael had sent the photo to his sister alone, closing the circle. She was not in the loop. Eve started to protest, but Cammie would not be deterred. "ONE! TWO! THREE! Everybody say cheese!"

Eve held up Micah and hid behind him like a coward. The irony wasn't lost on her. She was using Micah to hide from Rafael, in selfies and in real life. Cammie snapped the photo, examined it, grumbled something about needing more sun, added a filter and sent it on its way. Eve shuddered at the swoosh sound the phone made to confirm the message had been sent. Then Cammie returned her attention to the photo of her brother and father. "This isn't a small thing."

Eve agreed. That Rafael had brought his father to Manny's car shop was a truly amazing thing. It was his happy place. She had felt so honored when he'd brought her there.

"I had to work so hard to get these two together. It was tough enough to get them both in the same state. I would have never arranged for them to ride in the same car out of fear they'd kill each other."

"They look like they're having fun," Eve said.

"That is the miracle!" Cammie cried. "They've been at each other's throats for years. To see this... It's incredible. My family was shattered. My every effort to piece it back together was met with resistance. Rafael is just as stubborn as my father. For years, I sent him letter after letter, pleading with him to no avail. He said he was focused on his future and had no interest looking back."

Funny. That was how Eve felt at the moment, focused on her future. There was no looking back, no time to think of what might have been. This wasn't stubbornness, not in her book. She had good reasons to stay the course. But that picture of Rafael smiling with his father told a different story. He had yielded and, apparently, it had worked out for the best.

"What made him change his mind?" Eve asked, curious.

"The tenth anniversary gala of admitting women members into the TCC."

"No kidding!"

Cammie nodded. "Why does that surprise you?"

"It's just… He talks so much *shit* about the TCC."

Cammie laughed. "That means nothing! He's from Royal. The club has a special place in his heart. My father and I announced the official launch of our nonprofit that night by awarding college scholarships to kids of first responders and hospital workers. Rafe came back to stand by us. I was so moved. It showed me his heart, you know? And his friendship with you—"

"Has he talked about me?" Eve interrupted.

"I badgered him for information," Cammie said. "He cares about you, no doubt about it. Seeing you two together is one of the best things to come of this."

Eve's first instinct was to deny, deny, deny, but that would be a waste of time. "We won't be together for long."

"No?"

"I don't see a future for us, so there's no point dragging things on forever."

Cammie's eyes widened. "You don't see a future?"

"No, I don't," Eve said resolutely. "We don't want the same things out of life. It's more important to be with someone with whom you're aligned rather than not."

"Trust me," Cammie said. "Speaking from experience, I totally understand. It's a shame, though. It really is. I'm going to put the blame squarely on my brother. He's a tough nut to crack."

"It's not like that." Micah put a fistful of Eve's hair in his mouth. She struggled to free her curls from the baby's iron grip. "He's been wonderful."

"Yeah...he can be wonderful, but he can also be set in his ways. Then again, he can surprise you, like today." She held up the phone, indicating the photo. "As his meddling little sister, I'm going to ask you to give him a chance. Don't write him off completely. He may need time. He may need an infuriating amount of time. But he's so worth it. Look at us. Our relationship is way better than I could have ever hoped. I have a big brother again!" Cammie's nose turned red. She dabbed at her eyes with the corner of Micah's blanket. "Can you believe it? I have a big brother who wants to be in my life. And today my brother and my dad are out on some crazy joyride in a vintage I don't know what."

"A 1969 Camaro."

"Look how much you know!" Cammie exclaimed. She studied the picture. "And look at that interior! Love the color. It's beautiful."

"It is," Eve said, close to tears. "It's beautiful."

Twenty-Three

"This is a hell of a nice surprise!" Cammie exclaimed. "My big brother picking me up for a spontaneous outing. You're lucky I was here. I work from home most days, so I can care for Micah."

Rafael was glad she was game. He'd showed up at the foundation headquarters around noon with all of fifteen minutes' notice. She came skipping out of the building, wearing a sharply tailored business suit and swinging a shapeless tote bag. Rafael was leaning against the Camaro's passenger door. She gripped him by the shoulders and shoved him aside.

"The car!" she cried. "I get to ride in it, too!"

"Nothing but the best for my baby sister!"

She ran around to the driver's side. The top was down. "Look at it! How luxurious!" She ran her hands on the leather seats. "I love this tan color."

"Not tan," he corrected. *"Caramelo."*

"Ah, yes! It's gorgeous."

"Glad you like it."

"Give me the keys," she said. "I'm driving."

Rafael didn't see that coming. "Hell no!"

"Oh, hell yes!" she fired back. "I'm driving or I'm not going anywhere."

"Fine!" He tossed her the keys.

"Hop in!" she squealed.

Rafael did not hop in. He watched with amusement as Cammie got settled behind the wheel and adjusted the rear-view mirror. "How can I get me one of these?" she asked.

"You have to know someone who knows someone."

"Luckily, I know you. How soon can we get the ball rolling?"

"The sooner the better," he replied, and reluctantly slid into the passenger seat. "Then you can drive your own car."

Cammie pulled out her phone. "Let's take a picture and send it to Tobias."

"Oh, please!" Rafael moaned.

"Hey! I want this moment immortalized." She held up her phone. Rafael leaned close and held up two fingers. She snapped the photo, sent it along.

"Can we get back to business now?" Rafael said impatiently.

"What business?" she asked. "It's just lunch. Chill, already."

"We're not going to lunch."

"What?"

"We are *not* going to lunch."

Cammie scrunched her brows in confusion. "You pick me up at noon on a weekday and you are not taking me to lunch? How do you figure?"

"We're going to run an errand."

"There better be food involved with this errand because I'm starving. I left behind a totally fine BLT wrap in my mini fridge."

"Fine!" He caved for the third time. He wasn't in any particular hurry. He'd cleared his calendar for the afternoon.

But he was afraid that he would lose his nerve. "We're on an important mission. If you want lunch, swing by a drive-through."

"I know just the one." Cammie fired up the engine and put the car in gear. "I feel cheated, though. Dad said you took him out to get the best steak sandwiches, and I demand no less."

"I'll take you to my spot some other time."

"Where are you taking me?" she asked, while skillfully zipping through traffic.

Rafael couldn't rush the answer. When they arrived at the burger and barbecue joint, he proposed they sit at one of the picnic tables.

Cammie was ecstatic. "Now you're talking!"

They'd picked a table in the shade. Rafael pounded ketchup out of a bottle and covered his fries with the stuff. Cammie sipped her milkshake through a paper straw that wasn't up to the task. She set the cup aside. "What's the big hurry?"

"I asked you to come out with me because I need your help."

"Okay."

"It's delicate."

"Uh-huh."

"I'm not stepping onto your turf or anything—"

"Yes?"

"Eve and Micah—"

"Oh, God…"

The breeze picked up and tousled her red hair. Rafael's heart melted for her. "You know where I'm going with this?"

She reached out to squeeze his hand. "Eve and I had a talk."

"You did?"

"Yeah, well, not really. We have an understanding."

"Oh?"

Cammie nodded briskly. "Nothing definite, of course."

"And you're okay with it?"

"To the extent that I can be."

"There's nothing definite on my end, either," Rafael said, reassuring her the best he could. "I want to be prepared in case she'd like to bring Micah over for a night or a weekend or more."

Cammie straightened up. *"Ohhhhhhh."*

"That 'oh' long enough?"

"Not in this case! Tell me more." She reached for the milkshake again and sucked hard on the straw.

"She doesn't think there's room for the baby in my life. I need to do something concrete to show her. See what I mean?"

"I see."

"I was thinking about getting one of those basket thingies for Micah to nap in."

"A basket? So Micah is like a baby Moses drifting down the Nile?"

"What are you talking about? I see it on TV all the time! It's in every movie."

"You mean a bassinet," Cammie said. "Micah has outgrown those things. You need something sturdy and solid."

Rafael knew better than to argue with her. She was the expert in this case. "See?" he said. "That's why I need your help."

"First, I have a question."

"What's that?"

"Did you try telling Eve how you feel?"

"She knows how I feel."

"That's not what I asked," Cammie said. "Did you ever tell her in a sentence how you feel about her. Did you say 'I love you, Eve'? 'I can't live without you. Your problems are my problems. Your burdens are my burdens. You don't have to walk this road alone. I'm here for you.'"

Rafael looked down at his ketchup-smothered fries.

"Did you say any combination of those things?"

Rafael remained silent.

"Just to be clear—you did not tell her you loved her."

"I didn't! Okay?"

"It's not okay!" she cried, scaring away a crow. "Damn it, Rafe! You're doing it again."

"Doing what?"

"A Tobias move!"

Rafael pushed his food away, suddenly nauseous. He was a lost cause.

"You see what I mean, right? You skip the tedious communication part and leap straight into the take action part. You can't do that, buddy! You have to talk first, communicate your feelings and then together take proper action. Am I clear? Do you need a PowerPoint presentation on this? How can I make you understand?"

Rafael reached for a soggy fry. Cammie was having way too much fun with this. "You think this is a bad idea?"

"No," she said hastily. "I think it's a wonderful idea. We'll go and get all the stuff. You find someplace to stash it until you and Eve have that conversation. Sound good?"

Rafael studied his sister. She flashed him a devious little grin. "You're Tobias's kid, too," he said.

"I never said I wasn't." She stuffed her food in the to-go bag. "Come on! Let's get going!"

The sales assistant was handing out pink and blue sugar cookie samples from the bakery across the street. "For your next gender reveal party," she said.

Cammie declined. "I'm good."

"Yes, thanks," Rafael said. "I'll have hers, too."

"You've got a sweet tooth," Cammie observed. "I didn't know that."

Rafael took a bite of the blue cookie and grinned. "Now you know."

They wandered down the diaper aisle. "I'm so glad you're doing this. You have my full support."

"Thanks. That means a lot." Rafael paused to look around. "Think I might need some of these?"

"You can never have too many diapers, as I always say. Grab two sizes. That way you'll always be prepared."

Rafael did as instructed and loaded the cart.

"We'll need wipes. Lots of wipes."

He grabbed two packs of those.

"And maybe a Diaper Genie for cleanup."

"Seriously?"

"Trust me."

"You're a sweetheart, helping me like this. I'm not sure I deserve you."

"You probably don't." Cammie was rummaging through a bin filled with mini toy giraffes. "He likes to chew on these."

Rafael took the bin from her. "I'm trying to say thank you...for everything."

She offered him sunshine in a smile. "You're welcome... for everything."

He pulled his sister into a tight hug. "That was a lot of emotional heavy lifting."

"No kidding." She stretched up, kissed his cheek and snatched the blue cookie from him. "I'll take that, thanks."

Twenty-Four

Can a cookie heal a cracked heart? Eve wondered, staring into the display case filled with baked goodies. Maybe a cupcake? She was instantly drawn to the tres leches cupcakes topped with a strawberry nestled in a bed of creamy white icing. Why tres leches when her go-to cupcake was chocolate? She refused to answer that question and bought a whole pack of cupcakes instead of just one.

It was Wednesday. Eve had successfully avoided Rafael at work for two days straight. Or was he avoiding her? Either way, they were getting damn good at it. They kept open lines of communication via email but found ways to avoid face-to-face meetings or even run-ins by the elevators. Locking herself in her office was key. To avoid him at the residence, she locked herself in her suite. It was depressing as hell. The sooner she moved out, the better. Lately, her frequent calls to the real estate agent had gone unanswered. She was probably catering to more realistic clients.

Today Eve was going a little stir crazy, craving fresh air

and sunshine. She slipped out during lunch and spent the hour window-shopping. When she came across the bakery, the buttery, sugary scents lured her in. She walked out with the pack of cupcakes. However, standing at the corner waiting for the light to change, a sense of hopelessness drilled through her.

A tres leches cupcake was not going to take the place of Rafael's sweetly addictive kiss. It just wasn't. Nothing would. She loved him. The quiet and simple realization wrapped itself around her, lifted her when she stepped out distractedly into the crosswalk just when a car shrieked to a stop inches away. The light hadn't yet turned red.

Rafael was at the wheel of a convertible with a large blue teddy bear in the passenger seat. She tried to blink the image away. This had to be a love-induced mirage.

"Lady!" he called out to her. "What are you doing?"

She took a step toward the vision. "You're real?"

"Get in this car!"

There wasn't any room. The teddy bear occupied the front seat and the back seat was crammed with boxes. A mini crib, a bouncy chair, diapers and more diapers. "Did you just rob a baby store? What is all this?"

The only possible explanation was that he was on his way to a baby shower. She stood back, waiting for him to confirm that the loot was for an acquaintance or an employee.

"These are for Micah."

Eve stopped breathing, certain her heart wasn't going to take it. "What do you mean? He doesn't need all this."

Rafael removed his sunglasses. Eve's heart took another stumble. She had never seen him looking so subdued. She wanted to climb over the large bear to get to him.

"I thought," he said haltingly. "If maybe you and Micah wanted to spend the night or a weekend, we'd be ready."

"Awww!"

What else was there to say? Her heart was melting. Had he gone off and made plans without first consulting her yet again? Yes, but they were the sweetest, most lovely plans, and she wanted to be a part of them. She saw it clearly in her mind's eye, and in her rose the desire to make the dream a reality.

"I want to make this work," he said. "I'll admit, I don't have any magic solutions, but I want to try. What do you think?"

"Well… I think you might have gone overboard. Did you keep the receipts? Some of these things can be returned."

"It's Cammie's fault. She piled stuff in the cart," he said. "Besides, you can never have too much. Babies need stuff, Eve. That's the first rule of baby."

"What about this huge teddy bear?" Eve cried. The thing had a head the size of a watermelon.

Rafael shrugged. "Drake said Micah loved teddy bears."

"A tiny one," she said. "Did you buy this extra-large one to out-teddy Drake's teddy?"

His grin turned devilish. "Exactly."

Eve rolled her eyes. "Men!"

Blaring horns interrupted their exchange. The light had turned red then green again. "Eve, get in this car."

"Get that bear out of the way."

Rafael grabbed the blue teddy and flipped him onto the back seat. She hopped in and they took off, wheels spinning. At the next light, he reached for her hand.

"What do you have there?" he asked, pointing to the bag. "Sweets."

"Any caramel?"

"Nope," she said. "Tres leches cupcakes."

"Ah, sweet love," he said. "You missed me."

Eve tossed her head back and laughed. She'd missed him and the endless joy he brought to her life. He cupped her chin and drew her close. "I missed that laugh."

Her laughter died, quickly replaced by stillness. She had to say the words that were in her heart. She could not keep them locked away. "I love you, Rafael Arias Wentworth... whatever your name is."

His thumb swiped at a tear that had slipped out of the corner of her eye. He planted a kiss between her furrowed brows then gently, sweetly brushed his lips to hers. "I love you, too, darling," he whispered. "All your burdens are my burdens. All your problems are mine to solve. Everything you love, I love. From here on out, that is how it is, *mi amor*. Nothing can change that. Let me make you a home. It might not be conventional, but it would be for us."

A sailboat would feel like home if they were together. The room at an inn, her dreary efficiency, the residence at the guest ranch and the penthouse overlooking the Atlantic, any place they'd been together had felt like home. So long as Micah was welcome, she had no objections.

"Please say yes, my sweet."

Eve rushed to kiss him. "Like I can say no to you."

The honking resumed, more furious this time. Rafael growled like the wolf in black sheep's clothing that he was and put the car in motion.

"I think we deserve the afternoon off," he said. "Do you agree?"

"Absolutely!" Eve said. She kicked off her shoes. "Where to now?"

"The sunset."

"Where's that?" She'd never heard of the place. Was it a diner or a bar?

"We're in love," he said with that sparkle in his eyes. "We're driving into the sunset."

Epilogue

"I've called this meeting of the G-6 to inform you of some recent developments." Rafael sat at the corner of his desk and folded his arms across his chest, Eve at his side. Together, they faced Dan and Audrey, seated in the swivel chairs, and Bill and Lucas, standing behind them. "It's important to us that we keep everything aboveboard. We don't want to create any confusion."

"We also want to get ahead of any rumors," Eve added. "And we want everyone to feel comfortable."

"Any questions so far?" Rafael asked.

All four shook their heads. Dan glanced around the room, looking worried. Audrey gripped the armrest of her chair. Bill had gone pale. Lucas was snapping his gum. Rafael hurried to deliver the news before they imagined the worst. "Okay, here goes. I called you here to let you in on something. Eve and I are... We're in a relationship."

"We hope it doesn't make things weird," Eve said. "We will be as discreet as possible at work."

Rafael could feel her nervousness rush through him in waves. He draped an arm over her shoulders and tugged her close. She did not resist. So much for discretion!

This meeting had been her idea. She no longer wanted to sneak around, covering their tracks, and he didn't want things to get awkward at the office.

"Is that it?" Dan said.

"No, that's not it," Eve said. "We're moving in together. I'm moving into his suite. We will be living together, and my nephew will be staying with us part of the time. So... there's that."

"Wow!" Audrey let out a nervous laugh. "That's big news!"

"You'd think you guys were dropping a bombshell or something," Dan said flatly.

"I thought they were closing shop," Bill said, looking relieved. "Got me going there for a minute."

"You're in a relationship," Lucas said. "No shit?"

"Language!" Rafael scolded him.

"Yeah!" Dan said. "Show some respect."

Audrey was incensed. "Everybody *act* surprised!"

"Respectfully," Dan said, "we'll file this information in the 'no shit' folder."

Everyone broke out in hysterical laughter—everyone except Rafael and Eve. "You all are the worst," Rafael said.

"It was in the newspaper!" Audrey cried. "What do you expect?"

Eve covered her face with her hands. Rafael got up and cleared the room. "Everybody get back to work."

"Come on, everyone," Bill said. "You heard the boss."

"Congrats, you two!" Audrey said on her way out. "I knew it since day one."

"I called it," Lucas said.

They shuffled out of the office, shutting the door behind them. Eve turned to him, shaking with laughter. "Well... That was interesting. They were on to us this whole time."

"Looks like we were the only ones who weren't on to us," Rafael said.

"Seems anticlimactic, though," she said pensively. "Our big announcement fizzling out like that…"

Rafael frowned. Anticlimactic wasn't a word he wanted associated with their relationship. "We should do something to mark the occasion," he proposed. "What do you think?"

She snapped her fingers. "I know! Let's have sex on your desk. I've always wanted to."

There was his fearless Eve. Rafael slipped off his suit jacket. "Lock the door."

* * * * *

SECRETS OF A BAD
REPUTATION

JOSS WOOD

Prologue

James Ryder-White carefully folded the classy gold paper and placed it on his knee, mentally rolling his eyes at the square, red velvet box it revealed. Another Christmas, another pair of designer cuff links from Penelope…

His wife was not the most original present giver in the world. Then again, he'd gifted her with a black cashmere sweater and another solid gold charm to add to her already heavy bracelet. James knew she was as enthusiastic about his gift as he was about hers.

They'd been married too long, knew each other too well, and neither of them made an effort anymore. If they ever had.

James looked out the window of his childhood home—he and Pen occupied the right wing of his father's enormous mansion—and sighed at the wet sleet slapping the floor-to-ceiling windows. He loved Portland, Maine, with its arty vibe and excellent food scene, its centuries-old lighthouses, historic homes and edgy, independent shops and boutiques.

But this particular piece of craggy coastline was home. Low clouds obscured the jaw-dropping views of Dead Man's Cove. Ryder's Rest, his father's estate fourteen miles north of Portland, on Cousin's Island, consisted of a seven-bedroom mansion—every room in the house had a view of the bay—with heated pools, multiple decks and patios, and a garage big enough for ten automobiles.

It also boasted a drive-on stone pier and dock, three deepwater moorings, and over eight hundred feet of beach frontage.

James loved this house and property. The owner? Not so much.

He leaned back in his chair and briefly closed his eyes, wondering what his life would've been like had he not married Pen thirty-some years ago.

What if he'd had the guts to defy his father, to take a chance, to forge his own path? James ran a hand over his face, pushing his what-if thoughts away. He'd witnessed his father's ruthlessness—toward business rivals and members of his own family—so defying Callum had never been an option.

James also liked the money and the status of being a Ryder-White, so he remained a good little soldier. His obedience resulted in plump pockets and fat bank accounts. Putting up with Callum's crap allowed James to buy property and flashy cars and establish trust funds for his children.

His daughters now controlled the money he'd gifted

them, and Kinga's and Tinsley's fortunes were still, as far as he knew, intact.

Kinga, brown-eyed and blonde, sat down on the arm of his chair, interrupting his musings. James placed a hand on her back, grateful for the connection. Whenever regrets slapped him hot and hard, he reminded himself that if not for Pen, he wouldn't have two smart, lovely daughters. His marriage was far from a love match, but his two girls made any sacrifices worthwhile.

"Daddy, you're looking a little melancholy this lovely Christmas morning."

"I'm fine, Mouse."

And James supposed that he was. His marriage functioned, his children were healthy and successful. He wished he could add happy to that list, but Kinga was plagued by a life-changing event that had happened a decade ago and Tinsley was taking a long time to come to terms with her divorce.

Happiness: such a vague concept, and as hard to capture as the morning mist.

James felt Kinga straighten and he raised his head, softly sighing when he noticed his father—sharp blue eyes in a craggy face—standing by the fireplace, impatiently waiting for his family to pay attention. Callum was close to eighty, but he was fit and healthy, mentally and physically.

Callum caught James's eye and angled his head. James cleared his throat, and Tinsley and Penelope immediately stopped talking, their eyes wary. James understood the emotion—Callum had a habit of dropping new ideas—or orders—on the family whenever they gathered socially.

It wouldn't matter to Callum that it was Christmas; the Ryder-White reputation and businesses were always his highest priorities. Actually, James was surprised Callum had waited this long to raise Ryder International business.

"You will have noticed that I failed to give you all a gift this year," he said, his deep voice and cold blue eyes commanding attention.

Callum linked his hands behind his back, his nose in the air. Oh, God, here came the lecture. How many times had he heard it? A hundred times? Two hundred? More?

Probably.

"As you know, the first Ryder was William Ryder who arrived in Maine during the third settlement of this area. He was one of the original owners of property. He married the wealthy Lottie White, and we are directly descended from them. I've been reading up on genealogy and I want a deeper understanding of our family roots."

This. *Again.* The family tree stretched back three hundred years and their unbroken bloodline was a badge Callum wore with pride. But really, how much more was there to discover?

"Apparently, it is now possible to pinpoint where, geographically, our ancestors resided, and I want to know," Callum continued. "None of you have expressed an interest in our lineage and I am greatly disappointed in you all. To encourage that interest, my Christmas gift to you is a DNA test, so you can have a better understanding of your heritage."

James watched his father pull test tubes from a brown envelope and took the tube Callum handed him.

"Just swipe the swab on the inside of your mouth and put it back into the tube. Write your name on the label." Callum barked instructions, handing tubes to Pen and Kinga and Tinsley.

"I registered us on WhoAreYou.com." Callum spun the top of his test tube and pulled out a long Q-tip. "I will send off our DNA next week and soon we will have a complete picture of our origins."

"Technology is amazing," Callum added after he'd finished swabbing the inside of his mouth, sounding pleased. "WhoAreYou is the biggest and most popular company providing this service. I have distant cousins that are already registered on the site, so the site should throw up a match to them. I have asked to be notified if there are any DNA matches to me or any of you. It's a very good way to fill in some blanks on the family tree."

James felt the room swim. He stared at the test tube, his mind racing. How could he get out of this?

"This isn't difficult," Callum snapped, looking from him to Penelope, who held her test tube in her hand. "What's the problem?"

"No problem, Callum," James lied. He'd never been allowed to call him father. Or Dad.

James looked at his wife, noticing the annoyance in her eyes. She squirmed in her chair, and sent Callum a narrowed-eyed, I'm-not-happy look.

Callum replaced the swabbed-with-saliva tubes in the envelope. "Let's discuss business."

Blood and business, that was all that was important to Callum. "Have you made any progress tracking down the owner of that block of shares, James?"

James ground his back teeth together. Over the past three decades, Callum's obsession with the 25 percent stake in Ryder International he didn't control had mushroomed and he was more determined than ever to buy the shares back. But first they needed to discover who owned them.

"I'm still working on it."

"Work harder," Callum snapped. "Let's talk about Ryder International's centennial celebrations. The charity ball will kick off the year-long celebration," Callum continued. The ball was a $100,000-a-plate function, limited to two thousand very rich, very exclusive people, including princes and politicians. "I thought you girls would've nailed down a performer by now."

Kinga and Tinsley ran Ryder's enormous PR division together and did an excellent job. Their talent was something Callum routinely overlooked and rarely acknowledged.

"The performer I booked has canceled all her performances for the next six months for medical reasons," Kinga replied. "I'm still looking for someone."

"Well, I want someone a little controversial, someone who will attract attention and—what's that word?—*buzz*."

James felt Kinga stiffen. "And do you have any suggestions as to who might provide that for us?" she asked, her eyebrows raised.

"Griff O'Hare."

Kinga exchanged horrified glances with Tinsley and James didn't blame them. Even he'd heard of the bad boy singer, performer and actor with the voice of an angel and the impulse control of a toddler.

Kinga just closed her eyes and shook her head. "Happy damn Christmas to me."

One

Sitting in a booth in Ryder International's flagship bar situated in the famous Forrester-Grantham Hotel in Manhattan, Kinga Ryder-White tapped an impatient finger against her glass and scowled at the face of her Piaget watch.

Griff O'Hare was extremely late for their meeting but that didn't surprise her. She wouldn't hold her breath waiting for him.

Honestly, what was Callum thinking wanting someone so disreputable as the headline act at one of the most highly anticipated social events of the decade? Nothing good ever came of her irascible grandfather meddling in PR affairs.

Yesterday, when she was summoned to Callum's office, he'd gestured Kinga to look at his massive flat-screen TV. Her grandfather was watching YouTube, a surprise in itself. Her scowl deepened when she saw Griff O'Hare in the video—wearing holey-at-the-knees jeans and a red T-shirt—sitting at a piano in a music studio.

She couldn't deny that he was talented. And hot.

"I don't want to hire him, Callum."

Callum ignored her, pushed Play, and O'Hare's rich voice filled Callum's office, deep and dark and magical. She recognized the song and was marginally impressed that the bad boy of rock and roll could control himself long enough to give a creditable rendition of "Nessun Dorma."

When the video finished, Kinga had turned to Callum and shrugged. "I never said he couldn't sing. I said he isn't someone I want performing at the ball."

"I will make that call, not you," Callum had retorted, throwing the remote onto his desk.

Yes, *of course*. Because, in Callum's world, a woman couldn't possibly make a decision without having a male approve it. Kinga controlled her urge to scream. She and Callum had a hate-hate relationship: he hated her sassy mouth and lack of deference, and she hated the way he treated her father and his frequent dismissal of her and Tinsley's opinions.

She loved her job, loved the people she worked with… but couldn't stand her boss.

Callum had nodded to the screen. "That video has had over sixty-five million views in a month. The music world is speculating on when he'll return to performing."

She'd stared at the view count, her eyes skimming the comments. Ah, this was starting to make sense now. Griff O'Hare was unreliable, but he was a superbly talented, currently elusive rock star, and the world was clamoring for his return.

Callum Ryder-White wanted to be the person credited for bringing O'Hare back into the limelight by having his first performance in, well, *forever* be at the Ryder

International ball. Callum always wanted everything and anything that was new, shiny, exclusive and expensive.

He was, after all, the patriarch of the Ryder-White family, and he considered himself to be East Coast royalty. And kings wanted what they wanted…

Blergh.

Nope, hiring the unreliable O'Hare was far too risky. Kinga shook her head. "I'm not comfortable with his return performance being at my ball."

"*My* ball," Callum had corrected her. "My company, my ball, my decision. Meet with him, and make it happen. Or else find a new job. Now go away."

Kinga, knowing it was useless to argue, had left. But she couldn't help wondering if her grandfather was serious or if he was playing her, setting her up for failure. Callum did like to play manipulative mind games. Whatever he was up to, Kinga had no intention of risking *her* carefully planned event being spoiled when the entertainment failed to show.

Since that meeting with Callum she'd done her homework, conducted research on the guy and concluded that Griff O'Hare—once voted the world's sexiest man—was an ass.

Even worse, he was a bad boy ass.

Kinga had no time for either—bad boys or asses.

Kinga scowled, decided she'd give him another thirty minutes and then she'd move on. She didn't have time to waste on tardy one-time superstars who thought they were God's gift.

She liked New York City but she didn't love it; Portland—her proud little city, smaller, cleaner and far lovelier—was home. And she needed to get back.

On the point of leaving, she felt the atmosphere in the bar change, heard the buzz of excited voices and assumed her four-thirty appointment had deigned to join her. Lifting her head, she watched Griff O'Hare flash his famous half smile, half smirk at the excited waitress. Most of the men drinking in the luxury bar wore designer suits and thousand-dollar shoes—hair neatly brushed, ties precisely knotted and beards carefully trimmed—but O'Hare flouted the dress code with his faded jeans ripped at the knee, biker boots and a leather bomber jacket, a matte black helmet tucked under his arm. His nut-brown, naturally shot-with-gold hair was overlong and messy, and a thick layer of stubble covered his strong jaw.

A vibe of I-don't-give-a-crap rolled off him.

If she were honest, she'd admit her stomach did feel a bit mushy, her skin prickly. But that was just biology. She, like most women, was programmed by evolution to look for the fittest, strongest, most masculine guy in the room as a potential mate.

But Kinga, relentlessly single, needed more than an attractive face topping a ripped body. There were other, more important traits she required in a partner. Fidelity, a solid work ethic, intelligence.

But none of that mattered, since she no longer believed in love, didn't know if she ever had. But even if she did, and had, she'd never again risk losing a person she loved.

She knew how that felt and it wasn't an experience she needed to repeat.

O'Hare handed his helmet and his jacket to the simpering waitress and Kinga noticed how his navy blue T-shirt skimmed a wide chest and how the bands of the sleeves were tight against his big biceps.

With his seductive swagger and easy confidence, he screamed trouble.

Her ball was luxurious, classy, upmarket and elegant; she needed a performer who reflected those qualities.

O'Hare would not fill the bill. She just had to get through this meeting and bring Callum around to her way of thinking. She'd find someone else.

O'Hare looked around, saw her sitting in the booth, and their eyes collided. Heat skittered up her spine and lodged in her womb, warming the space between her legs. Her nipples contracted and she swallowed a heavy sigh.

Sue her, she was attracted. But only on a purely physical level.

Kinga watched as he looked around the bar for someone to stand and approach him. Deciding that it wouldn't hurt him to be kept waiting for a few minutes, she leaned against the back of the leather-clad booth, curious to see what he'd do. He looked around again and Kinga saw the flash of irritation at having his time wasted.

Welcome to my world, dude.

Enjoying herself, Kinga kept her eyes on him. When their gazes clashed again, Kinga felt the same slap of attraction. Damn, this was neither helpful nor convenient.

O'Hare lifted those swimmer's shoulders in a what-the-hell shrug and her stomach tightened as he moved toward her, his eyes not leaving her face. Stopping at her booth, he jammed his hands into the front pockets of his jeans, and Kinga inhaled his fresh air and healthy male scent and felt her head swim.

Keep it together, Ryder-White. He's just another guy and this is just another meeting.

That was like saying Hurricane Sandy was just another storm.

"Well, huh."

Kinga raised one eyebrow. "Sorry?"

"Your eyes are the color of fine, old whiskey."

"And have been since I was born," Kinga pertly replied,

telling herself not to blush. *Business meeting, Kinga! Be professional.*

He sent her a slow, hot, sexy smile and her stomach did a full, twisting forward tuck, something she'd never mastered in five years of gymnastic training. "I'm looking for a business associate but if I don't find him, can I buy you a drink?"

He flashed her a smile and looked a little confused when she leaned back against the leather banquette and raised an unimpressed eyebrow.

After thirty seconds of silence, Kinga nodded to the seat opposite her and narrowed her eyes. "No, O'Hare, you can't *buy me a drink*. But feel free to sit down. I'm Kinga Ryder-White and you are disrespectfully late."

Well, *shit*. Kinga Ryder-White looked like she'd swallowed a particularly sour lemon.

Not the reaction he generally received, Griff thought, a little amused. Having been a so-called heartthrob since his early teens, he found her get-over-yourself attitude refreshing.

Griff slid into the booth, his eyes sliding down her face and elegant neck. He leaned sideways to peek at the rest of her long, lean body. She was tall for a woman, five-eight or five-nine, but, topping out at six-four, he'd guess he still had four or five inches on her.

She was dressed in what he called Boring Corporate, a men's style button-down shirt, black tailored pants and spiky-heeled boots. Her makeup, if she wore any, was minimal and made her skin look flawless. Griff had dated enough women to know that natural look took hours to perfect.

Then those astute, exceptional eyes met his and he realized he wasn't dealing with a naive young woman or a pushover. She was not only sexy but also smart, determined and very, very wary.

"I thought I was meeting with Callum Ryder-White," he said, raking his hand through his hair.

"My grandfather instructed me to meet with you. I deal with PR, and I make the decisions around the Ryder centennial celebrations."

God, even her voice was sexy, containing a hint of rasp and smoke.

"Nice to meet you, darlin'."

The *darlin'* pissed her off and lightning flashed in her honey-whiskey eyes. He watched her run elegant fingers through her short, bright blond hair. It took a certain amount of confidence to wear her hair so short, but with her high cheekbones, straight nose and cat-like eyes, she pulled it off.

"You can call me Kinga or Ms. Ryder-White but can the darlin's, *darlin'*."

Because he always preferred sass to subservience, Griff smiled. He wanted to ruffle her very proper feathers, so he added some extra drawl to his next words.

"I don't object to you calling me darlin', but if we must be formal, then you can call me Griff," he said, his voice sounding rusty.

What was happening here? Why was he reacting like this?

He'd met princesses and supermodels, A-list actresses and B-list bombshells—slept with a number of them—and none of them had managed to scramble his brains or twist his stomach and tongue into knots. Yet this woman, in charge of PR for her grandfather's company, did.

And he couldn't work out why.

"Would you like coffee or a soft drink?" Kinga said, sounding brisk and businesslike.

Griff glanced at his watch, saw it was after four forty-five and decided he needed a drink. He looked at the collection of whiskeys behind the bar. "Whiskey, single malt. Preferably something old."

"This is a business meeting. Coffee, water or something soft?" Kinga asked through obviously gritted teeth. Damn, annoying her was fun. He liked the way she looked down her nose at him, how those extraordinary eyes flashed with disdain. For the first time in…well, forever, Griff understood the lure of the chase.

Keeping his eyes on her lovely face, he lifted his hand and, as expected, a waiter immediately glided across the room to where they sat. Griff ordered a dram of expensive Macallan Royal Marriage, neat, and asked Kinga whether she'd like to join him.

To his surprise, Kinga nodded, her eyes not leaving his. He instinctively understood that they were jostling for control and direction of this conversation and it was a battle he wanted to win.

So did she.

Despite their eye contact, Kinga's expression remained impassive and Griff found himself intrigued by her ability to ignore their attraction. He'd recognized her bolt-from-the-blue response to him. But she'd pushed it down and away, acting like it never happened.

Interesting.

God, how long had it been since he had to work to impress a woman? Fifteen years? Twenty? Maybe never?

Kinga Ryder-White was the most intriguing—and possibly exasperating—woman he'd ever met.

They sat in silence, neither prepared to look away, until the waiter delivered their drinks, the liquid in the cut crystal glasses the same shade as her eyes. Kinga lifted the glass, took a sip and delicately placed her glass on the table between them.

"Ready to talk business?" she demanded, tapping her finger against her tablet. "Is your agent here with you?" Kinga added. "Your manager?"

"No," Griff briskly replied. He had major trust issues and, after Finn's betrayal, he was taking his time finding someone to represent him. The Ryder-White gig was an offer Griff could negotiate himself, especially since he hadn't decided whether to make his comeback permanent yet.

"Why didn't you sign with someone else after Finn Barclay died?" Kinga asked, taking another sip of her whiskey. He'd expected her to take a slug to make a point, but she seemed to be enjoying the expensive drink.

Griff saw the curiosity on her face and released a frustrated sigh. He hated talking about Finn. To this day, nobody else knew Finn had died in a car accident because he was racing to the ranch to confront Griff about his decision to terminate their long relationship. Finn's treachery had taught him that the only person he could fully rely on was himself.

Eviscerated by how his association with Finn had ended, he doubted he could ever trust someone, anyone, again. It was why he'd stopped dating and why he was taking his time signing an agreement with another manager or agent.

"Well?" Kinga asked, tipping her head to the side, looking a little impatient at his lack of a reply.

Something made him want to tell her about Finn and Sian, about what had led him to this point. The impulse annoyed him. He never confided in anyone and God knew why he wanted to spill his soul to this uppity, in-your-face, sexy-as-sin female.

"None of your business," Griff told her, and he heard the annoyance in his own voice. That was okay, he was sure she could take it.

"Well, agents are the firewall between the artist and the client." Kinga handed him a smile that was part sweet, part sly. "It's so much easier to be frank with an agent than with the artist."

"I'm a big boy. I can handle it." He flashed a grin, enjoying the bite in her words, in her attitude.

Kinga acknowledged his words with a tilt of her head. She linked her fingers together, her gaze direct when her eyes met his. "My grandfather, Callum, seems to think you would be perfect to perform at the Ryder International ball. He likes the idea of being the one to relaunch you."

He considered telling Kinga the Ryder ball was just a venue, that he had other venues, other options to consider. He'd wasn't desperate, for God's sake. He didn't *need* to do the concert, to return to the stage.

One option would be to simply sell his songs to other artists, but singing, performing and entertaining had been his entire life, starting with his first role alongside his twin, Sian, in an extremely popular sitcom when they were seven. At eighteen, they both landed roles in the smash-hit musical, *Peter and Me*, and its popularity transformed them into international celebrities, with the soundtrack becoming the top-selling album for the next two years, going platinum four times.

Over the next decade, he'd run from project to project, enjoying having the world at his feet. Then his universe had fractured, and What Happened to Griff? became an oft-used headline as journalists tried to figure out why a hardworking, dedicated and easy-to-work-with artist had turned into a publicity-seeking monster.

Griff placed his ankle on his other knee and linked

his hands on his flat stomach. He was sure he knew the answer to his next question but decided to ask it anyway. "So you don't think I am suitable? Why not?"

"You don't fit the image for my ball, and you're not who I want to perform in front of many of our friends, family, guests, clients and colleagues, both local and international. They have certain expectations of the entertainment.

"You have a shocking reputation and haven't performed for a while." Well, he'd asked for an explanation and he'd got it.

Kinga didn't drop her eyes and Griff respected her take-no-prisoners attitude. "I'll be honest with you, Mr. O'Hare. I think hiring you would be a mistake and I intend to change my grandfather's mind."

Callum seemed pretty set on him, so Griff shrugged, knowing his casual gesture would frustrate her. Griff couldn't fault her for not wanting to take a chance on him. If he was in her position, he'd also have reservations about hiring a musician who'd trashed hotel rooms, closed down clubs, left with a different girl every night, racked up speeding fines in his superpowerful Ducati, dabbled in drugs and had three different children by three different women—all falsely reported but widely believed.

Most of his bad boy behavior was bullshit, a carefully constructed manipulation of the media. It was a simple equation: if he acted out, the media's attention focused on him and they ignored Sian, allowing his sister to fade from view.

He couldn't blame anyone for the bad press. After all, being bad was what he'd set out to do. And because he did everything well, he'd exceeded his own expectations.

Surprisingly, being wild and reckless took an enormous amount of time and energy. And he was sick of being portrayed as an asshole. It wasn't who he was, and he was ready for something new. Maybe performing at the ball would start to sway public opinion. To claw back some respect.

"You're not going to challenge me on that?" Kinga demanded, obviously impatient with him for taking so long to respond.

Griff wanted to tell her that it was an act, a well-choreographed show, but this was a secret he'd take to his grave. Only his family and his two best friends, Stan and Ava Maxwell, knew he'd spent the past few years diverting press attention away from his twin. If his actions were divulged, the press would try and discover what she was trying to hide. And them writing about Sian and her problems would be disastrous.

The press had all but forgotten Sian—thank God—and it was finally the right time to stage a comeback.

"No."

"You're a talented artist, Mr. O'Hare, and you have the voice of an angel."

Damned with faint praise. "Thank you."

"Those weren't my words. I read that quote somewhere," Kinga told him on a dismissive shrug. "Music isn't my thing. I can't hold a tune or keep a beat."

A million neurons in his brain died at the thought. "Everybody can hold the beat and sing a little," he protested.

"I'm music-impaired," Kinga assured him, waving a hand. "Anyway, that's beside the point. What I do know is PR, and hiring you would not be a good move for Ryder International. Unfortunately for me, my grandfather disagrees and thinks you are the bee's knees."

Her dismissive attitude shouldn't hurt—he'd heard worse over the years—but it still managed to prick his steel-hard hide. Damn her. Because he refused to let her see that her words had hit their target, he did what he normally did and resorted to flippancy.

"I often think about God and what he must've been thinking when He created bees," Griff mused, purely to wind her up. With her boss-girl demeanor, she radiated confidence and control and he was desperate to rattle her. "I can just imagine Him saying…give them the ability to make a substance that never spoils, a little sting and cute antennae. Oh, and give them kick-ass knees."

He thought he caught a hint of irritated humor but it flashed too quickly for him to be sure. She stared at him before shaking her head. "Are you done?"

"Probably not."

Kinga rolled those gorgeous eyes. "As I was saying, my grandfather thinks that being talked about—whether in a good or a bad light—is always better than not being talked about at all." She wrinkled her nose as if she were unable to believe anyone could be hoodwinked in such a way.

"I don't follow that school of thought. An association between Ryder and you is not in our best interests."

Another verbal blow. By the end of this conversation, he was going to look like a well-used punch bag.

"How did I come to your grandfather's notice?" Griff asked the question that had puzzled him from the moment he'd received Callum's first email raising the possibility of him performing at their ball.

Griff had no idea how Ryder-White obtained his private email address or how the man knew he was contemplating a comeback. He'd only shared that news with select people within the industry, and Callum Ryder-White had to have awesome connections, and deep pockets, to access that type of information. Griff wasn't sure whether to be pissed or pleased.

Performing at the intimate event—a ball for two thousand people was still a small gig—would be a good way to slide back into performing, to dip his toe into that always turbulent body of water. Along with returning to performing, he was also, finally, writing songs again, and was considering releasing a new album. But all these decisions had consequences, including increased press attention.

His return to work would also mean leaving Sian and her son for months at a time. He didn't know if that was a viable option.

"My grandfather adores Vinnie D'Angelo. The famous opera singer?"

Yeah, he knew who Vinnie was, had met him a couple of times, and genuinely liked the old guy. That was why he'd done a cover of "Nessun Dorma," Vinnie's favorite song, from the opera Turandot, for his eightieth birthday. That and because the piece was, instrumentally and vocally, a challenge...

"He saw the video you recently released and wasn't disappointed," Kinga explained.

Wow, that was a hell of a backhanded compliment. "Most people thought I nailed it."

"My grandfather has higher standards than most," Kinga replied, her smile a little flippant. She waved her words away, looking impatient. "Anyway, he saw that your fans are desperate for your return to performing—" Her expression suggested that she couldn't fathom why and the thought made him smile. He had no idea why her dismissive attitude amused him, but it did. "—and he figured it would be a publicity coup to have you perform at the ball."

"But you don't feel that way."

She widened her eyes, trying and failing to look innocent. "Whatever gave you that idea?"

His mouth twitched as he tried not to smile.

It took everything not to give her a big-ass, 'got you',

smile. "Then, *darlin'*, you have a huge problem because your grandfather has already offered me the gig.

"But I never sign anything or agree to take on a project before meeting the people with whom I'll be working," he added.

She worked hard to contain her shock, but she recovered quickly, determination quickly replacing the annoyance in her eyes. "I'd prefer to book someone with a little less charisma and a great deal more reliability," she informed him, her voice six degrees cooler.

He heard her unspoken words... *Selfish, childish, out-of-control.*

The words, and the implication, so often repeated in the press, hit him like another gut punch. His amusement faded and it took all his effort to keep his expression genial. He wasn't the type to spill his soul, but again he felt the urge to explain himself. To explain that the person she saw wasn't who he was. He wanted to tell her that the bad boy act was just that, an act, and he was so damn sick of being seen as problematic. All he wanted to do was write music, perform, be himself again.

Why her and why now? She was prim, buttoned-up, haughty and direct, but Griff had the uncomfortable sensation she was the only one who could get him to spill his secrets.

Despite his attraction to her, Griff knew he should get up and walk—hell, run—away. He'd find another way to stage his comeback. He instinctively knew this woman was dangerous, to his heart and his mind.

But he also needed this gig, not for the money—he had enough for ten lifetimes—but because music was what he did, and being a performer was who he was. He'd been someone else for so long...that he wanted this opportunity to be himself.

He'd sacrificed his reputation, his music and his career for his sister and her son, and now that she was stronger, he was ready to come back. Performing at the Ryder International charity ball was a good move for him, a classy move. A good, tasteful, move.

Suddenly, horribly, he was no longer convinced that he held the upper hand here.

Not because she was being difficult and not because she wasn't enthusiastic about him performing but because…

Crap. He ran a hand over his face.

…Because something about this woman resonated with him. She was a melody he had to put lyrics to, an unwritten song hovering on the edge of his subconscious.

She was a new instrument he'd yet to master, a song he'd yet to sing. A score that needed to be notated…

Damn. He was in serious trouble here.

Two

Kinga stared at him, her fists bunched, cold with shock and dismay.

Because really, there was no way she'd heard him right. There was no way he *already* had an offer, because she'd explained to her grandfather, in precise detail, why hiring Griff was a terrible idea. Callum was hardheaded but he wasn't stupid…

Could the stubborn old goat have done this? Already made the deal? Set her up? Would he really put her in such a tenuous and unacceptable situation? Sure, he wouldn't have thought twice about it.

What the hell was she going to do?

And why the hell did her heart triple-thump and her lady parts thrum every time her eyes connected with Griff's?

He was a very good-looking guy, she accepted that. She liked his messy hair, square jaw covered with three-day-old stubble, his straight nose, the small scar on his right cheekbone. She knew, from pictures, that he had two delicious dimples, but despite his practiced smiles, she'd yet to see them.

His body was fantastic: wide shoulders and chest, a trim waist and big arms that strained the fabric of his expensive T-shirt. But it was his eyes that enthralled her. Kinga could lose herself in the deep green, the color of fir forests on a cold winter's day.

Highlighted by dark brows and thick lashes, they held a million secrets, none of them good. The thought occurred to her that his easy manner and relaxed demeanor lulled people into believing he was the devil-who-didn't-care, an unrepentant bad boy, but his eyes reflected an unexpected intelligence. They suggested there was a lot more to the man than his wild exploits.

Kinga gave her herself a mental slap and reminded herself that it didn't matter who or what O'Hare was; he wasn't suitable to be the headline act at *her* ball.

O'Hare performing at the ball would cause the press to sit up and take notice of the charity event, sure, and then Callum would take credit for being the visionary who'd given O'Hare a second chance *if* Griff behaved himself and turned in a decent performance.

If he messed up, Callum would blame her for the bad publicity, for hiring him. She'd be the one in the firing line. Family or not, Callum looked after himself first.

Kinga looked down at her bunched hand and released her cramping fingers. No, hiring Griff was too risky and she was risk averse. Bad things happened when she stuck her neck out and deviated from the norm. As she very well knew.

"So, to be clear, you haven't signed the contract yet?" Kinga asked, her voice, annoyingly, shaky.

"No, but I probably will. It's a classy event, a decent amount of people, and it's for charity, which will make me look good."

"Does that mean you are donating your fee?" Kinga demanded, leaning forward. Maybe she could make a little lemonade from lemons…

He grinned, white teeth flashing. "No, Ryder International will pay me for performing."

"Marvelous," Kinga muttered. *Jerk.* She sat back and folded her arms across her chest, vibrating with annoyance. "I intend to get my grandfather to change his mind."

"I think you know you won't," Griff told her, sounding amused, "but feel free to try.

"Oh, and good luck explaining to the press why you rescinded your offer to hire me," he added.

Kinga snapped her head up, her eyes colliding with his. "What the hell do you mean by that?"

"If you make this process difficult, I will send a press release to the mainstream media, telling them that I am thrilled to announce my comeback, starting with a performance at your ball."

Kinga linked her hands together and squeezed. "You can't do that without my permission!"

Griff leaned forward, his gaze intense. "Understand this, Ms. Ryder-White. I do not need your damn permission to do or say anything. I received an offer from the head of your organization, with a contract for the gig. I am going to accept that offer. This is my career, not yours."

"But it's my ball, dammit!" Kinga hotly replied. "And I'm pretty sure you don't want to work with me."

"If you become too annoying, I'll ask Callum to make someone else my liaison. Callum mentioned your temper and suggested I might prefer to work with your sister."

Tinsley was sweet, nice, quiet. And how stupid was

it that she felt hurt at hearing Callum's words on Griff's lips. She looked down at the table and hoped he hadn't noticed her expression.

"Look at me, Kinga."

Kinga reluctantly lifted her eyes to his, hoping hers held fire, not pain. Griff stared at her, his expression impassive. "I'm your headline act—you might as well get used to it. Callum wants me, and from what I've read, he normally gets what he wants."

He was, unfortunately, right. And once Callum made up his mind, there was little hope of changing it. And, like his rare collection of illuminated manuscripts, the ring that once belonged to Marie Antoinette and his rare 1953 Jaguar, Griff was another shiny object to collect, use and forget about. He'd get the praise and publicity for luring Griff back into the spotlight and he'd enjoy that momentary thrill. It didn't matter that hiring Griff might not be in Ryder International's best interests. It would be up to others, like her, to manage any potential fallout.

If Griff had a contract offer from Callum, then she was locked into having him as her headline act. Instead of arguing with him, she needed to switch gears and start thinking about how to manage the press, how to spin his comeback into positive publicity for Ryder International. To protect the company, her job and herself.

She'd have to draw up a whole new publicity campaign. But the first step, obviously, was to ensure that he didn't do anything asinine between now and Valentine's Day.

Kinga rested her arms on the table and locked eyes with him, hoping her expression looked as fierce as she felt. "I'll make you a deal."

"This should be interesting," he drawled, amusement lifting the corners of his mouth. Right, so she didn't intimidate him at all. *Great.*

"I will not fight Callum on this and, believe me, I could. It might take some time but he would, eventually, listen to me." No, he wouldn't, but O'Hare didn't need to know that. "And we can easily afford to break your contract, pay you for any inconvenience caused. As far as the bad publicity that would generate, I think that a lot of people would understand why we felt we couldn't afford to take a risk on you."

Kinga thought she saw a flash of pain cross his face but it came and went so quickly she couldn't be sure. But she did have his attention and that was all that mattered. She'd push her agenda while she had the upper hand. She suspected she wouldn't retain it for long.

"I control the publicity, *all* the publicity, including how we frame the story of your comeback." Griff started to speak but Kinga jumped in before he could. "You don't have a manager anymore and my sources in the industry tell me you don't have a publicist, either. Consider my PR services part of your remuneration package."

"I am perfectly able to manage my publicity," Griff said, his voice dangerously soft.

Kinga snorted. "No, you're not. And since your comeback intersects with my ball, I'm going to be the one controlling that narrative." She drilled her finger into his muscular forearm and ignored the fire when she touched him. Her uncontrollable attraction to him was very damn inopportune. And annoying.

"All you need to do is behave yourself. And because I don't trust you to do that, you will relocate to Portland, Maine, where I live and where Ryder International has its headquarters so I can keep an eye on you."

"No," Griff countered. "If I make it to Portland, it will be because I *want* to be there and not because you issued a royal decree."

Kinga frowned at him, wondering if he knew that the local press called her and Tinsley Portland's princesses, or whether his off-hand comment was just a coincidence.

"I want you in Portland, it's where our business is based, where the Ryder-White's have lived for generations," Kinga stated, momentarily distracted by the interest in his eyes. God, he was want-to-jump-you-hot.

She wondered what he'd do if she put her mouth on his, whether the heat swirling between them would erupt into a firenado.

She rather suspected it would. The flames between them were sky-high and if he were anyone other than, well, *him*, she might be tempted to explore their crackling chemistry. Even to the point of suggesting they get a room…

The thought shocked her.

She wasn't an impulsive person. She didn't make quick decisions. Her impulsive behavior at the New Year's Eve party a decade ago had led to tragedy, so she analyzed everything, considered all options, worked all out the possible outcomes and consequences. Only then did she act.

"I want you to relocate to Portland," Kinga repeated her suggestion.

"That's not going to happen." Griff's insolent smile pulled her back to reality.

"Chin up, darlin'," he drawled. "I realize you are a boss girl, but not everyone is always going to fall into line with your wishes. Maybe I've been sent to remind you of that."

She'd never admit it to him, or anyone, that she suspected he was right. That her vociferous opposition to Griff just made Callum more determined to have him perform. Callum liked shaking her up, making her feel off-balance and out of control. He liked the idea of his grandchildren working in the family business but would far prefer she and Tinsley were male.

Callum wasn't a fan of strong, successful women.

Mind games—Callum was a master at them. But she wouldn't let him, or any other man, get the better of her. Kinga forced herself to drop her shoulders, to send him a cool smile. "I think this whole process would run smoother if we worked together so I would greatly appreciate your presence in Portland, Mr. O'Hare."

Where she could keep her beady eye on him.

It galled her to admit that she'd lost this first battle between them—she had no doubt there would be many more—and she knew it was time to retreat. Picking up her tablet and bag, she slid out of the booth, a little surprised when Griff stood, too. The man, surprisingly, had manners...

"I need to leave now to catch my flight," she said, digging into the side pocket of her tote bag for a business card. She handed it over and watched him tuck it into the back pocket of his jeans. "I'll pick up the tab and let you go back to doing what you seem to do best."

"And that is?" Griff asked, laughter back in his eyes.

"Picking up random women in bars."

Griff dipped his head and Kinga had the wild thought that he was about to kiss her. She should step back, retreat, but her feet refused to cooperate. She wanted him to kiss her, she realized; she wanted to know how he tasted, whether his big body was as muscled as she expected.

Dear God, this wasn't good.

But instead of kissing her, Griff's warm, whiskeytinged breath drifted over her cheek before stopping an inch from her ear.

"Just to be clear, I wasn't trying to pick up a random woman. I was trying to pick up *you*. See you soon, darlin'."

Kinga stared at his broad back as he walked away, wishing that she could give in to her impulse to throw the heavy crystal tumbler at his head.

Maybe she should just order another drink. She sure as hell could use one.

Feeling a little shaken, Griff strode across the lobby, helmet tucked under his arm. Looking around, he realized that instead of heading for the exit, he'd walked deeper inside, to a reception area dotted with comfortable couches and...

Holy crap, a Fazioli Aria.

Griff immediately crossed the harlequin floor to the piano and watched the pianist's elegant fingers dancing across the keys. She was young and pretty but all of his attention was on one of the most luxurious, insanely expensive pianos in the world. He was a Gibson guy, but he'd taken piano lessons and knew his way around the keyboard.

The redhead saw his approach, her eyes widening when she recognized him. To her credit, she didn't stumble or stop, but simply raised an eyebrow. Her mouth lifted into a half smile. "Griff O'Hare, hello. Do you play?"

Griff nodded. "Guitar is my first love but I've been known to lose hours massacring Mozart or Bach."

She segued into Henry Mancini's "Moon River" and her smile turned flirty. "Feel free to join in..."

Griff looked around and grimaced. That would attract more attention than he was looking for. "No, thanks. It's a beautiful instrument."

"They have another in the ballroom."

"Two Faziolis?" Be still, his beating heart.

"The owners of this place don't spare any expense. I'm Alice, by the way. Are you checking in?"

"I've just come from a meeting," Griff replied and internally grimaced at the flirtatious glint in her eye. He knew what was coming next—it was as predictable as the sun rising in the east.

Three, two, one...

"Would you like to meet with me as well? I'll be done in ten minutes."

He was such a freaking genius. "Thanks, but I can't," Griff told her, allowing his hand to skim over the upraised lid. "Nice meeting you, Alice."

Conscious of eyes following his progress across the lobby, he fought the urge to walk back into the Ryder International bar situated in a prime position just off the main lobby and engage Kinga Ryder-White in some non-business conversation.

I-wonder-what-you-taste-like and *I'm-desperate-to-see-you-naked* conversation. But her frosty looks and don't-go-there attitude told him he had more of a chance of becoming pregnant than he did of persuading her into his arms and his bed.

And maybe that was life's way of telling him he should put all his energy into this comeback performance. Deep in thought, Griff nearly ran into the back of a petite gray-haired lady. After muttering an apology, he stepped through the lobby doors and headed to where he'd parked his Ducati a few blocks away. He liked walking, and riding his loud and powerful bike up to the valet station was just asking for unneeded attention.

Jamming on a pair of sunglasses and a ball cap he'd tucked into the inner pocket of his jacket, he dodged tourists and New Yorkers, walking swiftly, still deep in thought.

His thoughts, as they often did, centered on his sister, his twin. It had been nearly ten years since the doctors first diagnosed Sian with schizophrenia, yet it felt like yesterday. Directly after the diagnosis, and because she'd wanted out of the industry, Sian had retreated to his horse ranch in Kentucky, shunning company and raising a lot of gossip in the press.

After some salacious speculation about his sister, Griff and his manager, Finn, had agreed that they needed to divert press attention from Sian. Finn accepted that Griff's transformation into a bad boy was the way to go. He also insisted that Griff embarking on a "Raising Hell" tour was necessary. Griff hadn't wanted to leave Sian, but Finn promised to look after his twin while Griff toured. Yet, while he was away, what Griff had believed to be a father-daughter relationship had turned sexual and Sian had gotten pregnant.

Griff still struggled to believe that the man he'd considered to be his second father—his parents had died when he and Sian were in their early twenties—and his mentor could have turned an avuncular relationship with Sian into something sexual, especially knowing how vulnerable his sister was.

Bastard.

Sian didn't see it the same way he did, and frequently told him that her liaison with Finn had been consensual, that she went into the affair with her eyes wide open. But Griff, deeply protective of his twin—to her immense frustration—couldn't help but think that Finn had taken advantage of her need for comfort and reassurance. Her need to feel normal and attractive and like the sexy woman she was before she was diagnosed.

A lot of advantage…

But, on the plus side, Griff had managed to keep the

press away from all of Sian's private life. Nobody knew Finn was Sam's father, that Sian had mental health issues or that she was a mother. He'd managed to snow them all and that had been, after all, his primary objective. Given the same set of circumstances and presented with the same choices, he'd do it all over again.

She was his twin, the person he shared life with before life and he'd rearrange the heavens for her if so required.

Griff walked up to his bike, whipped off his cap and jammed on his helmet. Knowing he was well disguised, he straddled the bike and watched the passing traffic, both pedestrian and vehicular.

He'd do it all again, of course he would. He'd do anything to protect Sian and Sam and never considered them a burden or a drag.

But he was so damn sick of being portrayed as an attention-seeking publicity hound, the bad boy performer.

He'd once been respected as a consummate professional and he desperately wanted to restore his reputation. It was, he thought, the right time to do that. Sian was stable and the entertainment industry wasn't focused on her anymore. Sam was thriving. Griff was thirty-five years old and he'd been keeping a low profile lately—well, a lot lower than before—and this ball, elegant and exclusive, would set the tone for his comeback and whatever came next in his career.

He could do the concert, see how he was received, and then decide what path to follow.

And bonus, he'd be working with the stunningly sexy Kinga Ryder-White, she of the long, lanky body, short, bright blond hair. And eyes the color of secrets and sass.

Yeah, so far the Ryder International ball was turning out to be a damn good deal.

Penelope

Watching from the windows of their private sitting
room situated in one of the two wings of Callum's sprawling mansion, Penelope watched James walk up the path
from the beach, his hair windblown and his cheeks pink
with cold. But no matter the weather, whenever they came
to Ryder's Rest, he'd take his to-go cup of coffee to the
beach and spend some time staring at the sea.

Her husband was a creature of habit, Penelope thought.
She liked that about him. Unlike her, James was an open
book.

Penelope poured herself another cup of coffee and
flipped open her crocodile-skin diary to check her schedule for today. She had Pilates at eleven, lunch with friends
at one and a meeting with the Ryder Foundation CEO at
four to discuss the many requests for funding and grants
that the foundation regularly received. It was always hard
to prioritize need and so many people needed their help…

Pen hoped she managed to concentrate long enough to
make a meaningful contribution to the discussion.

Her thoughts, since doing that stupid DNA test, had
been scattered and her attention span was minimal. Picking up her coffee cup, she walked back over to the window and stared down at Dead Man's Cove, thinking back
on her life and the choices she made.

And the consequences of those choices.

But in time, she'd learned to live with the guilt and the
emptiness, and she'd devoted herself to raising her two
girls as best she could. Now in her late fifties, Pen had
thought that the past was far behind her and that her secret was safe.

Callum's "gift" of a DNA test had flipped that belief
on its head.

Penelope heard James step into the room and turned to look at him. His blond hair was tousled, and he looked tired and stressed. No, she corrected, James was always stressed. Working for his demanding and unappreciative father was difficult beyond measure. He looked like his uncle, she realized with a pang.

"Morning, Pen."

Penelope returned his subdued greeting. They hadn't been in love when they married; the union had been, to an extent, an arranged marriage. Her parents were friends of the Ryder-Whites—and she'd been considered suitable, rich, educated, and of the right social class to join the Ryder-White clan. Callum never suspected she was anything other than another debutante in her early twenties, an educated, innocent, wealthy man's daughter who had, like so many of her friends, spent a year abroad.

But somehow, despite the massive secret she kept from him, she and James had made their marriage work, by becoming friends first, then lovers, then parents.

They'd raised two beautiful girls, and if James had had an affair, or a few, he'd been discreet. She wasn't emotional about her marriage or her husband, and fully expected him to stray: it was what men—her father included—did.

Her marriage was stable. They were rich, popular, respected…semi-famous. She didn't want anything to change and the secrets of her life before James to be revealed.

"Are you okay, Pen?" James asked, coming up to stand beside her.

Pen started to tell him she was fine, but on seeing his worried eyes, shook her head. "Not really. Are you?"

James shrugged. Pen sighed, knowing James wasn't one to rock the boat. Her husband's sweet nature and his hatred of conflict were why Callum treated him like a servant. Her father-in-law was a bully, and like all bullies, he only respected people who stood up to him.

"Just tired," James lied. "I feel like I'm on a treadmill and there's no getting off."

When she looked at him, she frowned at the emotion in his eyes. Working for his father had worn him down, and she wished, sometimes desperately, that they could run away, start again.

But unfortunately, some things followed you wherever you went.

James stared out the window, his square jawline taut. With his thick blond hair turning silver, blue eyes and fit body, her husband was still a gorgeous man. She was lucky to be married to him, lucky to enjoy the fabulous lifestyle he provided, to be respected and even, occasionally, feted.

That could change…

No, it *would* change. It was best to be prepared.

Once a month, Callum insisted on a family meeting to be held around the two-hundred-year-old dining table at Ryder's Rest. After they were done discussing Ryder International and Ryder-White business, they adjourned to Callum's reception room to drink sherry while his housekeeper set the dining table for a four-course dinner followed by port and, if they felt so inclined, a hand of cards or a game of billiards.

It was all very Downton Abbey. Every family member's attendance was mandatory and, being so busy, Kinga and Tinsley chafed at the wasted time and mentally mocked their grandfather's pretensions.

He was not a bloody duke or a member of the peerage. This wasn't aristocratic England, for God's sake.

But because no good ever came of rocking the boat, Kinga gritted her teeth, drank his revolting sherry and followed Tinsley to her seat at the dining table where they'd discuss business over dinner.

Tinsley glanced around, and seeing that her grandfather was preoccupied at the other end of the room with pouring himself another whiskey, nudged Kinga with her elbow. "You're looking very militant, Kingaroo. What's up?"

"A thousand and one things," Kinga muttered, flipping open the cover to her iPad. Not least of which was the fact that she couldn't stop thinking about that man-devil, Griff O'Hare. He popped into her thoughts all the time and then she spent a few minutes remembering the color of his eyes, the width of his shoulders, the way his jeans cupped his very nice package...

Dear God, she was losing her mind.

"Whose stupid idea was it to have a yearlong celebration of everything Ryder International?" she demanded, sounding irritated.

Her dad stopped next to her seat and dropped a kiss on her head. "Yours, darling."

Kinga twisted her lips. "And, except for the notion of hiring O'Hare to sing at the ball, it was the stupidest idea ever."

Tinsley sent her a sympathetic look and jerked her chin. Kinga turned her head to see Callum approaching his chair at the head of the table. He'd exchanged his suit jacket for one of his many vintage smoking jackets, this one a rich burgundy with black velvet lapels. Callum sat down, opened his leather folder and picked up his Montblanc fountain pen, one of only six made in the world. The unlined paper on which he made notes was hand-crafted and his whiskey glass was made in Bohemia. Callum was a blue blood and nothing but the best was good enough for him.

Griff was annoying, sure, but at least the man wasn't pretentious. And why was she thinking about him?

Callum cleared his throat and his pale blue eyes landed on James. "Why have you made no progress in establishing who owns the block of shares that are out of my control?"

James gave his father the same answer he did every time he was asked this question. "Callum, the shares are held in a trust. The trust is confidential." James lifted up his hand. "All we can do is send letters—as we have been doing—via the trustee's lawyers and hope he responds. If he doesn't, our hands are tied."

Callum released a low growl. "What the hell was Benjamin thinking leaving those shares to someone out of the family?"

Ah, that might be because you, Callum, flipped out when he told you he was in love with another man. Karma, as she'd learned, never lost an address or failed to deliver.

Kinga caught Tinsley's eye and rolled her own.

"Would it help to hire a private investigator to look into Benjamin's life at the time that he bequeathed the shares?" Callum demanded.

Kinga saw frustration in her father's eyes. "We did that, and the only person close to Ben at the time was the man he briefly lived with, the man he wanted to marry." James shook his head at Callum's look of distaste. Unlike Callum, her parents were tolerant and accepting. They'd taught her and Tinsley that love was love.

"I had the PI dig into his life, but Carlos lived simply, a solidly upper-middle-class life. If he had access to Ben's wealth, he would've at least paid off his mortgage. He didn't. The investigator found no indication that Carlos controls those shares, but we don't know who else might."

"Can we please move on?" Penelope demanded.

Kinga frowned at her mom's terse tone. "Mom? Are you okay?"

"We keep beating the same dead horse! The shares are out of our reach. Maybe it's time to accept that!" Penelope muttered.

Callum narrowed his eyes at his daughter-in-law. "If I simply accepted what I was told, I would not own a ten-billion-dollar company, Penelope. You would not be wearing Chanel or sporting a five-carat diamond or driving the latest BMW."

Penelope pushed her fingertips into her eye sockets. "Yes, I understand, Callum. Sorry."

Stop apologizing, Mom! You didn't do anything wrong. Kinga shook her head. She saw the glint in her grandfather's eye as he looked at her mom's bent head, the small smile on his lips.

Callum loved putting people in their place; he got a kick out of knocking people down, especially women. So why was she still working for the man? Why didn't she just leave?

Kinga sighed. Because, while she didn't like her grandfather, she loved the business, loved her demanding and interesting job and she thought that, maybe, she could draw some of Callum's fire from her father.

"I sent you a copy of Griff O'Hare's signed contract, Callum," Kinga said, wanting to move the meeting along. Damn, even saying his name made her feel squidgy, off balance. What was wrong with her?

Callum scowled at her, and Kinga knew he was debating whether to scold her for hijacking his agenda. "I saw that. And I am pleased with the publicity his comeback has generated."

So was she…for now. "But if they'd spend a little more time talking about the ball and the Ryder Foundation and less about Griff O'Hare's exploits, I'd be grateful," Kinga said.

"I'm still being touted as the person who persuaded him to come out of retirement, so I have no issue with the press coverage," Callum told her.

Of course, he didn't. But when O'Hare messed up, Callum would throw Kinga to the press wolves. Despite frequently telling the world that his family meant everything to him, her grandfather always put himself first.

"I have some ideas about the songs I want O'Hare to sing," Callum stated.

Kinga swallowed her groan. She and Griff had exchanged at least a dozen emails arguing about who had creative control over his set list, with him threatening to walk unless she butted out. So she'd butted out.

Now Callum, who obviously hadn't read the contract, wanted to butt back in.

"That's not going to happen, Callum. Griff won't tolerate any interference with his creative control of the performance," Kinga told him, enjoying his shocked expression. In Griff, Callum might just have found someone equally stubborn. The thought amused her. And turned her on.

Honestly? Everything about O'Hare turned her on.

"That's not acceptable. I will have my way."

"Not this time you won't," Kinga shot back. "If you interfere, he walks and we don't have a performer."

"Who the hell drew up that damn contract?" Callum shouted, his face flushed with temper.

Kinga leaned back in her chair and smiled. "You did, Callum. I sent you a memo detailing my concerns, and control of his set list was one of them. I was surprised to see that you signed it with no alterations."

"I...what...how—" Callum blustered.

Tinsley kicked her ankle and Kinga's smile faded. Right, baiting the bear was never a clever tactic.

"Have you received the DNA tests back yet, Callum?" Tinsley asked him, changing the subject yet again. Kinga sent her a grateful smile.

"This family seems to forget that I have an agenda to follow," Callum retorted. "But to answer your question, no, I have not. The laboratory sent me an email telling me that there was a snafu and our results would be delayed."

"All of them?" James asked. Kinga heard the note of doubt in his voice and didn't blame him. She could understand there being a problem with one sample but five? At the same time?

"Must we swipe the inside of our mouths again, Callum?" James asked.

"I would've told you if that was what was required."

Kinga pulled a face at Callum's terse tone and hauled in a series of calming breaths. It was going to be a long meeting and an even longer evening.

Three

Two weeks had passed since Kinga and Griff's initial flurry of email-based arguments about the set list and publicity. Despite reaching out via emails, text messages and leaving messages on his voice mail, Kinga hadn't heard a squeak out of him in over ten days.

She needed to talk to the man. She needed to discuss the ball, press releases, interviews...

She also wanted to know whether she'd seen sadness flicker across his face or simply imagined the sexual interest she saw in his eyes.

She couldn't stop thinking about him, wondering what he was doing, whom he was with...

Kinga shook her head, surprised at the fast, hot flame of jealousy travelling across her skin. She'd met him once—one time!—and he had her acting like an idiot.

God knew what would happen if she spent more time with him.

Sitting in the corner of her comfortable couch, Kinga closed the report she'd been reading and moved her machine from her lap to the coffee table in front of her. She pulled her feet up onto the couch and wrapped her arms around her knees, her eyes invariably drifting toward the heavy silver frame on the mantel of her fireplace.

The photo was taken a week or two before Jas died. They'd spent a weekend skiing Saddleback Mountain and they'd asked a cute ski instructor to take their photograph. Their noses were pink from the cold, their eyes sparkling, their smiles boldly declaring that they were young, beautiful and invincible.

Jasmine had been a ray of sunshine, could make friends with a lamppost and, within a day of reaching the ski resort, knew a dozen people by name. She was the eternal optimist, a free spirit, someone thoroughly in love with life. The daughter of a prominent senator and his equally charismatic wife, Jas had been born with confidence, ebullience and the ability to persuade a rock to crumble. They'd met in kindergarten, bonded immediately and, with them both attending the same exclusive private school, forged an unbreakable friendship.

Determined, intensely bright and vivacious, Jas pulled Kinga, reserved and a little shy, out of her shell, and it was because of Jas that she had a social life.

Jas made her braver and bolder.

Then Jas died...

Kinga wished she could remember Jas without having to recall the soul-destroying events that occurred a decade before. But that was impossible and her mind wandered down that all too familiar, dark path.

It's all good, Kingaroo, I'll be fine.

Kinga sighed at the sound of Jas's voice in her head. It hadn't been good and nothing was fine.

The memories were as vivid today as they'd ever been. Kinga could still recall the fear in Jas's mom's voice when she called on the first day of the new year. She'd asked whether Jas had slept over at her house, because she hadn't returned home that night. She remembered rushing to the Garwood house and screaming at the police officers, trying to get them to believe Jas wasn't a runaway, that she hadn't left home for places unknown. Walking Cousin's Island, paralyzed with fear as she papered windows, poles and cars with missing-person flyers.

Stopping now and again to cry and pray her heart out for Jas's swift return. Wishing she'd never left Jas at that party...

A few days later they found her body, lying under snow in a ditch on the side of the road. The police determined it was a hit-and-run and the culprit had never been identified.

Jas's on-off boyfriend, Mick Pritchard—the boy who grew up next door to Kinga and whom she'd known even longer than she'd known Jas—told her, and anybody who would listen, that she was to blame for Jas's death.

He was right.

Kinga placed her face in her hands, desperately wishing she'd hung around and given Jas a lift home as she'd promised she would. That instead of leaving with some long forgotten boy, she'd stayed, seeing in the new year with her best friend.

Kinga reached for her wine, draining the last inch in one long swallow.

She was still close to Jas's parents but the loss of their daughter had changed them in ways that were almost impossible to understand. Her father, Seth, still served as Maine's senator but, to Kinga, it was like the light within him had dimmed. Viola, Jas's mom, rarely left their sprawling estate.

Kinga missed Jas but she also missed the loving, fun people who'd once been Jas's parents. But thankfully, they'd never blamed her for what happened that night.

Unlike Mick, who was relentless in his attacks. He'd confronted her after the funeral and, over the past ten years, on each anniversary of Jas's death, he sent her either a text message, a voice message or an email, sometimes all three, reminding her that Jas would be alive if it weren't for her actions. And he always, always sent her the link to the sales video on his company website…

"When I was twenty, I lost the love of my life, Jas Garwood, Senator Garwood's only daughter, in a hit-and-run accident. Her best friend, Kinga Ryder-White, was supposed to see her home from a New Year's party and failed to do so. Jas chose to walk and, in the mist and rain, was hit by a vehicle. I have chosen to dedicate my life to helping others by providing security services."

She didn't need Mick's reminders. She lived with the consequences of her actions every single day. She had not only lost her best friend, but she was the reason the Garwoods had lost their only child.

Jas's death had changed Kinga, too. She never, ever allowed herself to act rashly, seldom made new friends or dated. She analyzed every decision she made, overthought everything.

And she'd vowed she would never voluntarily love someone so much again.

She loved Tinsley and her parents—but loving your family was baked in from birth, wasn't it? To voluntarily love, or to fall in love, meant taking the risk of letting someone down, making another mistake. Being hurt.

She would never allow that to happen again.

Knowing that she had to stop thinking about Jas, Kinga jumped up and turned the silver frame to face the wall.

The memories and regrets were strong tonight, and not seeing Jas's laughing face might keep her thoughts from returning to that awful time so long ago.

She needed to think of something else, someone else. She could think about Griff O'Hare...

Like you weren't thinking about him just ten minutes ago.

Annoyed with that mocking inner voice, Kinga walked over to her window and placed her hand on the pane, idly watching the wicked weather outside. It was snowing, again, and the weather people were predicting another winter storm to roll in later.

She wondered how Griff, when he finally dragged himself to Portland, would cope with their weather. She knew he owned an island off the Florida Keys, a ranch in Kentucky, houses in Malibu and Nashville, apartments in Manhattan and London, but she didn't know which of his many properties was his primary residence.

If she did, she'd find him and drag him back to Portland by his hair, cave girl style.

They needed to finalize the PR strategy, but let's be honest here, she couldn't wait to look into his forest green eyes, to watch for those sexy dimples, to hear his deep drawl saying her name. Kinga sighed. She couldn't believe she was at risk of falling under the spell of a bad boy.

Nothing was going to happen between them, Kinga told herself as a big SUV turned the corner into her street.

She turned away from the window, reminding herself that she didn't make connections, take risks, make impulsive moves.

It wasn't what she did, who she was.

Griff pulled up to the third of four redbrick buildings on Congress Street and turned off the engine to his rented

Mercedes SUV. Placing his arms on the steering wheel, he looked up at the imposing building with its stained glass inserts above the front door, the original slate roof and tall chimneys.

He looked to the right and noticed the discreet signage indicating that the property next door was a boutique hotel.

It looked glamorous and expensive and Griff wasn't surprised that the granddaughter of the town's richest man lived here. It was perfectly situated, smack bang in the arts district, and he'd noticed many upmarket restaurants and trendy shops nearby. It was also a short walk to Portland's famous harbor.

From the little he'd seen from his after-dinner stroll earlier, he rather liked this small, vibey, unpretentious city. He liked the Old Port, an appealing old harbor town with amazing architecture and cobblestone sidewalks. He'd never visited this part of the world before but knew that spending time here wouldn't be a hardship.

Admittedly, Kinga Ryder-White was, for him, one of the city's main attractions.

Leaving his vehicle, Griff pulled his jacket off the back of the driver's seat and shrugged it on, trying and failing to ignore the icy splatters hitting his hair, face and shoulders. If he was going to stay in Maine any length of time, he was going to have to buy himself a big-ass umbrella. After locking his car, he walked across the road—being careful to avoid puddles—and strode up the steps to stand under the portico at the entrance to the building. There were only three apartments—K Ryder-White and T Ryder-White lived in apartments A and B, while C didn't have a name attached—and Griff jammed his finger on the buzzer of the apartment belonging to Kinga.

"Yes?"

It was one word but he heard the fear in her voice. He should've given her some warning that he was coming over but he'd landed in Portland just a few hours before, grabbed some food and decided he couldn't wait until morning to see her. She'd been on his mind since he left Manhattan.

A most unusual circumstance.

"It's Griff O'Hare."

"What the hell? It's after eleven, O'Hare." Kinga told him, sounding pissy. Man, he loved her irritated rasp.

"You've left at least two dozen messages telling me to get in touch." Griff smiled, his forearm resting on the wall above his head. He grinned, enjoying the fact he could rile her so easily. "This is me, getting in touch."

"This is you, being a pain in my ass," Kinga shot back.

Griff chuckled, loving her sass. "Apparently, we've got lots to discuss, so let me in, darlin'. It's colder than a witch's—"

Kinga interrupted him to mutter something indistinguishable but definitely uncomplimentary. He grinned when her door clicked open.

Griff walked into the pretty lobby dominated by an old, intricate chandelier. It was a small area and he couldn't help wondering what happened to the wooden staircase that would've once dominated the space. The U-shaped lobby held three identical, and old, wooden doors, a small lemon tree in an ornamental pot and a wooden bench with plump black-and-white cushions.

He turned to knock on Kinga's door but before he could, she opened it, standing there in a pair of men's-style flannel pajamas, in a pretty mint-and-white check. She wore chunky socks on her feet, her short hair was messy and her face free of makeup.

She looked, as Sian used to say, *uh-maz-zing*.

"It's late, O'Hare," Kinga said, leaning her shoulder against the wooden doorframe. "Go away and we'll meet in the morning."

Griff glanced at his watch and shrugged. "You weren't sleeping," he pointed out. She might look like she was ready for bed but she didn't look remotely sleepy. Griff suspected she'd been working when he leaned on her buzzer.

Griff turned at the sound of a door opening behind him and in that doorway stood a gorgeous woman with long, straight, coal black hair, pale, creamy skin and navy blue eyes. Sexy as hell, but she didn't nudge his I'm-attracted-to-her needle. However, the whiskey-eyed beauty with the sharp tongue, still glaring at him, sent it revving into the red zone.

"Griff O'Hare, meet my sister, Tinsley."

Tinsley, dressed in blue jeans, thick socks and a cable-knit sweater, mirrored her sister's pose against the door-frame and uttered a cool, "Hello."

"It is ridiculously late, Mr. O'Hare," Tinsley stated. Like her sister, she was equally unimpressed with his late-night visit. And with him.

Griff looked from one sister to the other and shrugged. "On the West Coast, we normally only start our evening around about now."

"And get up at noon," Kinga snapped. "Some of us have real jobs that start early."

She had no idea of the time and effort it took to reach his one-time level of success. Rising early, hitting the gym, learning lines, filming, rehearsing or recording. When one worked fourteen-or sixteen-hour days, the only time to socialize was from eleven onward.

He wanted to defend himself, something he hadn't had the urge to do in a very long time. Damn, that was the second time he wanted to explain and had no doubt it wouldn't be the last.

He returned his gaze to Kinga and saw she was looking past him to Tinsley. The two sisters seemed to be having a silent but intense conversation.

What was he missing here? Whatever they were discussing, they gave off enough of a vibe to make him feel he'd overstepped. He raised his hands and put some distance between himself and Kinga's door. "You're right, it's late. We can meet in the morning."

He turned to Tinsley to tell her that it was nice to meet her and caught her shocked expression when Kinga ordered him, "Come on in."

"Would you like me to join you, make coffee or something?" Tinsley asked, her eyes not leaving her sister's face.

Kinga sent her a soft smile. "No, we're good. Thanks, Tins."

Tinsley's eyes widened again in surprise and Griff knew he was missing a lot of subtext. He didn't like it.

He started to demand an explanation but then remembered he hated people asking him personal questions, so he pushed down his curiosity.

After nodding to Tinsley, he walked into Kinga's apartment and heard the door shut behind him. Turning, he saw Kinga eyeing the four locks on her door, as if trying to decide whether to lock them or not. Four locks? Wasn't that excessive?

A thought occurred, one that burned a hole in his stomach. "Are you scared of me?" he demanded.

Kinga slowly turned, and when she faced him, she cocked her head to the side, as if trying to figure out her answer. Griff held his breath, waiting for her reply. If she was even remotely uneasy, he'd leave.

One hint of hesitation and he was gone.

A soft smile passed through Kinga's lovely eyes but Griff knew it wasn't directed at him. "I'm not," she said, sounding amused. "You annoy me and irritate me but, surprisingly, you don't scare me."

Okay. Well, good.

Kinga released a tiny chuckle and brushed past him. His nose filled with her scent, something light and subtle and thoroughly sexy. It wasn't perfume...shower soap, maybe? Shampoo?

Disconcerted, Griff followed her into her open-plan living, dining, kitchen area. A staircase was to his right, and her walls were covered with abstract works of art that were both playful and thought-provoking. Cream couches holding bright, jewel-colored cushions sat next to the bay window, and he looked through the glass coffee table to the Persian rug tossed over the old hardwood floor. The back wall of the kitchen was exposed red brick.

There were fresh flowers on a side table and roses in a round glass bowl on the mantel next to an ornate silver frame, its face to the wall. He frowned. What was up with that?

Griff looked around and whistled. "This place is fantastic."

Kinga padded over to the kitchen and turned her slim back on him to take two fat wineglasses from a slim cupboard next to a stainless steel fridge. "Thanks. My dad dabbles in real estate and he found this place and converted it into three apartments. As you noticed, Tinsley is opposite me and there's a much smaller third apartment behind us both. We bought the building from my dad a few years back."

"And I presume you rent the other apartment?" Griff

said, taking off his coat and draping it over the back of the closest sofa.

Kinga poured red wine into two glasses, her shoulders lifting in a small shrug. "The hotel next door occasionally rents the apartment from us if they have a family group they can't accommodate. It's fully furnished, so it works for both of us."

Griff took the glass she held out and when her fingers brushed against his, he felt the unmistakable current of attraction run up his arm. Judging by the way her eyes widened, she was feeling it, too.

Good to know. And bad to explore because they were about to commence their working relationship.

Griff knew engaging in a physical relationship would be a lot more fun. And satisfactory.

Kinga placed her glass on the coffee table and shifted from foot to foot, her eyes going to the stairway. "Can you give me five minutes? I'd like to change into something a little less informal."

"Don't bother on my account," Griff told her, sitting down at the end of her comfortable sofa. He placed his ankle on his knee and took a sip of the wine, sighing at its complexity. Like her taste in buildings and interior decor, Kinga's taste in wine was exquisite.

"Nice. What am I drinking?"

Kinga hesitated before perching on the sofa opposite his and lifting her wineglass to her lips. She sniffed, took a sip and sighed. "Ah, this is a bottle of 2005 Vieux Château Certan."

"It reminds me of Château Pétrus from the same year."

Kinga smiled. "It's supposed to. My dad is a wine buff and he has a case of the Pétrus. He won't waste the truly excellent stuff on Tinsley and me—apparently our palates aren't sophisticated enough—so he finds reasonable alternatives for us." Kinga crossed her legs and placed her elbow on her knee and her chin in her hand. "Are you a wine connoisseur?"

He had, so he'd been told, one of the best wine cellars in the country and, like whiskey, he enjoyed a glass of the good stuff. But never more than one or two. Drinking too much and too often was like flirting with a very slippery slope and he preferred to avoid the fall. Griff shrugged. "I like wine."

Kinga's direct gaze didn't drop from his face. She sipped again before nailing him with a hard look. "Why are you here, O'Hare?"

He couldn't tell her that she'd been on his mind constantly, that every time he saw an email from her, or a text message, or heard an increasingly irate voice message, he fought the urge to drop everything and fly out to her. That no other woman had ever taken up so much of his mental energy and that when he saw her standing in her doorway, dressed in her cute pj's, he'd felt like he'd taken his first proper breath since leaving New York City.

That waiting until morning to see her had been impossible...

Griff pushed his hand through his damp hair and took a huge gulp of wine. He didn't know what was happening here, but he had to get his thoughts under control. He wasn't looking for a partner, or a significant other or even, right now, a part-time lover. Sex would be great, but not if it came with complications, and Kinga embodied the word.

"You told me you wanted to see me," Griff eventually responded, keeping his face bland.

"Our conversation could've waited until the morning."

Griff couldn't pull his gaze off her lovely brown eyes and his heart rate picked up. What was it about this woman? Why did she make his extremities tingle, his mouth dry, and, yeah, his cock harden? She wasn't the most beautiful woman he'd ever laid eyes on. She was definitely the bossiest. But he still found himself constantly thinking about her, wanting to know what made her smile, what made her sigh.

He sipped his wine, slid down farther in the seat and rested the back of his head against the back of her couch. Her apartment was warm, she was pretty to look at and he had a glass of red in his hand. His home life was in order. His nephew, Sam, was his happy self. His sister, Sian, was stable, and Eloise, his former au pair and now his right hand, had everything under control.

He could relax. Just a little.

"Tell me about the ball," Griff suggested and smiled when she scooted back in her seat and tucked her feet under her butt. She held her wineglass to her chest, but her eyes lit up at the question. It was obvious the project was important to her.

"The ball is to be held in six weeks, on February fourteenth, as you know."

"If you're planning on a red-and-white theme with a million hearts, I might throw up," Griff told her. He couldn't think of anything more obvious.

Kinga released a little snort. "Please, I have better taste than that. The nod to Valentine's Day will be very subtle—Belgian chocolate hearts on the table, a swag bag filled with champagne and caviar, expensive bath products and lingerie. A heart-shaped pendant from Tiffany, a gold-plated pen for writing love notes." Kinga informed him.

Love notes? Did anyone send those anymore?

"Vouchers for romantic getaways, handwoven cashmere rugs, designer scarves and bags."

Wow, pricey. "Kind of like the swag bags they give away to the Oscar nominees?"

Kinga nodded. "The same firm who does those are doing ours, but because there are so many more people at our gala, they are just a smidgeon—" Kinga left a small space between her thumb and index finger "—cheaper. And I'm not exaggerating, our swag bag sponsors want our guests to use and purchase their products and are willing to donate accordingly. One Instagram post, one tweet and they've recouped their initial investment. You know how it works."

He did. He'd been paid big money to endorse products and the companies were always happy with the bump in sales.

"I read somewhere that the profits from the ball are donated to charity?" Griff said, enjoying their suddenly noncontentious conversation. Despite her saying that she didn't have any musical talent, her voice was melodic, a little edgy, like an expertly played saxophone piercing the late-night silence.

"We have sponsors but there are huge costs, obviously. Food, drink and talent being the top three most expensive items." Her amazing eyes pinned him to the sofa. "You are exorbitantly expensive, O'Hare."

Griff didn't bother to tell her that he'd quoted Ryder International a lower hourly rate than he normally charged because the profits from the event were going to charity. And if she was trying to make him feel bad about his re-muneration, she was going to have to wait a while. He'd worked his ass off for more than twenty-five years to com-mand the prices he did.

"We're hoping to raise around a hundred million for our foundation. My mom is the family representative on the foundation's board and that's her goal."

That was seriously impressive. He wasn't a slouch at donating. He quietly funneled considerable amounts to causes he believed in—fighting climate change and promoting literacy were two of his favorites—but this was next-level philanthropy. It inspired him to up his game.

Kinga leaned forward to put her wineglass on the coffee table, creating a gap between her pajama top and her chest and giving Griff a view of small but beautiful breasts.

God, he wanted her.

Kinga looked down at her clasped hands. "The Ryder name is associated with luxury and class and elegance. Our drinking establishments can be found in some of the most expensive and exclusive hotels all over the world. We host a ball for charity every year but this one, because it's our centenary year, has been designed to be our biggest and best one ever. It's a big deal.

"That's why I've been so vociferous about your involvement. I can't help but be scared that you will ruin our hard work and our reputation by doing something stupid, O'Hare."

He'd been called selfish and irresponsible, out of control and inconsiderate, and he'd trained himself to let the insults roll off his back. But her words, quietly uttered, hurt a lot more than they should.

Would she understand his reasoning for doing what he did? Would she understand his need to protect his twin? And weren't those stupid questions to ask himself, because he couldn't tell her or anyone else the truth?

"I will not tolerate you, or anyone else, derailing my event," Kinga added.

Griff looked at her pugnacious expression and sighed. "Would you believe me if I told you that I have no intention of doing anything of the sort?"

Kinga held his eyes and for half a heartbeat, Griff thought she might say that she did. Then her eyes cooled and she shook her head. "I believe you'd try, but you're impulsive and headstrong and I don't think you consider the consequences of your actions so, no, I wouldn't believe you."

He'd known that his past would come back to bite him in the ass and here it was, merrily snacking away.

Kinga picked up her wineglass and drained it, her eyes not leaving his face. "So, where are you staying while you are in Portland?"

He was grateful for the change in subject. "I booked the Portland Harbor Hotel."

"I know it well. And are you going to stay there until the ball? You'll be inundated by the press and you won't have a moment's peace," Kinga pointed out.

Situation normal, Griff thought.

Kinga scrunched up her nose. "But I suppose that's a given wherever you are."

Unfortunately.

"So, are you going to be sticking around until the second week in February?" she asked, a little wistfully, suggesting that she already knew the answer to the question she'd asked him weeks before.

"I'm leaving tomorrow, after our meeting."

He needed to get back to his stud farm in Kentucky. Eloise was scheduled to take a four-day break and he needed to be around for Sam. Sian was a good mom, she loved her son but her condition required an extra set of hands and eyes. Nevertheless, spending time with Sam, and his sister, was one of his favorite things to do.

"But I need you to be in Portland until the concert."

Right, he could tolerate her bossiness—it amused him

and he never allowed anyone to push him where he didn't want to go—but now she was being imperious. "Nope."

"What?"

Griff smiled at her. "Oh, sorry, that didn't come out right. No can do, *princess.*"

He silently admitted that temporarily relocating to Portland did make sense. He should be on hand to give input into Kinga's decisions around his publicity and his favorite band members would be a lot more amenable to relocating to Portland than to his stud farm for practice sessions. But Sam and Sian came first and he couldn't leave Eloise with them on her own for weeks at a time.

Griff watched, amused, as annoyance filtered across Kinga's face and settled in her eyes. "If you are going to perform at *my* ball, I need you to be close at hand."

"No, you want to keep me out of trouble." Griff stood up abruptly and walked around the coffee table to place one hand on the arm of her sofa, bending down to look into her lovely face.

Kinga didn't bother to deny his words and Griff appreciated her honesty. She lifted her chin to stare at him, raising her arched eyebrows. She was trying so hard not to show any reaction, or her attraction, but Griff had enough experience with women—probably too much—and noticed her flushed skin and the erect nipples pushing against her pajama top. There were more subtle hints, too: her eyes had turned richer and darker, warmer, and she swallowed a few times, as if looking for moisture in her mouth. Her nails also burrowed into the thick material covering her couch and she sucked in a couple of harsh breaths.

But she never, not once, dropped her eyes from his. Stubborn, gorgeous woman.

"Or maybe you just want me close because you're ridiculously attracted to me," Griff murmured, his eyes dropping to her sexy, wide mouth.

"Dream on."

"Shall we put that notion to the test and see who is right?" Griff asked her, lowering his head so that his lips hovered over hers.

"I—"

Griff searched her face to make sure he wasn't reading her wrong—he never forced himself on anyone, ever—but before he could cover her lips with his, Kinga surprised him by grabbing a handful of his sweater and pulling him down. She arched her back and their mouths connected and...

Boom! Magic happened and his world imploded. All those crazy clichés he usually disdained suddenly made sense.

Yeah, this.

Judging by the way her tongue slid into his mouth, she was very into him. Maybe just as much as he was into her.

Damn, he was about to make this very complicated indeed, but he couldn't help himself. He'd been dreaming about doing this for what felt like a lifetime. But complicated was for later. Right now he wanted to take however much Kinga was offering.

Placing his knee on the cushion next to hers, Griff gripped the back of her head and tipped her head up to an angle he preferred. His lips danced along hers and he allowed his tongue to trace the seam of her mouth, coaxing her to open up, to let him in. At the same time, Kinga's hands moved from his clothing to his shoulders, she released a breath and her lips parted beneath his. Testing her response, needing to know if she was on board with where this was going, he pushed his tongue into the tiny gap, waiting for her reaction. Kinga, because she kept surprising him, widened her lips and her tongue tangled with his, as desperate to explore him as he was to discover her.

She was delightful, saucy and spicy, fierce and feisty, and he could kiss her for hours, days. Needing more, Griff hiked up her top, needing to feel her smooth skin under his broad hand. Smooth, soft, fragrant…gorgeous. His fingertips skimmed over her ribs and she released a tiny laugh into his mouth and Griff realized she was ticklish. Keeping his touch firm, he explored her tiny waist, her flat stomach and, leaving her skin, ran his hand down her hip, over her flannel-covered butt.

He fought the urge to pull her top over her head, to taste what he knew would be lovely nipples, to discover the honey between her legs. But, remembering her locks and her sister's concern, he wouldn't push. She'd only granted him permission to kiss her; the next move would be all hers.

As if hearing his thoughts, Kinga stiffened and pulled her mouth off his, pushing her hands against his chest to give her some space between them. Too much space…

But because he was a gentleman, even though few people knew it, Griff bounded to his feet and jammed his hands into the back pockets of his pants. He was sporting a massive erection but figured Kinga was an adult and should know that it was a natural outcome of a scorching hot kiss.

And yeah, thanks to his two-year-plus break from sex, he was rock-hard. And desperate to play. But Kinga's tense face was one big stop sign and he was backing off.

Kinga wrapped her arms around her bent knees and looked up at him with those wide, intense brown eyes. With her just-had-the-hell-kissed-out-of-her lips and flushed cheeks she looked stunning…

Man, he wanted her.

Almost as much as he didn't *want* to want her.

Griff rocked on his heels and looked around the room, wanting something to distract him from the gorgeous woman with her witchy eyes, to make him fight the urge to kiss her again.

The heavy silver photo frame facing the wall caught his eye again and he frowned at his surge of curiosity. Why have a photo if you weren't going to look at it? Who inspired such deep feelings in her that she couldn't bear to look at their image?

Why was he so fascinated by everything to do with her?

Right, he should go, right *now*. This was getting out of control.

But they hadn't touched on business yet.

"Would you like to join me for breakfast tomorrow at the hotel?" he asked. "Around eight?"

Griff saw that Kinga was still trying to get her brain into gear. Then the fogginess in her eyes cleared and she shook her head. "You'll be mobbed and we won't be able to finish a sentence. No, come to my office. I'll send you the directions—" she narrowed her eyes at him "—if you promise you'll read the damn text."

"I read every text you sent, sweetheart. I just stopped responding when you started repeating yourself."

"You didn't respond to any of my most recent ones!"

Griff winced. Hadn't he? He'd meant to, but he'd had his hands full with a colicky mare, a distracted Sian and a rambunctious Sam. The little spare time he'd had, he'd worked on choosing and testing his set list for the ball.

Not wanting to get into another argument, he dropped a kiss on her nose. "Get some sleep, sweetheart. I'll see you in the morning."

"Don't be late. I have a full day and can't wait around for you."

Kinga rubbed her forehead with her fingertips in a gesture Griff was coming to realize displayed her anxiety. He sent her what he hoped was a reassuring smile. "Relax, Kinga, it's all good."

Kinga's huge eyes flew up to collide with his. Color receded from her face and she seemed to shrink in on herself. "Don't say that!"

It's all good?

Why on earth would she object to that? But it was obvious the phrase disturbed her because he heard the pain in her voice, saw it in her eyes.

"I'm sorry?"

Kinga waved his apology away and stood up, wrapping her arms around her waist. "Ignore me, I'm just tired and it's been a very long day."

Yeah, he didn't buy that for a second. Knowing he couldn't push her, Griff started to walk away. He took two steps before stopping. After a short, internal debate around whether to vocalize his thoughts, he spoke. "I know you don't trust me, Kinga, but I won't let you down, I promise."

She didn't know it, but he seldom made promises, and the ones he did make, he always kept.

When he pulled back to look at her, her eyes reflected her skepticism and Griff realized it was going to take more than a sentence or two to get her to believe him.

And he was shocked at how much he wanted her to have faith in him.

Four

Griff looked at himself in the reflective surface of the elevator and picked a piece of lint off his camel-colored jacket. In an effort to be taken seriously by the oh-so-stern Kinga, he'd worn dark blue jeans and a cream cable-knit sweater under the jacket.

He felt overdressed and a little stupid.

Good clothes wouldn't make her trust him… Or trust that he was the performer she was looking for, Griff amended. Despite their fiery kiss last night, a business relationship was the only type of relationship he could have with her. She wasn't, he knew, the type to have one-night stands or flings and he wasn't looking for anything permanent or complicated.

He had, so they said, baggage. A high-stress job, a bad reputation, a family with challenges.

He and Kinga were also, as he reminded himself, work-ing together and her cooperation would ensure whether his comeback was a resounding success or a career-crushing failure.

There were more important things than her mouth under his, his hands on her spectacular body...

But because Griff was always brutally honest with himself, when he kissed her, or touched her, or even laid eyes on her, he tended to forget that salient point.

As much as he wanted to, he wouldn't misbehave today. Today he would show her that he could be professional. They'd talk about the publicity around the ball and how to manage the buzz his return would inevitably create.

He would not think about her spicy taste, her smooth skin...

The elevator doors opened and his phone vibrated. Stepping out, Griff pulled the phone from the inside pocket of his jacket and looked at the screen. He smiled, genuinely pleased to hear from his older half-sister.

Jan was born when his mother was seventeen and, because she was thirteen years older than him and Sian, and was already at college when he and Sian started in the industry, the press didn't know about her. She was his favorite secret, and she and her husband were among a handful of people who knew about Sian's condition and the lengths he'd gone to to protect her from the world.

"I'm about to go into a meeting, sweetheart. Can I call you when I'm done?"

"I'll make this quick," Jan assured him. She went on to explain that she, her husband and kids wanted to take Sam and Sian away with them for a few days and that Eloise would join them after her long weekend.

Jan's husband, Pete, an extremely wealthy, famous CEO, would hire a private jet to ensure their complete privacy.

"Where are you heading?" Griff asked, though he suspected he knew. Jan and Pete, with his blessing, had built a huge mansion on the opposite end of the island he'd purchased years ago, two nautical miles off Key Largo, completely overshadowing the modest bungalow he normally stayed in when he went down there.

It was their second home and they were spending more and more time in the Keys. Because they homeschooled their late-in-life kids, Griff suspected it would soon become their permanent abode. And that was fine by him.

"We might stay longer and Sam and Sian can stay as long as they like. You know how my girls adore having Sam around," Jan added. Jan's daughters, seven and five, considered Sam to be more of a baby brother than their cousin.

He trusted Jan and her levelheaded, down-to-earth husband to help Sian and Sam while Eloise was away. And Eloise would be happy to join them after her break. She loved the island.

And he could stay in Portland...

He told Jan to make the arrangements, told her that he'd pick up the tab for the private jet and said goodbye, feeling a little guilty for feeling relieved that he didn't have to rush back to Kentucky. He'd been given some freedom, a little me-time, and he had no intention of wasting it.

It would give him a chance to, unhurriedly, work out the set list for the ball, to start practicing, to meet with the musicians he wanted for his band.

And to get to know Portland's Prickliest Princess a little better...

He bolted out from behind a pillar in the parking lot, scaring the hell out of her.

Kinga, in the process of opening her car door, let out a

small scream and slapped her hand against her chest, gathering every bit of courage she had to face Mick Pritchard.

"Mick," she said, leaning back against her car, hoping he didn't realize that her legs were shaking and that she was terrified.

You are not eighteen anymore, Kinga, and he wouldn't dare punch you again. Not here, in the Ryder International garage, with cameras everywhere.

"What are you doing here?"

"I thought we needed to chat."

"I thought vicious emails and text messages were more your style," Kinga snapped, her anger chasing away a little of her fear.

Mick slid his hands into the pockets of his expensive coat. He was doing very well for himself. His coat was cashmere, his shoes were designer, as was his suit. But Kinga wasn't impressed and she'd lost all respect for the boy she'd grown up with when he'd backhanded her after Jas's funeral. For that, she'd never forgiven him.

He'd not only blamed her for Jas's death but, by assaulting her, he'd taken away her trust in men, in people generally.

"I wanted to tell you that I am entering politics. I am going to run for mayor of Portland. I plan to run on a law-and-order ticket, making our town safe again type of thing. I have a big press conference announcing the news next month."

Kinga's heart sank. Jesus. Why was life punishing her?

"And you're asking my permission?" Kinga sarcastically asked, knowing her statement was the exact opposite of the truth.

Mick snorted. "As if. No, I want you to get me an audience with Jas's father so that I can explain my intentions. He's not taking my calls and he won't meet with me."

Mick had to be desperate if he was reaching out to her. Kinga narrowed her eyes and crossed her arms over her chest. "That could be because you've used his daughter's death in your company's promotional videos. Why do you want to see him?"

When he didn't answer, a thought crossed Kinga's mind. Her mouth dropped open. "Oh my God, you want him to endorse you!"

Mick didn't look even remotely embarrassed. He simply shrugged. "It's politics, Kinga."

"It's *sick*, Mick! You've spent years capitalizing on her tragic death and you want her father to simply forget that? You son of a bitch!" Kinga shouted, furious beyond belief. "No, I will not pass on your message, but I will warn him about you. Maybe Seth will campaign against you."

Mick's strong hand shot out to grip her forearm and his fingertips dug into her skin. "Be very careful, Kinga."

Kinga, refusing to show her terror, jerked her arm from his grip. "Don't you ever lay hands on me again, Pritchard! I am not that sad, young girl I once was!"

His eyes narrowed and his expression darkened. She recognized that look—she'd seen it before, seconds before he struck her.

"Everything that happens in this garage is filmed and recorded, Pritchard, and if you hit me again, this time I won't hesitate to press charges."

His fist bunched tighter and Kinga held her breath, knowing he was fighting for control, but after a minute, maybe more, his hand relaxed.

"Leave me, and the Garwoods, alone, Mick."

"I stopped listening to you the moment I realized it was your fault Jas died," Mick coldly informed her.

There was no point in arguing. It was, after all, the truth. Knowing she was either going to cry or collapse, Kinga abruptly turned and yanked open the door to her car, sliding into her seat and immediately locking her doors. She hit the start button, slapped the car into Reverse and watched Mick in her rearview mirror as she sped out of the garage.

A half hour later, exhausted and emotional, Kinga pulled her car into one of the three parking spaces outside her home and cursed the weather. She'd yet again left her umbrella at work. Hard raindrops, containing flecks of snow, hit her windshield. She considered the distance between her car and the front door and wondered whether she had the energy to make it to her door.

She was that tired.

She'd fought off a panic attack since leaving the parking garage, and now that she was finally home, she could feel its cold fingers dancing up her throat, squeezing. She knew she was safe, that Mick wouldn't hurt her again but, despite a decade passing, she could still hear the awful sound of his hand connecting with her cheekbone, see the fury on his face. The spittle in the corner of his mouth, the anger in his eyes...

"You stupid bitch! You let her die. She was my everything! I had plans, dammit!"

Kinga leaned her forehead on the steering wheel, her heart rate inching upward. Lifting her hand, her fingers bounced up and down and her throat tightened. It was after eight and she didn't need to experience a panic attack in her car on one of the coldest evenings of the year.

Her first goal was to get inside, but her front door was a hundred miles away. She was short of breath and incapable of movement. Getting there seemed an impossible task. She knew she had to move, but the feeling of impending doom, of sheer terror, wouldn't allow her to open the door or climb out of her car.

Kinga turned her head and looked at her cell phone lying on the passenger seat next to her. She brushed her finger over the screen and saw that her last call was to O'Hare fifteen minutes ago… She'd asked something about the press conference they'd scheduled for tomorrow to formally announce his comeback but couldn't remember what.

Her memory was always spotty when she felt like she was dying. But she did know Tinsley and their best friend, Jules, were out of town and her parents would take more than a half hour to reach her.

She needed someone right now and, somehow and strangely, it felt right for her to call Griff.

He answered almost immediately. "Will you please stop fussing, princess? I've done a million press conferences before."

Kinga swallowed, tried to speak and swallowed again.

"Kinga?" His voice sharpened and she could easily imagine him sitting up, his eyes narrowing. "What's wrong?"

"Can you come?" she asked, her voice thready. "To my apartment?"

"On my way," Griff instantly responded. "Do you need help? Should I call 911?"

"No. I'm fine." Sort of. "I just need some help." *Getting to my front door.*

When he got here, he'd realize she wasn't the strong, always-in-control woman he thought she was. Kinga cursed herself for her impulsive decision to call him. What the hell had she been thinking? He was a business associate, not a friend.

"Look, don't worry, I'm fine. I'll make a plan."

But looking into the dark, she didn't know if she could.

Jas had died in the dark, a short distance from her home. Kinga's head swam…

"Shut up," Griff ordered, his tone harsh. "I'm coming."

The minutes—hours, years—passed and Kinga held the steering wheel in a death grip, finding it increasingly difficult to get air into her lungs, feeling like the car was closing in on her. A short, sharp rap on her door made her jump and she turned to see an indistinct blob standing outside her car. She screamed and fumbled for the button to check whether she'd locked the car, forgetting that she always, always locked her car.

"Dammit, Kinga, it's me, Griff!"

She looked at him through the rain-wet window and it took a minute, maybe more, to recognize his face, hair plastered against his head, his dark green eyes worried and his normally sensual mouth stern.

Griff tapped on the window. "Open the goddamn door, Kinga."

Kinga hit the locks and Griff pulled the door open, and the shock of cold air had her gasping.

The sound of her seat belt releasing sounded like a gunshot and then she felt two warm hands on her face. She stared into Griff's eyes, wishing she could breathe.

"What's wrong with you?"

She just managed to whisper the words. "Panic attack."

"Right, I want you to breathe with me. In for four, hold it…" Kinga listened to the command in his voice, his eyes a lifeline in a topsy-turvy world. "Now blow out in a steady stream. I'm here, sweetheart, I've got you. Right now, all I want you to do is breathe in and out," Griff told her, his gaze warm and sympathetic and his voice oh-so-steady.

"You've stopped taking deep breaths, honey. Come on now. In for four, hold it and release in a long, steady stream."

Kinga concentrated on his words and closed her eyes, sucking in air. She held her breath before releasing it in as long a stream as she could. It took three or four, maybe more, times before she felt her heart rate dropping and her tight chest easing. Kinga placed her hand on Griff's shoulder and she felt his warmth through his leather jacket and the ice in her veins started to dissolve...

A few more minutes passed and eventually, she felt the last tendrils of fear flee, felt like she could breathe properly. As oxygen hit her brain, Kinga started to take in some details. His car was parked in Tinsley's space, the door open and the light on, and it looked like he'd barreled out of the vehicle without locking up, as if he'd rushed to get to her.

He sat on his haunches outside of her car, snow falling on his bare head, but his eyes fixed on her, his expression sympathetic.

"You okay now? Chest and throat loose?"

Kinga nodded. "Yeah." She shivered, feeling the wind whipping around her legs and rustling her short hair. "God, you must be freezing," she stated.

Griff shrugged and stood up. "I've been warmer. Let's get you inside, sweetheart."

The endearment sounded good on his lips, like it belonged there. Kinga looked at the strong, tan hand he held out to her and placed her palm in his, allowing him to help her out of the car. Knowing that her knees tended to be a bit liquid after a panic attack, she held on, not wanting to fall facedown onto the snow-covered pavement.

Debilitating tiredness would soon follow and she hoped to be in her apartment before it struck.

Griff ducked into her car and picked up her bag, snagging her car keys from the ignition. He slammed the car door closed.

"I'll come back and sort out my car and get your laptop," Griff told her, wrapping his arm around her waist. "Have you got your keys?"

"In my coat pocket." She leaned into him, happy for his support, and let out a squeal when he picked her up and cradled her against his broad chest. "Griff, I can walk."

"I'm sure you can, but I'm freezing and would like to get inside before I turn into an icicle." Griff strode across the small patch of lawn and hurried up the steps leading to the front door of her building. He asked her for her code, punched it in on the keypad and used his shoulder to push the door open. Two paces later he was at the door to her apartment and, balancing her on his upraised knee—God, the guy was strong—dug around in her coat pocket with his free hand to pull out her set of keys.

At her direction, he found the right key, turned the knob and walked into her home. Kinga inhaled the warm air and the subtle scent of fresh flowers and beeswax polish. This was her safe place, her sanctuary. She relaxed immediately. Nobody could hurt her here.

Exhaustion washed over her in a steady wave.

She glanced over to her still open door, tasted panic again—Mick's furious face popped up on the screen of her mind—and reminded herself that he wouldn't be foolish enough to follow her home, to push his case. Besides, right now she had her very own, very brawny bodyguard. Not wanting to lose this sense of security, she rested her head against Griff's wet chest and sighed. She'd take being wet above being scared any day of the week.

Kinga felt his lips in her hair before he loosened his grip on her and allowed her feet to drop to the floor. He gently lowered her to sit on the closest sofa and dropped to his haunches again, concerned. "Better? Want some tea or something?"

He ran his hand around the back of his neck and Kinga realized that he was wetter and colder than she'd thought. His jeans were dark with rain, his hair was slicked back and his lips held a tinge of blue. "You should get out of those wet clothes," she suggested, her voice still weak.

His lips quirked. "Are you trying to get me naked, sweetheart?"

His teasing made her smile. "I'm trying to ensure that you don't get hypothermia, O'Hare."

Kinga yawned and she covered her mouth with her hand. Then she yawned again.

"Exhaustion often follows an extreme panic attack. Let's get you to bed."

Kinga wanted to make a joke, say something witty and funny but couldn't muster the mental strength to think of anything. She just wanted to sleep. But the door was open and anyone could walk inside…

"Can you shut the door, hit the locks when you leave?" she asked, and cursed the tremor in her voice. Despite knowing how weak she sounded, she couldn't stop her next sentence. "Will you check, and check again, that I'm locked in?"

Griff's face hardened. "At some point, we're going to have a chat about what's got you so scared, Kinga." Then his expression lightened and Kinga noticed that his eyes were as warm as the hand cradling her cheek was cold. "Would you sleep better if I stayed here?"

She wanted to brush away his offer, tell him she was an independent woman, that she could take care of herself. But her actions tonight completely negated that statement, and she would sleep better knowing he was within shouting distance.

Why was she so comfortable with him?

"Kinga, do you want me to stay?"

She wanted to lie, to tell him to go, but she was too tired to make the effort. "Yes, please."

She'd deal with the consequences of her impulsive decision in the morning. Because, as she knew, every action had consequences.

The next morning, after a night spent in her spare bedroom, Griff used Kinga's espresso machine to deliver a much-needed hit of caffeine. Taking his cup back to the living room, he decided to satisfy his curiosity and picked up the heavy silver frame Kinga had turned to face the wall.

It was a perfectly normal photograph of Kinga—much younger, with long, braided hair—and a dark-eyed, dark-haired girl, both beaming at the camera. They wore beanies and huge smiles, and there was nothing in the photograph to explain why she couldn't look at it.

He was now more curious than he'd been before.

Not good.

Griff heard footsteps on the stairs, replaced the photograph and walked over to the window to pull back the drapes. The weather was continuing its dismal streak. The rain and snow had stopped but the clouds were low in the sky, as if deciding whether to dump more moisture on the already soaked land.

"Morning."

Griff turned to look at Kinga, dressed in black jeans and a black cashmere sweater under a black-and-white houndstooth jacket. Trendy black-and-white sneakers covered her feet. He sighed at her don't-ask-me expression but was unable to get her pale, terrified face out of his mind. He was so used to Kinga's quick mouth and her in-your-face attitude, and seeing her vulnerability last night had shaken him.

What in God's name could've happened to cause his alpha boss girl to have a panic attack? Not for the first, or fiftieth, time he wondered what Kinga was hiding behind her I-can-do-anything-and-be-anything facade?

"You're looking better," Griff told her.

Kinga sent him a wry smile. "I could hardly look any worse."

Griff watched as she made herself coffee, waiting for an explanation he knew wouldn't come. He leaned against the state-of-the-art gas cooker, crossing his legs at the ankles.

After giving her a minute or two to get some caffeine into her system, he spoke again.

"Do you get panic attacks often?"

Her eyes collided with his, and he smiled at the soft expletive she didn't mean for him to hear. Ah, so she'd been intending to fudge her way out of the experience, obviously hoping she could spin a BS story.

"Ah, I—" Kinga pushed her hand through her hair, making the short ends stand up on one side. It was a cute look on her. She wrinkled her nose and when her shoulders slumped, Griff knew she'd given up on the idea of finding a fake explanation for what had happened. "I haven't had one for a few years, thank God." She sipped her coffee, wrapping both hands around the mug.

"What triggers them? Is it a specific event or general anxiety?"

His first memory of Sian having a panic attack was when they were eight and about to do a live segment for a Christmas special. She'd passed out and the producers had rearranged the lineup to put them later in the program. Someone, possibly Finn, had given her something to calm her, and Sian was able to sing.

Looking back, he cursed both Finn and their parents

for pushing them so hard to constantly perform. He'd been able to cope with the pressure but Sian, who was by far the better musician, vocalist and performer, didn't enjoy the limelight. Her biggest dream growing up was to be a normal kid doing normal things.

Griff raised one eyebrow, silently reminding Kinga that she hadn't answered his question about what triggered her panic attacks. Kinga ignored his silent demand and changed the subject. "We need to get moving. Your press conference is in an hour and you still need to change. And shave."

He rubbed his hand over his not-too-heavy stubble.

"And please wear something nice."

Yep, the princess was back. Griff was both sad and relieved. And while a pair of old jeans and a T-shirt sounded great—clothes he felt incredibly comfortable in—he had planned to wear something similar to what he'd worn yesterday, business boring.

It was his first press conference in years and, annoyingly, it would help if he made a good impression.

"Are you nervous?" Kinga asked him, her lovely eyes meeting his. He didn't do morning-after conversations, but he had no problem with Kinga being the first thing he looked at in the morning. He rather liked her face...

And her body.

Recalling her question, he shrugged. He wasn't, not particularly. And especially not if he compared it to the flat-out terror he'd felt when he heard Kinga asking him for help.

And, as he said, he'd done what seemed like a million press conferences before.

But none of them had been this important...

He was, officially, about to launch his comeback and he needed this morning to go well. Or as well as it could.

It was going to be a helluva story and, since it was *his* life and *his* career, Griff figured he was facing a barrage of ugly questions.

Luckily, with Sian being in the Keys, she'd be far away from any reporter wanting to get his sister's reaction to his comeback plans. As per normal, they wouldn't find her. The island's ownership was hidden behind a couple of LLCs and they wouldn't trace her through Jan, who had a different maiden name and married surname than them. Jan was also married to a reclusive Fortune 500 CEO who took his privacy very, very seriously.

Sian and Sam would not be caught up in the press hype. And that was all he cared about.

"They are going to ask a lot of rude and intrusive questions. Don't answer them, just move on," Kinga told him, her expression worried. She glanced at her watch. "We have fifteen minutes or so before we need to leave, so we can do a dry run."

"A what?" he asked, heading back to the coffee machine. He needed, he estimated, a gallon more to feel human.

"Why did you divorce your first wife four months after you married her?" The question was like a bullet, but he saw the curiosity in her eyes.

"Because I was twenty-one and thought I was in love. Greta didn't love me, she just needed to marry to extend her working visa and I was a means to that goal," Griff told her, surprising himself by giving her the unsanitized version.

She had a way of pulling the truth out of him.

"Wrong answer. Rather tell them that you refuse to discuss your private life," Kinga informed him.

"I wasn't answering them, I was satisfying your curiosity," he remarked, before turning back to the machine.

"I'm not curious."

Griff finished making his coffee, and when he faced her again, he raised both his brows, watching as her cheeks colored. The hell she wasn't curious...

"So she got her visa extended and filed for a divorce?"

Griff lifted his cup to hide his smile. "Pretty much."

His ex was now one of the highest-paid actresses in the business, happily married, and hated, as much as he did, any references to their super-brief wedding. He'd forgiven her a long time ago, knowing that his ego and pride had taken a hit but not his heart.

Kinga pulled in a deep breath. Picking up a teaspoon, she held it to her mouth, mimicking holding a microphone. "Has Stan Maxwell forgiven you and Ava? Do you regret kissing your best friend's wife in that New York nightclub?"

Like the rest of the world, Kinga believed his and Ava's excellent acting. If there was one story he deeply regretted manufacturing, the Manhattan club episode would be top of his list. It had all happened so fast, triggered by a reporter who'd continuously hassled his then-publicist for a response to allegations that Sian was both depressed and pregnant.

They needed a massive story to counteract the one the reporter was planning on publishing and, desperate, Griff had sought Stan and Ava's advice. Trusting his two best friends implicitly, he'd explained that his bad boy routine was just a ruse and that Sian was, indeed, suffering from serious mental health issues. And that she was three months pregnant.

They'd immediately asked how they could help, and it was Ava who suggested they anonymously tip off the reporter, that he be the one to catch them cuddling. Ava and Stan's relationship was fantastically secure, and as one of the world's golden couples, they could withstand gossip. The reporter got the scoop, Sian was ignored and Griff became, in the eyes of the world, a class A prick.

He desperately wanted to explain to Kinga that he wasn't the disloyal, marriage-wrecking bastard the press portrayed him to be.

But he couldn't. Nobody could know...

"Back off, darlin'," he quietly suggested.

Kinga snorted, not at all intimidated. "They are going to ask."

In his previous life, when he spoke in that tone of voice, people—including his ex-manager— immediately backed down. Not Kinga. And he liked that about her. He just didn't like her nosiness.

"I can deal with the press." He saw that she was about to argue, and spoke before she could. "Have I pressed you about your panic attacks? Demanded to know who is the dark-haired girl in the silver frame? Asked why you can't bear to look at her?"

Kinga wrinkled her nose, something she tended to do, he realized, when she didn't have an immediate answer or solution.

She sat down and slumped back in her chair. "Fair point. I just don't want you to be caught flat-footed this morning."

Griff hid his smile. It was a decent excuse and he admired her quick mind. But, bored with the interrogation— he was about to do this again in a couple of hours—Griff decided to give her something else to take her mind off business.

And her panic attack.

Walking around the kitchen island, he gathered the material of her thin sweater in his fingers. Wrapping it in his fist, he gently pulled the fabric, silently asking her to stand up. Once on her feet, she inched closer. She might not want to work with him, but she was attracted to him.

As he was to her…

"What are you doing?" Kinga asked as he closed the gap between her mouth and his.

"I'm tired of arguing with you and I'd much rather do this. Wouldn't you?"

When she nodded, he kept his kiss gossamer soft, giving her the choice to take their kiss deeper or not. Only she would know whether she wanted hard and intense or light and lingering, so he didn't push. Kinga placed her hands on his chest and tipped her head to the side, her body taut. He traced the seam of her lips with his tongue, and on a puff of sweet air, her lips parted and invited him to take the kiss deeper.

Pulling her into him, Griff wrapped his arms around her and felt her body liquefy, her tension dissolve. It would be so easy to light that fuse—to take their kiss deeper, to fall into passion—but Griff knew that wasn't what either of them needed.

Sometime in the future, God willing, he'd have her naked and panting, but not this morning. Beneath her prickles and her snark, she was tired and vulnerable and no man with any honor took advantage of that.

And despite what the world thought, honor was still important to him.

Griff eased back with great reluctance, his mouth lifted from hers, and his thumb slid against her bottom lip.

"Let's get moving, Kinga. And we'll pick up this discussion later."

Kinga stepped back and smoothed down her sweater. When her eyes met his, they were, once again, filled with annoyed determination. "We most certainly will. For the record, I don't like your high-handed manner of changing the subject, O'Hare."

Griff smiled at her. "And just for the record, I still want to know why you have panic attacks."

Her mouth opened and snapped closed, and when she remained silent, Griff thought he just might have won this round.

But with someone as intriguing, enigmatic and plain sexy as Kinga, who the hell knew.

Five

Right, well…

That went as well as she'd expected it to.

In the small meeting room adjacent to the conference room where they'd held the press conference to announce Griff's comeback, Kinga sank into a chair, put her elbows on her thighs and stared at the carpet below her feet. She felt like she'd gone ten rounds with a sumo wrestler.

Sitting next to Griff, she'd been asked a few questions about the ball, and how far Ryder International had come in a century, but most of the questions, and *all* of the interest, had been directed at Griff. The room had been fascinated with his return to the limelight.

And despite her telling the press that his private life was off-limits, he'd been bombarded with questions about his past.

"Why did you divorce Greta after four months?"

"Have you racked up anymore DUIs?"

"Stan Maxwell threatened to sue you when pictures of you and his wife kissing in a corner of a notorious New York nightclub were leaked to the press. Did you settle out of court and how much did you have to pay your former best friend?"

"Who is your current girlfriend, Griff? And have you cheated on her yet?"

"Is Sian thinking about making a comeback as well? Where is she? Why haven't we seen her for years?"

The rude, intrusive questions were machine-gun fast and had Kinga feeling weirdly protective, a stupid reaction because Griff was the last person in the world who needed or wanted her protection. Throughout the torture session, she'd worked damn hard to keep her expression bland.

Griff, to his credit, had handled the press with aplomb and good humor. He ignored the rude reporters, repeatedly telling the big crowd that he'd only answer questions about his comeback, his upcoming performance at the Ryder ball, and his future career plans.

They'd persisted, but Griff just handed the offenders hard stares and took the next question. After an hour of watching the reporters pummel Griff, Kinga had called the press conference to an end.

If she felt like she needed a shot of tequila before lying down, then Griff had to feel like he'd been run over by a tank.

Frankly, it had been a brutal twenty-four hours. She always felt drained after a panic attack and she'd had to spend extra time on her makeup earlier to cover the dark stripes under her eyes. Her thoughts kept bouncing from wondering whether Mick would ever leave her be—she'd received another text message from him this morning demanding another meeting—to how sweet Griff had been when she'd called him the night before.

Griff was, reputedly, everything she didn't need in her life: a hard-living bad boy and a self-absorbed celebrity. But she'd still called him. He'd arrived quickly, provided his strength and support and had, to her surprise, stuck around. And, as he'd pointed out, he hadn't peppered her with questions. He'd respected her privacy.

She hadn't respected his.

In her defense, she desperately wanted to understand what drove him, what motivated him, why he acted like an entitled, spoiled superstar.

Because Kinga was starting to suspect that he wasn't as bad as he was reported to be.

She had no evidence to back up her suspicions, but she had a gut-deep feeling that she, and the rest of the world, were missing some crucial information.

The door opened behind her and Kinga turned to see a relaxed-looking Griff walk into the room, followed by...*holy shit*, Stan Maxwell, the front man of one of the world's most famous rock groups, Milestone. His wife, the ex-supermodel turned actress Ava Brandon, was at his side. Ava wore tight, ripped-at-the-knee jeans, Doc Martens boots and a twenty-thousand-dollar designer jacket.

Stan, as was his habit, wore black. Black jeans, black V-neck sweater, black high-tops.

Kinga slowly stood up, her eyes darting from Griff to Stan to Ava and back to Griff. Why were they all here, together? Weren't they supposed to hate each other? Her brain struggled to make sense of their obvious affection for each other as Stan had his hand on Griff's shoulder and Ava's smile reflected both worry and concern.

They were unaware she was in the room. And as Kinga watched, Griff pulled Ava into a hug, wrapping his arm around the model's waist and holding her head against his shoulder. "I can't believe you guys are here. Jesus, this is an unexpected treat, but please, for the love of God, promise me nobody knows you are here."

"We've gotten good at fooling the paparazzi," Stan replied. "We used the back entrance and the staff corridors. We watched the press conference in the limo."

"But what are you doing here?" Griff asked, as Ava stepped away from him to take her husband's hand.

"You didn't think we were going to let you face that rabble for the first time without us being here, if only in the background, giving you moral support, right?" Ava asked, a hand on her slim hip.

Kinga stared at them, trying to wrap her head around the fact that the participants in Griff's most notorious scandal were in Portland, in this room.

"We put out a fake story that we're going to our cabin in Vail so anyone looking for us will look for us there. But honestly, since our wedding and you falling off the face of the earth, the press attention has lessened considerably," Stan stated.

"Thank you for being here," Griff said. "I can't tell you how grateful I am, and how much I appreciate all that you've done—"

"Hi! You must be Kinga," Ava loudly stated, cutting off Griff's words. Kinga couldn't decide if Ava was being rude or if she was trying to stop Griff from continuing his sentence.

Griff whirled around and his eyes widened on seeing her. She saw a hint of panic in his deep green gaze before his expression slid into impassivity. "I thought you'd left, Kinga," Griff said, rubbing the back of his neck. "You said you were heading back to your office."

"I thought I'd take a minute to decompress and this room was handy," Kinga explained. She sent Ava and Stan a quick smile. "I'm Kinga Ryder-White. I handle Ryder International's PR and publicity."

Stan held out his hand to shake Kinga's and introduced his wife. Kinga suppressed her burning questions. Why they were still friends if Griff kissed Stan's wife in a New York nightclub and was then photographed leaving her apartment the next morning? Stan had threatened to sue Griff. Was this some weird ménage à trois? Why did Kinga feel she was missing something big?

She tried to act normal. Well, as normal as one could act when in the presence of two incredibly famous musicians and an actress/model who was as well-known for her climate change activism as she was for her lovely face and gorgeous body.

Griff gestured for them all to sit. "I appreciate you being here," he told his friends, sitting next to Kinga on the two-seater couch, his thigh pressing into hers. "How do you think the press conference went?"

Ava looked at Stan before speaking. "The news that you are returning to work is explosive and everyone will run the story. But with the good comes the bad, and they will dredge up the past."

Kinga turned her head to look at Griff's profile, noticing that his jaw was tight with tension. "For what's it worth, I thought you were wonderful. You were completely professional, and you handled the questions with humor and class," she told him.

Griff smiled, his expression amused. "Thank you. I've been doing this for a long, long time, Kinga." Turning to his friends, he gestured to Kinga. "Kinga has spent the last week dreading this press conference. She was convinced that I'd lose my shit and embarrass her and Ryder International."

"I did not say that!" Kinga vehemently retorted. When

Griff raised his eyebrows in protest, Kinga tossed her hands up in the air.

"You thought it," Griff said, and Kinga heard a note in his voice she couldn't identify. He couldn't be feeling hurt at her lack of faith, could he? No, she was letting her imagination run away from her.

Ava rested her forearms on her thighs and checked her watch. "The car will be here to collect us soon." She looked at Griff. "What are your plans today? Stan and I have meetings in Manhattan later, but we've been invited to Frodo's tonight. Geraint wants to test his new menu on us. We're sneaking in the back door and using the private dining room. Do you want to join us?"

Kinga had grown up wealthy and was used to a certain amount of local fame, but these people were in a league of their own. Frodo's was a multi-Michelin star restaurant in Manhattan and Geraint Du Pont was its lauded, avant-garde chef. Normal people were required to wait eighteen months and to take out a personal loan to eat his creations.

Griff looked at Kinga. "Well?"

Kinga frowned, surprised. "I'm invited?"

"Sure," Ava said, her expression friendly. "But we'd need to leave quite soon if we are to make our meetings. The Gulfstream is waiting at the airport."

Griff looked at her, waiting for her response. She was so tempted, but there was no way she could just blow off the rest of the day to take a jaunt with these superstars. She had a ball to organize and a to-do list as long as her arm to get through. "Uh, thank you, but I really can't."

Ava's smile reflected her disappointment. "Pity, I was looking forward to getting to know you better."

Why? Kinga ran her fingers across her forehead, trying to make sense of what was happening. Griff had had an affair, a one-night stand, a *something* with his best friend's wife. Yet here they were, all acting like the paparazzi hadn't caught him with his mouth on hers or her hand on his butt. Maybe they'd all forgotten?

Ava looked at Griff and then smiled at her husband.

"She has that what-the-hell-is-happening look," she said, unfurling her long body and standing up. Stan followed her to his feet and immediately wrapped his arm around her waist, sending Kinga a sympathetic smile.

Kinga shrugged, following the others to her feet. "I admit, I'm a bit thrown by this dynamic."

Griff glared at his friends before looking at Kinga, his expression impassive. "I'm sorry you can't join us. I think you would've enjoyed Geraint's food."

She was sure she would've too.

"Bring me back a Lombardi's pizza and a slice of cheesecake from Junior's," Kinga joked.

"I'll see you tomorrow, sweetheart," Griff said.

God, her heart melted like an ice cube under a blowtorch every time he called her an endearment in his raspy, sexy voice. "Have fun," Kinga told him, unable to keep her eyes from darting to Stan's big hand on his wife's hip.

Ava stepped forward, took Kinga's hands and placed a kiss on her right cheek, then her left, before holding her own cheek against Kinga's to speak in her ear. "There's always a story under the story, honey. The truth is never simple and seldom found on entertainment websites."

Ava stepped back and smiled at her. "I hope we meet again." Turning to her husband, she held out her hand, which Stan took. "New York, baby?"

"Anywhere with you," Stan said, his smile soft and loving. "But honestly, I think Kinga's idea of Lombardi pizza and New York cheesecake is a far better idea than the bite-size concoctions Geraint serves."

"Monster," Ava told him.

Griff's fingers briefly hooked with Kinga's as he walked past her. "We'll catch up later," he told her.

Kinga nodded and crossed her arms over her jacket, wondering what the hell had just happened.

They weren't just missing something about Griff O'Hare. Kinga suspected they all might be missing *everything*.

That afternoon, Kinga attended a hastily convened meeting between the top management of Ryder International in Callum's private boardroom. They touched on quarterly returns and Ryder's expansion into China and Japan, but most of the attention—Callum's especially—was on the upcoming ball and the other celebrations to mark their hundred years in business.

Kinga was particularly excited about Tinsley's new project: a specialty cocktail competition. Ryder International bars, in the US and overseas, employed specialty mixologists to serve both mundane and unusual cocktails to their guests. The mixologists could enter either as a team or on their own, but they needed to create four new cocktails inspired by four different events over the last one hundred years. There would be regional, national and international winners.

At Tinsley and Kinga's request, Callum increased their centenary celebration budget by another twenty million, which was both surprising and helpful. Possibly because Griff's fee to sing at the ball was astronomical. Nobody else had a problem with Griff or was even remotely worried about him or his antics spoiling their launch event.

Even her anxiety about his performance was rapidly receding...

Now, thinking back on her intense, fast-paced day, Kinga sat on her sofa in her apartment and told herself, yet again, that it didn't matter whether her perception of Griff was changing. The world considered him a vain, self-absorbed bad boy and that was the image she had to work with.

And despite having more confidence in Griff, there was no getting away from the fact that he had failed to show up for performances a few times before.

What if he did that again?

She wanted to believe him when he said he wouldn't let her down but how could she? The best predictor of future behavior was past behavior, so…

She had to protect her event. She could not allow herself to become complacent.

And that meant having a backup plan.

If she had made a backup plan to get Jas home, her friend would still be alive.

Pushing away those dark thoughts, Kinga ran through a list of artists and entertainers she used regularly. As soon as she got Griff's set list, she'd hire a vocalist to be his understudy, ready to step in if anything went wrong.

And she wasn't just overplanning when it came to Griff; she had contingency plans for *everything*. She was splitting the catering between three different companies—so that if one had an issue, the others could step in. She'd hired more bartenders than necessary to ensure great service, knowing that if a few didn't show up to work, the guests' enjoyment wouldn't be compromised. She had a second florist on standby and, on a personal level, she had three ball gowns in case she spilled wine or food on herself.

This ball was being touted as one of the entertainment events of the decade—she would not allow anything or anyone to spoil it.

Kinga heard the beep of a message landing on her

phone and quickly picked it up, relieved that it wasn't a voice mail from Mick again. He'd briefly and insincerely apologized for ambushing her in the parking garage and asked her, again, to intervene on his behalf with Senator Seth Garwood. He'd also, interestingly, asked whether she planned on disclosing his lack of control to the press— she presumed he meant revealing how he'd punched her. He reminded her that if she did, it would be a "he said, she said" situation.

No, she was keeping quiet about that. She didn't need any interest from the media that wasn't directly related to the ball. Besides, she'd never told anyone about Mick's lack of control. Tinsley and her parents would be hurt and furious if they found out.

No, no good would come of saying anything. But Mick didn't need to know that.

Other news of the day was that Callum still hadn't received the results of their family's DNA tests, and he was not happy. Her blue-blooded grandfather was obsessed with the Ryder-White family tree and their reputation as one of the state's first families. Kinga knew he was itching to discover other links to some of the area's, and America's, founding families.

Her father and mother, it had to be noted, were also surprisingly invested in the outcome. Why did they suddenly seem to care about DNA tests and who was related to whom?

God, she didn't know if she could cope if they started banging on about blood and the importance of the family tree. Callum's obsession with legacy was more than enough. Neither she nor Tins cared whether Mr. X arrived during the second or third settlement of the area, or whose daughter married whose son. It was bloody ages ago, and her grandfather's obsession with the Ryder-White line, when they had so much to achieve, was just silly, in her opinion.

She was busier than most of her family, and both Mick Pritchard and Griff O'Hare were giving her indigestion for wildly different reasons.

Kinga scowled. Griff O'Hare was an enigma and she wasn't fond of puzzles. She liked her men straightforward and, well, let's be frank, a little pliable. Beta men were a fire suit, a measure of protection, because she knew she'd never fall in love with a man she could boss around.

She didn't like change or risk or danger, and Griff O'Hare, damn him, was all three wrapped up in one luscious package.

He was a man whose kisses set her soul on fire and who made her feel out of control.

After what happened with Jas, control was paramount. Kinga would never risk loving and losing someone again.

Like her best friend, Griff was a charismatic, pull-to-a-flame creature. She had to be on guard around him. Her attraction to Griff, to the wildness she sensed in him, was dangerous. If she lowered her guard, she could make a mistake that could have enormous consequences.

To her ball, to her reputation and, if she weren't very, very careful, her heart.

So, no more kissing, touching or wondering what he looked like under his clothes.

Kinga yawned and closed the lid to her laptop. It was way after midnight and she should climb the stairs and go to bed. She had a long day tomorrow. With O'Hare invading her dreams and providing her with some X-rated fantasies, sleep wasn't something she was getting a lot of lately.

Kinga placed her laptop on her coffee table, switched off the table lamp and stood up. She padded over to the door to check that all four locks were engaged—she knew they were locked but she wouldn't sleep unless she'd checked. About to turn to walk up the stairs, she heard a sharp rap on her front door. With her heart trying to escape through her throat, she stood statue-still, wondering who could be banging on her door at—she glanced at her watch—twelve thirty in the morning.

Another knock and Kinga heard Griff's soft voice calling her name. Kinga bent over, placed her hands on her thighs and breathed deeply, trying to push the panic away. God, maybe she should've stayed longer in trauma counseling.

Pulling in a deep breath, and telling her heart to calm the hell down, Kinga checked her peephole and sighed. Even distorted, Griff looked lovely. She flipped open her locks, pulled the door ajar and immediately inhaled the divine scent of garlic, melted cheese, herbs and fresh tomato.

Griff held a pizza box in his hand and a cake box in the other, both bearing the logo of the famous restaurants in New York.

He'd heard her request and had made the effort to fulfill it.

Holy crap, who was this man?

Kinga opened the door and took her time examining Griff. He wore faded blue jeans and a light blue open-neck shirt. His buttoned waistcoat was a deep brown and his jacket a rich cream. Classic, brown Oxford leather shoes covered his feet. His coat and scarf lay on the wooden bench pushed up against the outer wall of her apartment.

He looked amazing, as yummy as the pizza smelled.

Kinga lifted her eyes to his face and her stomach lurched at the now-familiar half smile she saw on his face.

"You brought me pizza and cheesecake," Kinga stated.

She reached for the pizza box, suddenly conscious of how hungry she was. "Thank you. That's sweet… Gimme."

Griff flashed *that* smile, the one that revealed those amazing dimples and, after a bit of tugging, allowed her to take the flat box from his hands. Kinga turned and walked back into her apartment, flipping open the lid. In a well-practiced move, she held the box with one hand, lifted and folded a slice of pizza, and had the slice in her mouth before she reached the sofa.

Sinking to sit cross-legged on her coffee table—she didn't want the greasy pizza anywhere near her silk sofa cushions—she closed her eyes as the intense flavors hit her tongue.

If there was no New York–style pizza in heaven, she wasn't going.

Kinga heard Griff close her door, heard the locks turning and then saw him cross the room to sit on the sofa in front of her. He placed the box of cheesecake on the table and tried to tug the pizza box from her tight grip.

"You dined at Frodo's. You shouldn't be hungry."

Griff scoffed at that statement. "Geraint's portions are bite-size and, while stunning, were just enough to satisfy an overweight flea." He tugged at the box again. "Have a heart, Ryder-White, my stomach is eating itself."

Kinga released her grip on the box and Griff helped himself. Like her, he folded his pizza in half and took a huge bite, demolishing half the slice. Without talking, Kinga and Griff steadily made their way through the bulk of the pie, only talking to murmur their approval of their late-night treat.

There were two slices left in the box and Kinga picked up a napkin to wipe her greasy hands. She still wanted cheesecake, but was rapidly running out of room. Griff, big and bold, didn't have that problem. She leaned back on her hands and dropped her legs off the coffee table, her knees on the inside of Griff's. She felt sated and a little sleepy, and her eyes wandered over Griff, taking in his strong neck, the stubble on his cheeks, the intensity of his eyes. He had a tiny drop of tomato sauce on his lovely, pale blue shirt and Kinga used her index finger to scoop up the drop before it stained.

Except that the stain was dry.

She frowned and sat up straight, her eyes narrowing. "Mine wasn't the first pizza you ate tonight, was it, O'Hare?"

"I have no idea what you are talking about." Griff's innocent look didn't fool her for a second.

Kinga leaned forward and bent to the side to look in the direction of his ass.

"What are you doing?" Griff asked, puzzled.

"Checking to see if your pants are on fire," Kinga retorted. "Mmm, let me guess. While you were at Frodo's, you and Stan sent a minion to Lombardi's to order a couple of pies. One or two of which you ate on the plane on the way home. Or in the taxi on the way to the airport."

Griff grinned at her. "Busted."

"And then you ate half of mine!" Kinga pointed at the box, struggling to keep from smiling. "You jerk!"

Griff popped the last bite of his slice into his mouth and when he swallowed, he shrugged and smiled at her. "At least I brought you a whole pizza. I was tempted to eat some of it on the way over here."

"Lucky for you that you didn't," Kinga tartly responded.

"I could've not brought you any at all," Griff pointed out, that sexy smile still on his face.

It really was a sweet gesture. Had she thanked him properly? And thank him she should. Kinga leaned forward and touched her lips to his in a brief kiss. She placed her fingertips on his strong jaw before pulling back. "Thank you for the pizza," she softly told him. "It was a very nice of you to think of me."

"Even if I did eat most of it?" Griff asked, his voice raspier than normal.

"Even so," Kinga said before tapping her fingers against that sexy stubble. "But the cheesecake is mine."

Griff captured her fingers in his and gently, so very gently, kissed the tips. "Bet I could persuade you to share."

"Bet you couldn't."

This was, after all, Junior's cheesecake. She might not be able to finish a whole pizza pie, but she could scarf down an entire cheesecake with no problems at all. It was her superpower.

Griff's eyes darkened to intense green, the color of Maine woods after a hard rain. Kinga felt her throat tighten and her nipples harden. She was old enough, experienced enough to know that he was contemplating eating her sweet treat in a very nonconventional way.

It surprised her to realize she didn't have the slightest objection to combining food and pleasure...

Oh, there were a million reasons why sleeping with Griff was a mistake but, by all things holy, she couldn't remember one. The ache between her legs needed to be assuaged; her skin craved his touch. Her mouth needed his on hers—immediately—and her hand itched to strip those beautiful clothes from his stunning, masculine body.

Even her mind, normally so clear-thinking, was silent.

"Tell me what you are contemplating, Kinga," Griff asked her, scooting forward and wrapping his big hands around her thighs, just above her knees.

"I'm thinking that you would like to lick cheesecake

off me," Kinga whispered, surprised by her low, raspy phone-sex voice.

"You'd be right," Griff replied. "I've been having cheesecake-inappropriate thoughts since boarding the damn plane."

Feeling like she was operating outside of herself, Kinga flipped open the lid of the cheesecake box and, using her finger, scooped up a blob of filling and slowly sucked it off her finger. Griff's eyes followed her actions and Kinga dropped her gaze to see his erection tenting his pants.

Griff was a big man, everywhere.

"My turn," Griff said, echoing her actions. He smeared some filling down her neck and took his time licking her clean. Kinga heard someone's hard breathing, realized it was hers, and shuddered. She'd only sucked her finger and felt his lips on her neck, she shouldn't be this turned on...

Yet she was. And she had no intention of stopping...

Griff snapped off a corner of cheesecake, popped it into his mouth and then kissed her, deeply and with complete confidence. A million taste bombs exploded on her tongue. The tart tang of the cheesecake, a hit of sweetness, Griff himself.

As their tongues danced and dueled, Kinga went to work on his clothes, of which there were too many. She pushed his jacket off his shoulders, undid the buttons to his waistcoat and pushed both garments down his arms and flung them away. Under his thin cotton shirt she could feel his hot skin and, not wanting to waste time fiddling with buttons, she yanked it out of his jeans and pulled it over his head, exposing his gorgeously hard, tanned, muscular chest to her hands, eyes and mouth. Pulling back, she looked down to see a light smattering of hair, a darker trail snaking over his ladder-like stomach to disappear under the band of his jeans.

His hands were under her jersey, confident fingers exploring her breasts and stomach and, while she loved his touch, it was more important to trace the ball of his muscled shoulder with her tongue, to smear cheesecake across a flat nipple and lick it off, to hear him shudder and feel him squirm.

This hot, sexy, alpha man was completely under her spell and Kinga felt powerful, connected to the source of ancient, feminine wisdom and strength.

She was never the aggressor in sex, and rarely allowed her dates to go this far, but with Griff, she felt safe and… free. Free to explore, to be the initiator. He was strong enough, confident in his masculinity to allow her to take the lead…

Kinga stood up, pushed the coffee table away and put the cheesecake box on the floor, in easy reach. Kneeling between Griff's legs, she placed a palm on his chest and forced him to lean back. He watched her through hooded eyes as she tackled his soft leather belt and then the buttons on his jeans.

"You seem to be doing all the work, baby," he murmured, his hand cupping her cheek.

Kinga sent him a cheeky smile before placing her palm on his thick, steel-hard cock. "Do I look like I have a problem with that?"

"No," Griff replied, lifting his hips to push into her hand. "I love the way you touch me, Kinga."

His cotton underwear was a barrier, so Kinga pulled down his boxer briefs and there he was, six or seven inches of masculine glory. Dipping her head, she blew against his shaft, inhaling his fresh, clean smell. After nuzzling him and teasing him with eager fingers, she fumbled for the cheesecake box and scooped up a little filling, creating a cream-colored strip down the center of his shaft.

"I certainly hope you're going to lick that off," Griff muttered.

Kinga looked up at him, her lips quirking when she saw his forearm across his eyes, big biceps bulging. His breathing was shallow and the cords in his neck tightened.

Oh, yeah, she was so in control here. She liked it. Of course she did, control was her thing...

But she'd never exerted control in this particular way. Up until now, fellatio wasn't in her box of sexual tricks. Oral sex was so very intimate, more so than regular sex, and she'd never hit that level of comfort before...

Strange that she wanted to share this with Griff, that he was the man who made her feel so at ease...

Griff, gorgeous and hot, made her act differently. Later, when her brain returned to normal, she'd work out what that meant. And how to protect herself. But right now, all she wanted was to taste him. Using her tongue, Kinga licked off the filling, surprised at how hot he was, how hard. She'd heard the expression, velvet over steel, and while it was a cliché, it was a perfect description for his lovely erection.

Her hand enveloped him and she licked around the tip before taking him into her mouth...

"That's it, no more," Griff muttered, launching himself up. Using his strength, and he had lots of it, he lifted Kinga to her feet, pulled down her yoga pants and ordered her to take off her thin jersey.

Still trying to get her bearings, she hesitated and looked down, her eyes slamming into Griff's. All pretense of teasing and fun was gone—he was now a man on a mission. Hopefully that mission was to make her scream...

Then, as she stared at him, his eyes softened and his hands came to rest on her hips, his thumbs drawing patterns on her skin. "Do you want this, Kinga? Do you want me? Because if you want to stop, this is a good time."

Did she want to stop? *No*.

Should she? *Hell, yes*.

But she knew she wouldn't. She wanted to know what making love with Griff was like. If she walked away now, she'd regret it forever.

Griff must've seen something on her face—eagerness? consent?—because his mouth curled up into that sexy smile-smirk. "Good, because we haven't finished eating the cheesecake."

Kinga looked down at the mangled cheesecake and smiled. "No, we haven't, have we?"

Griff's expression turned serious again. "Does that mean I can make love to you?"

Kinga didn't hesitate. She just nodded before lowering her head to brush her mouth across his. "Yes. Let's do a threesome…you, me and the cheesecake."

His laughter created a deep warmth inside her and she couldn't help her long sigh as he undid the front clasp of her bra and gently pulled the cups aside. The heat of his mouth tugging on her nipple raised her temperature further and she clasped her hand to the back of his head, arching her back as he pleasured her.

He lifted his head to speak, his expression rueful. "I need you, Kinga, but I'm not carrying any condoms. Got any upstairs?"

That was easy to answer. "No."

Disappointment flashed in his eyes, across his face. She couldn't bear the thought of stopping now, not knowing what making love to him would be like. She needed to know him. "But, if you can promise me you're clean, I am on the pill."

He placed his hand on his chest and nodded. "I am, I promise."

She swallowed, suddenly a little shy. All she could do was nod.

Griff didn't hesitate, taking her mouth while dropping his jeans and underwear. He slid his hands between her legs, his thumb brushing her most sensitive area. Pulling back to look at her, he lifted her leg, held it across his hip and nudged her opening with his cock, sliding inside her.

She gasped, entranced by the look in his eyes and the wonder on his face. She'd never had a man look at her like that, ever...a combination of heat and wonder and pleasure and satisfaction. Like she was all his birthdays and Christmases rolled into one.

Being the object of such intense fascination sent tingles up her spine, and she felt that lift of the wave, the need to soar, then crash.

Kinga could feel Griff's tension, heard his groan and then he spun her around to sit her on the back of the couch, lifting her legs. It was instinctive to wind her legs around his waist, to arch her hips into his and with one deep thrust, he hit a spot that sent her skyward before exploding into a Catherine wheel of sparkles and sensation.

She heard his shout, felt his shudder but her world was still whirling and spinning. This was good sex, no, this was spectacular sex.

This was a mind-blowing, soul changing, impulsive coupling that could, if she wasn't very, very smart, shake the foundations of her world.

And, in doing so, could upend the stable, controlled life she worked so hard to create.

Griff O'Hare was a game changer but she couldn't

let him change her. As she'd realized earlier, he was risk and danger.

Her arms wrapped around his neck, Kinga silently prayed to find a way to protect herself.

Six

Penelope

Penelope looked down at her six-carat diamond engagement ring, surrounded by emeralds from ancient Ceylon, now Sri Lanka, passed down through the Ryder-White clan to the wife of the oldest son. She was the fifth—or was it the sixth?—Ryder-White wife to wear the magnificent and irreplaceable jewel.

Like so much else about her life, she both loved and hated it. Loved that the jewel was rare and stunningly expensive, hated it because it was another stupid Ryder-White tradition and neither of her daughters would one day wear the ring. Her father-in-law had made it clear that it was on loan to her.

Bloody Callum.

Through force of will, Penelope kept her spine steel-rod straight, her clasped hands resting on the cheap vinyl table in a diner on the west side of town. She'd refused coffee, asked for water, and pushed away the menu with one finger, the tip of which was perfectly painted in bright fuchsia.

This wasn't her usual milieu. She didn't know how to relate to blue-collar folk but this meeting required anonymity and discretion. Nobody would expect Penelope Ryder-White, society wife and fundraising maven, to frequent this slightly grubby, riotously busy truck stop on the edge of town.

Penelope removed her designer sunglasses, carefully folded them and tapped the edge of the frame against the table. She'd been waiting for five minutes already and her contact was late. She abhorred tardiness and would wait for, precisely, another five and then she would leave. And then she'd find another private investigator, someone who could, at the very least, be punctual.

Finding an investigator wasn't hard; finding one who could give her quick results was trickier. Callum was becoming increasingly difficult. Things were changing and she needed information to anticipate and head off trouble.

A middle-aged, curvy woman holding a coffee cup dropped onto the bench seat opposite her and shoved her own, cheap sunglasses into bright red hair. With her deep green eyes, freckles, a wide mouth and lack of makeup, she looked like any other suburban housewife.

Penelope raised her thin eyebrows in displeasure. "Excuse me, that seat is taken."

Amusement flashed in her eyes. "Ms. Ryder-White, I'm KJ Holden."

She was KJ Holden, reputed to be one of the best investigators in the city? This woman was a whiz at tracking down missing people and family members?

She didn't think so.

"You?" Penelope demanded.

With an annoyed sigh, KJ lifted her bottom and pulled a thin wallet from the back of her pants. After flipping it open, KJ eased a card from a slot and pushed it across the table. The card told Penelope that she was a registered PI and bail bonds agent.

Right, so much for assumptions. "You must get that a lot," Penelope said. It was as close as she could come to an apology. People of her ilk and wealth weren't in the habit of dropping *sorrys* like snowballs.

"Normally people are politer," KJ said on a false smile.

She was feisty, too. Penelope rather liked that. Her daughters were feisty and fierce and she liked that they were strong and independent women. Like Callum, Pen looked down on pacifists and suck-ups. Her husband was, unfortunately, both.

"I'm not going to be able to help you if you don't tell me what the problem is, Ms. Ryder-White."

Penelope tucked her hair behind her ears and fiddled with the diamond stud in her ear. "I understand that you have a good reputation for finding the missing, but also for making connections between people and companies."

"I do," KJ replied. Her words weren't a boast but a statement of fact.

"Did you ever work on the Jas Garwood case?" Penelope asked, curious. Jas's hit-and-run death had turned Kinga into a tightly controlled, fearful adult.

KJ shook her head. "I specialize in looking for the missing. However, I know the detective working the cold case and there are no leads on the driver of the vehicle. They've chased down everything, I don't think there's anything to be found." KJ tipped her head to the side. "Your daughter was her best friend, right?"

Penelope nodded. "Since kindergarten. Jas all but grew

up in our house and the Garwoods consider Kinga their second daughter."

"I'm very sorry," KJ said. She tapped her finger against her coffee cup and wrinkled her nose.

Pushing her coffee cup away, she leaned back in her seat and met Penelope's gaze. Her face and body might fool people into thinking she was a harried mom, but her eyes had seen trouble and were a hundred years old. Those eyes reassured Penelope that this woman could get the job done.

"What can I do for you, Ms. Ryder-White?"

Ah, could KJ give Penelope's father-in-law a personality transplant? But this woman was a PI, not a fairy godmother with a wand.

Penelope bit her bottom lip, unsure if she should proceed. Would she be opening up Pandora's box? Would hiring a PI make everything better or worse? She didn't know…

But living on eggshells was driving her insane.

"Ms.—"

"Give me a minute," Penelope snapped. She just needed some time to *think*.

For what felt like forever, she'd been waiting to hear from the son she'd given up for adoption thirty five years ago. Once he turned eighteen, she'd expected a phone call asking for an explanation, asking who his father was. It was a long time to wait…

And a long time to worry about whether her youthful, scandalous affair would come to light.

She and her lover had been guests at a beach house in the Hamptons. She'd been intrigued by the much older man, flattered. She'd felt sophisticated, so very grown-up. He'd been stunningly good-looking, funny and, as a shy girl with overprotective parents, she'd been easily charmed out of her clothes. But on leaving the Hamptons, he'd ghosted her. She'd never felt so scared, so alone in her life. Like the Ryder-Whites, her family were East Coast blue bloods…rich, wealthy, stunningly *correct*. Girls from her social standing didn't get pregnant. Appearances had to be maintained.

That hadn't changed in three-plus decades. Appearances were still everything.

Gathering all her courage, she'd told her parents she was pregnant, clever enough to know that she could never name the father of her unborn child. As she expected, they assumed she'd had an affair with the pool boy or the gardener, someone much lower down the social ladder. She didn't bother to correct them.

After they stopped shouting, they flew into action.

Tickets to England were bought, an apartment in London rented. Numb, sick, sad and overwhelmed, she allowed them to contact the Knightsbridge adoption agency, met with the officials. Her parents wanted a completely closed adoption. She refused to sign any papers until she had their agreement that her son, should he wish to do so, could contact her when he was an adult. She lived in anticipation—and dread—of receiving a call, a letter, an email… something.

She'd heard nothing.

That baby would turn thirty-five soon, in less than a month.

Eighteen months after leaving London, she ran into her lover and during a furious argument, told him she'd given his son up for adoption. She'd never, before or since, seen anyone that angry. He'd demanded to know where the baby was, vowed to track him down. She tried to explain that the adoption was completed, that he had no chance of getting the baby back but he, being who he was, refused to accept that. The best she could do was give him the name of the adoption agency in London.

That was the last time she saw him and she had no idea what plans he put in place, what measures he'd taken after that to find his son. Not knowing almost drove her mad.

And why hadn't her son reached out? Wasn't he curious about the circumstances of his birth? Did he know and was just ignoring her? Had he chosen not to find out? And if so, why?

She couldn't live with uncertainty anymore, she had to find him, and when she did, she needed a private investigator who could do a deep dive into his life. Was he the type to exploit his connection to the famous family she was a part of? If yes, she needed to mitigate the fallout.

She never wondered whether he'd had a good life and a decent education, as the adoption agency they used only dealt with the extremely wealthy. And she tried not to think about whether he was happy and loved. She hoped he was, but since she couldn't do anything to change his circumstances, she always pushed those fears away. What good did it do to worry about something she couldn't change?

But she couldn't help wondering about him, who he was. Was he married or did he have kids? Was she a *grandmother*? What did he do for a job? Was he healthy? Did he look like his birth father or her?

Penelope rubbed her forehead and rolled her shoulders. Those questions, like a million more, were unproductive and useless. Unless he got in touch with her—and with every year that passed that possibility became more remote—she'd never know.

But she couldn't stop thinking about possible connections…and the consequences of her youthful actions. Penelope believed in having advance warning, a backup plan. And yes, if she could swing it so that she came out with her reputation intact—keeping her secrets—that would be a huge win.

"I need you to find a child I gave up for adoption a long time ago," Penelope told KJ, pushing the paper across the table.

She ignored the PI's raised eyebrows and the surprise flashing in her eyes. Yes, she'd had a baby when she was still a teenager, many had and many would. "It was a closed adoption, so I have no information on him."

KJ read the document and when she lifted her eyes to Penelope's again, she looked skeptical. "That might be difficult, especially since this adoption agency is based out of London. What's the deadline?"

"Yesterday."

"Of course it is," KJ said, releasing a heavy sigh.

Penelope was done with this conversation, with wading around in the muck of her past, and with this dreadful diner. "I've written down everything I know about him and the circumstances of his birth. Do not bother to contact me looking for more information. There isn't any." Penelope tapped the table with her index finger. "Find him, and I will pay you triple your rate with a big bonus."

KJ picked up the paper, read through the scant information again and raised her eyebrows. "Are you sure you want to kick over this rock, Mrs. Ryder-White?"

Penelope narrowed her eyes. "I wouldn't be meeting you here if I wasn't."

"I make a point of reminding my clients that the truth doesn't always set them free," KJ told her, flicking the paper with her thumbnail.

But secrets could also bury you alive, Penelope thought, before ending the meeting.

Kinga followed Studio Portland's manager down a wide hallway and thanked him when he opened the door to a vast studio space and gestured for her to enter. Stepping inside the huge room, she took in the action: scruffy band members milling about on the full stage, others setting up equipment, someone banging away on a set of drums.

Not seeing Griff, she turned in a full circle, observing the wooden area in front of the stage for dancers, the natural lighting flooding in from the bank of large rectangular windows to her left. She eventually found Griff sitting on a couch at the back of the room, a writing pad on his knee and a sexy pair of wire-framed glasses on his gorgeous face.

Kinga leaned her shoulder into the wall, taking a moment to study the man she'd slept with a week before. She hadn't seen him since he left her apartment very early the next morning, slipping out of her bed with a kiss on her forehead and zero explanations. They'd spent a crazy, wild, hot night together—God, it had been the best sex of her life—but she hadn't wanted any morning-after awkwardness. Neither had she wanted to discuss how they were supposed to act going forward.

He'd left Portland and this morning she'd received a message informing her he was back. She tapped her fingers against her heart, feeling both excited to see him and confused about how to act. While he was away—she had no idea where he'd gone, and refused to ask—they'd exchanged many work-related text messages, and if she could carry on having a text-based relationship with him until the ball, she would. It was so much cleaner, easier.

Safer.

If they kept their distance, she could pretend he was just another artist—one of the many she'd dealt with over the years—and not someone who rocked her sexual world.

Kinga lifted her fingertips to her forehead, wishing she could get his beautiful body, and the way he made hers sing, out of her mind. She hadn't had a decent night's sleep since he'd spent the night in her bed. Despite washing her linens and her towels, she could still, strangely, smell his citrus cologne, taste cheesecake on her tongue and hear the deep rumble of his voice. In her dreams, he often made love to her. Frustratingly, her subconscious always took her to the brink before waking her up. She was horny, tired and deeply frustrated.

Not that she'd ever let him know that.

He was such a contradiction, Kinga thought, happy to watch him. He had a rock star vibe, completely confident and effortlessly stylish, but still managing to exude an alpha male, don't-screw-with-me attitude. He was charming and had a wicked sense of humor, but below the surface, she sensed dark and turbulent waters. Kinga suspected he had a complicated backstory, depths that had never been explored, feelings and thoughts that went unuttered.

There was Griff O'Hare, the wild musician, stupendously talented, and there was the real Griff, private and intense and so very…real. She could dismiss and ignore the artist, but the man behind the facade fascinated her.

Like the rest of the world, Kinga wanted to know why he acted out, what motivated his bad boy behavior, why he'd given up music and performing to hibernate on his ranch for a couple of years. She wanted to know about his family—never discussed by him—and she wanted to know whether he'd ever thought about changing careers. Was he where he wanted to be? Was he living the life he wanted?

Was she?

Good question. Kinga stared down at the toes of her spiky-heeled, thigh-high boots. Callum had carved out a space for her and Tinsley at Ryder International, but despite her MBA, her two degrees and years in the business, Kinga knew neither she nor Tinsley would ever be promoted into the CEO position. Neither, sadly, would her dad.

She adored her father, but James was too soft to make the hard decisions a multinational company needed. Someone who operated at that level needed to be focused, unemotional, fiercely intelligent and, to an extent, ruthless.

Her father was intelligent but emotional, and unlike Callum, James didn't have a ruthless bone in his body.

Years ago, after leaving college, Kinga had campaigned hard to get her grandfather to consider her as his successor but he'd either brushed her off or laughed at her ambitions. She was a woman and, as such, lacked the "balls" the job needed—his expression. Her ego had been hurt and her pride scorched, but when she pushed both away, she realized that she didn't really want the responsibility or the stress of leading Ryder International.

She didn't want to end up old and brittle, a workaholic, putting profits above people. Cold, disengaged, soulless.

She didn't, in other words, want to be like Callum.

Kinga felt her phone vibrate and looked at the screen, smiling when she saw her sister's number. "Hey."

"Why did you support Callum's decision to appoint Cody Craigmyle's company to co-create and manage the cocktail competition?"

Kinga winced at the venom in her sister's voice. "Because his quote was very competitive, he has experience in running international events, does fantastic work and has never, *ever* let us down."

Tinsley didn't respond, so Kinga spoke again. "He's also someone we've known most of our lives and we trust him."

"*You* trust him," Tinsley muttered.

Kinga shook her head. Even as teenagers, Tinsley and Cody had been combative, but since her divorce from Cody's younger brother, JT, their animosity had ratcheted way up. Before marrying, Tinsley and JT had been an item through high school and into college; the Ryder-Whites and the Craigmyles were close friends and trusted business associates. And best of all, Callum had approved of and promoted the marriage. Kinga had thought that JT and Tinsley had a good chance of making it over the long term.

They hadn't. Now Tinsley was single again, her ex was living in Hong Kong and had remarried and—pouring peroxide onto her torn-up heart because Tinsley had begged him to start a family—had a baby on the way.

Tinsley's marriage was over and she never spoke to JT anymore. Tinsley and Cody, however, would not stop arguing. Kinga wondered if Tinsley was taking out her hurt and anger over the divorce on Cody. But she wasn't brave enough to suggest that to Tinsley. Kinga just wished the two would stop bickering or, if that was impossible, to leave her out of it.

They exhausted her.

"The contracts have been signed and you are overseeing the mixology competition, so you're going to have to work with him," Kinga told her sister.

"I don't want to," Tinsley said, sounding like the sulky five-year-old she'd once been.

"Deal with it, babe," Kinga told her before disconnecting the call. Shoving her phone back in her leather tote bag, she looked up to see Griff looking at her from his seat on the couch, that sexy smirk on his face.

Kinga walked over to him, conscious of the heat in his eyes. She'd pulled on thick black tights and a gray turtleneck sweater dress that ended six inches above her boots and Griff seemed fascinated by the space between her hem and her boots.

"Hi," he said, standing up as she approached him. To her surprise, he placed his hand on her forearm and bent his head to drop a kiss on her temple. "How are you? You're looking tired."

There was genuine concern in his voice and interest in his eyes and because of both, Kinga answered him honestly. "I *am* tired."

"Working like a demon?" Griff said, gesturing for her to sit next to him on the leather sofa.

She couldn't tell him that most of her exhaustion was due to her vivid sex dreams, so Kinga just sat down and crossed her legs. She looked toward the stage, where the musicians were gathering, laughing and joking.

Kinga gestured to the stage. "I see you have a band."

Griff sat down next to her and rested his forearms on his thighs, turning his head to look at her. "Yeah, most of the musicians I like to work with were available, thank God. The backup singers are new to me but they have experience."

Kinga looked at the notepad he'd tossed on the table, saw the pages covered in his chicken scratch and what she thought might be lyrics.

Despite not wanting to invade his privacy, she nodded to the writing pad before looking away. "Are you writing again?"

Griff's sigh was long and loud. "Mmm. I've been thinking about releasing an album of my compositions."

Kinga swiveled on the couch to face him. "That's fantastic!"

Griff grimaced. "It might be, if I knew if the songs were any good."

It was so strange to hear the usually confident man sound so uncertain. "I'm sure they are great, Griff. I mean, the last album you released went platinum."

"That was a while ago, Kinga," Griff responded, looking troubled. "And I had a cowriter." He placed his hand on the notepad. "This is all me…"

"I can't imagine how hard it must be to put your creations out in the world," she mused. "I suppose it must be like having a baby and putting his picture on social media and asking the world to comment on whether he's ugly or not."

Griff stared at her for a long time, his surprised expression eventually turning to amusement. "That's exactly what it feels like. I couldn't put it better myself." Griff took his glasses off and put them into the top pocket of his untucked button-down. Today's jeans were faded and thin, authentically aged, and he wore trendy, expensive sneakers on his feet. His hair was all over the place, probably because he'd spent the morning running his hands through it.

"How are your rehearsals going?" Kinga asked him.

"Good, mostly. I'm a bit rusty," Griff admitted. "It should go better now that I've finalized the set list."

"Will my grandfather approve?" Kinga asked him, knowing that Callum had very definite ideas on what music he wanted Griff to perform.

"I've gone for jazz and classic standards, very similar to a concert I did in London. But I've tossed in a couple of modern songs to keep the younger crowd happy."

Kinga twisted her lips. "I should warn you that my grandfather is planning to watch some of your rehearsals."

"That's not going to happen," Griff told her, his expression implacable. "Nobody watches me rehearse. Nobody but the band, dancers and crew are allowed into my practice studio."

"I'm here," Kinga pointed out.

"Not for long," Griff told her on a smile. He checked his watch, which was high-end and overly complicated. "I'm about to kick you out—the session starts in five minutes."

Kinga pouted and fluttered her eyelashes at him. "Just a few songs, please? I'll be as quiet as a church mouse."

Griff squinted at her. "Mmm. One song and then you leave."

Kinga bounced up and down, thoroughly excited. But if she only had five minutes, she needed to discuss business with him. Pulling her tablet from her bag, she powered it up before looking at Griff again. "Uh, a couple of quick questions. I've managed to book you onto a hugely popular morning talk show next week to discuss your comeback and the ball."

Griff looked like he'd rather be hanged, drawn and quartered. "The least favorite aspect of my work."

"Interviews are a necessary evil. So, what questions are off-limits? Same as for the press?" Kinga asked. She needed to produce a publicity pack for the talk shows and included in the briefing would be a list of dos and don'ts. Some interviewers pushed for more, but most respected the celebrity's privacy. None of them wanted to run the risk of losing trust and not being able to book interesting guests.

Griff rubbed his hand over his stubbled jaw. "Uh, same

as last time. I definitely don't want to answer any questions about Sian."

His twin and his former costar. Kinga didn't know anything more about her than the man on the street. And she was curious, dammit.

"And I refuse to answer questions about my manager, his death or to comment on the rumors surrounding a supposed bust-up between us. They often try to sneak that question in."

Kinga heard devastation in his voice and noticed fury in his eyes. She tipped her head to the side, wondering, as so many did, why he refused to talk about the man he'd once called his second father, his mentor and his best friend. "Okay," she said.

"No questions about former lovers, my acting out, or that night in Phuket."

Kinga frowned. What was he talking about? "What happened in Phuket? I didn't read anything about you visiting Phuket."

Griff grinned. "Ah, so you did read up on me?"

Kinga handed him a cool, get-over-yourself-smile. "I read the basics, O'Hare. I didn't do a deep dive into your life."

Griff dared to peek at her butt. "Now whose pants are on fire?"

"Jerk," Kinga muttered. She looked into his eyes, saw the desire blazing within them and placed her hand on her heart, silently telling it to slow the hell down. They'd made love, yes, but she was a modern woman. One hot, wild night did not a relationship make; it didn't even mean that he wanted a repeat.

It was just sex...

"I've been thinking about you," Griff told her, taking her hand and squeezing her fingers.

She couldn't deal with him looking and sounding so sincere. It gave her ideas and those she didn't need.

"You don't have to lie to me, O'Hare. I know exactly what that night was."

"And what was it, Kinga?" Griff asked her, his voice surprisingly gentle.

Kinga attempted a casual shrug, hoping to sound blasé. "A wild night, a step out of time, something that wouldn't be repeated."

"It was wild, it was unexpected," Griff admitted. "It's also a night that I can't stop thinking about. I can't stop thinking about *you*."

Yeah, she didn't believe that for one second. And she was a little disappointed that Griff was treating her like a dumb groupie and not an intelligent, independent woman. Unlike a groupie, she wouldn't simper and melt when he used his sexy voice and bedroom eyes.

She wasn't romantic or impulsive. Starry-eyed and naive hadn't been her since she was eighteen and her world flipped upside down. She far preferred to see things how they were, not how she wanted them to be.

"You don't believe me," Griff stated, his voice low but intense.

Kinga heard a guitar riff, a drum roll and, glancing toward the stage, saw people taking their places. "You need to go. They're waiting for you."

"I am paying their salaries. They can wait until I am ready," Griff growled, and it was hard to miss his frustration. "Look, I didn't call you because I was out of town. I had…something to take care of."

Had he been called away by a woman, a longtime lover or a casual hookup? Did he leave to interview for a better job offer than what they'd offered for the ball? Was he about to ditch her? Or had he done something stupid while he was away, something that was still going to come to light?

Stop, Kinga, you're overreacting and overthinking. Just...

Stop.

She held up her hands, palms forward. "Griff, it's fine. I didn't expect you to call. I understand that this is, apart from one night, a completely professional relationship."

"Except that I want another night and possibly another night after that," Griff stated, his tone firm.

Kinga stared at him, unsure that she'd heard his words correctly. "Sorry?"

Griff bent down to speak directly in her ear and his breath warmed her neck. "I'd very much like to share your bed again, Kinga. Any chance of that happening?"

She pulled back to stare at him. She'd genuinely believed that he'd moved on to his next conquest, that she was just another woman on a long list. Why her?

She was tempted to throw caution to the wind and nod furiously, but her pride, and a healthy dose of wariness, wouldn't let her. She was about to ask him whether she could give his question some thought, when her phone rang. Deeply grateful for the interruption, she frowned at the unfamiliar number on the screen and answered.

"This is Edward, Senator Garwood's assistant. Hold for the senator please."

Kinga was very surprised to receive a call from Jas's father. He was in Washington and, as far as she knew, busy with a Supreme Court confirmation. Why was he calling her? She'd barely finished the thought when the answer popped into her head.

Mick Pritchard...

"Kinga, it's Seth."

Kinga heard his deep voice in her ear and smiled, as

she always did. Jas's father loved his daughter and, because Kinga had been a fixture in his home for most of her life, loved her, too. "Uncle Seth. It's good to hear from you. Is everything okay?"

"That prick is back."

Seth rarely swore and his description of Mick told Kinga how upset he was at Mick's return.

"I know. He's called a few times and ambushed me in a parking lot. He wants you to support his bid for mayor."

"I'd rather shove a hot stick covered with fire ants up my ass," Seth told her, his voice vibrating with anger.

That would be a no, then. Just as she'd expected.

"The thing is, he managed to con his way onto the grounds of my house and Viola let him in. He told her that he wanted to talk to her about Jas, to reminisce. She's not making much sense, but it's obvious that he's upset her and she's having a meltdown."

Kinga knew what he was asking, without him having to say the words. Viola, sensitive and emotional, had a hard time regulating her emotions, even before Jas died. Now, few people could talk her down when she was in an agitated state. Seth was one of them, Kinga another.

"I'll go and see her, try and get her to calm down, maybe take a nap?"

Kinga heard Seth's relieved sigh. "Thank you, Kinga."

"I'll go now. Do you want me to call you and let you know she's okay?" Kinga asked, standing up and reaching for her bag.

"Please. You can get me on this number." Kinga heard the frustration in his voice and could easily imagine him pacing the floor of his office. Seth adored his wife and missed her terribly when the Senate was in session. "I swear, if I get my hands on that self-serving prick, I will rip his arms off."

"You and me both," Kinga told him. "I'll speak to you soon."

Kinga disconnected the call and abruptly dropped back down to the couch, feeling like someone had punched her in the gut. Looking down at her hands, she noticed that she was trembling. She had to pull herself together and make the trip across town to Cousins Island. Immediately. Viola needed her and she wouldn't repeat her mistakes and let her—or Seth—down.

But, God, the fear of failure was always there. And so was the urge to panic, dancing under her skin.

Kinga hauled in some much-needed air and saw a bottle of water in front of her face. Taking it, she cracked the lid, only to realize that it was already open. She took a big sip, then a deep breath, another sip, and felt a fraction calmer. She could do this...

Standing up, she picked up her bag and pulled it over her shoulder. Handing Griff the water bottle, she told him she had to go and, her arms wrapped around her waist, walked to the door.

All this was her fault.

The tendrils of panic grew stronger and she did not want to be behind the wheel of a car if an attack struck. If she became immobilized on the road, she could kill herself or someone else. And when she saw Viola, she needed to be clear-eyed and in control. She needed to do her deep breathing and calming exercises, but that meant having to hire a ride.

Kinga scrolled through her phone, eventually finding the contact number for the taxi company she routinely used. They were more reliable than a ride share service. She dialed, ordered a taxi, and when the dispatcher asked for a pickup address, she went blank.

She had no idea where she was...

Kinga felt her phone slide out of her fingers and lifted her eyes to look at Griff, his green eyes reflecting his confusion and concern. "Cancel the taxi, I'll drive you."

She looked around the room, seeing the musicians waiting for Griff, and shook her head. "You can't, all these people are here, you have a practice scheduled!"

"As I said, I'm the boss and pay their salaries." He looked across to the stage, sliced his hand across his neck and immediately, the band members realized that their session was canceled.

"Where do you need to go, baby?" Griff gently asked her, sliding her phone into the open pocket on the outside of her bag.

Kinga thought about lying but didn't have the energy. "I need to go to Senator Garwood's house on Cousins Island. It's about twenty minutes away. Will you take me?"

Seven

A couple hours later, Griff followed Kinga into her apartment, gently closing the door behind him. He watched Kinga shrug out of her coat, hanging it up on the coatrack before turning to face her front door. He thought she was about to ask him to leave, but she turned the four locks on her front door instead.

She still looked pale, Griff thought, though not as white as she'd been when she joined him in his car after spending forty-five minutes within Senator Garwood's mansion. Griff rocked on his heels, desperate to pepper her with questions but not wanting to upset her further.

He wasn't particularly surprised that Portland's princess was on friendly terms with the state's first family, but he couldn't understand why the visit would upset her so much.

Deciding to give her some space, Griff looked at the raindrops hitting the windowpane and sighed. So far, Port-

land had two weather settings, snow and rain, both accompanied by wind. Kinga's apartment had great central
heating but there was nothing like a fire to raise spirits.
Wood sat in a neat pile next to the period-correct fireplace, so he walked over to the hearth and grabbed a
handful of kindling.

Knowing that Kinga needed something to do, he asked
her to make him a cup of coffee and set about adding logs
to the hearth. By the time she returned with an espresso
from her high-end machine, he had a healthy fire burning in the grate.

Kinga held out her hands to the warmth. "Thank you.
I can't remember when last I used the fireplace."

Griff placed his cup on the table behind him and gently pulled her into his arms. Holding her, he wondered if
he had any right to ask her the questions burning a hole
in his brain. After all, he hadn't told her, or anyone, why
he'd abruptly left Portland the morning after spending an
enthralling, smoking-hot night in her bed.

No one besides his immediate family knew that in Key
Largo, Sian had decided to take an early-morning swim,
which wouldn't have been a problem if she'd stopped,
turned around and headed back to shore. She hadn't. If
Pete hadn't seen her when he stepped out onto his balcony
shortly after waking up, Sian would've been halfway to
Australia by the time they discovered her.

And dead.

Pete, a strong swimmer, had guided her back to shore
and they'd immediately contacted her psychiatrist and
Griff. A few hours after hearing from Pete, and after a
detour to pick up Sian's therapist, he was on his way to
Key Largo.

After spending hours with Sian, Dr. Warfield concluded that Sian experienced a rare schizophrenia-induced

delusion. Her meds were adjusted, and by the time Griff left the island a week later, Sian was happier and chattier. Her disease was a roller coaster, Griff thought for the umpteenth time.

With Jan and Pete insisting that Sian, Sam and Eloise remain on the island with them, he'd hired a psychiatric nurse to monitor Sian for the duration of her visit. After the therapist left, Griff had hung around for a few more days, playing with and watching over Sam and catching up with his sisters and brother-in-law, telling them about his return to performing.

Sam was in his element, completely spoiled by Jan's girls, and it was obvious that he wasn't suffering from any lack of attention in Jan's household. They doted on him and Griff suspected that when Sam returned home, he might have a bit of a monster on his hands.

Thank God the press had no idea that Sian and Sam were in the Keys.

Walking backward, with a fragrant and soft woman still in his arms, Griff lowered himself to the nearest sofa and pulled Kinga down to sit on his lap. She curled up against his chest, her face in his neck. He rubbed her back and waited for her to speak.

He wouldn't force her to talk. He hated being interrogated and suspected she did, too.

Griff yawned and played with the edges of her supple boots. Thinking she'd be far more comfortable without her footwear, he eased the stretchy boots off her legs. Pulling her closer to his chest, he placed his hand on her thigh, his thumb drawing patterns on the inside of her knee. "Better?"

"Mmm, thanks."

He was curious, sure, but he could just sit here with this woman in his lap, her perfume wafting up to his nose, with the fire crackling and the rain turning to sleet as it smacked the windows. Sliding down a little, Griff rested his head on the back of the sofa and idly hummed the melody to a song he'd been working on earlier.

"That's nice," Kinga murmured.

"I thought you said you aren't musical," Griff gently teased her.

"I'm not, but that doesn't mean I can't enjoy a nice tune."

Griff's lips twitched at the hint of haughtiness in her voice and hoped it meant she was feeling a little better, a tad stronger. He decided to risk a probing question. "Can you tell me why you rushed over to Senator Garwood's house in the middle of a Tuesday afternoon?" he asked.

Kinga shot up and winced. "Oh, God, I spoiled your practice session and you wasted all that time. I'm so sorry… The band and rental of the studio must be prohibitively expensive and I took you away."

Griff pulled her back down, tightened his arms around her and dropped a reassuring kiss in her hair. He was one of the highest-paid artists in the industry, and one afternoon's wages and studio rentals were less than petty cash to him. Not that he'd tell Kinga that—he'd sound like a boastful jerk.

"You were upset and you needed someone to drive you. I'm sorry I couldn't deliver you to the door, but reporters were hanging around and that would've started a media story neither of us needed," he added.

When he approached the senator's impressive gates, he'd seen a blond-haired man talking to the sizable number of reporters on the sidewalk. Judging by Kinga's feral growl, he assumed she recognized him but she gave no explanation of who he was or why he was there. Grateful the journalists weren't paying the traffic any attention, and for the tinted windows of his car, he drove past, turned down a side road and suggested that Kinga walk the short distance to the house. Telling her that he'd pick her up at the house when the coast was clear, he had spent the next forty-five minutes in his car, catching up on returning calls and emails and trying to ignore his growing curiosity.

Thankfully, the press had departed by the time Kinga was finished and he could pick her up without any cameras flashing or people yelling his name.

"Thank you for thinking of that—I certainly didn't. And thank you for driving me," Kinga said. She lifted herself off his chest and rested her back against the arm of the sofa. She tucked her clasped hands between her thighs and when her eyes met his, he winced at the pain he saw within those honey-colored depths. "So…"

Griff didn't push her when she hesitated; he just waited for her to continue. When she did, her voice trembled. "The girl in that photo, the one on the mantel…that's Jas, Senator Garwood's daughter. She was my best friend, and we bonded on our first day in kindergarten. Tinsley and I are close now, but we weren't when we were kids. When she was sixteen, Tinsley and JT fell in love and they became inseparable and she didn't have much time for me. But Jas was always there—she was my soul sister and the other half of me. I don't know if you can understand that…"

He'd grown up in the limelight, on stages and TV and movie sets, and Sian had been his constant companion. And to an extent, his only friend, so, yeah, he understood. "I have a twin, remember?"

"Right," Kinga pushed her hand through her hair. "Ten years ago, Jas had just broken up with her boyfriend, Mick Pritchard, for the fourth or fifth time that year. We went to a New Years' party not far from Jas's house and my parents' estate... Well, it's my grandfather's estate..."

She was rambling and Griff let her go at her own pace.

"Callum wants you to come to dinner on Friday night, by the way," Kinga said, and he blinked at her unexpected change of subject.

He lifted his eyebrows. "Will you be there?" he asked. If he could hold Kinga's hand under the table, he might consider it. Otherwise, there was no way he'd endure a meal with her cold, austere grandfather.

Kinga looked affronted. "Of course I will. There's no way I'd let you face my family alone."

He smiled at her protective attitude and didn't bother telling her that he'd been dealing with difficult, egocentric and self-important people most of his life. He'd decide about whether to accept her grandfather's invitation later; right now he wanted to hear the rest of Kinga's story.

"You were telling me about your friend..." he prompted.

Kinga turned her head to look out the window and his heart clenched at her desolate expression. "I told her we'd see in the new year together and I promised her a lift home, but a guy I was into arrived at the party. He wanted me to leave with him and Jas encouraged me to go, as a lot of our friends were there and she was having fun. I told her to phone me if she needed a ride, but she told me that it was all good..."

Ah, the phrase she so hated. Griff swallowed, dread creeping over him. He thought he knew where this was going.

"She never called and I presumed she got a ride home with one of our many friends at the party. Someone remembered seeing her at the house around four a.m. We now know she left on her own and that she was a little drunk. It was a misty night, but it was a road she was familiar with. Jas loved to walk at night and her house was only a half mile down the road. My house was a half mile in the opposite direction. She was so close to home, Griff."

"But she never made it."

"Initially we thought she'd been taken by a predator and we immediately put up missing person flyers and Seth—Senator Garwood—hired a private investigator. A few days later, they found her body in a deep ditch, covered with snow. She was a victim of a hit-and-run collision."

Griff's hand tightened on her knee. The poor kid. Kinga started to speak but then snapped her mouth closed, misery in her eyes and all over her face.

She didn't need to say the words; he understood what she couldn't say. She blamed herself. Kinga, protective and loving, felt responsible for her friend's death. It wasn't logical but, in her mind, she'd left her friend at a party, after promising to take her home, and it was her fault Jas was gone.

Kinga wasn't responsible but Griff knew that was a conclusion she'd have to come to in her own time. It might take another decade or it might not happen at all.

After a few minutes' silence, he spoke again. "And the rushed visit to the senator's house today?"

Kinga rubbed her hands up and down her face. "That would take a bit more explanation."

Griff waited while she decided whether or not to give him the whole story, knowing that, to an extent, it was a referendum on whether she trusted him or not. He wanted her to trust him, he realized. He wanted her to hand him her thoughts and fears, her hopes and dreams. He wanted to be the place, and the person, she felt safest with.

Yeah, this connection to Kinga was turning a lot more complicated than he'd expected...

Not clever, O'Hare. He was halfway down that slippery slope and his brakes weren't working.

Kinga played with the hem of her dress, her thoughts in the past. "Earlier, I mentioned that Jas had a boyfriend. I grew up with Mick—I've known him all my life and so did Jas. Mick and I were friends, and at times, we were really close. Along with the Craigmyle boys, I considered him to be the brother I never had."

Kinga folded the hem of her dress up an inch, and then another inch, revealing more of her slim thigh covered in a thin black stocking. Were they fancy stockings, the ones held up by those strappy, lacy garter things?

Griff cursed himself, reminding himself that he was listening to Kinga tell him about one of the worst periods of her life and that he should be concentrating on her story, not her lingerie.

Get a goddamn grip, O'Hare.

"Jas and Mick hooked up when they were seventeen and they were on and off, as I said. They were off at the time she died. That's why he wasn't at the party." Kinga hauled in a deep breath. "For those first few days when we thought she was missing, Mick was beside himself, crying, on his knees praying... He was desperate to find her. As you can imagine, the networks picked up on the story pretty quickly. Seth's popular, Viola's beautiful and Jas was brilliant. It was...well, very newsworthy."

He'd seen coverage of some of the more high-profile murder and missing investigations and understood that certain stories got more coverage than others. A famous and much-liked politician's beautiful and brilliant daughter going missing? That would bring out national and international reporters...

"You were telling me about the boyfriend..." Griff prompted Kinga.

"Mick took every opportunity to talk to the press. Looking back, I now realize he was milking the situation. On day two of her being gone—she was found on day three—he started blaming me, telling anybody who'd listen it was my fault."

Griff winced. What a bastard.

But he still didn't understand what any of this had to do with her visit to Garwood's house this afternoon. He told himself to be patient and listen.

Kinga tensed and Griff knew he was about to hear something he wasn't going to like. "After her funeral, I was at home, alone... I can't remember where my parents were. Mick arrived and he started yelling at me, telling me that I destroyed all his plans, that he'd intended to marry Jas, that she was his ticket.

"I didn't know what he was talking about and I started yelling back, I was so sick of his crap. I told him that Jas had said they were done, permanently, and that she was glad to have him out of her life." Kinga hesitated, then softly told him that she'd been punched.

It took Griff a few moments for the red mist in front of his eyes to clear. "I'm sorry," he carefully asked, "did you say he hit you?"

"Mmm-hmm. He's a big guy and I fell to the floor. It hurt like hell."

Griff released a low growl. "Please, please tell me where I can find the prick so that I can rip his limbs off."

Kinga placed her hand on his and squeezed. "He was the blond-haired guy outside the Garwood house today, talking to the press." Kinga pulled her bottom lip between her thumb and forefinger, deep in thought. A minute later she dropped her hand to speak again. "It's all starting to make sense, actually."

He was glad she thought so, because he didn't have a

damn clue. All he knew for sure was that if he was alone with Pritchard, one of them would die and it wouldn't be Griff. Kinga was tall but slim, and the guy he'd seen earlier was six-four and bulky. God, even a pulled punch from him would've stung like a bitch. He could've broken her cheekbone, made her crack her head when she hit the floor...

"He's the owner of a private security company with offices here and in Boston. On his website is a video promoting his services and telling the world why he got into private security, to help people because his, and I'm paraphrasing, love of his life was killed in a hit-and-run accident. In the video, he also names and blames me. Every year he emails or texts me on her anniversary to reinforce that message."

The sniveling cockroach.

"I've been able to ignore him mostly, but now he's back and he's launching a bid for mayor, and he wants Seth's endorsement. He ambushed me in a parking lot recently, telling me that I owe him, and demanding that I set up a meeting with the senator."

He what? What the f—

"Now I think that back then, he was planning on using Jas to ride Seth's coattails," Kinga mused. "Seth can't stand him because he's refused to take that video down. We believe he's capitalizing on Jas's death. Mick went to see Viola today, Jas's mother. She's never fully recovered from Jas's death and mostly stays at home. She told me he bullied his way into the house, and immediately demanded that she talk to Seth, that Seth owes it to Mick to endorse him for mayor. She was distraught and scared and it took me a while to calm her down."

"Is the guy clueless?"

"He's something," Kinga admitted. "He tipped off the

press and that's why they were there. I bet you that he hinted at an announcement about him entering politics to tease them. He would've told them he was visiting Viola as Jas's boyfriend, showing his respect on the tenth anniversary of her death. The press will pick up on the story—they love anything to do with Seth and Jas."

Griff lifted his hand to hold her chin, making sure she was looking at him when he spoke again. He wanted no misunderstandings about this. "If he comes anywhere near you, I want to know about it, Kinga."

Kinga shrugged. "I appreciate the sentiment but the last thing you can afford, from a PR point of view, is to get into a showdown with Mick Pritchard, Griff." Kinga shrugged. "I can handle him."

But she shouldn't have to, and Griff wanted to make it very clear to Pritchard that any fight he picked with Kinga meant taking on him, too.

"I. Want. To. Know." Griff enunciated each word.

"Fine," Kinga huffed, but in that one word, he heard the exhaustion and emotion in her voice. She came across as tough and together on the surface, but his amber-eyed pixie was a lot more vulnerable than she allowed the world to believe. Feeling tenderness rise up inside of him—well, he thought it was tenderness—he wrapped his arms around her, pulled her in close and kissed the top of her head.

While he was in Portland, for as long as this lasted, she was his to protect.

Griff lifted his hand to stroke her cheek with the tips of his fingers. "I'm sorry this happened to you, Kinga, so sorry that you lost your friend."

Kinga blinked away her tears. "I still miss her, Griff. As much today as I did ten years ago."

Griff nodded, understanding grief didn't die over time.

It changed, sure, but it never went away. He still missed his parents.

"I know what loss is like, how it can rearrange the world. Death, and the emotions it brings, is never simple and comes in so many different shapes and forms."

Kinga rested her forehead against his. "I'm so grateful you are here. Thank you for staying."

"Always a pleasure," Griff murmured back. And it was. Honestly, there was no place he'd rather be than holding Kinga.

Pulling back, she looked into his eyes and he watched, fascinated, as sorrow turned to desire. His eyes darted to her mouth and back to her eyes and liquid want invaded his veins, warming him from the inside out.

Kinga straddled his thighs, lowering her head to position her mouth above his, but Griff's hand on her shoulder stopped her from lowering her head. "Problem?" she asked, frowning.

Time to be the good guy. Frankly, it sucked. "I want you, Kinga, but you're vulnerable and still upset. Maybe it's not a good time."

Kinga rested her palm on his cheek, her thumb swiping over the stubble on his cheek. "It's a great time. I need you, Griff, I need to feel alive and connected and…"

Loved.

Kinga looked into his mesmerizing eyes, shocked that she'd nearly allowed the L word to escape. Love wasn't something she'd ever imagined for herself, not in any shape or form. Love was a story society had been fed for far too long and it didn't exist, not really. Friendship did, as did companionship. Attraction, obviously, and flat-out lust. Couples hooked up for a variety of reasons—in her parents' case it was an amalgamation of wealth and power—but love? No, that was a myth.

"Are you sure, Kinga?" Griff asked, searching her face.

"Very," Kinga told him, sitting up and grabbing the edges of her dress to pull it over her head, exposing her torso to Griff's appreciative gaze. He lifted his big hand to her breast, his tan hand a lovely contrast to her pale skin and pale pink bra. Griff sat up and put his mouth to her nipple, tugging her into his mouth, his hand going down the back of her panties to explore her butt cheek. The thought that she shouldn't be feeling like this, not with Jas dead, popped into her brain. But she also knew that Jas would be the first person to tell her carpe diem, to seize the day and all that.

Besides, Jas would not be the type of girl who'd kick a sexy, sweet man out of her bed.

Griff pulled away, his expression a little fierce. "I'm going to make you feel so good, Kinga."

Yes, please. She could live with that.

Griff asked her to lie back down and when she did, he hovered over her, taking his time, looking at her. Unable to wait, Kinga cupped the back of his neck and pulled his head down, needing his kiss, his tongue in her mouth.

While he fed her kisses, Griff unhooked her bra and dropped it to the floor. He moved his hands down her body to stop at her ankles, before sliding them back up her body. After removing her tights and caressing her calves, knees and thighs, his hand went back to her butt, his skilled fingers sliding under her bottom, probing to stroke lightly between her legs. Kinga allowed her thighs to fall open, and she wondered if Griff would notice her damp panties.

Still kissing her, alternating between take-her-to-heaven kisses and gentle nibbles, Griff's hand skated back up and then down her chest and over her stomach to rest his palm on her mons. Kinga pulled in a harsh breath as he moved his mouth from hers to her bare breast, and his fingers slid underneath the band of her panties to access her warm, wet and secretive places.

"Let's get rid of these, okay?"

Not able to speak, she heard his gentle command to lift her hips and felt the fabric slide down, and then it was gone. Griff's fingers drifted through her small patch of hair and his fingers—urgent now—slid over and into her folds, unerringly finding her clit, causing her to release a turned-on moan. She pushed into his hands, needing more and needing it now.

"That's it, baby."

One finger probed and entered her, his thumb caressing that center of pleasure until she whimpered into his neck, begging for release. Kinga felt that wave of pleasure lifting her, fully in the grasp of lust's primal power. Griff bent down to kiss her breast again, to suck her nipple to the roof of his mouth and Kinga knew that she was close to coming, that the wave was about to crash. Sensing her approaching climax, Griff pulled back and slowed down, murmuring compliments against her mouth and skin.

He could've been speaking Swahili or Spanish, she had no idea. All she cared about was his trailing mouth on her body, his tongue dipping into her belly button, his big body hovering over hers, his mouth on her mound, his hands holding her legs apart.

That wave swelled again, shooting her up, and she hovered on its crest as he sucked her bud into her mouth. She waited, sobbing and begging his name, and when his fingers slid into her channel, she screamed, dropped and flew.

She tumbled, caught up in a maelstrom of warm, wet pleasure.

When she found solid ground, came back to herself, Kinga pulled him up and cradled his head into her neck, half sobbing from the pleasure of the experience.

"Best orgasm ever," Kinga whispered in his ear and felt his lips curve against her skin.

"That was just the warm-up act," Griff told her, lifting his head to grin at her.

"I'm so glad I bought a ticket to this gig," Kinga teased him. "But wonderful warm-up acts put pressure on the main performer. You're gonna have to up your game, O'Hare."

"Not a problem," Griff assured her.

And it wasn't. Griff O'Hare, yet again, gave her an incredible one-man show.

Eight

On Saturday morning, Kinga sat across from Griff in the Ryder International Gulfstream as they made their way to Manhattan. In one of their many conversations lately, Griff had mentioned he'd like to see the venue for the ball and to meet with the sound people she'd hired. After making space in her packed schedule, Kinga commandeered the Ryder International jet to fly them to New York City.

She'd booked them into a suite within the luxurious, iconic Forrester-Grantham Hotel. Having attended Columbia University, she wanted to show him her favorite spots in the city. Hopefully, his presence would go undetected by the press.

Either way, it would be nice to get away from Portland, the press, the Mick situation and her uptight family for a day or two.

Kinga stretched, thinking that dinner at Callum's house last night—postponed from the previous week—had been a shit show. Her parents had been visibly tense and had barely spoken to each other the whole evening. Or to anyone else.

Callum had banged on and on about the delays in the DNA test, and Cody Craigmyle, a favorite of both Callum and her parents, had attended, exchanging barbs and insults with Tinsley like street vendors trading produce.

The only time Kinga relaxed during the whole evening was when Griff sat himself down at Callum's Steinway and played some jazz tunes from the fifties and sixties. Callum and James smoked cigars, Penelope made her way through another glass of chardonnay and Tinsley and Cody glared at each other from opposite sides of the room.

Her family was frequently tense and uptight but not normally that bad.

Kinga watched Griff scribbling in a notepad, glasses on his nose and humming a tune, oblivious, she was sure, to her presence. She crossed her legs, remembering how he'd held her hand under the table last night, telling her to relax when she tried to whisper an apology for her family's bad behavior. And curled up into the corner of Callum's sofa, listening to him play, had made her feel like she'd spent the day at a spa or on a sun-drenched holiday. Loose, relaxed, pretty damn happy. Griff O'Hare, the bad boy of rock and roll, could calm her down, boost her spirits...

She also found herself telling him things she'd never shared with anyone before. Nobody else knew that Mick had hurt her, that he sent her ugly texts and voice messages every year, that he still blamed her for Jas's death. She hadn't come close to sharing that with anyone, not even Tinsley. All her sister knew was that she'd had a scary encounter with a guy, resulting in her feeling skittish around men she didn't know.

So, why did she tell Griff?

Kinga rolled her head to the side to look out the window, clouds below them, wishing she was touching him, needing the connection. He had a million secrets, none of which she was privy to, and Kinga knew she felt more for him than he did for her.

That was a fine way to get her heart shattered.

What was it about him that so intrigued her? He wasn't the first good-looking guy she'd encountered. Was it his bad boy streak that attracted her? Maybe. But Kinga suspected he wasn't as spoiled or self-serving as the media made him out to be.

He could be hard-ass and humorous, intellectual and impossible. He was smart and savvy and very, very talented. But it was his ability to be both alpha and tender, stubborn and sweet that had her all tied up. He got her, in ways that nobody ever had since, well, Jas. Feeling that sort of connection terrified her. If she were smart, she'd bail now, while she still could, while her heart was still reasonably intact. Her brain thought that was a pretty good plan; her body wanted more of him.

Her heart, well, who the hell knew what that stupid organ wanted?

Kinga heard Griff shift in his seat and turned her head to look at him. She caught his eyes and slowly responded to his soft smile. He stood, crossed the space between them and dropped into the seat next to her. His mouth drifted across hers in a can't-wait-for-more kiss. Pulling away before they both got carried away, Griff leaned back in his seat and placed his hand on her knee.

His thumb stroked her through the material of her skinny jeans and his eyes were tender. "You doing okay?" Griff asked her, half turning to face her.

"I should be asking you that," Kinga pulled a face, "after our less-than-fun dinner last night."

"Is your family normally that…uptight?"

Kinga wanted to lie but couldn't. "They aren't known for being warm and fuzzy, but normally they are better behaved." She placed her hand on top of his, pushing her fingers between his. "Since Christmas, my parents have been acting weird. Something is going on with them."

"Like?"

She could tell him her suspicions. After all, he was privy to her biggest secrets. "I wonder if they are finally talking divorce."

Griff looked surprised. "And that doesn't upset you?"

Kinga pulled her hand away and lifted her leg to drape it over his lower thigh. His hand curled around her knee and she leaned back against the padded armrest. "Actually, sometimes I wish they would go their separate ways. Theirs has never been a love match. They don't fight but they're not happy, either. But Callum wouldn't approve, so I doubt a divorce would ever happen. My dad is big on getting his father's approval."

"Because he's next in line to inherit?"

She liked Griff's blunt questions, the way he said what he thought without pussyfooting around the issue. "I'm sure that's part of it. But I don't think he'll ever be Callum's successor. I love my dad, Griff, but he's not tough enough to be the CEO of an international company worth a few billion. My mom, on the other hand, is tough, but she doesn't have the skills needed for the job."

"And you do."

Kinga nodded. "I do. But I don't want the job. I love what I'm doing now. The CEO position is twenty-four seven and I don't think I have the temperament for it, either."

Griff smiled. "Fair enough." He picked up his bottle of

water, unscrewed the cap and took a long sip. "Why didn't your dad leave the business, pursue another career?"

Pfft. In Callum's world, that wasn't possible. James was his son and his son belonged in Ryder International, even if it meant chipping away at his soul every day. With Callum, doing things any other way than his way was never an option.

Kinga took his water bottle from his hand and sipped. Replacing the cap, she considered her words. "My grandfather is as tough as old leather and it's his way or the highway. I'll give you a classic example of how controlling he is…

"He had a brother, Ben, who was fifteen years younger than him. From what I can gather, rumors always abounded about Ben's sexuality and Callum couldn't accept that his brother was either bisexual or gay. Ben was, in Callum's eyes, embarrassing the family name.

"Callum and Ben ran Ryder's together at that time, but Callum wouldn't stop nagging Ben to find a wife and have a son. Ben finally confirmed all the rumors and told Callum that he'd fallen in love with the man he wanted to be with. Callum couldn't accept it, and he tried to force Benjamin out of the business."

"Harsh."

Kinga agreed.

"There was a huge family ruckus. It affected my father's relationship with Callum because my dad publicly supported his uncle. Ben died in a car crash before my parents married, I don't think my mom met him. Anyway, the authorities said he was speeding, that he had to have been distracted to end up dying in a one car accident. I think that my dad quietly blamed Callum for Ben's state of mind. He and Ben were close and my dad refused to obey Callum's order to cut him out of his life, and Callum has never forgiven him for taking Ben's side. Callum didn't even go to Ben's funeral when he passed away."

"That's quite a story," Griff said.

"Yeah, my grandfather is ruthless, controlling and old, *old* school. In fact, and don't take this the wrong way, I was surprised he had you around for dinner. My grandfather doesn't generally have much time for supposed degenerates and reprobates."

A strange look crossed Griff's face. "Maybe he hasn't read the tabloids."

Kinga snorted. "My grandfather is as sharp as a tack—he's sure to have read them. Anyway, you survived and he wasn't particularly rude to you. And I'm sorry that you had to hear about the entire history of the Ryder-White clan. Congratulations on not falling asleep."

"Hopefully those DNA tests come back soon. If they don't, he might blow a gasket," Griff said, his dimples flashing. "And, for the record, I've yet to meet a parent, or grandparent, I couldn't charm."

Kinga patted his shoulder. "Apart from being gorgeous, you are also incredibly modest and self-effacing."

Griff's laugh, sexy and low, rolled over her. "You are very good at keeping my feet on the ground, Kinga."

"It's tough but I'm up to the challenge," Kinga replied, keeping her voice light. She couldn't let him suspect that it was a job she wouldn't mind doing for a long time. The thought made her feel icy cold.

She'd never give a man, *anyone*, that much power over her. No, it was better to be like her parents, uninvolved and unemotional. They weren't blissfully happy but they *were* reasonably content. Reasonably content was all anyone could ask for, right?

Asking for more was looking for heartbreak.

She should end this, sooner rather than later. Maybe

Griff would hand her a way to ease out of his life with the minimum of drama. They did, after all, still have to work together.

"Changing the subject... Have you heard from that prick again?" Griff demanded, annoyance tingeing his words.

"Mick?"

Unfortunately, she had. He'd left a voice message, apologizing for going to Viola's and begging for a meeting with Kinga to clear the air. He suggested dinner at his house and the thought made her want to vomit.

Was she imagining the red in Griff's eyes? Deciding not to tell him about the dinner invite, she deflected. "I heard from one of my journalist friends that he's sent out an invitation to a very exclusive cocktail party. My source says he's been teasing a big announcement, but his political ambitions are an open secret."

"When is this cocktail party?"

"Uh, on the second, I think. At one of the restaurants downtown. Very smart, very ritzy. The media is invited, too. My friend says most of them are going only because of the free snacks and an open bar."

"So he's going to get his time in the spotlight?" Griff asked.

"Sounds like it. If the press doesn't make a big song and dance about his bid, he'll find it harder to break into the news cycle and to get his face before the public." Kinga frowned at him, suspicious. "You aren't planning on gate-crashing his party, are you?"

Griff raised one arrogant eyebrow. "And give him the press coverage he wants? Hell, no. Though I wouldn't mind meeting him in a dark alley and seeing how he likes to be on the receiving end of *my* fist," he added.

Maybe it wasn't politically correct, but there was something lovely about having a strong, protective man in her corner, prepared to stand between her and the world.

But…

But Griff was temporary, someone who wasn't sticking around. She couldn't start relying on him.

Besides, she was a strong and independent woman who could handle herself.

And don't you dare forget that, Ryder-White.

Griff turned his head and looked at Kinga's delicate profile, soft and vulnerable and relaxed. This trip to NYC was an unexpected pleasure. After they were finished with work, he planned on taking her to a little restaurant in Brooklyn, a ten-seater Italian joint that served the best shrimp and lemon risotto he'd ever tasted. And amazing tiramisu. Maybe they could get takeout and have another threesome…

The last one, with the cheesecake, had been a bunch of fun.

Griff hoped he'd be able to fly under the radar in the city and, if he took the normal precautions, ball cap and sunglasses, hopefully nobody would know he was there. He knew Kinga had booked a suite at the hotel but he wondered if that was wise as chambermaids and bellhops were a frequent source of information for the paparazzi.

And if the press found out he was sleeping with Kinga Ryder-White, their lives would be untenable. She was a good girl, Portland's princess, and he was Hollywood's favorite bad boy. It wouldn't be the first or the hundredth time his love life was dissected for the titillation of the public, but he was pretty sure Kinga—or her father or grandfather—would not appreciate the invasion of her privacy.

Nor would her family appreciate the fact that she was mixing business with pleasure...

Kinga was so different from anyone he'd dated before. She was supersmart and very independent, sophisticated but not hard. A little more vulnerable than he was comfortable with. All his previous lovers understood that, by being at his side, there was always the chance their affair would hit the tabloids. For some, the notoriety was an added inducement, hoping they'd be able to leverage the publicity into something bigger and bolder.

Kinga was not like that. She was different, in a hundred ways, all of them pleasurable. Griff looked at her, blonde and beautiful but not in a centerfold pinup type of way, and his heart thumped against his rib cage, while his stomach attempted a backflip.

He'd been in lust before—many times—but no one had ever made his internal organs quiver.

Not that he was in love with Kinga Ryder-White—it was an unrealistic, silly concept, but she affected him in ways no woman ever had. He didn't like it.

Then again, there were a million things he didn't like but couldn't change.

Griff heard the ding of a message landing on his phone. It was a video clip of Sam on the beach, chasing seagulls and whooping like a banshee. Seeing Kinga's curious expression at the noises coming from his phone, he angled his screen and pushed Play again.

"That's Sam, my nephew."

Griff almost looked around to see who had said his words, who was using his voice. Astounded that he'd told her something so incredibly personal, he immediately turned his head to look out the window, unable to meet her eyes.

"Sian has a child?"

He'd opened the door, allowed her to walk inside; he couldn't shut her out now. He wanted to but manners dictated that he had to, at the very least, give her a small explanation.

"Yes, but I've helped raise him since he was born. Sian lives on my Kentucky ranch and Sam and I are very close," Griff added, pushing his hand through his hair, wishing he'd kept his mouth shut.

"He's very cute."

"He's my world."

And he was sharing his existence with Kinga.

His stomach dropped, as heavy as an iron bar.

He'd just exposed himself. Worse, he'd exposed his family to a woman he barely knew and wasn't sure he could trust. Not because Kinga was untrustworthy but because he didn't trust anybody, not with information about Sian and Sam. He'd never even brought a woman home to meet his family; the thought had never crossed his mind. It wasn't what he did, who he was.

He and Sian had had their fights because he was so very protective—she'd, on more than one occasion, accused him of smothering her—but it wasn't because he didn't trust or respect her. She was his sister, damn it. The person he shared a womb with; he couldn't *not* look out for her. "He looks like you. How old is he?" Kinga asked. He looked at her and saw more questions in her eyes, including the one she most wanted to know but dare not ask…

Who was the father of Sian's child?

He dropped his head to look at the floor, unsure how much to tell her. He quickly tallied up the pros and cons. If he said nothing and she let the information slip about Sam, he might be able to refute her words, to dismiss her claim.

But if he gave her more, and she let all of it slip, the

media's interest in Sian would be reignited. And if the world found out Finn was Sam's father, the internet would explode.

And Sian would be hounded... His sister wasn't ready, might never be strong enough, for so much concentrated attention.

It all came down to whether he trusted Kinga or not. And really, how could he? He liked her, her body enthralled him and he enjoyed her quick mind. But realistically, he hadn't spent enough time with her to trust her with his most explosive secrets.

"You don't trust me."

Griff raised his head and looked into her pale, wounded face. "Try not to take it personally. I don't trust anybody. I should never have told you about Sam."

"Why did you?" Kinga quietly asked him, nervous fingers drumming on her thigh.

He jerked a shoulder up. "I'm not sure, actually. It kinda slipped out." Griff looked into her lovely eyes and saw her hurt and disappointment. Dammit. He never meant to make her feel either emotion. How could he explain his fears without insulting her? "I have a lot of trust issues, Kinga."

She nodded. "I'm sure you do. I'm sure growing up in a superficial world with superficial people has scared you, made you wary."

"Not everyone in the industry is shallow and superficial. I've met some lovely people, like Stan and Ava."

"But more people let you down than supported you," Kinga pointed out. He couldn't argue with that. And the person he trusted the most, with his career and with his sister, had done the most damage.

Before he could reply, Kinga spoke again. "And you

don't know whether your impulsive confession will back-fire on you spectacularly."

Yeah, well. *That*.

"I'm not a groupie, neither am I easily impressed with stardom," Kinga told him, sounding pissy. "I thought you understood that." She pushed a finger into his shoulder. "I went to bed with Griff, the man, not Griff, the star. I don't even like Griff, the star with the stunning voice."

Ouch.

But the pain was clean, sweet rather than jagged. And in her eyes, he saw that she spoke the truth. But he needed to hammer home the point.

"If the press found out Sian has a son, the ramifications could be devastating, Kinga," Griff said, his voice as cold as an Arctic storm. He saw her eyebrows lift and knew she thought he was being melodramatic. But he couldn't explain. That level of trust had died with Finn.

"Your secret is safe with me, Griff. I'd never betray you," Kinga stated, and Griff knew that she'd try to keep that promise. That didn't mean she would.

"If it helps relieve your anxiety, I'm not an impulsive person," Kinga explained. "I always have a backup plan, maybe two. I overthink everything and I never, ever make quick decisions. So the chances of something slipping out, as you say, are minimal."

"I know I sound like an asshole, but…" Griff rubbed the back of his neck. Kinga placed a hand on his shoulder and squeezed.

"I get it, Griff, I do. The less I know, the less you'll stress," Kinga nodded. "But…" she added, pulling her bottom lip between pretty teeth, "…given your trust issues and my fear of doing something stupid, maybe this is a good time to have a conversation about us…"

She was going to tell him something he didn't want to hear, like she couldn't see him anymore.

"I can't keep doing this."

Was he a genius or what? Griff cocked his head, silently asking for more of an explanation. Kinga twisted the ring on her middle finger, a colorful concoction of brightly colored stones.

"You've slipped under my skin," she admitted, her frustration obvious.

And he had no problem admitting, to himself, that she was deep under his...

"It normally takes me ages to feel comfortable with somebody, longer if that person is a man. And I've never felt as comfortable with a guy—or anyone since Jas—as I do with you. That scares me because I can see myself falling for you and I don't want to do that. I don't want to risk falling for anyone. I can't risk losing someone I lov— like, again. I can't do it. I don't *want* to do it."

Griff stared at her, unable to believe they were having this conversation thirty thousand feet in the air.

"I'm thinking that we should stop this, Griff, before it runs away with us," Kinga ran her hand through her hair. "We both know it could never work."

Did they know that?

"Explain it to me..."

Kinga's expression was pure who-are-you-kidding? After hesitating, she sighed and lifted her shoulders, allowing them to drop quickly. She lifted her leg off his and withdrew from him, putting as much space as possible between them.

Shit.

"You live in Kentucky, and in Nashville." She wrinkled her nose. "In fact, I don't even know what property you call your true home."

He loved his homes in Nashville and Malibu but also loved being on the ranch in Kentucky. He loved spending time in Key Largo... Asking which place was his true home was a good question and one he didn't know the answer to.

"I am a Mainer," she said. "I will always want to live in Portland. My job is there and my family is close by, even if they are occasionally a little odd. You're impulsive and free-spirited, I'm...not. I hate the idea of living my life in a fishbowl and that's where you need to be, in the public eye."

To a point. He'd proved these past two or so years that he could lead a low-key life.

Griff opened his mouth to argue with her and snapped it closed, unable to believe he was about to put forward a case about why they should be together, stay together.

"I have a ball to organize and after that's done, I have other projects that will take up my time. I'm burning the candle at both ends, juggling sleeping with you and trying to stage one of the biggest functions of the decade and my career. My concentration is shot and I'm rapidly heading toward burnout. I can't afford to screw up, Griff. This is a once-in-a-lifetime event for Ryder International. We both should put all our energies toward making the ball a success. You because it will make your comeback easier if you nail your performance, me because, well, I don't want to disappoint myself or my family.

"You've got to admit that there's nothing we can build on, Griff. No common friends, no common city, God, I can't even sing!" Kinga wailed.

Funny, he so didn't care. He forced a smile onto his face. "Yep, that's a deal breaker."

"I'm being serious, Griff."

"I know."

And she was right, Griff reluctantly admitted. There were just a couple weeks—three? four?—before the ball and he needed to get his head in the game and start rehearsing his ass off. He needed his performance to be his best yet. Because he hadn't done this in a while, he was rusty. With Kinga being so busy, too, he'd be lucky to get scraps of her time, and he was far too selfish and demanding to be content with that.

But he knew he was going to regret letting this extraordinary woman leave his life.

He knew that truth like he knew his name. She was the first person who'd ever made him consider more…a relationship, a life together, building a future.

Ridiculously, he wanted her to meet his twin, Sam, his older sister and his brother-in-law. He already knew that Eloise, wise and wonderful, would love Kinga.

But what choice did he have but to agree with her to call this quits? She already knew too much and if they carried on seeing each other, he knew he'd tell her more, possibly everything, and she'd be the keeper of all his secrets. If she betrayed him, she'd not only devastate him but Sian and Sam, too. The stories would dog Sam his entire life. This wasn't just about Griff…

And she wanted out. He'd never been dumped before…

It sucked.

But Kinga was right. They should end this before things turned deeper, more intense. It would be better this way: a relationship always hit roadblocks, dived off cliffs, tore apart souls, eventually.

"So, are we going to go to the hotel, check out the function room and fly back? If that's the case, I might spend an extra few days in the city."

Kinga lowered her lashes and hauled in a deep breath, and Griff watched her cheeks turn pink. "Well, I was thinking we could go our separate ways tomorrow. That is, if you want one more night…"

More than he wanted his heart to keep beating.

Relief crashed over him, hot and sweet. Thank God. And screw the Italian restaurant, he was keeping her in bed for as long as he possibly could. He had memories to make…

He cradled her cheek in the palm of his hand and dropped a gentle kiss on her temple, holding his lips there, breathing her in. This was the start of twenty-four hours of trying to imprint her body, her smell, the wonderfulness of her on his soul. "In case I forget to tell you tomorrow, I have loved every second of being with you."

When he pulled back, he saw the sheen of tears in her eyes. She covered his hand with hers, holding his in place. "If this were another time or place, if we both didn't have so much damn baggage…"

"Yeah. If only…" Griff pulled back, knowing that if he started kissing her, he wouldn't stop. Then again, if this was all the time they had, he was wasting it.

"Does this plane have a bedroom?" he asked, seeing the heat in her eyes.

"It does," Kinga told him, after sucking his bottom lip between her teeth and releasing it with a plop. "But unfortunately, we're descending and will be landing in ten or so minutes."

Griff captured her chin in his hands and gave her a hard kiss, trying to ignore the desire in her eyes. How was he supposed to let her go when she looked at him like that? "Bed first, ballroom later?"

Kinga stroked her finger along his jaw, loving the scratchy feel of his stubble. "It's a deal, O'Hare. And, Griff?"

"Yeah?"

"In case I forget to mention it, I had the best time, too." She smiled, releasing a small, forced laugh. "Thanks for showing me a different way to eat cheesecake."

Thinking about wearing a black tuxedo, black tie for my performance on the 14th.

Sounds perfect, Kinga replied.

Brief emails and text messages were how she and Griff communicated these days and, over the last three weeks, many days had passed without them touching base at all. She set up the publicity events, he attended them and always managed to steer the conversation back to Ryder International's hundred years in business, their ball and the Ryder Foundation.

Remaining calm, he charmed the interviewers, insisting that he was still exploring his options career-wise and hadn't decided on a clear path.

It wasn't a path she would be walking with him...

Another message popped up on her screen: I'm thinking of dressing the backup singers in bright red sequins with white collars and big, heart brooches.

Knowing he was teasing—because, well, he knew she'd disembowel him if he did that—Kinga responded with a tongue-out emoji and returned her attention to her laptop sitting on the coffee table in front of her, needing to make sense of her master list for the ball, a detailed, massive, color-coded document.

Sitting on the cozy two-seater couch in her office, Kinga felt the familiar burn and reached for the box of antacids on the table next to her. She popped out four, chewed them and prayed for them to work. Her heart was on fire; there was a huge boulder sitting on her chest and a massive, invisible python was wrapped around her ribs.

Her stress-induced indigestion would pass. She just needed the ball to be a success and, after the fourteenth, she would feel like herself again. She was slated to take a two-week holiday, but she'd yet to decide where to go or what to do. Frankly, what she most wanted to do was hole up in her apartment and sleep for a week.

She missed Griff.

No, she missed him *desperately*. Missed his intelligent eyes and rough voice, his agile mind and his truly excellent body. They barely knew each other, had barely scraped the surface of what made each other tick, but Kinga knew he had the potential to be someone special in her life.

Hell, he already was.

The truth was that she was mourning a relationship that was never fully formed, and the love she felt for a man she could never be with. He was the one she wanted at her side, the one she couldn't live without, the puzzle piece she'd been missing.

But she'd sent him away because she was scared… scared to try, scared to love, scared to lose.

But since he wasn't in love with her, what choice did she have?

Kinga looked up as her office door opened and she pulled up a smile as Tinsley walked into her office and dropped into the seat next to her. She placed her hand on Kinga's back, and Kinga tipped her head sideways so it connected with her sister's.

"It's late, sweetie. Let's go home," Tinsley suggested.

Kinga frowned at the darkness beyond her window and glanced at her watch. It was past nine already—where had the time gone? And what had she accomplished? Not that much…

Tinsley leaned forward and picked up the box of antacids, her navy eyes concerned. "This box was full this morning, Kinga."

Yeah, she was pretty sure she had an ulcer but she had no time to get it checked out. After the ball, she would, as she told Tinsley.

"Let's hope it doesn't perforate before then," Tinsley muttered.

It wasn't a cheerful thought and Kinga hoped so, too. That would suck.

"Did you get the invitation to Mick's cocktail party?" Tinsley asked.

Kinga pulled a face. "I did."

She'd finally confessed Mick's actions to Tinsley and her confession had resulted in a few lectures about keeping stuff to herself and being stupidly independent.

"Are you going?" Kinga asked her sister.

"Hell, no!" Tinsley's smile was just this side of evil. "And I'm telling everyone I can think of not to go, either. Mom, Dad and Seth are also encouraging all their friends and connections—and between us, we know everyone— to boycott the function and his mayoral campaign," Tinsley said, looking smug. "I don't think he's going to have much support. If only we could get the press to boycott him as well."

"It's a story connected to Jas and those will always sell," Kinga told her. She squeezed Tinsley's knee. "But thank you for doing that."

Tinsley smiled before her expression turned concerned. "How are you, Kinga?"

She started to insist that she was fine before admitting she was tired of lying, tired of trying to be strong. This was, after all, her sister. And her best friend. "I'm stressed about the ball and overworked, but mostly I simply miss Griff."

Tinsley didn't look pleased and Kinga couldn't blame her. She wasn't happy that the bad boy of rock and roll had caused such emotional chaos, either.

"It was never anything serious, but it also feels like it was. I'm not sleeping much. I'm often awake at three a.m., bawling my eyes out, missing something I never had. Missing someone who was never mine."

Tinsley thought for a moment before wrapping her arm around Kinga's shoulders. "Would it help you if I reminded you that he's a bad boy rebel, a Peter Pan, someone who'll never grown up? He's done a million stupid things, he's irresponsible and selfish, and if he messes up at the ball, his career will be over, forever."

"But that's the thing, Tins. After our first meeting, I never thought of him in those terms again. He's never been *that* guy, to me. Sometimes I think he's better at *playing* the bad boy, than *being* the bad boy."

"Really?"

Kinga shrugged. "I can't explain why but I know the rebel persona is not who he is, not really." The real Griff was tough but tender, alpha to his core but considerate, too. A little sweet, a little arrogant, flawed and fabulous. A guy who adored his sister, was obviously in love with his nephew, who kept in constant touch with his family.

And she missed him with every breath she took.

Kinga waved her hands in front of her face, trying to

dry the tears in her eyes. "Let's talk about something else, anything else. Tell me something to distract me, Tins."

"Okay." Tinsley leaned back against the arm of her chair, folded her arms and lifted one arched eyebrow. "Let's see…the parents are still acting weird and if they ask me one more time why the DNA tests have been delayed, I might lose it. And today I heard that Garrett Kaye will be attending our ball."

Garrett Kaye was the wealthy venture capitalist son of Callum's personal assistant, Emma. Kinga felt a little of her misery recede at this news. They'd only met him a few times over the years and, while fabulous-looking, he was tight-lipped, introverted and frequently abrasive. But he was one of the richest men in the country and his attending the ball would give it another level of cachet. If Garrett Kaye thought the ball worth attending then it had to be something special…

"That's great news."

Tinsley smiled. "He's not bringing a plus-one, so we'll put him at the same table with the other singles, like Jules. And Sutton Marchant, Cody and others."

Sutton Marchant was a mega-wealthy ex–international trader who'd found fame when his debut novel hit the New York bestseller list. Kinga had met him years ago in London and found him bright, fantastically good-looking and quietly charming. Garrett Kaye probably wouldn't contribute much to the conversation but Sutton and Jules, their best friend and world renowned mixologist, would keep their table entertained when Griff wasn't performing.

Griff…her thoughts always went back to the man who'd upended her world.

Nine

In Key Largo, Griff lay on his back on a lounger in swim trunks, Sam curled up next to him, fast asleep. It was late afternoon, and his nephew was exhausted after a day on the beach. Griff felt like he could drift off, too.

But he knew that as soon as he closed his eyes, his brain would kick into high gear and sleep would scuttle off like a crab. God, he was tired.

He and his band had been practicing flat out and their performance was practically flawless. They'd worked out the kinks, rearranged the set list, added some songs, dropped others. Knowing they all needed a break—and that if he didn't leave Portland he wouldn't be able to resist rocking up on Kinga's doorstep and begging her to let him in, take him back, make it work—he'd told his crew to take a long weekend and headed down to the Keys.

But Kinga was always with him…

Griff sighed. Even if she wanted him in her life, and

as far as he knew she didn't, he still couldn't tell her the truth about his past. And Kinga deserved someone who was all in, someone who trusted and loved her enough to open the closet door and show her all the skeletons inside.

He couldn't do that, not when all the skeletons he'd helped bury weren't his...

To distract himself from thoughts of his brown-eyed pixie, Griff thought about the news sites he'd visited earlier: the news from Portland and the East Coast was the same as it ever was. He read lots of articles reporting on the ball and on his comeback, but there were a few about what was being touted as the party-before-the-ball, Pritchard-the-Prick's event. The press was speculating that he was going to announce his decision to enter politics—like that world needed more scumbags.

He hoped Kinga was okay, that she wasn't being hassled or harassed. God, why had Griff left Portland?

He sighed, lifted his bottle to his lips and sighed again. Suddenly noticing the silence, broken only by waves hitting the beach, gulls and Sam's soft snore, he looked around and found four sets of eyes on him.

"What?" he demanded, placing his empty beer bottle on the table beside him. He wouldn't mind another, but that would mean disturbing Sam, who'd only just nodded off.

Griff looked over the rails of the balcony to the white sands and clear water below and considered going for a run or hitting the state-of-the-art gym downstairs after Sam woke up. But he'd done both already today and was still waiting for a rush of endorphins.

He was starting to believe his happy hormone was called Kinga Ryder-White.

Griff rubbed the skin above his heart in a futile attempt to close the hole that was growing bigger by the day. Crap, he missed her. He missed her smile, her scent, her raspy voice and take-no-shit attitude.

He was grieving the end of something that had never really begun.

"Fool."

"We've been telling you that for years," Sian said, and Griff realized that he'd spoken aloud. Marvelous. And because he'd opened the door, they'd step on in and pepper him with questions...

Three, two, one...

"Why are you grumpy?" Jan demanded.

"You look like the dog ate your homework, dude," Pete commented.

"What's been happening in Portland that's made you so depressed?" Sian asked him. She was doing really well on her new medication. She seemed to be enjoying mothering Sam and she was interacting with the family more than she had in a long time.

Maybe his twin was on her way to stability... Oh, he couldn't kid himself—she'd have setbacks and episodes for the rest of her life, but if she could remain as upbeat as she currently was, he'd consider that a massive win.

Unlike him, who was feeling anything but positive.

He didn't know where he wanted his career to go but knew he was done, forever, with acting like the irresponsible man-child the world thought he was. He also knew he would never take on a movie role, act in a play, release an album or do a performance unless the project resonated with him.

He wanted to work at his craft and create a legacy people could respect. He wanted to be the type of man who deserved a woman like Kinga, someone she could be proud of...

Yet he knew that no matter where he went or what he

did, his past would follow him. It was now a part of his persona, not easily discarded.

He closed his eyes and released another long stream of air.

Eloise, sitting beside him, patted his hand. "I've known you since you were a child, Griff, and I don't think I've ever seen you so blue. Why don't you tell us what's worrying you?"

Uh, that would be a hard no.

He was the protector of his family, the one responsible for making the ship sail smoothly. He'd pull himself off the rocks, just as soon as he got his head together. But until then, he'd pretend, as he always did, that nothing was wrong.

"I'm fine, Eloise. Everything is fine."

"Not, it's not!" Sian whisper-shouted, obviously not wanting to wake Sam. But her voice crept up to normal levels as she spoke. "You and I need to talk, twin."

"Nothing to talk about," Griff eyed her, noticing the militant look in her eye. "I *am* fine."

"Bullshit!" Sian replied, leaning forward. She caught his eye and Griff saw she was clear-eyed and determined. Strong...

His heart surged with pride.

"Look, I know that I haven't been well for a long time and I accept I have issues and always will. But the new medication I'm on is helping, a lot. I don't feel as disconnected as I once did. A few years ago, I didn't care whether I lived or died, whether you or Sam or Jan lived or died. I might feel like that again in the future, and I really am going to work hard not to feel like that, but today I feel like myself."

Griff smiled at her. "I'm glad you are feeling stronger, twin. You and Sam are my priority, you know that."

"I do."

Good, conversation over. Time to get another beer—

"But Sam and I aren't the only people in this family who deserve to be happy," Sian told him. She smiled as Jan sat on the arm of her chair, their older sister silently offering Sian her support. "You deserve to be happy, too, Griff."

Griff thought about protesting but didn't have the energy. Happiness…it was such an intangible emotion. The closest he'd come to the emotion were those few nights he'd spent with Kinga…

Why did everything come back to her?

"I want to set the record straight, Griff," Sian stated, her tone and expression resolute. "I want to tell the world my story, the whole story."

Not happening. Not ever.

Griff looked from Jan to Pete, and neither looked surprised at Sian's announcement. So, this wasn't the first time this issue had been discussed.

"No," Griff declared. "Not a chance in hell."

"I can do it with or without you, Griff."

Her warning shocked him, causing him to rise abruptly. Sam tipped to the side and Griff caught him before he woke up and gently lowered the boy to the cushion. When he was certain Sam was comfortable, Griff walked over to the railing, gratefully snagging the beer Pete held out to him.

"I don't understand why you want to expose yourself, Sian. Why you'd want to undo years and years of hard work," Griff muttered. Years of *his* hard work.

She hit him with a clear-eyed look. "I want to tell the truth, the real truth. I want to set myself, and you, free. I still have a voice, a loud voice, and I can be an advocate for people with mental health issues. But to use that voice, to do some good, I need to be honest. I *must* be honest. And so do you... The world needs to know why you did what you did, that all your crap was to take the focus off me. I needed your help back then, I don't need it as much now. I'm stronger, better, *bolder*. If we tell the truth, the weight will be lifted off both of us. You can reclaim your name—"

"I don't care what the world thinks about me!" Griff told her. Outside this group, and Stan and Ava, he only cared about the thoughts and feelings of one person, just *one*.

He just wanted to tell Kinga, not the entire freakin' world.

"The press will go insane, you will be stalked and hounded." Griff pushed his hand through his hair. "You won't be able to move without being ambushed by a reporter with a camera."

This was such a bad idea. He couldn't believe that Jan and Pete supported this BS.

Sian shrugged. "We've discussed that. The ranch is completely secure and so is this island. I've spoken to my therapist, Griff, and I intend to be very careful about how I wade into this unknown territory. I mostly intend to work via social media, and I will be extremely cautious about any public appearances. Sam, his happiness, safety and security, will always be my top priority. Everything I do will be carefully vetted and screened by my therapist and my security team."

"You have a security team?" he asked, sending Pete a what-the-hell look.

"No, but I will get one," Sian told him, looking earnest. She stood up and walked over to him and placed her hand on his bare forearm. "I want to reclaim my life, Griff. I *need* to reclaim it."

He didn't like it at all. "Okay, I hear you. But you don't need to explain the past. Just put out a press release saying you have had difficulties and that you intend to be an advocate for people with mental health struggles."

"And be accused of being just another celebrity who won't get her hands or reputation dirty?" Sian scoffed and shook her head. "No, I either do this properly or I don't do it at all."

This was Sian—feisty, determined and difficult to sway once she'd decided on a course of action. Griff pulled his eyes off her stubborn face to look at the trio watching them interact.

"I presume you've had the same argument with her?" he asked.

Jan nodded. "We've covered the same ground, many, many times."

"I'm afraid we have two choices, my dear," Eloise said. "We can either support her and stand by her side, or we can watch her do this on her own. I vote for the first."

Sian started to talk, but Griff held up his hand, asking her to give him a minute. He needed to think. Sian was going to expose his bad boy life as a sham, tell the world why he acted like he did, and after that, there'd be no secrets to keep. He couldn't help feeling excited at having that burden lifted.

It would no longer be his burden.

Maybe it never had been.

Sian was going to do this, with or without him, and he was damned if he wouldn't stand by her side. He'd always thought she was talented, very smart, but today he was so very proud of her strength, in awe of her courage.

Man, he was so very proud to be her brother. Her twin.

And sometime in the future, when the furor died down and his life settled into a new type of normal, maybe he could ask Kinga out for dinner, start afresh, with no secrets between them.

A guy could only hope.

Griff narrowed his eyes, a thought occurring. Maybe, just maybe, he could kill a flock of birds with one supercharged stone...

"Are you sure you want to do this, Sian?"

Sian rolled her eyes before solemnly nodding. "I am very sure, Griff. If I could do it today, I would."

Right, well...

Griff looked into her eyes, so like his own. "If you are certain, if you are irrevocably committed to this path, can I ask you to do something for *me*?"

It was past six and Kinga promised herself an early night, vowed not to work until the early hours of the evening. She was even thinking about leaving her laptop here in her office, to force herself to take a break.

She was still debating whether she'd curse herself for such a radical move when Tinsley flew into Kinga's office, her expression confused.

"News!" Tinsley dramatically announced.

"Good or bad?" Kinga asked her overexcited sister, unable to summon much interest. God, she had to pull herself together. Since she and Griff parted ways, nothing much raised her blood pressure.

"I drove past the restaurant where Pritchard is hosting his cocktail party and not only is there a dearth of guests, but I also can't see any members of the media, either."

"They are probably all inside the restaurant, Tins."

Tinsley sat on the edge of her desk. "They aren't. As I drove past, I saw three reporters leaving the venue, moving fast. I think something else has happened to take the spotlight off Pritchard."

Kinga shrugged, not particularly concerned. Mick was a jerk and she refused to let him affect her life anymore. Jas was gone. Kinga still loved her and she was pretty sure that wherever Jas was, she still loved Kinga, too. It was time to release the guilt…well, as much as she could.

"What could've happened to drag their attention away from Pritchard? O'Hare is still out of town, so it can't be him," Tinsley stated, frowning. "It's got to be a big story."

Her sister was curious, and Kinga knew she wouldn't leave until she knew what was happening and where. Tinsley hated being out of the loop.

"Contact your sources," Kinga told Tinsley, pulling her phone out of her bag. Scrolling through her contacts list, she called one reporter, didn't receive an answer, and called another. Judging by Tinsley's face, she wasn't getting much joy, either.

Frustrated, Kinga punched out a text message, staring at her phone as she waited for a reply. A minute later her phoned vibrated, indicating an incoming message from one of her favorite journalists.

Sian O'Hare is giving a press conference at the Portland Harbor Hotel. Heady stuff. The place is packed, every reporter ever born is here. Guess that's the O'Hare pulling power.

WTH? Kinga replied. Is Griff there?

Griff and Stan and Ava. Wow. He did a great job snowing us.

What on earth did that mean? Kinga read out the messages to Tinsley, who looked equally astonished. Kinga tried to imagine why Griff would call a press meeting without telling her and felt her stomach twist into a tangled knot. What if he was pulling out of the concert? What if he was announcing his retirement, telling the world he was going on a retreat to find inner peace?

Kinga verbalized her fears to Tinsley, who frowned. "If that's the case, then I'll personally track him down and drag him back to Portland by his hair. Let's go find out what he's up to, Kingaroo."

Kinga followed Tinsley to her car, her stomach burning and her head pounding.

I won't let you down.

Kinga remembered his words and his determined eyes and her shoulders dropped and her tension eased away. She didn't know what this was about, but Griff wouldn't let her down. He'd said he'd be there for her and he would be.

"He won't disappoint me, Tins," Kinga told Tinsley as she negotiated her way through the evening traffic to the Portland Harbor Hotel.

"Okay," Tinsley said, sounding doubtful, slipping her car between a delivery van and an SUV.

"It'll be okay, I promise."

Tinsley tossed her a quick look and then a smile. "Of course it will, because my sister—cautious, analytical and very wary of making mistakes—would never fall in love with a man who would let her down."

Kinga considered Tinsley's words, and when they sank in, she smiled. Damn straight. He might not love her and he couldn't give her the life she wanted—to shelter in his arms, to make babies with him, to live and love and laugh with him—but she was too smart to fall in love with someone who was flaky and foolish.

No, whatever this was about, Griff would still perform at their ball the following weekend.

Tinsley pulled up next to the corner entrance of the redbrick hotel, telling her that she'd find a parking space and meet her as soon as she could. Kinga nodded, exited the vehicle, and raised her hand in apology to the driver in the car behind them. Adjusting her bag on her shoulder, she entered the lobby of the lovely hotel and walked up to the front desk, asking where the press conference was being held.

Ten minutes later, she slipped into the biggest of their conference rooms, her eyebrows lifting at the number of people in the room. A feminine voice was talking about being an ambassador for mental health and the journalists were entranced by whatever she was saying, heads lifting and falling as pens flew across notepads. Unable to see Griff, his sister or anyone else, Kinga edged down the wall until she was at the front of the packed crowd. Standing behind a diminutive journalist with a fearsome reputation, she looked at the table in front of her, her breath catching as her eyes fell on her favorite X-rated fantasy man who was wearing a...

Kinga squinted, unable to believe her eyes. Was Griff wearing a suit? Yep, dark gray, with a white shirt and patterned tie in greens and blues. He was also clean-shaven, his hair was neatly brushed, and he looked like a Wall Street trader, someone who frequented Ryder's Bar in Manhattan.

She far preferred him in ripped jeans and a tight T-shirt.

Her eyes danced over the rest of the table. Ava Maxwell sat between Griff and her husband, looking as she always did, indescribably lovely. Stan wore his usual black and his expression was both bored and forbidding. Griff's arm rested on the back of his twin's chair, a clear signal that she was under his protection.

Sian was the feminine version of her brother, with darker hair, green eyes and the same sexy mouth. She was tall and thin, and while her mouth was pulled up into a practiced smile, her eyes looked tired.

Griff kept his eyes on her profile and, as if hearing her thoughts, leaned forward to speak into his microphone. "I think that's enough for today, folks." When the room responded with collective disappointment, he shook his head, his expression hardening. "You guys have enough for several articles and any other questions can be directed to our publicist…"

They had a publicist? Since when? And why didn't she know about it?

Griff cleared his throat and the room quieted down. "I would like to remind you about my upcoming concert at the Ryder International ball. I would be grateful if you could mention the ball, that all the money raised through this project will go to the Ryder Foundation and that donations are always welcome."

Without missing a beat, Griff looked straight at her, his smile going from practiced to personal. He winked at her and her insides liquefied.

God, she loved this man. She didn't know what was happening or what bombshells he'd just dropped, but, in front of a dozen cameras, he'd given the ball some truly excellent press.

Bonus points for the bad boy—he'd denied Mick his spot in the sun by calling this press conference at the same time Mick wanted the press at his function.

Griff made some concluding remarks and, all around her, the press started to exit the room. She stayed where she was, watching as Griff, his sister and two of the biggest faces in the celebrity land walked in the opposite direction to a door guarded by two black-suited bodyguards.

Kinga scrubbed her hands over her face, still in the dark. She'd discover the reason for this get- together shortly. Hell, she just had to step outside and anyone would tell her, but for now, she was content to stay where she was. She needed a minute to get her bearings.

She'd been right to trust Griff. He hadn't let her down and wouldn't. He'd be behind the microphone at the ball and as soon as his performance ended, he'd be completely out of her life.

Her heart, struck by an invisible but heavy hammer, shattered anew at the realization. Fighting the urge to drop to her knees, she sucked in a couple of breaths, terrified she was heading toward a panic attack. Oh, God, she'd forgotten how painful it was to love and lose someone and she most definitely didn't need the reminder.

Needing to find Tinsley, Kinga blinked back tears. She was about to follow the last of the stragglers out of the room when she saw one of the beefy security guards approaching her, his expression impassive.

"Ms. Ryder-White?"

"Yes?"

"Mr. O'Hare would like to see you. He's asked me to escort you to his executive suite."

"Okay, thanks. Just give me a minute, I need to tell my sister I've been delayed."

Kinga banged out the text message, shoved her phone in her bag and nodded to the man-in-black. Kinga's breath evened out and her heart settled. She knew Griff would be leaving her life after the ball, but that wasn't tonight. As long as the broad-shouldered man was leading her to Griff, she'd follow him anywhere. O'Hare was, after all, her personal pot of gold at the end of the rainbow.

The security guard knocked on the door to the suite and it opened a few seconds later. Had Griff been waiting for her? Was he as anxious to see her as she was to see him?

Griff gestured her to enter and nodded to the guard standing behind her. "Thanks, Reynolds. Appreciate your help."

Griff closed the door behind the guard and Kinga's eyes drifted over him. He'd shed his suit jacket and his tie was pulled from his open collar. His hair was now ruffled, as if he'd shoved his hands through it. Frankly, he looked exhausted.

Kinga couldn't help lifting her hand to his cheek, feeling the beginnings of his fast-growing beard. "Are you okay? You look shattered."

"I am tired... That was the hardest thing I've ever done," Griff told her. Placing a hand on her lower back, he guided her into the exquisitely decorated sitting room and suggested she take a seat. "Do you want a drink?"

"No, but you look like you need one," Kinga said, sitting down on the edge of a gray couch. Placing her forearms on her knees, she watched as Griff, obviously distracted, poured himself a shot of whiskey and tossed it back. He then poured another two shots into heavy tumblers and walked back across the room to her, handing her a drink she'd told him she didn't want. Kinga thanked him, placed the drink on the glass coffee table and softly suggested that he sit down.

Griff shook his head and stood behind the chair opposite her, his forearms—sleeves of his shirt rolled up—resting on the top of the chair. Instead of explaining why he'd requested her to come up to his room, he just stared at her, his eyes troubled and his expression brooding.

Unable to contain her curiosity, Kinga spoke. "I have no idea what's going on, why the press pool looks like you just handed them the moon."

"I didn't, Sian did," Griff replied, his voice raspy. His voice always took on that growly quality when he was tired or feeling stressed or emotional. Kinga cocked her head, waiting for him to speak.

He sipped at his whiskey and frowned at her. "It's a long, complicated story."

She didn't have enough patience for long and complicated. "Give me the highlights."

Griff nodded. "Uh...so, in our early to midtwenties we were flying high. If anything, Sian was flying faster and higher than me—she was always the more talented twin." He said those words without any rancor or jealousy. Instead, his voice held a healthy dose of pride.

"You're a pretty talented guy, O'Hare," Kinga pointed out.

He shrugged. "But Sian was next-level good. She was exploring more facets of her talent and people were starting to notice. She was frequently compared to some of the greats, Garland and Hepburn, and was widely considered, by the industry heavyweights, to be a once-in-a-generation performer."

Okay, she hadn't known that.

"Long story short, Sian had always struggled with anxiety and depression, but a few years back she started to behave erratically and, because the press paid so much attention to her, they quickly picked up that something was amiss. They hounded her and the rumors started flying about her using drugs." Griff's frown deepened. "It was, after all, the most logical conclusion."

"But she wasn't," Kinga softly interjected.

"No, she was diagnosed with a mild form of schizophrenia," he said, staring at the glass in his hand. "Her interest in performing declined and she became a bit of a recluse. Her psychiatrist recommended she retreat from the limelight permanently and try to live a life as calm and normal as possible."

"Pretty impossible when you are one of the world's hottest and most recognizable stars," Kinga commented.

"The burning question on everyone's lips—the press, our friends and our colleagues—was why a talented performer at the height of her career would bail? The media interest in her...well, exploded. Finn, our manager, and I both knew we had to do something to change that."

Oh, God, she thought she knew what he was about to say, but because she could be wrong, she waited for him to continue.

"Stan and I have been friends since we were teenagers and he suggested that I start behaving like a spoiled, selfish asshole to pull the attention off Sian."

Ding! Ding! Ding! All at once, everything fell into place and Kinga knew her instincts were spot-on.

Griff looked at her, a puzzled expression on his face. "You don't seem surprised."

"I'm not," Kinga told him, picking up her glass and taking a small sip. "For a while now, I've felt that you were playing a role, that you're not who the press portrays you to be."

Griff looked astounded at her almost casual comment. Kinga hid her smile behind her glass and gestured for him to continue. "Carry on with the highlight reel, O'Hare," she told him.

"Finn told me he'd take care of Sian, that he'd keep an eye on her while I went on a tear. We set up a worldwide tour and I caused chaos," Griff reluctantly admitted. "The press attention shifted off Sian and onto me. I behaved like a jerk, but it worked, they bought it."

"And Sian was allowed to fade from view."

Griff stood up and jammed his hands in the pockets of his pants. "Essentially. But Sian is tired of being in the shadows and she wants to help fight the stigma around mental illness. She called the press conference to talk about her diagnosis and explain that I acted like a jerk to protect her. It was her truth to reveal."

"I'm with you so far, but I still don't understand how Stan and Ava fit into this picture."

"The story of Ava and me having an affair was bullshit, and it was a way to give a persistent reporter a scoop."

"So you didn't have a thing with her?"

"Of course, I didn't!" Griff snapped, looking affronted. Then his expression changed to resignation. "Look, all that happened between us was what everyone saw in that club. Sian was pregnant and she'd been spotted, somewhere, I can't remember where, and some intrepid reporter was going to run a story about the baby and her depression. We needed something big and bold to minimize that news, so Ava suggested we fake a hookup. I was reluctant, but Stan agreed with Ava. He's always been super protective of Sian—she's like a little sister to him. We set it up immediately and it worked. The news spread like wildfire."

Kinga couldn't resist asking her next question. "So, what was it like kissing the world's most beautiful woman?"

Griff glared at her. "Stan told me that if my hand landed anywhere other than her back and if my tongue passed her lips, he'd castrate me. I believed him." He shrugged. "Honestly, it was awkward and...*wrong.* Thank God we are both decent actors, because there wasn't a flicker of chemistry between us."

She heard his unspoken words...not like the firenado that sprang up between them.

But Kinga couldn't be distracted by the heat in his eyes, the quirk of his sexy lips. There was still so much ground to cover. "Okay, your make-out session with Ava was a scam, but why were they at the press conference? They didn't need to be, not really."

Griff flushed and Kinga thought it was the first time she'd seen him flustered. "Ah, that was for you, actually."

"Me?" What on earth was he talking about? She had nothing to do with his past or their press conference.

"I was reasonably sure the press would drop everything, including Pritchard's cocktail party, to attend Sian's press conference. But I wanted to be certain they would. Because Stan and Ava are seldom in the public eye and never engage with the press, I *knew* every reporter with a heartbeat would attend the press conference if they were there."

Kinga placed her hand on her heart as it flung itself against her rib cage. He'd asked his friends to change a habit of the past few years to deny Mick the publicity he so desperately wanted…and it was all for her. How… sweet. A little Machiavellian but very sweet.

"I don't know what to say," Kinga whispered.

Griff's face hardened and she knew his anger was directed at Mick and not at her. "Friends don't act as he did, and I was happy to put a metaphorical foot on his throat. Besides, Stan is working on a new album and Ava punted her climate change foundation, so they were happy to be there."

"No, they weren't," Kinga countered.

"No, they weren't, but I asked, and they stepped up to the plate. It's what friends do," Griff said on a soft smile.

Yeah, it was what friends did. And by arranging this press conference to coincide with Mick's opening night, Griff had sent him, and her, the message that nobody messed with the people he cared about. And he did care about her, she knew that.

But there was a universe between friendship and love.

"Thank you," Kinga said, her chest and throat tight.

"There's something else you need to know, something media-land doesn't know. It might come out later, or not, but I want to tell you. You'll be the only person who knows, outside of my family and Stan and Ava."

God, he sounded so serious. What on earth could top what he'd already told her? And why was he confiding his secrets to her?

"We can't go forward until everything is in the open," Griff stated, his eyes on hers.

Did he want to go forward? What did that mean?

Kinga clasped her hands together and waited, holding her breath.

"I told you that I left Sian under the care of our manager, Finn. Well, he cared for Sian a little too much. Sam is his biological child."

Holy hell...*what*?

"I was furious. I've always believed that she was in a terrible place, mentally, and that he took advantage of her. Sian says it wasn't like that, that she never felt bullied or coerced." Griff said, his voice saturated with pain and anger. "I was incandescently angry, still am to an extent because she was vulnerable."

He rubbed his palm up and down his jaw. "Anyway... when she was diagnosed, I gained power of attorney over Sian's financial affairs and I fired him the moment I heard. He was on his way to meet with me when he wrapped his car around a tree."

Oh, Griff.

"I was there when Sam was born. Sian suffered from terrible postpartum psychosis and I did all the heavy lifting with Sam, the midnight feedings and the diaper changes. I heard his first word, watched him take his first step. He's Sian's, but in some ways he's also mine. He'll always be a big part of my life."

His love for his nephew radiated from every pore. Seeing his tenderness and unembarrassed adoration for Sam made Kinga fall in love with Griff a little more. If that was even possible.

"From that moment on, I resolved never to trust another person outside of my family and Stan and Ava," Griff said, hoarse with emotion. "Then you came along..."

Kinga stood up slowly, feeling unsteady on her feet. "You trust me?"

Griff's intense eyes didn't leave hers as he slowly nodded. "Trust you implicitly, love you more."

For a moment Kinga thought she'd heard him say he loved her. *Wait!* Did he say he loved her?

"What...what did you say?" she asked, her tone polite.

Griff scrubbed his hands over his face. "I'm in love with you. I know that's not what you want to hear, but I didn't want you to leave my life without you knowing how I feel." He looked a little lost and confused. "I've never felt this way about anyone before, so, yeah, I thought you should know."

Kinga plopped back down on the couch, her legs wobbly and her heart climbing up into her throat. She couldn't believe what she was hearing, couldn't fathom the idea that all her biggest wishes and dreams were within reach.

"Wow...um, that wasn't what I expected," Kinga managed to push the words out.

"I know. It wasn't what I planned, either. I was going to do a comeback concert, release a new album, go on a tour. Maybe pick up a small film role to ease my way back into acting," Griff explained. "Then you dropped into my life and all I can think about is putting my ring on your finger, keeping you in bed for a month, making babies with you."

He looked uncertain and completely out of his depth. "I don't suppose there's a chance you might be interested in any of those?"

Feeling off-balance and knowing she couldn't walk to him on sky-high heels without falling flat on her face, Kinga bent to the side and slowly removed one heel, then the other. Standing up, she carefully circumvented the coffee table, then the chair to stand in front of him. She placed her hands on his chest and, almost instantly, her wobbly world steadied. She felt strength, and love, and happiness flow through her. From him to her and back again.

"No, I wouldn't be interested in one of those," she slowly told him, lifting her mouth to his. She caught the flash of disappointment in his eyes and, not wanting to cause him a moment of pain, hastily added, "I'm interested in all of it."

Shock flashed in Griff's eyes. "What?"

Kinga's laugh was a little tremulous. "You love me, right?"

"Right." His emphatic nod accompanied the word.

"And I love you. You are my…well, you're everything important. You are where I can lay down my insecurities and my fears, my flaws and my failures." Kinga watched as his eyes softened with joy, felt his fingertips digging into her hips. A smile returned to his sexy mouth, and she continued, "You are good sex and quick quips, your arms are where I feel safest and your heart is as big as the sun." The words fell from her lips, a jumble of the good and the glorious. "Oh, I'm making a mess of this! But believe me when I tell you that I love you. Deeply, madly…"

She pulled a face. "And deeply and madly is not what I do, generally."

Griff's hand on her back pulled her to him so that her breasts pushed into his chest and his erection lay hard against her stomach. "I've missed you so much, sweetheart."

Kinga brushed her lips across his, her mouth curving into a smile. "I've missed you, too." His thumb swiped her bottom lip and Kinga watched, mesmerized, as desire jumped in his eyes.

"What are you thinking, O'Hare?" she asked, as she slowly pulled his shirt out from the back of his pants.

He cupped her ass and squeezed. "That you are the best thing that ever happened to me, that I can't wait for the rest of our lives and that your clothes would look much better on my bedroom floor."

"Shall we test that theory?" Kinga asked him, her hand sliding up his spine.

"Oh, we very much shall…" Griff promised her, scooping her up and holding her against his chest. "But I warn you, it might take a lifetime of experimentation to reach a conclusion."

Kinga sighed, kissed his neck and smiled. She loved and was in love…

Life didn't get much better than this.

* * * * *

COMING SOON!

We really hope you enjoyed reading this book. If you're looking for more romance, be sure to head to the shops when new books are available on

Thursday 3rd March

To see which titles are coming soon, please visit

millsandboon.co.uk/nextmonth

MILLS & BOON

MILLS & BOON

THE HEART OF ROMANCE

A ROMANCE FOR EVERY READER

MODERN

Prepare to be swept off your feet by sophisticated, sexy and seductive heroes, in some of the world's most glamourous and romantic locations, where power and passion collide.

HISTORICAL

Escape with historical heroes from time gone by. Whether your passion is for wicked Regency Rakes, muscled Vikings or rugged Highlanders, awak the romance of the past.

MEDICAL

Set your pulse racing with dedicated, delectable doctors in the high-pressure world of medicine, where emotions run high and passion, comfort a love are the best medicine.

True Love

Celebrate true love with tender stories of heartfelt romance, from the rush of falling in love to the joy a new baby can bring, and a focus on the emotional heart of a relationship.

Desire

Indulge in secrets and scandal, intense drama and plenty of sizzling hot action with powerful and passionate heroes who have it all: wealth, status, good looks…everything but the right woman.

HEROES

Experience all the excitement of a gripping thriller, with an intense romance at its heart. Resourceful, true-to-life women and strong, fearless me face danger and desire - a killer combination!

To see which titles are coming soon, please visit

millsandboon.co.uk/nextmonth

LET'S TALK

Romance

For exclusive extracts, competitions
and special offers, find us online:

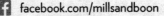

facebook.com/millsandboon

@MillsandBoon

@MillsandBoonUK

Get in touch on 01413 063232

For all the latest titles coming soon, visit

millsandboon.co.uk/nextmonth

MILLS & BOON
A ROMANCE FOR EVERY READER

- **FREE** delivery direct to your door
- **EXCLUSIVE** offers every month
- **SAVE** up to 25% on pre-paid subscriptions

SUBSCRIBE AND SAVE

millsandboon.co.uk/Subscribe

WANT EVEN MORE
ROMANCE?
SUBSCRIBE AND SAVE TODAY!

'Mills & Boon books, the perfect way to escape for an hour or so.'

MISS W. DYER

'Excellent service, promptly delivered and very good subscription choices.'

MISS A. PEARSON

'You get fantastic special offers and the chance to get books before they hit the shops.'

MRS V. HALL

Visit millsandboon.co.uk/Subscribe and save on brand new books.

JOIN THE
MILLS & BOON
BOOKCLUB

* **FREE** delivery direct to your door

* **EXCLUSIVE** offers every month

* **EXCITING** rewards programme

50% OFF
YOUR FIRST
PARCEL

Join today at
Millsandboon.co.uk/Bookclub

JOIN US ON SOCIAL MEDIA!

Stay up to date with our latest releases, author news and gossip, special offers and discounts, and all the behind-the-scenes action from Mills & Boon...

 millsandboon

 millsandboonuk

f millsandboon

It might just be true love...

GET YOUR ROMANCE FIX!

MILLS & BOON
— *blog* —

Get the latest romance news, exclusive author interviews, story extracts and much more!

blog.millsandboon.co.uk

MILLS & BOON
MODERN
Power and Passion

Prepare to be swept off your feet by sophisticated, sexy and seductive heroes, in some of the world's most glamourous and romantic locations, where power and passion collide.

Eight Modern stories published every month, find them all at:

millsandboon.co.uk/Modern

MILLS & BOON
MEDICAL
Pulse-Racing Passion

Set your pulse racing with dedicated, delectable doctors in the high-pressure world of medicine, where emotions run high and passion, comfort and love are the best medicine.

Eight Medical stories published every month, find them all at:

millsandboon.co.uk

MILLS & BOON
True Love

Romance from the Heart

Celebrate true love with tender stories of heartfelt romance, from the rush of falling in love to the joy a new baby can bring, and a focus on the emotional heart of a relationship.

Four True Love stories published every month, find them all at:

millsandboon.co.uk/TrueLove